Penny White

and

THE HUMILITY

OF HUMANS

Penny White # 9

Chrys Cymri

Cover Design: Cover Couture (www.bookcovercouture.com)
Photo (c) Shutterstock/Creativa Images
Photo (c) Shutterstock/Supertrooper
Photo (c) Shutterstock/LarsZ
Photo (c) Shutterstock/Maksim Shmeljov
Photo (c) Shutterstock/ventdusud
Photo (c) Shutterstock/Aleksandar Mijatovic

For Kara

I hope you still love unicorns
when you're old enough to read this!

This is a work of fiction.
All names, characters, businesses,
places, events and incidents are either the
products of the author's imagination
or used in a fictitious manner and any resemblance
to actual persons, living or dead, or actual events
is purely coincidental.

Chapter One

Gentle waves chimed across the golden sands, touching my bare feet with warm water. The blue skies, the green hills, and the birds which wandered the shoreline all added to the beauty of the place. But my eyes were drawn to a far more glorious sight. I never tired of watching my husband flying towards me, his hide shimmering between black and green in the bright sunlight. On his left foreleg glittered a gold bracelet, twin to the one on my left wrist.

The dragon tipped his right wing and began to spiral down to the beach. I placed a hand on my hat, holding it firmly as Raven landed twenty feet away. A blast of air from his wings blew across my chest, and then fine sand stung my sunburnt legs.

Raven walked towards me, grumbling under his breath as his weight made his feet sink deep into the soft sand at every step. There were disadvantages to being nearly twice the height of a horse. When he reached my side, I lifted a hand to touch the warm skin near his red-rimmed nostrils.

After a moment, he said, 'No air thin places over this island, either.'

'Land crossings?'

'Several,' he acknowledged. 'But those would only lead through to the Earth equivalent.'

'Not much of a help,' I agreed. 'Especially as I don't have my passport with me. Or any way of explaining how I've ended up in--remind me what Caribbean island we're on now?'

'According to Cornelius, the inhabitants call this island "Taino",' Raven said. 'I have no idea what that is on your world.'

'I don't either.' I sighed. 'There are times when I really miss Google.'

'The lack of air crossings is strange,' Raven added. 'Do we continue to look at the next island, or shall we finally ask Clyde to create a crossing for us?'

I started to walk along the beach, heading towards a clump of nearby rocks. 'That leaves us with the problem of explaining how we got back to Lloegyr without using a ship.'

'The good citizens of Lloegyr,' Raven pointed out, 'might have no idea that these islands lack air thin places. Using Clyde doesn't necessarily mean revealing his secret.'

'I know, I know, maybe I'm just being paranoid.' The boulders were dry, and one had a flat area just the right height for me to on and rest my feet. 'Would you mind giving me some shade? Goodness, if this is the temperature in January, I really don't want to be here in the summer.'

Raven chuckled. 'I like the warmth.'

'It was a nice change not to be shivering at Christmas.' I touched my reddened legs. 'Pity I've run out of sun lotion. I'd better dig out my long trousers and just get used to sweating during the day.'

'Christmas,' Raven said slowly. 'I would've liked to have been able to give you a better present.'

I laughed. 'We were together. That's the best present you could've given me.'

The dragon arched his neck. 'I shall remember that when it's your birthday.'

'Oh, no,' I said, wagging a finger at him, 'I expect something quite spectacular for my birthday.'

'Noted, precious Penny.'

'Good.' I smiled up at him. His ears and horns were curled towards me, his jaws slightly open in a grin of his own. 'Let's go back to *The Morning Star*. Time we had a chat with Clyde.'

I used the boulder to give me easier access to Raven's neck. The burnt skin on my legs chafed against the dragon's hide, and I bit back a groan. It was my own fault for deciding to wear shorts.

Fortunately, the soft sand meant that Raven couldn't make his usual back-jarring spring into the air. He inflated his gas chamber, and pushed off gently from the ground. I gripped the neck spine in front of me as his long wings swept down on either side, taking us away from the beach.

The Morning Star was anchored just a short flight away, the three tall masts currently bare. Several sails were spread out on the wooden deck, and were-puffins bent over the ivory cloth as they worked on repairs. Crew members waved feather-covered arms at us as Raven circled the ship. He landed carefully on the upper deck, pulling in his wings to avoid hitting the webbing which ran up to the masts' cross bars.

Johno walked over to the steps leading up to the top deck. Although he was in biped form, grey feathers covered the were-albatross's chest and legs. His black eyebrows were drawn close together. 'Youse guys find a crossing?' he asked in his soft Australian drawl.

'Struck out here as well,' I said as I slid down from Raven's neck. 'I don't suppose Doethineb has anything for sun burn, does she?'

'Strewth, you did cook yourself,' the captain said, peering at my legs. 'She might. That sheila keeps all sorts of clobber. I'll whistle for her.'

'I'm going below,' I told Raven. 'I'll be back later.'

It was much cooler inside the ship. I walked down the steps, careful to keep one hand on the rail. The sickbay was just along the corridor. I let myself in and took a seat on the single bed. Fresh herbs hung on racks set into the wooden walls, and I felt my nose twitch at the spicy smell.

The were-penguin bustled in a minute later. Although she wasn't physically able to speak English, she understood the language. Or perhaps the state of my legs spoke for themselves. The thick grey salve she produced provided immediate relief. I took a jar away with me and carried it down to my cabin.

Clyde was resting on the top bunk, hidden away in his dark shell. As I placed the jar into a drawer, I heard him mutter something in Welsh. I straightened, and found that his eyespots were fixed on me. 'You worked late?' I asked sympathetically.

'Night watch,' the snail affirmed. More of his body emerged, the calm blues and greens tinged with grey.

'I admire your work ethic,' I said. 'But if we hit any more storms, promise me you'll stay in the cabin, please?'

The lack of response told me that no such assurance would be forthcoming.

'Raven didn't find any air thin places,' I continued. 'I think we've tried long enough. As he pointed out, it's unlikely that anyone in Lloegyr would know that this area doesn't have them. So, maybe after a day or so to pack up and say our goodbyes, could you take us back to Saint Raphael's?'

Clyde's body pulsed blue and purple. 'No.'

I stared at him. 'I beg your pardon?'

'Bishop.'

'Of course Bishop Aeron will have a fit when I tell her that I've married Raven,' I agreed. 'But sooner or later we'll be back in Lloegyr.'

'Honeymoon.'

My face warmed. 'That's very kind of you, but Raven and I have had a great few months in the Caribbean. We're ready to head back now. We don't feel the need to stay any longer.'

The sound of wings announced Morey's presence a moment before the gryphon landed on the top bunk. 'Well? Did Raven find any thin places we can use?'

'No air ones,' I said.

Morey cocked his purple-grey head at the snail. 'Then it's time we deployed our personal vortex manipulator.'

'Clyde and I were just discussing that. Seems he's not keen.'

Morey fluffed his head feathers. 'I beg your pardon?'

'Bishop,' the snail said. 'Honeymoon.'

'Sooner or later, Penny's going to have to face the music,' Morey snapped. 'And, in the meantime, I've been away from my wife for nearly four months. Don't punish me just because you want to be nice to Penny.'

Clyde reared up. Multiple colours pulsed through his body, and his tentacles twisted in the sign language he had picked up from James and Jago. I rubbed my forehead. 'I can't follow any of this. Where's Jago?'

'Somewhere,' Morey said glumly. 'He's still moping.'

'It was hard for him to accept the truth about Dancer,' I reminded him. 'And he also has to think of what he's going to say to Bastien, once we're back.'

'True.' Morey sighed. 'He's still very young, and it's been hard for him to realise how wrong he was. You think you know everything at that age.'

I grinned. 'So what's your excuse now?'

'Very funny, Black.' Morey turned to Clyde. 'Look, if you don't want to take all of us back, at least let me visit Taryn. I know I can't stay, not without being asked some awkward questions. But if I could at least let her know I'm still alive, that would help.'

'Would you consider that, Clyde?' I gave him my biggest smile. 'That's not too much to ask, is it?'

The snail's eyespots studied me, then Morey. 'Will do.'

'And could I come with you to England?' I asked. 'I'd like to try to contact James. So that he knows I'm still alive. Don't worry, I'm not about to try to sneak back to Lloegyr without Raven.'

Clyde's colours settled down to calm blues and greens. 'Okay. Tomorrow. Afternoon.'

'Afternoon?' I asked. 'Oh, because tomorrow's Sunday.'

'Yes. Church.'

'We need to keep in mind the time difference,' I said slowly. 'I know that the USA is around five hours behind Greenwich Mean Time. How about an early church service and we go through after that? Okay?'

'Yes.'

'We'll want to create the crossing on land,' Morey said. 'If we do it on the ship, and *The Morning Star* moves, we might end up with a thin place over the sea.'

'Noted. I'll ask Raven to fly us over to the island.' I held out my arm to Morey. 'Come on, let's leave so Clyde can get some rest.'

Over the weeks I'd been offering a Communion service on a Sunday morning, my congregation had steadily grown. Raven peered over my shoulder from his place on the upper deck. I stood on the lower deck, behind a table holding a plate of hardtack and a mug of fruit juice. Morey, Clyde, and Jago stood on the deck, as well as a dozen crew members. Cornelius sometimes hovered in the middle distance, but the praying mantis was missing this morning.

Before my iPhone had yet again run out of battery, I had copied out a Common Worship service. A slight breeze fluttered through the handwritten sheets, held firm under my Bible, as I lifted mug and plate into the air for the end of the Eucharistic prayer. "'By whom, and with whom, and in whom, in the unity of the Holy Spirit, all honour and glory be yours, almighty Father, for ever and ever.'"

'Amen,' the others intoned, before we started the Lord's Prayer together. 'Our Father, who art in heaven...'

I distributed the bread and then took the juice around. The were-puffins, Jago, and Raven each bent their head for a blessing. Morey helped me to consume the excess hardtack and liquid before I gave the final blessing and dismissal.

The crew members wandered back to their work. Jago and Morey flew up to the crow's nest. Massen came forward to carry away the plate and mug. I gave the were-puffin a thankful smile before climbing up the stairs to join Raven.

'That was an interesting portion from the Bible,' the dragon commented. 'That Jeremiah person seemed very angry at God.'

I cast my mind back to the Old Testament reading. 'You mean, the bit that started "O Lord, you have seduced me, and I was seduced"?'

'Yes, particularly the part when he said the day on which he was born should be cursed.' The skin around his muzzle was creased, a sign that he was thinking hard. 'I thought people in the Bible only ever said nice things to God.'

I laughed. 'I'll have to show you the Psalms. There are plenty of people annoyed at God in those.' I paused a moment before asking, 'Do you feel some sympathy with Jeremiah? You've told me that you find God terribly inconvenient. But now that the Noble Leader's spirit is gone, I thought you'd no longer need to keep close to God?'

'I suppose not,' Raven said slowly. 'But church seems to have become a habit. I think I'd miss it, if I didn't attend.'

'Now that I'm leading services again,' I admitted, 'I realise that I'd been missing that part of my life.'

'And it is very much part of your life.' Raven blew soft warm air across my face. 'So, as your husband, it needs to be part of mine.'

'I think it's only fair to tell you that not all clergy spouses feel that way. Alan certainly didn't. He only came to church at Christmas and Easter.'

'I'm not like Alan.'

I recalled my all-too-human first husband and laughed. 'You're quite right about that.'

'So when we're back in Lloegyr,' Raven continued, 'I will be asking Bishop Aeron to confirm me. I'd like to be able to take communion from my wife's hands.'

I placed a hand on his muzzle. 'That's lovely. But will you ask before or after we tell her that we're married?'

'Why should that matter? I'm proud to be your husband.' Raven glanced down at the gold band glittering around his green-black foreleg. 'If she refuses to confirm me, then we'll just have to approach your Nenehampton bishop. Will he be against our marriage?'

'There's nothing in the Church of England's canon law preventing a priest from marrying a dragon,' I said confidently. 'And, let's face it, if I ever served a human congregation again, they won't be able to see you anyway. Not many humans have the Sight.'

'Will you be allowed to return to work at Saint Raphael's?'

'I can't see why not.' I shrugged. 'Llewelyn was happy enough to ask me to marry him, and that too would have been against official church policy. It would still have been a mixed-species marriage. I suppose it really comes down to how Llewelyn will feel about me choosing someone other than him.'

'The were-wolf has always seemed like a good man to me,' Raven commented. 'But I'll not show myself to him until you've explained matters.'

I winced. 'Maybe I'll speak to him first. It'll prepare me for the far more difficult conversation with Bishop Aeron.'

A flash of purple-grey drew my attention. Morey dropped down from the mast to land on the nearby gunwale. 'I asked Jago if he wanted to pop over to Lloegyr to see his mother. The lad's turned me down. I think he's worried about bumping into Bastien, and he hasn't worked out yet what he's going to tell the rat.'

I lowered my voice. 'Well, nothing really happened between him and Dancer, did it? Just a lot of flying around and preening, as far as I could tell.'

'There was emotional involvement,' Morey said. 'That's already crossing a line, and Jago knows that. At any rate, I'm ready to go when you are.'

'Let me pack a lunch,' I replied. 'Then I'll ask Clyde if he's ready. You're still happy to fly us over, Raven?'

The dragon extended his wings. 'As ever, preeminent Penny, I am at your disposal.'

I hurried down to the galley. Massen smiled as I hovered by the door, and quickly slid hard tack and salted fish into a banana leaf. I thanked him as I placed the packet into a coat pocket and hurried back to the upper deck.

Johno handed Clyde up to me after I'd settled on Raven's neck. I placed the snail inside my coat. Although the morning's warmth was making me sweat, I had no doubt that it would be much colder in England and I wanted to be prepared. Morey hovered in the air, waiting for us.

Raven made a careful take-off, avoiding webbing and masts as he leapt away from the ship. We passed several were-puffins rowing a small boat towards *The Morning Star*. Greenery filled the space around the seats. Herbs, I decided, and various types of fruit and vegetables. The former destined for the sick bay and the latter items for my dinner plate, no doubt.

The bright blue sea and white sands gave way to palm trees. Raven circled for a moment, his head sweeping from side to side, looking for a good place to land. We touched down in a grassy clearing. Several birds and a large insect flew up, all screeching protests in a language which I didn't understand. 'Sorry!' I called out.

I placed Clyde on Raven's neck before I dismounted. The snail crawled down to my upstretched hands, and I lowered him to chest level. Morey thumped on to my left shoulder a moment later. 'You can take me straight to Saint Raphael's, can't you, Clyde? You have to have some sort of connection with a place, don't you?'

'Or someone he knows has to have a good connection,' I said. 'That's how he managed to take us to New York.'

'Simply because you'd visited there?'

'Well, no, not really.' I coughed. 'It appears Clyde can cut a crossing through to wherever I've left part of myself.'

'A part of yourself?' Raven asked. 'Like blood?'

'No.' I felt my face flush. 'Wherever I've been caught short.' My companions looked puzzled. 'Where I didn't find a loo in time. Where I've defecated.' A chuckle from both gryphon and dragon made me glare at each one in turn. 'You knew full well what I meant, didn't you? You just pretended not to know.'

Morey laughed. 'I've never understood this human embarrassment over a natural biological function.'

'Humans can be very strange,' Raven agreed.

'You're the one who decided to marry one,' Morey said.

'Indeed,' the dragon said. 'And I have no regrets.'

'When you two are finished talking about me,' I commented, 'maybe we could concentrate on our trip?'

'Yes,' Clyde grunted. 'Now.'

'My iPhone battery is flat,' I said. 'I'd like to phone James to let him know I'm still alive. So first I'd like to go somewhere to recharge it. Then Clyde can take you across to Saint Raphael's.'

'EBM?' the snail asked.

'Yes,' I agreed. 'Earls Barton Man.'

'That man never gets a break,' Morey muttered. 'Did you say he's now sheltering a manticore?'

'Along with other Lloegyr refugees.' I strode away from the dragon, the long grass catching against my boots. 'I'll call for you, Raven, when we're back. Okay, Clyde. Earls Barton, here we come.'

Chapter Two

I lifted the snail high and he opened his jaws. The air shimmered as his teeth cut through the barrier between two worlds. Tucking Clyde under my arm, I ducked my head and stepped from Daear to Earth.

The cold hit me immediately. I shivered as I buttoned up my tattered coat. Morey fluffed his feathers. 'At least it's not raining,' he said, pointing his yellow beak at the cloudy sky.

'Yet,' I said wearily, recalling too many dreary English winters. The back garden was quiet and empty. 'Looks like the refugees are hiding from the weather.'

'I think there's more to it than that,' Morey said slowly. 'If a manticore were here, I'd definitely smell him.'

'I'll ask EBM.' I placed Clyde on the damp ground. 'I guess you'd best go together. If the search dragons seal up the crossing, you'll need Clyde along to cut a new one. Just make sure you come back here to collect me.'

Morey chuckled. 'Don't worry, Black, we won't leave you behind.'

Clyde reared up and made his second crossing. I watched them disappear through the opening, one much too small for me to even consider following them. Taking a deep breath, I marched up to the small house and knocked on the back door.

A smell of roast chicken and boiled potatoes wafted out as EBM opened the door. My stomach grumbled at the contrast to my packed lunch of hard tack and salted fish. 'Hello, sir,' I said brightly. 'May I come in?'

'You again,' the man grunted, stepping aside. I walked in, immediately pulling off my coat as I drank in the warmth of the house. 'Coffee?'

'Yes, please,' I replied, trying not to sound too desperate. I hadn't enjoyed a cup of my favourite morning drink since my November visit to New York City. 'How are you? And your visitors?'

To my great pleasure, the man poured ground coffee into a filter machine. 'Now, about that. I have a bone to pick with you.'

Bearing in mind how often I'd disturbed this man's life, I would have expected a whole skeleton. 'Go on.'

A small table rested against a wall. The man brought over a mug along with a pitcher of milk, and nodded at the nearest chair. I obediently took a seat. 'Last time you came, you charged out of here when that black car turned up.'

'I had my reasons,' I said cautiously. 'Who was in it?'

'A rather large were-bear.'

I nearly spilled my coffee. 'How did you know that's what he was? A were-bear?'

'The dwarves told me afterwards,' the man admitted. 'I could see there was something odd about the chap, the way he suddenly looked so different when he turned his head. Fair made my stomach turn, I tell you.'

'Weres do the same to me,' I said. 'It's like there's some sort of a shimmer around their bodies.'

The man nodded. 'That's it. Anyways, he knew all about you. Said this Minister without Portfolio, Sue Harkness, wanted very much to see you. You'd skedaddled by then, so I told him she was plumb out of luck. He got a bit shirty and wanted to know why you were here and what you said to me.'

I took a sip of coffee, and took a moment to revel in the thick roast swirling around my tongue. 'What did you tell him?'

'To get off my property and take his attitude back to London.' The man sniffed. 'Last I heard, an Englishman's home is still his castle. No one comes to my door and demands I answer his questions.'

'Unless it's the police, I guess.'

'Don't trust them either,' the man grumped. 'Well, except that Peter you used to be with. I phoned him afterwards. He came over with a vet, nice woman called Jenny, and they said that I'd best move out the refugees staying with me.'

A chill moved down my spine. 'Did Peter say why?'

'They're in danger.' EBM removed his glasses to give them a quick polish. 'So some of us have started up this network, see, called the "Friends of Aslan".'

'"Friends of Aslan"?'

The man glared at me. 'Well, we couldn't call it "Friends of Lloegyr" now, could we? Far too obvious.'

I bit back my words. The man's face was lined with worry, and his hair looked greyer than I remembered. It suddenly occurred to me that he was paying a high price for becoming involved with the problems of England's sister country. 'The network is trying to help Lloegyr refugees?'

'That's the point of it, yes,' he said. 'Seems someone is rounding them up, wherever they find them.'

I glanced through a window to the grey and damp back garden. 'Is that what happened here?'

'Of course not,' EBM growled. 'I'd never have allowed that. We managed to move them to a safe place. Well, all of them except Philip.'

'The manticore?'

'That's the one.' The lines around the man's eyes deepened. 'He just couldn't make his mind up, whether to stay or to go. The van had to leave without him. Me and the missus went off to do the shopping one day, and when we got back, he was gone. The lock on the side gate was busted, so I think the government just came and took him.'

'You're sure it's the government?'

That earned me another hard stare. 'Of course. Who else would it be?'

'Sue Harkness,' I muttered bitterly. 'That's why we need to keep the existence of Lloegyr secret. It's the only way to protect its citizens.'

The thump of the man's fist on the table made me jump and coffee spilled across the scarred wood. 'No, that's exactly why as many people as possible need to know about Lloegyr.'

'But if they do, more might try to exploit that country.' I shook my head. 'I've met them. Businessmen who want to take over parcels of land. Government ministers who see advantages for our military in using the crossing places.'

'The reason they'd get away with that is because hardly anyone else knows.' His tone was fierce, and I found myself leaning back in my chair. 'Prove to the great British public that there's this other world, and the people there are under threat. They'll protect them.'

'Really?' I asked. 'Do you think humans are willing to accept that they aren't the only intelligent beings in the universe? And that these other beings are worthy of protection?'

'Seems to me you're the one who could use a dash of humility, Miss "I know what's best for everyone",' the man retorted. 'What gives you the right to decide who knows and who doesn't know?' Before I could answer, he continued, 'I tell you something else. After that winged unicorn gave me and my wife this blasted Sight, I found out that my memories had changed. When I think back to the first time I saw you, for example, I can now see the dragon and snails that were there. Other people in the "Friends of Aslan" say the same. I bet there's all sorts who've come across people from Lloegyr and didn't realise it. If they had the Sight as well, they could help us. And God knows we could use the help.'

The sudden weariness in his tone made me lean forward in sympathy. 'What's been happening?'

The man rubbed his eyes. 'Like I said, round-ups of Lloegyr people. Some of us in the network, we're certain we're being followed. One of them, June, one of those who set us up, she's disappeared. We do have good people on our side. Bishop Nigel, he's been a brick. But he's like you, "Don't tell anyone, keep it all quiet.'"

'Could you please send the Bishop a message?' I asked. 'Let him know that Penny White is still alive.'

'Certainly.'

'And you said your wife has the Sight as well?'

'She saw the unicorn from our bedroom window. Even took some photos.' He eyed me. 'Are you wanting to use my phone again? I'm not sure it's secure. I bet government people listen in.'

'I'm only here to recharge my iPhone, if that's okay.' I pulled the mobile out of my coat pocket. 'I need to plug it in, though.'

The man did so for me, and without prompting also poured me another cup of coffee. 'Is it safe using that?'

'Sue Harkness has the number,' I admitted. 'I'll use the phone just before I leave.'

'Good. I don't need to give them another reason to call around here.'

'Understood.' I gave him an apologetic smile. 'I'm waiting for someone to cross back from Lloegyr. Do you mind if I stay in your kitchen a little bit longer? It's very cold outside.'

The man nodded. 'I need to get on. Let yourself out when you're ready. By the way, we have a website and social media set up for the "Friends of Aslan". I won't try to teach you all the code words. But if you do need to get hold of us, leave us a message to say that you need to speak to Mister Tumnus. That's me.'

'Mister Tumnus.' I narrowed my eyes. 'That's the first person Lucy met in Narnia. Are you one of the main people in this collective?'

'Someone had to be,' he said, sounding defensive. 'We had to do something to protect these people. "Whatever you did for one of the least of these brothers and sisters of mine, you did for me." I think Jesus meant it when he said we're supposed to look after each other.'

My throat was tight and I felt tears prickling my eyes. 'And I don't even know your name.'

The man rose from his seat, and so did I. We shook hands. 'It's Colin. Colin Shoemaker.'

'Colin Shoemaker,' I said solemnly. 'I'm proud to know such a good friend to Aslan.'

Colin gave me the Sunday paper to read, and I was working my way through the travel section when I saw Morey and Clyde reappear. I collected my iPhone, noting that the two hours I'd waited hadn't been totally wasted. At least I had a fully charged mobile.

I tightened my coat around my chest before going back outside. A cold wind swirled through my hair, and I tucked the brown strands back behind my ears. Morey was fluffed, and Clyde was shivering. 'Just a moment,' I said as I opened up my contact list and clicked on my brother's number.

Just like the last time I'd tried, I only heard a dead tone on the other end. I ended the call, and stared at my phone. Whom else could I contact? I had Skylar's number, but no conversation with that vampire was ever brief. I resorted to a text. *Hi, it's Penny. Only briefly in England, going back to Lloegyr. Please tell James I'm still alive.*

'Okay,' I said as Morey leapt up to my shoulder. 'Time to go back. Clyde, can you find the thin place you made earlier?'

'Yes,' he said smugly, pointing his eyespots at a place near the bushes. I pushed my hand through, wriggled my fingers in the welcome warmth, and then took us to the other side.

The clearing was dragon-free. I retrieved the pocketknife from my trouser pocket. Then a sudden thought hit me. 'Peter and Jenny came together to visit Earls Barton Man.'

Morey's tail slapped against my back. 'To do what?'

'To tell him to send his refugees somewhere else, for their safety.' I looked down at the pitted handle of the knife. 'Do you think Peter and Jenny could be, well, together?'

'I suppose that's possible,' Morey replied.

'Peter and Jen,' Clyde said confidently, still tucked up in my left arm.

'Where's a chair when you need one?' I muttered.

Morey sighed. 'Come on, Black. You've moved on. You're married, for goodness sakes. You didn't expect Peter to pine after you forever, did you?'

'Not forever. But a decade or two would've been nice.'

The gryphon chuckled. 'Go on. Call your husband.' Then his feathers slicked. 'And once we're back on the ship, I'll tell you what I saw at Saint Raphael's.'

I put Clyde down and opened the blade half way. While we waited for the dragon to appear, I dug out my dry and salty lunch. I'd emptied my water bottle by the time Raven appeared in the sky, wings spread wide as he glided towards us.

'Successful visits?' he asked the moment his feet touched down on the grass.

'An interesting one, at least for me,' I said. 'We'll talk about it once we're on *The Morning Star*. You'd better seal up this crossing.'

Raven sliced his sharp teeth across a toe, and splattered red blood at the thin place. Then he lowered his neck, enabling me to place Clyde between two spines before I clambered up. Once the snail was tucked inside my coat, the dragon kicked us upwards. Morey opted to fly alongside, placing himself in Raven's slipstream.

Johno waved at us from the crow's nest as we landed on the top deck. 'Arvo!' He changed briefly into albatross form to soar down to join us. 'We set sail tomorrow,' he said once he was back in biped form. 'Time to say hooroo to this island.'

'We'll be ready,' I promised as I placed Clyde on the gunwale before shedding my coat.

'Bonza.' And he flew back up to his viewpoint.

Morey hopped up to join the snail. 'Any of you see Jago around?'

Raven lifted his head and sniffed the air. 'No sight or smell. Why?'

'It'll become clear in a moment.' Morey lowered his voice. 'I hoped that Taryn would be at Saint Raphael's, as today's Sunday, but I didn't think it was a good idea to have a thin place opened up in our flat. That could cause awkward questions when a search dragon called to seal it up again. So Clyde cut one through to the woods. He went off to hunt, and I headed towards the house.'

'Blackbird,' the snail said, and released a happy burp.

'And it took me ages to sneak over,' Morey continued. 'It looks like Saint Raphael's is undergoing major expansion. There are three new barns and another stone building going up near the main house. The number of not-weres has tripled. I also saw at least four clergy wandering around.'

'Saint Raphael's has been struggling financially,' I said slowly. 'But Llewelyn did say that he'd found a new benefactor, remember? You asked who it was, Morey, but Llewelyn said the person wanted to remain anonymous.'

'I finally managed to slip into the house and upstairs without being seen,' the gryphon continued. 'Taryn was in the flat, and we had about an hour together. She wasn't best pleased to hear that the ship wouldn't be heading back until May. I promised I'd ask Clyde if we could risk another crossing in a couple of weeks if we're still stuck out here.'

The snail waved his tentacles. 'Okay.'

'I left by a window.' Morey paused, his eyes sweeping the ship before continuing. 'I thought I was in the clear, and I started back to the woods. Then I heard Llewelyn's voice, so I hid behind those boulders near the front of the house. And guess who he was talking to? Bastien.'

Raven grunted. 'Perhaps the rat has decided to live there.'

'Could you hear what they were saying?' I asked.

Morey shook his head. 'Not much of it. They were too far away. I did hear one word I recognised. "Letherum".'

Raven growled. 'Wasn't that what was used against the vampires at Llanbedr? It made their children lose their bat shapes and fall into the river.'

'Yes, it was,' I said, shuddering at the memory. 'Tarkik and his crew also used it against the resident akhlut. It froze the were-orcas into their wolf form. Both those times, it was released as a gas. The tablet form is what Saint Raphael uses to settle not-weres into one shape rather than a mixture of two. It also works as a pain killer for some species.'

'Helping?' Clyde suggested. 'Supplies?'

'I never asked how the Guild sourced its letherum.' I glanced at the gryphon. 'Morey?'

'No more than I asked where the bandages came from or who was the supplier of our morning bacon.' Morey lifted his wings in a shrug. 'I was there as a clergyperson, not a quartermaster.'

'We could be making too much of this,' I said. 'There could be an innocent explanation. Maybe letherum works as a pain killer on rats, just like it does on humans.'

'None of us trust the rat kings,' Morey agreed. 'But something about the way Llewelyn and Bastien were speaking to each other just seemed, well, off. I'm not going to say anything to Jago.'

'You have nothing to go on,' Raven said. 'But my question to you is this. Is letherum valuable?'

'I don't know.' I again turned to Morey. 'Llewelyn keeps the Guild's supplies locked away, but I thought that was to stop people from helping themselves to the drug. Is it rare?'

Morey's feet shifted on the wooden top of the gunwale. 'I've never spent much time thinking about it. Letherum has such a specialised use that I never came across it until we met not-weres. I know supplies are controlled. Taryn once told me that the medics at her police station keep notes anytime they use it.'

'If the supply is monitored,' Raven persisted, 'and if someone wanted access to letherum, surely they would approach a place which is permitted to stock it. No doubt such a institution could demand a high price.'

I stared at him. 'Llewelyn's not a drug dealer. I refuse to believe that. I think you're putting two and two together to make five.'

'Two and two does not add up to five,' Jago said crossly, landing a moment later beside his father. 'What're you all talking about?'

Chapter Three

'Our trips to England and to Lloegyr,' I said quickly. 'Did you hear? Morey saw Llewelyn.'

'I only heard the bit about wrong maths,' the small gryphon replied, his purple-blue crest rising far above his head. 'Did you see Mam, Tad?'

'I visited her, yes,' Morey said. 'I couldn't stay for long, but I told her we were both well and that it might be awhile before we're back home. She wasn't very happy about that, I have to say.'

'And we might still find an air crossing,' I pointed out. 'I do wish we knew what formed them. That might help. Land thin places always seem to be formed where a lot of people have been killed. But the ones in the air? I can't think that snail sharks made all of those, particularly as only rare lefties like Clyde seem to be able to do it.'

'I simply use them,' Raven said. 'I've never pondered what brought them into being. I still think we could risk using Clyde and going back to Lloegyr. How would anyone there know that this area lacks air crossings? You are the one putting two and two together to make five, erroneous Penny.'

'Clyde?' I asked. 'How do you feel about it?'

The snail's body flashed with various colours, and he added to his explanation with his sign language. Jago told us, 'Uncle Clyde thinks that the further away we are from les Etats-Unis, the more likely people are to think that air crossings won't have been closed off by search dragons. He suggests we have one last look at the next island. If Raven can't find any air thin places there, then he'll create a crossing.'

I rubbed my forehead and told myself that this was Clyde's decision to make. 'Fair enough. One more island. Enjoy the winter sun while we can.'

'And when we get to the next island,' Jago said, 'I'm going walkabout.'

'And what's that when it's at home?' Morey asked.

'It's something Captain Johno told me about.' Jago stepped away from his much larger father to look into his eyes. 'It's something people do in

Australia, where he comes from. When a young person is trying to work out who they are, they go out into the wilderness on their own for awhile. That's what I'm going to do.'

My stomach squelched. Never had Jago seemed so small. I reached out to lift him into my hands. He rested comfortably on one palm. 'On your own? In a place which has who knows what? Is that safe?'

'I've flown the nest,' Jago retorted. 'I can look after myself.'

Morey leapt over to my shoulder. 'Normally I wouldn't worry about the ability of any of my eyasses to protect themselves. You all come from a strong line of hunters and fighters. But, unlike your brother and sisters, you won't hunt or fight. Penny's right to be concerned. How are you going to feed yourself?'

'These islands have plenty of fruit, Tad.'

'And what if something attacks you?' Morey pressed. 'Will you remain committed to non-violence, even if that means you'd be killed?'

'That's what I need to know.' Jago's eyes, one brown and one blue, flicked between me and Morey. 'Dancer, she said that I'm not a real gryphon. Okay, they didn't hunt, the hummingbird-gryphons, but they were ready to protect themselves and their crops. She said she didn't know what I am, and I don't think I know either.'

'You're a *griffwn glas*,' Morey said gruffly. 'And, more importantly, you're my son.'

'How long do you plan to be gone for?' I asked, trying another tack. 'I mean, what if *The Morning Star* is ready to set sail and you're not back yet? I'm not certain Johno would want to wait around for you.'

'I'd go looking for him,' Raven answered. 'I can find Jago.'

I bit my lip. 'Are you certain?'

The dragon lowered his head. His jaws opened, and he wiped his large blue tongue across Jago's body. As the gryphon spluttered, his grey-blue feathers and fur darkened by dragon saliva, Raven said, 'I am now.'

'Did you have to do that?' Jago asked, his claws digging into my fingers as he tried to shake himself dry.

Raven chuckled. 'Perhaps not. But best to be sure.'

'Come on, Jago,' I told him. 'I'll take you below and you can have a bath.'

'I only had one a month ago,' the gryphon complained. 'Thanks a lot, Uncle Raven. And I've already agreed with the captain that I'd be back in three days!'

'Just be grateful that one lick was enough,' I said as I started down the steps to the lower deck. 'I had to shed blood so he could find James for me.'

'Really?' The mention of Jago's favourite human made his crest rise. 'What was that all about?'

And so I began the tale of a desperate hunt for my brother, which led us to invade a dragon's longhouse and face a murderous matriarch. The tale so enthralled the gryphon that he endured a sink bath without complaint. After I'd sent him back outside to dry in the sun, I noted that a large feather had detached from his crest and was gleaming against the metal basin. I lifted it free and carried the feather to my room, where I patted it dry and placed it carefully into a drawer.

The clank of the anchor chain woke me. I opened my eyes to semi-darkness. The low amount of light coming through the cabin's windows told me that dawn was still only a promise. I stifled a groan and swung my legs out of my bed.

Morey and Jago were curled up on the top bunk, both asleep. No sign of Clyde. The snail was probably working alongside the crew. *Or,* I mused as I changed into outdoor clothes, *is he now part of the crew?*

I went to the galley to find some breakfast. As I'd expected, Massen had laid out the supplies of hard tack, fish oil, and hot water. There was the unexpected bonus of a small jar of fruit jam. I only allowed myself enough to cover one piece of dry bread. Morey and Jago would want some as well.

Colin had given me a packet of ground coffee before leaving me alone in his kitchen. I placed two spoonfuls into a mug, poured in hot water, stirred, and waited for the grains to settle. No milk, and despite my best efforts several grinds still slipped through to catch in my teeth. But it was coffee, and I closed my eyes in order to better enjoy the caffeine rush.

The sun had risen by the time I went up on deck. Wind strained against the large sails, sending *The Morning Star* at a good speed across the open ocean. The island was already no more than a smudge behind us.

I made my way carefully to the top deck, keeping my knees loose to counter the rocking motion of the ship. Raven touched his nose to my shoulder in welcome, then lifted his head again to look towards the bow. I glanced down to see Clyde pulling on a rope, adding his weight to that of two were-puffins.

Low-lying clouds on our left announced that land was nearby. The ship continued to plough on. This island was obviously not our intended destination. Despite the wind, temperatures were rising along with the sun. I removed my coat and tied the arms around my waist.

A flash of grey and black drew my gaze to the crow's nest. Johno stood in the large basket, his eyes scanning the horizon and shouting down the occasional command to his first mate. A much smaller creature hovered near the captain's head. I lifted a hand to shield my eyes, squinting as I tried to work out what it was.

'A flying rat,' Raven told me. 'I can't quite hear what she's saying, but she sounds very worried.'

Johno held up a feathered arm, and the rat landed. The were-albatross bent his head close. Then he turned. 'Emblyn, turn hard to port! Ship in danger!'

The first mate called out a series of commands, involving specific instructions relating to sails and directions which I only half understood. I moved quickly to grip the wooden top of the gunwale as *The Morning Star* made a sharp course adjustment. The sails snapped at the wind as we aimed towards the island on our left.

The rat flew away from the captain and circled towards the deck. Johno changed into bird form and headed towards the shore. I held up my arm, and the rat landed on my wrist. Her black bat wings trembled above her grey body, and she panted heavily. 'Would you like some water?' I asked, first in English and then in Welsh.

'Water,' she repeated in an accent I couldn't place. I dug into my coat pocket and pulled out my bottle. The rat allowed me to put her down on the gunwale, and I poured water into my left palm. Her whiskers twitched as she drank deeply.

'Once you've caught your breath,' Raven said, 'perhaps you could tell us what you said to the captain.'

The rat cocked her head and flicked her long ears. 'Boat *emergencia grandes rochers.'*

'Do you understand us?' I asked.

'*Sí, por supuesto,*' she replied. 'You speak *aon teanga.*'

'That's Scottish Gaelic,' Morey said as he landed on my shoulder. 'It means "one tongue". Seems to me she's using words from various languages. *Podemos tener tu nombre?*'

'*Mi nombre es* Emala,' the rat said, giving us a slight bow.

'I'm Penny,' I responded. 'This is Morey, and the dragon is Raven.'

Emala nodded at us each in turn. 'Crew on boat *en peligro* by *costa*. Help from *capitano* and ship.'

'That's what's we're doing, going to help,' I agreed. Land was coming into view, another island with sandy shores and a green-hilled interior. 'All ships help each other in emergencies.'

Jago landed on my free shoulder as I finished speaking. 'A rat! Hello, my name is Jago, and it's great to see you.'

'Her name is Emala,' I told the small gryphon. 'We're heading over to help a boat in trouble on, well, I think large rocks is what she said.'

'My boyfriend is a flying rat,' Jago told Emala. Then his crest drooped. 'Well, I hope we'll still be friends once I'm back home and told him everything. Who's your rat king?'

Emala cocked her head. 'What is "rat king"?'

'*Rey rata?*' Morey attempted. '*Roi des rats? Rata reĝo?*'

'I don't think it's the words that confuse her,' Raven said. 'I don't think she even understands the concept. Maybe there are no rat kings here.'

'If so,' Jago said, his voice trembling, 'maybe a rat doesn't need a rat king.'

'Bastien would have been bound to a rat king from birth,' Morey said gently. 'I should think that's rather different to growing up without one.'

We were nearing the island. A clump of dark rocks rose from the sea between us and the shore. Waves crashed against the jagged sides, sending spray high into the air. *The Morning Star* turned to the right and headed along the coast.

A large albatross hovered in the bright sky. I followed the angle of his grey head, and saw the small wooden boat which was bobbing near the rocks. A half-dozen people sat inside, a mixture of genders and skin colours. They sank their oars deep into the water as they fought against the tide. I took a sharp breath. There was no shimmer around their bodies, so they weren't weres. They were all fully human.

Johno flapped back to *The Morning Star* and changed to biped shape. Emblyn stepped away from the ship's wheel and the captain gripped it himself. Johno said a few words to the first mate, and she hurried over to us. 'The boat be too close to the rocks,' she called up. 'We cannot get close. Raven, be thou willing to assist?'

The dragon straightened and extended his wings. 'What do you want me to do?'

'There's a *corda* on the boat,' Emala said quickly. '*Tirez* on the *corda*.'

'I understand.' Raven leapt from the ship, ducking around webbing and sails before aiming himself towards the shore. Emala headed after him, her black wings a frantic blur.

The humans in the small boat saw Raven approaching and shouted out in hope. The fact that they welcomed him made me wonder how and when they'd encountered dragons before. Most humans, in my experience, showed far less enthusiasm the first time they were confronted with a large reptilian predator.

'*Corda!*' Raven shouted out. 'Toss out a rope!'

The man at the bow obeyed, uncoiling a thick brown cable and throwing it out across the heaving water. Raven's chest expanded as he filled his gas chamber. With his weight now lightened, he was able to reduce the pounding of his wings to drop nearer to the ocean surface. It took a couple of attempts, but he managed to snag the rope in his foreclaws.

Emala flew over to his head and said something into his ears. Raven backwinged, pulling the boat away from the rocks. But rather than bring the crew over to us, which is what I'd been expecting, he tugged it parallel to the shore. The vessel stayed afloat, and I released a breath, relieved that it obviously hadn't been damaged. The humans pulled in the oars and slumped, looking exhausted.

As they, and *The Morning Star*, continued along the coast, we left the rocks behind. A wide sweep of sand came into view. A wheeled cart stood near the shore, half-submerged in the water. The man on board waved and shouted at

Raven, and the dragon changed direction to start pulling the boat towards him. I glanced at the animals harnessed to the cart, and rubbed my eyes before looking again. Even before I saw the silver horns, the bright glow of the white hides told me that I was looking at a pair of unicorns.

As the boat drew near to the cart, the humans in the vessel called up to Raven. He released the rope, and they took up their oars. The man in the wagon leaned out as they drew near. He grabbed the gunwale, and the boat was brought up against the back of the cart.

The humans shouted thanks to Raven in various languages. The dragon dipped his wings, then turned to fly back to us. Oars were stowed on board, and the crew rose from their seats to transfer their cargo to the cart.

'I don't understand,' Jago said, leaning out from my shoulder. 'Do you see what they've been carrying? It's rocks. What do they want with rocks?'

Johno handed the wheel back to a crew member before once again becoming an albatross. Emala had landed on the row boat. She moved over as the captain joined her, keeping his wings out for balance as his webbed feet struggled for purchase on the narrow gunwale. A couple of the humans halted their work to listen in on the conversation and add a few words of their own.

The warmth of dragon flame told me that Raven had returned and was emptying his gas chamber. He landed a moment later. 'Well done,' I told him. 'A good rescue.'

'Barely tested my wings,' Raven replied modestly, but he still arched his neck with pride.

Johno dipped his head, and launched himself from the boat. 'Cut sails!' he commanded as he drew near. 'Drop anchor!'

Emblyn issued the necessary commands as the captain rose back into the sky. 'Curiouser and curiouser,' I said as Johno headed inland. 'It'd be nice to know what's going on.'

'I could head off after him,' Morey suggested, shaking out his wings.

'Let's hear from the rat first,' Raven said, pointing his snout at Emala. She had left the boat and was heading back towards our ship.

'*Muchas gracias,*' Emala said as she landed on the gunwale. 'Much *aide* needed for the dam.'

'Dam?' I asked. 'You have a dam?'

'Above our *ville*. A *stoirm mhòr* damaged it.'

The humans in the boat had resumed their seats. With loud snorts, the unicorns put down their heads. They tugged the cart from sea to shore and then on to rough-cut planks laid across the sand. The dark wood eased the passage over the beach and to the grasslands above. Deep ruts cut through to dark soil, and spoke of many earlier journeys.

'The rocks are to repair the dam?' Morey asked. 'How bad is the damage? Are lives at risk?'

'*Beaucoup de dégâts,*' Emala said solemnly. '*Très dangereux.* Your *capitano* looks for himself.'

Unicorns and cart had disappeared into the woods. An empty wagon was making its way down to the shore, this time drawn by a unicorn and a brown-skinned horse. The shimmer around the horse's stocky body told me that I was looking at a were. A second row boat had managed to avoid the rocks and the mix of humans and weres on board were heading towards the beach.

As we waited for Johno to return, we took it in turns to ask questions of Emala. In her mixture of English, Spanish, French, and Gaelic, she informed us that the village held several hundred people. Trying to elicit species' names seemed to confuse her. 'People, people,' she insisted. *'Los ciudadanos. Les habitants. Caraidean.'*

'Like us?' I asked, pointing around at myself, gryphons, dragon, then over at the crew.

'Oui.' Her head turned and she nodded at Clyde. 'And *siorc seilcheag.'*

Morey brought his beak near my ear. 'My Gaelic is a bit rusty, but I think she just said "snail shark".'

I kept my voice low as well. 'Let's not say anything to Clyde until we know for certain.'

Trying to find out where the villagers had come from also proved difficult. 'Leave it,' Morey finally said. 'Perhaps she just thinks that her community has always existed.'

'We may have more answers in a moment.' Raven pointed ears and horns at the rapidly approaching were-albatross.

Johno changed into biped form the moment he landed. 'All hands on deck!' he called out. 'All-crew conference!'

'Should I go get Cornelius?' Jago asked. 'If everyone's supposed to be up here.'

Morey sniffed. 'Do you think he'd be bothered? That insect is only interested in himself.'

'He should still be here.' Jago flew to the lower deck, waiting until the last of the were-puffins had emerged from the ship before going below. All twenty-four crew members stood ready and waiting. Twenty-five, if I included Clyde.

Johno climbed halfway up the steps to the upper deck. The grey feathers covering his scalp gleamed in the bright sunlight. 'Oi, you lot. I had a gander at this dam of theirs. It's stuffed. There's a big hole in the front and their village is only a mozzie's leap away. They need heaps of help.'

Emblyn stepped forward. 'What needs doing, Captain?'

'Good onya,' Johno said. 'But what do the rest of youse reckon? This won't be an easy flight. There's rocks to shift and nippers to move.'

'Nippers?' Massen asked. 'There be chicks?'

Johno dipped his head in a jerky nod. 'Plenty in their village, just below this here dam. If it goes they're carked.'

'No chicks be let to die,' Massen said firmly. Behind him the rest of the crew clucked and muttered agreement.

Raven let out a heavy sigh. 'Fit me up with my harness and a net. I can help carry stone up to the dam. I assume they're using it to patch up the hole. You'd best come with me, Penny. I want someone I can trust to make sure everything's fastened properly, and you're good with knots.'

'I'll go with the were-puffins,' Morey said, lifting his head from a quick conversation with his son. Jago had reappeared at some point and was sitting on the gunwale, Cornelius at his side. 'Help move villagers to safety.'

'We'll need a skeleton crew,' Johno reminded everyone. 'Clyde, Doethineb, you choose three others.'

Snail and were-penguin made their way through the group. Jowan, Doethineb's husband, was first to her side. Another mated couple were chosen, and the five withdrew to the ship's bow.

'You too, Jago,' Morey told his son. 'Stay here and keep an eye on the ship.'

'But I want to go with you,' Jago protested. 'I can help.'

'How?' Morey's voice was gentle but determined. 'We might need to airlift people to safety. I don't think there'd be many you could help with.'

Jago opened his wings. 'Right. Well, then, I might as well start my walkabout.'

Morey leaned forward, his claws digging through my shirt and into my skin. 'Right now? We don't know why the dam's been damaged. It might not be safe.'

'See you later, Tad.' Jago leapt away, his flight steady and strong as he left the ship behind.

'Let him go,' Raven said as Morey growled, lifting his own wings. 'He's not a puffling.'

'Maybe not, but he's not an adult either,' Morey snapped. To my relief, he flew down to the gunwale, easing the pain in my shoulder. 'You don't understand. You've never had children.'

'I brought up James after our parents died,' I reminded the gryphon. 'I understand.'

Morey dipped his head in a mute apology. 'All right. Let's get to work.'

'I'll go fetch the harness,' I said. As I turned to the stairs, a thought struck me. 'Where's Cornelius?'

'He came up with Jago,' Raven said slowly. 'But I've not seen him since.'

'No doubt made himself scarce when he heard there's work to be done,' Morey muttered. 'I'll find out where the crew keep the nets.'

Chapter Four

Raven shook himself from nose to tail. 'Harness feels secure. Have you checked out the net?'

I inspected the four corners of the closely woven mesh. The black material was artificial, a reminder that there had been a trade of sorts between Lloegyr and Britain. 'Yes, it seems strong enough. I'm going to tie it on your side for now. Until we can report in at the village, I'm not certain whether we can help more by transporting stone from wherever they find it or from a closer point. If they're happy to still use the boats and carts, that saves your strength for the last bit.'

'Indeed.' He held still as I climbed up to his neck. 'At any rate, there is at least one other dragon on this island.'

'How do you know? Did you get some sort of tingly feeling?'

Raven chuckled. 'Of course not. The wind shifted and I smelled her midden.'

'Humans, dragons, unicorns, weres, snail sharks,' I commented. 'I wonder what other species also live here?'

'Time to find out.' And he lifted us from the deck.

We flew over the beach and followed the track which led across the grassland. Another pair of unicorns were pulling at the cart below us, the human on board clutching at several stones to stop them from rolling out. Emala caught up with us, and I pointed at my shoulder, saying, 'You've done a lot of flying today. Why not hitch a lift?' She landed a moment later.

The ever-present palm trees were joined by other trees and low lying bushes. I leaned over for a closer look. The growth looked far too regular to be natural. Several fields nearby made me think of planned agriculture. This part of the island bore all the hallmarks of a settled community.

The cart tracks turned to the left. Raven tipped his wing and took us right. A collection of wooden and clay brick buildings, topped with woven roofs, came into view. Above, and to the left, rose the dam. The concrete panels had broken away on the right-hand side, exposing the soil infill underneath. A yellow dragon was dropping stones from her foreclaws into the gap. Several carts waited at the base of the dam, all filled with rocks.

'We should send puffins back for another net,' I called out to Raven, glancing back at the black and white birds flying behind us. 'That dragon can only carry so many stones in her feet at a time. She won't have a harness, but she should be able to snag her claws through the webbing.'

Raven grunted his agreement. I turned to shout my suggestion to the crew. Four were-puffins split away from the flock and headed back to the ship.

I studied the dwellings as Raven angled us towards a clear area near the largest building. My rough estimate was at least a hundred houses, erected in a variety of styles. Longhouses were set alongside round cottages. Square homes clustered to one side. Some had ornate front gardens, set with grey stones and flowering plants. Others revealed more practical owners, with neat rows of vegetables growing from weed-free soil.

Johno had landed in the clearing before us. Several villagers waited nearby. A unicorn, her grey hide marked with the impression of harness straps, stood next to a deeply tanned human man. A heavily-maned lion panted nearby, the shimmer around his body telling me that he was a were. Another were, in the form of a blue and yellow parrot, perched on the lion's back.

Raven touched down nearby, his claws rattling against a flooring of flat stones. I forced myself to keep quiet and wait for instructions, telling myself that I wasn't in charge. Johno was the captain of *The Morning Star* and the crew which had volunteered their help. The puffins crashed down behind us, reminding me that landing wasn't their strongest talent. Morey made a polite enquiry of the lion, and landed next the parrot.

'*Diolch am gynnig eich cymorth,*' the man said, startling me with his use of Welsh. '*Fe'i gwerthfawrogwn yn fawr.*'

'We know it's important to fly as a flock,' Johno replied in the same language, although I could see Morey flinch at his rough accent. 'This here dragon is Raven, and he's ready to carry rocks to your dam. Penny, that's the human, she'll be assisting him. The crew and I are ready to help you move to safety.'

There was one advantage to Johno speaking in Welsh, I reflected. It meant he dropped all of his Australian slang. The parrot translated the captain's words into a mixture of English and other languages, which led me to suspect that Welsh wasn't widely known. When we had a moment, I wanted to find out more about the origins of this community.

The unicorn dipped her head in a nod. '*Muchas gracias.* If Raven could help Clodagh we'd all be *taingeil.*'

Emala hopped down as Raven took off. As we rose away from the village, I kept my gaze on Johno as he split his crew into smaller groups and the were-puffins headed towards the houses. Morey fell in alongside them.

Villagers were already carrying youngsters and personal items away from their settlement and heading towards higher ground. It looked like a long slog up the hill, and I felt some guilt at my far easier assignment.

The yellow dragon was standing beside one of the rock-filled carts when Raven landed nearby. A net rested at her feet. I loosened the one which Raven was carrying and slid from his neck. 'Clodagh? Raven, and Penny. Do you prefer English or *ydych chi'n siarad Cymraeg?*

'Prefer Gaelic,' the dragon grumbled. 'English will do.'

'For us too,' said a human woman standing by the cart. 'I'm Sabine. You want *les rochers* in this?'

I nodded. 'The dragons will be able to carry more at a time.' I unwound my net and brought it over to the cart. To my relief, the back of the wagon was a hinged panel. Sabine lowered it, which meant we could push stones on to the webbing rather than toss them in one by one.

'That's enough,' Raven decided when the mound was around two feet high. He marched over and positioned himself above the netting. 'Hook it up.'

I attached the back corners to the harness. 'I think you're better off holding the front. Then you can decide when to let it go.'

Raven slid his golden claws through the material and filled his gas chamber. Slowly and carefully, he rose into the air. The webbing stretched, and smaller pieces of stone fell through, but the net coped with the weight. The dragon flew off towards the dam.

Sabine and I spread out the second net and repeated the exercise. Clodagh, who was slightly larger than Raven, asked for more stone to be added. Then she hooked all ten fingertoes through the netting before flying off with her burden. I wondered which dragon would feel the greater strain, Raven who had a harness to spread the weight across his body, or Clodagh who carried it all with just her legs.

Carts came and went, pulled by teams of unicorns and were-horses which looked increasingly weary as the day went on. The humans handling the wagons shared their lunches with me, and directed me to a nearby stream when my water bottle ran dry. Between dragon visits, I managed to find out that the dam had been built fifty years previously. A recent bad storm had damaged the visible front and, it was feared, the other side as well.

'We don't know how to repair *les dégâts*,' one man told me wearily, rubbing at his dark forehead. 'We need *hora* to move the *ville*.'

The day was drawing to a close. My arms were aching from the long hours of shoving stones and rigging nets. The dragons and those working on the carts looked equally tired. I glanced at the man standing nearest me, and managed to remember his name. 'Thiago, I think it's getting too late to do much more.'

He nodded, pulling a grubby rag from his trouser pocket to wipe his face.

'*Sí.* More *mañana.*'

I glanced at Raven, noting with concern where the harness had rubbed his skin raw. '*Mañana,*' the dragon agreed. 'We'd best go to the village, Penny, and see if the crew is ready to return to the ship.'

Suppressing a groan, I pulled myself up to his neck. Raven took us upwards, his leap lacking its usual vigour. I glanced back at the dam as we flew away. The rocks thus far added to the broken side looked like an inadequate response. Water lapped against the top, and I wondered how much more might run in from the surrounding hills.

Puffins were already in the air when Raven pulled up to hover over the village. Johno and Morey still remained on the ground, deep in discussion with the two weres. The lion was in biped form, and the parrot clung to his bare shoulder.

Morey looked up as the dragon's shadow touched clearing. After a few last words, he flew up to join us. 'Everyone has been evacuated,' he said as he landed on my shoulder. 'We'll be moving more possessions tomorrow. How's it been going at the dam?'

'I'm not sure how much good it'll do, adding rocks to the front,' I admitted. 'And no one has any idea if there's damage on the other side.'

'That should be easy enough to check out,' Morey said. 'Send somebody down wearing the mer tail.'

I grinned. 'What a great idea. I could do that first thing tomorrow.'

Morey cocked his head. 'How good a swimmer are you?'

'I've done a bit,' I said defensively.

Raven's chuckle thrummed against my legs. 'Valiant Penny, there are others equally able to risk their lives for a higher cause. We have no need for anyone to use the mer tail. There's a were-penguin on *The Morning Star.* I should think Doethineb is the best suited for the job.'

'Used to swimming in treacherous waters,' Morey agreed. 'We could bring her tomorrow. Pack the mer tail, Black, if it makes you feel any better.'

'No, you're right,' I said. 'And I should think she'd have better underwater sight than me.'

The Morning Star was a welcome sight as we swooped across the shore. I was sweaty and my shirt and trousers were grimy with dust and mud. A quick sponge bath, change of clothing, and then I'd speak to Johno and Doethineb about inspecting the dam.

Raven, of course, wasted no time in relaying his suggestion to the were-penguin. Everything had been arranged by the time I returned to the top deck. The next morning I felt every muscle in my arms complain as I helped Doethineb up to the dragon's neck. Even in biped form, the were-penguin's head only reached my shoulders.

I climbed up to place myself one spine behind her. Although I'd rubbed

THE HUMILITY OF HUMANS

ointment into Raven's hide the evening before, the welts from the harness still looked painful. He'd decided that he'd carry any further nets full of stones in the same way as Clodagh, by threading the webbing through his feet. We still carried the harness, just in case the other dragon wanted to try using it.

The morning sun was weak, fighting its way through high clouds. I could only hope that the island wasn't facing another storm. We didn't need yet more water racing down to the reservoir.

A cart was already halfway up the incline from the beach. I felt a sense of helplessness on the villagers' behalf. All this effort could be for nothing if the water levels rose further and either leapt over the top of the dam or forced the walls to collapse. At least everyone was now safe on higher ground.

The dam came into view. Raven hovered for a moment by the loading area so I could drop off the harness. Then he took us over to the dam, his claws only a dozen feet away from the damaged area. 'Have a good look,' he told Doethineb. 'We need to know if it's the same on the other side.'

The were-penguin grunted. We would have to wait until we were back with the crew to find out what she'd seen. Her fellow were-birds had no difficulties in translating her squawks and snorts.

Raven flew low over the water. Waves lapped against the top of the dam. Doethineb leaned down and studied the situation. She pointed at an area to our left then upwards. 'Back off about twenty feet,' I told the dragon. 'And go up to around the same height.'

Once Raven was hovering over the spot, Doethineb carefully rose from her seat to stand on the dragon's neck. She leapt off, gracefully turning in the air and changing into penguin form. Her orange and black beak hit the water first, followed by her long body. The resulting splash and ripples dispersed quickly across the dark liquid.

Raven flew over to the nearby bank and landed heavily. 'Are you okay?' I asked, laying a hand on his warm skin.

'Tired from yesterday,' he admitted. 'Saving myself up for starting up again today.'

We watched for signs of Doethineb. I wondered anxiously how long penguins could hold their breath under water. A few bubbles broke the surface, which I decided to take as a sign that she was still alive. To our right, Clodagh had resumed her work on the dam. Stones thumped against soil and broken concrete.

After what felt like hours--but my wristwatch assured me was only fifteen minutes--the black and white head of a penguin emerged from the water. She looked around, spotted where Raven was waiting, and swam over to join us. Water slid from her body as she climbed onto land and waddled up the slight incline.

I slid from Raven's neck and held out my hand. She shimmered into human form and placed her cold fingers into mine. I pulled her up to stand next to me. 'Did you find anything?'

Her head bobbed in a nod. She pointed down the hill. The message was clear. She needed to tell us what she'd found. I gave her a heave up the dragon's side, and quickly followed suit.

The moment I was settled in my usual seat, Raven launched himself from the bank and angled us towards the village. I saw the net waiting for us by the cart and felt a pang of guilt. The correct course of action would be to leave Doethineb with the village leaders and return to our work on the dam. But I knew full well that I would wait to hear her findings.

The were-parrot and unicorn broke off their conversation with Morey and Johno as Raven landed in the clear area. Behind them villagers and were-puffins were hard at work, removing possessions from the houses. I noted with relief that nearly all of those who had come back down to the village were able to fly. If the dam should suddenly collapse, they had a good chance of saving themselves.

Doethineb began to speak the moment Raven's claws touched the stones. Johno bent his head, listening intently. The parrot, also in biped form and covered with red and blue feathers, shifted impatiently from foot to foot. The unicorn acted more patiently, tail flicking across her hindquarters.

'The other side of the dam is a goner,' Johno reported solemnly. 'Lots of cracks. Chucking stones on this side is a boondoggle. More water, and the whole thing could go.'

'We need to drain off the water, somehow,' I said. 'Large buckets, carried by the dragons?'

Raven grunted. 'Water, rocks, it's all the same to me. But I shouldn't think that just two of us could remove enough water to make any difference.'

Morey flew over to my shoulder and lowered his beak to my ear. 'We know someone who could create a hole under the water.'

It took me a moment to work out what he meant. 'A thin place acting as a drain?'

'Precisely.' Morey lifted his head. 'We have an idea, but it means returning to the ship. Doethineb, you coming with us?'

The were-penguin bobbed her head.

Raven took off again. Although the sun was battling on, the clouds were starting to thicken. 'I smell rain in the air,' Morey confirmed as I looked anxiously upwards. 'We need to drain that water.'

'Clyde has to have been somewhere first,' I reminded him, glancing at the feathered figure of Doethineb in front of me. None of the crew knew of the snail's talent, and I preferred to keep it that way. 'What are we going to do, lower him into the water?'

Morey chuckled. 'He can also just use a connection with someone he knows. Weren't we talking the other day about how you, Penny, can establish that sort of connection?'

I felt my face redden. 'You want me to, I mean, am I to visit the loo and…?'

'Or I could do it,' the gryphon said. 'Seeing as I'm not as bothered as you about these things.'

'No one else needs to sully the reservoir,' Raven told us. 'Clyde has worked with many members of the crew. We'll just ask one of the were-puffins to dive deep, and he can make the connection with him or her.'

'Why not have Doethineb do the dive?' I asked.

'Because once the drain is opened,' Morey said, 'whoever is on the water side is going to be sucked through. You want someone who can fly out of the way. So we want the crossing to be high enough in the air to give the puffin time to do so.'

I wished I could think of a different solution. Perhaps, with enough time, one would come to me. But we didn't have that luxury. 'We'll want a volunteer. And the puffin needs to know the risks.'

The few crew members who had remained on *The Morning Star* glanced up as we approached. I waved at Clyde as Raven landed on the upper deck. The snail climbed up the steps and I dismounted to crouch beside him. 'The dam is very weak, and we think it could break at any time. The idea is that we'll send a crew member to the base of the dam, and you'll cut a thin place through to somewhere else on the island. The water will then drain out.'

Orange and greens pulsed through the snail's body as he considered the idea. 'Yes.'

'It means,' I continued, glancing down at the were-puffins on the lower deck, 'that more people will know about your ability to create thin places.'

'Necessary,' Clyde said firmly. 'Save lives.'

I gave his shell a rub and straightened. 'Hello, everyone! We need a volunteer. And it could be dangerous.'

The were-puffins looked at each other. And, almost as one, they all moved forward. 'Any of us be willing,' one said gruffly. 'Take yer pick.'

Their willing trust made my eyes prickle. 'Kayna,' I said, recalling that she was one of the few puffins who had decent landing skills. 'Can I explain to you on the way over?'

A quick swap of penguin for puffin, and then we were heading back to the dam. To her credit, Kayna quickly took in what was being asked of her. Other than checking how close she was to be to the dam itself, and agreeing to the height of the air drain, she didn't probe too deeply as to how the crossing was to be formed. She did glance back once at Clyde, who was tucked up safely against my chest.

Raven only hovered over the dam long enough to allow Kayna to fly down to the surface. 'Give us ten minutes,' he called down to her. 'I know where to take us. Wait ten minutes, then dive down.'

'I hope puffins know how to mark time,' Morey grumbled from his place on my shoulder.

I glanced at my wristwatch, wondering the same. Raven headed to our right, rounding the hill and heading back towards the coast. Seven minutes after we'd left the reservoir, we reached an area of grass and palm trees. There were no signs of habitation or agriculture. Raven took us upwards, hovering around a hundred feet above the ground. 'Here. Have Clyde make the crossing to one side of us.'

I lifted the snail from my chest. Morey gave me a nod and left my shoulder. My legs ached as I clenched them tight around the dragon's neck and leaned out to my left. 'Ready, Clyde?'

The snail opened his teeth and sliced at the air below us. The moment water began to gush through, Raven tilted his right wing and pulled us away. A small body appeared in the flow, squawking as she was carried through the waterfall. Kayna fluttered free. Morey flew to her side, but the puffin quickly righted herself. My heart rate calmed down again as she flew over to us.

'That should do,' Raven said with great satisfaction. 'Let's check out the reservoir, then go to the village with the good news.'

Although I shared his pleasure over the successful outcome of our plan, I brought Clyde close and held him tight. I could only hope that no one on *The Morning Star* thought to ask, or even worked out, what role Clyde had played in today's events.

Chapter Five

A quick circle over the reservoir revealed that the airy waterfall was working. The water level had already gone down, and the damage on the inside of the dam was plain to see. The thin place would have to be left open. I could only hope that the island's inhabitants would simply become accustomed to the strange phenomenon.

'You can stop hauling rocks!' Raven called out to Clodagh and the workers on the carts. 'The water is emptying. Come down to the village!'

Kayna and Morey went on ahead of us. By the time we landed, the news had already spread. The were-parrot flashed past us, bright wings pounding as he flew towards the dam. Johno followed close behind him. Villagers and crew put down their burdens, looking both hopeful and confused. My heart sank as I wondered how we were to explain what had happened.

'It be a mystery to me,' the were-puffin was telling nearby listeners, Morey standing next to her. 'Swimming I was, near the dam. A hole opened, and I be sucked through.'

'It's enough that it's happened,' I said quickly. 'You can all move back home again.'

'That would be a relief,' the unicorn said. She took a step forward. 'In all this *emergencia,* no *nombre* have been given. Mine is Clely.'

She was obviously one of the rare unicorns who used contractions and gave her name. I tucked Clyde carefully under one arm and slid down from Raven's neck. 'Mine is Penny. This is Raven.'

Clely's eyes flicked from dragon forefoot to my left wrist. 'Your husband, I see.'

'Yes,' I said, bracing myself for her reaction.

'You've met my *mari,*' the unicorn continued. 'The were-lion, Bernal.'

For once, my school French proved to be useful. *Mari* meant 'husband'. 'And that's accepted here?'

Clely stared at me. 'Why wouldn't it be?'

The dark-skinned man we'd met on the first day panted as he joined us. 'It is *certo?* The dam is now safe?'

'Rory has flown to see,' Clely told him. 'Gaspard, these are Penny and Raven.'

'Morey,' my Associate said, dipping his head in a bow.

'And this is Clyde.' I held up the snail shark.

'*Siorc seilcheag,*' Gaspard exclaimed, sounding genuinely pleased. 'The others are on the hill.'

'Others?' Clyde repeated, tentacles waving excitedly.

The parrot came back into view, Johno close behind. 'Water's gone, water's gone,' the were-bird called out, the albatross adding, 'Just inches left at the bottom!'

'Our *ville* is quite empty,' Gaspard said, an ironic lilt in his deep voice. 'Stay, *s'il vous plaît,* and when we are again to home, *àm pàrtaidh* with us. *Mañana?*'

Johno glided down to join the group. 'Bonza, I like a cracking shindig. We'll first help you lot move back. We can stay on a couple days.'

'That also gives time for Jago to come back,' Morey commented, his voice strained.

I felt a stab of guilt. In all the activity over the past two days, I'd not given Jago much thought. 'How about we give him until tomorrow afternoon, and then Raven could go looking for him?'

Morey flew up to my shoulder. 'Maybe just to scout out where he is. Jago'd never forgive me if we brought him back before he's finished with his great adventure.'

'Not adventure, mate,' Johno corrected. 'He's on walkabout. You don't mess with that.'

'So long as nothing messes with my son,' Morey growled.

'If something does,' Raven promised, 'we will avenge him together.'

Morey didn't look much comforted by the dragon's statement.

The less hurried pace of restoring the village finally gave us time to come to know the people we'd helped. Clely and Bernal became my guides, showing me their small house and the unicorn's well-kept grazing area. What few possessions they had were still in a jumble by the door, but I could see that they kept a clean and normally tidy abode.

'Many came here from *ailleurs,*' Bernal said as we walked along one of the paths through the village. 'Ships, blown by storms. Others from les Etats-Unis.'

He strode away to help a were-tiger who was trying to lead a child and carry several sacks at the same time. The cub squirmed as Bernal scooped her into his arms, but a quick purr from her father calmed her down.

'When we were there,' I said, 'we were told that humans are always removed from that country. They're shipped over here?'

'Yes, and not only humans,' Clely replied. 'Others also fell through *des fissures entre les lieux* before the *fissures* were closed.'

I fought my way through the French. 'Do you mean thin places? A shimmer in the air which leads from one place to another?'

'*Sí.* So we gained many of your kind.'

The sun was setting on a village transformed from morning despair to evening joy. As we passed house after house, the inhabitants talking excitedly, some of them even singing, I was struck by the integration. Unlike the towns and cities in Lloegyr, the different species hadn't segregated themselves. Unicorns lived side by side with weres. Clodagh's long house stood near that of a human family. 'You all seem to be happy to live alongside each other,' I commented as the dragon lowered her head to a toddler squealing for attention.

'We are all *ville,*' Clely said. 'Look. Your friend has found the *siorc seilcheag.*'

Clyde and a dozen other snail sharks sat on the grass outside a round-walled hut. Most of his new friends were several times his size, and I was once again saddened by all he had sacrificed in order to bring peace between two warring armies of snail sharks. Without Jago or Cornelius, I had no way of knowing what the group was saying to each other. But the bright colours told me that they were delighted to be together.

I glanced behind me. The human child was gripping Clodagh's nose in an attempt to stand. The dragon's ears and horns were twisted, telling me that the grip was uncomfortable, but she made no attempt to stop the toddler. 'So there's no problems living with humans?'

Clely glanced at me. 'Why would there be?'

Indeed. It looked like I'd found a community in which all the species happily co-existed. Perhaps there was hope for the humans stuck in Llanbedr? Over time, could they start to integrate with others in that city? Then I reminded myself that, at times, even Lloegyr's native species struggled to accept one another.

A sudden rise in voice levels made me halt. Angry words rose from the area behind us. In the midst of the babble, I heard a Southern drawl. 'If your brain was dynamite you still couldn't blow your nose! Let me out of this here cage before I knock you so hard, you'll see tomorrow today!'

I turned and rushed in the direction of the commotion. A number of villagers stood in the clearing, stomping hooves and shuffling feet. A basket had been turned into a pen. Cornelius was trapped inside, his forelegs snapping open and shut as he shouted curses at his captors.

'Let him out,' I panted as I pulled up nearby. 'He's with us.'

'This *insecto grande?*' Gaspard spat. He lifted his foot, and for a moment I feared that he was going to kick the basket.

'Stop! Stop now!' Jago batted around the man's head. 'Leave him alone!'

'Yes,' I added. 'Whatever's he's done, I'm certain we can sort it out.'

—

'I've done nothing,' the praying mantis stated indignantly. 'I was wandering through some pastureland, minding my own business, when this ruffian leaped out and shoved me in this here cage.'

Jago flew over to land on my shoulder. 'He's right, Auntie Penny. Cornelius wasn't doing anything wrong.'

'It's an *insecto grande*,' a were-wolf growled. 'No one can trust an *insecto grande*.'

'If I had a dog as ugly as you,' Cornelius retorted, 'I'd shave his butt and make him walk backwards.'

'And this isn't helping matters,' I said quickly. 'Cornelius has travelled with us for some time. Please let him out.'

Gaspard caught my eyes. 'Do you trust it?'

I always found it difficult to offer a lie in response to a direct question. 'I don't know what your issue is with insects, but I'm certain Cornelius hasn't done anything to deserve imprisonment. If you'll let him go, we'll take him back to the ship.'

'The *insectos grandes* captured me in les Etats-Unis,' a unicorn stated. 'Hobbled my legs and put me on a ship to this island.'

'Same with me,' Gaspard said. 'They are no friends to us.'

Morey landed on my other shoulder. 'So you'll be glad to be shot of him. Like Penny said, we'll happily take him back to our ship.' He leaned out to speak to Jago. 'And it's good to have you back, son.'

I looked around for Raven and couldn't see him. As I pulled out my pocketknife and half extended the blade, I told the gathering, 'It's been a long day and we all need our rest. When we come back tomorrow, we'll leave the *insecto grande* on *The Morning Star.*'

Raven landed a moment later. 'What have I missed?'

'It's time to head back,' I said wearily. My good mood had evaporated in the heat of the villagers' anger. *Dear God,* I thought, *why can't I ever find somewhere that's free of prejudice?*

Gaspard looked around at the other villagers. Then he nodded. 'But the *insecto grande* stays in its *jaula.*'

'Fine,' I replied over Cornelius' renewed protests. 'Raven, could you please fetch your harness?'

The delay was unwelcome, as the people around me were still muttering angrily in various languages. But I was already going to have to hold Clyde for the flight back. I couldn't try to clutch a praying mantis as well. The basket would just have to be attached to the harness. It wasn't the first time Cornelius had been transported in such a fashion.

Our flight started a general exodus of the crew from the village. Promises were made to return for the celebrations the next evening. Part of me had soured on the idea, but I tried to put my feelings aside. A priest was often called to attend social gatherings, and although some of those were less welcome than others, the ministry of presence was always important. The villagers wanted to express their thanks to us, and so I would be there.

By the time we arrived at *The Morning Star*, Jago seemed to be clinging to my shoulder through sheer willpower alone. I transferred him to Raven's neck before handing Clyde down to Johno. 'Coming, coming,' I told a grumbling Cornelius as I dismounted. 'You wouldn't want me to do this too quickly and accidentally drop you.'

'Certainly not,' the mantis snapped as I lowered the basket to the deck. 'Not when you've made it abundantly clear how much you value me.'

I'd pulled out my penknife, ready to cut the string which had been used to tie off the top of the basket. But I paused to look into the insect's large compound eyes. 'What do you mean? I defended you.'

'Really?'

'Of course.' I opened the blade and worked on setting him free. 'I'd do that for anyone.'

The top was open. I leaned back so Cornelius could extract himself from the woven fibres. The mantis emerged, looking physically undamaged. 'So you did it because I'm an "anyone". Not because I'm Cornelius.'

'I'm not quite sure what you mean.'

The triangular head turned as he looked from me, to Raven towering over us, to Morey sitting on the nearby gunwale, to Clyde resting by my feet. 'I'm not part of this merry gang, am I?'

Morey snorted. 'You've never even tried to be.'

Cornelius opened and shut his wings. 'Well, I feel like I've been chewed up and spat out. I'll leave y'all to sing your little songs around the campfire.'

Clyde made a sad noise as the mantis flew to the lower deck and disappeared down the hatch. 'He doesn't make it easy to be liked,' I reminded the snail, rubbing his shell. 'And I'm still not sure we can trust him.'

'Cornelius does what's best for Cornelius,' Morey reminded me. 'We've seen that time and again.'

Jago dropped down to my shoulder. 'But he doesn't. Not always.'

I looked at him. 'Something you want to tell us about? From your journey?'

The small gryphon looked away. 'He helped me. That's all.'

I nodded. 'Well, I wait to see that for myself.' Suddenly I'd had enough of living on a ship, wandering from island to island. 'Raven, how do your wings feel? Because, if you're up to it, let's fly out tomorrow morning to see if we can find an air crossing to help us go home. And, if not, then maybe it's time we asked Clyde to create one.'

The views were breathtaking. Rain had fallen overnight, and the clouds pulled away by early morning. I stood on a small boulder, looking out across the rounded green hills. The sea gleamed in the distance. From this vantage point, there was no sign of any habitation. *The Morning Star* and the village were on other side of the island.

'Plenty of land thin places,' Raven said on my left. The additional height provided by my perch meant that our heads were nearly level. 'But no air crossings.'

'I can't think that the inhabitants of les Etats-Unis send search dragons over to close those up. Not all the way out here.'

'Or that they would do so and then leave the land ones open,' Raven agreed. 'So it's up to Clyde now. If you feel it's a risk worth taking.'

'It's like you said, how would anyone know that we didn't just find a thin place? We're pretty remote out here.' I placed a palm on his warm skin. 'It could be dangerous for us back in Lloegyr.'

'*Cadw ar Wahân?*' Raven arched his neck. 'I have no fear of *Cadw ar Wahân.*'

'We know they're willing to kill those in mixed-species relationships,' I reminded him. 'That's why I have the mer tail, remember? *Cadw ar Wahân* killed Auiak's wife.'

'Did Llewelyn not tell you that the Guild of Saint Raphael's is safe from *Cadw ar Wahân?*'

'Yes, although I didn't have chance to ask him why. We were in the midst of discussing a wedding ceremony.'

'The chaplain of Saint Raphael's,' Raven noted, 'has various questions to answer.'

'But maybe not all at once,' I said quickly. 'It's probably the only place I can work, after Bishop Aeron finds out I'm your wife.'

Raven grunted. 'You lead a complicated life, convoluted Penny.'

'Should've thought of that before you married me,' I said with a grin. 'Now you're part of it.'

'Gladly,' he replied. 'So, tomorrow afternoon? We have the celebration to attend tonight, and the crew will want some time to express their farewells.'

'And I'll need to pack. Not that I have very much.' I touched one of the wounds on his chest. 'I'm sorry, but you're going to have to wear the harness again.'

'For the last time, I hope.' Raven shifted his feet. 'Let's return to *The Morning Star*. I'll ask for some more of Doethineb's ointment. It soothes the pain.'

'So,' I finished telling Clyde, seated beside him on the lower bunk bed, 'I don't think it's risking too much, going from here. Raven will seal up the crossing on the other side. Are you willing to take us back to Lloegyr?'

Colours flashed through the snail's body and he wriggled his tentacles. Jago, peering down from the top bunk, translated, 'Yes, little risk. Time to go home.'

Home for him, perhaps. I wondered if I even had a place to return to back in England, if and when I ever did. The Church might have found a new priest for my parish and moved my belongings out of the vicarage. Would I be in the uncomfortable position of asking my brother for room and board?

'Let's go tell Johno,' I said. 'Jago, you coming?'

The gryphon hopped down to my shoulder. 'Do you think the captain will be upset?'

'I should think he's used to passengers coming and going,' I replied. 'How are you, by the way? Did the walkabout do, well, whatever you hoped it'd do?'

'It was interesting,' Jago said slowly. 'But, yes, I think so.'

'Fair enough.' I'd walked along the corridor as we spoke, and we'd reached the stairs to the deck. 'If you ever want to sit down for a chat, just let me know.'

'Yes, Auntie Penny, I will.'

Johno was standing near the main mast, his gaze fixed on several crewmembers in the webbing. 'Is everything okay?' I asked.

'Just having a gander,' the captain assured me. 'Youse ready for the knees up? It'll be a real ripsnorter.'

'We'll head over soon.' I cleared my throat. 'We have access to an air crossing, on the other side of the island. So we'll head back to Lloegyr tomorrow.'

Johno clapped a feathered hand on my shoulder. 'So youse be saying hooroo.'

'It's been great sailing with you,' I started awkwardly.

The captain waved my words away. 'Youse all going?'

It hadn't occurred to me to think otherwise. 'I should think so. I'll have to check about Cornelius. I mean, he wouldn't want to stay on this island, but I don't know where else he might want to go.'

Johno dipped his head. 'Poor bloke has nowhere to lay his head.'

'And whose fault is that?' I winced at my sharp tone. 'If he wants to go back with us, we'll take him. Then it's up to him what he does next.'

'He should come back with us,' Jago said. 'I mean, he's not family, but he has helped us.'

'Sweet as,' Johno said. 'And now time for the shindig!'

'I'll stay here,' Jago told me. 'I didn't help the villagers.'

'You could still come--'

'I think someone should keep Cornelius company.' And he launched from my shoulder and went through the hatch.

Ten minutes later, I reached down from Raven's neck to accept Clyde from Johno's hands. Morey hovered nearby, looking impatient to be off. Most of the crew had already flown ahead, squawking happily. Doethineb sat in front of me, her husband standing by Raven's shoulder.

The were-penguin said something to Jowan. He looked up at the dragon.

'Doethineb wanted to thank you for giving her the experience of flight.'

Raven glanced back at us. 'You're welcome.'

Although his wings pulled evenly at the air as he took us towards the village, I could still sense the weariness in his body. I'd ask Clyde to cut the thin place close to Saint Raphael's. It would be good to save Raven from any more long flights for awhile.

The villagers might still be settling back into their homes, but they had made quite an effort for the celebrations. Torches had been lit around the clearing, providing light as the sun set. Tables covered with food filled one side. Several people sat nearby, tuning various small musical instruments. Raven found a clear space to land. Gaspard hurried over and helped Doethineb down before taking Clyde from me. I slid down to find the man giving Raven a deep bow. 'May I have the *jouissance* of your *esposa's* company?'

'You misunderstand,' Raven said. 'She's my wife, not my property. You'd do better to ask her directly.'

'I'm very happy to go with you,' I told Gaspard. 'Lead on.'

The frown around his mouth eased as I laid a hand on his arm and allowed him to escort me away. 'It was meant politely, *señora,'* he assured me.

'And that's how I took it,' I said. 'Was there something in particular you wanted to show me?'

'Yes. This.' We stopped at a table near the musicians. Wooden cups stood alongside small barrels and clay bottles. With a flourish, he poured a clear liquid into one of the cups and handed it to me. 'Please, drink. It is from my own still.'

The smell hit my nostrils. 'Moonshine,' I said weakly. 'Homemade spirits.'

'I grow the crop on the hill.' Gaspard poured a sample for himself and knocked it back. 'Yes, very good.'

The strong smell of the alcohol made my knees tremble. Just the one drink, what harm could it do? And the man was so proud of what he'd made. It was almost rude to refuse. My hand shook as I stared down at the sloshing liquid. *Oh, God, help me, help me, help me…*

'You're very kind,' I said quietly. 'But I don't drink. I mean, not alcohol. I'm sorry about that.'

'But why, *señora?'* Gaspard glanced back at Raven. 'You cannot be *avec un enfant?'*

'No, I'm not pregnant.' I forced myself to hand the cup back. 'Do you have any juice?'

As the man poured me something which looked orange and sweet, I realised that this was going to be my life from now on. How many social events would I spend turning down drink? It was bad enough in Lloegyr. In England, no celebration occurred without alcohol. Could I really remain sober for the rest of my life?

As I turned from the table, Raven caught my eye. His head cocked at the barrels, then at the drink in my hand. I gave him a quick shake of the head. His ears and horns pointed forwards, showing that he was pleased. Yes, I could do this. I had someone in my life worth more than the rarest whisky. And I walked back over to my husband.

Chapter Six

'So, it's really up to you,' I said awkwardly. The leather sacks containing my possessions rested on the floor next to my feet. I stood in the doorway of Cornelius' cabin, still waiting for an invitation to step over the threshold. 'I'm assuming you don't want to stay on this island--'

'Most definitely not,' the mantis said from his perch on the lower bunk bed.

The Morning Star is planning to head back to Lloegyr in May. If you want to go back to les Etats-Unis, they'll try to find a ship going there and meet up to transfer you over.'

'Which would you advise, Father Penny?' From the insect, my title sounded like an insult. 'I'm in need of spiritual direction.'

He was definitely in need of something, but I curled my fingers into my palms and managed to bite back my words. Carefully taking a deep breath, I told him, 'If you ever really want a real talk, just ask. In the meantime, you need to decide what you want to do. We're leaving after lunch.'

'I can't go back home.' Cornelius opened and shut his forelegs, the spines lining the inside rasping loudly through the cabin. 'They'll only find me another mate to feed on me. None of these islands have anything to offer. I might as well go back to Lloegyr. At least no one will try to eat me over there.'

The Southern twang had all but disappeared, leaving him to sound almost English instead. 'I'm certain you could stay at Saint Raphael's,' I offered. 'Llewelyn, the chaplain there, can find a place for you.'

'With the rest of the freaks?'

'Not-weres are not freaks,' I said firmly. 'And you'll not be welcome if that's your attitude.'

'Don't worry, I know I'm too poor to paint and too proud to whitewash.' Cornelius turned his back to me. 'I'll be on the deck after lunch. Just have my cage ready.'

I picked up my belongings and continued down the corridor. A nagging sense of failure made me walk slowly, and I wondered if I should go back and talk to the praying mantis. Then the task of heaving two sacks through the hatch demanded my attention, and I pushed the thought to one side.

Massen put on a special lunch for my last meal on board. I could only assume that'd she found someone on the island who grew potatoes, because she served up fish and chips. Morey and I squabbled good-naturedly over the last few of the perfectly fried potato chunks. I gave the were-puffin a hug as we left the galley.

The crew was lined up on the deck as I climbed the steps. The ship was still at anchor, the masts bare of sails, and for a moment I felt a pang at not seeing *The Morning Star* riding the wind one last time. *Alan would have loved this ship,* I found myself thinking as I joined Raven on the upper deck. And, somehow, thinking of my first husband as I stood next to my new one felt like the closing of a circle.

Ointment was slathered on Raven's wounds before the harness was put back in place. Cornelius and Clyde had already entered their containers. Raven held still as I checked the attachments, Morey and Jago watching me from the dragon's neck. The larger gryphon's feathers were fluffed with excitement. His son, however, looked less enthusiastic about returning home.

Johno joined us and turned to face his crew. 'Are they leaving us? That's be right. To have them here has been great.' He now looked at us. 'Youse guys now have to shoot through. But youse welcome back on *The Morning Star* any time.'

I formally shook his hand, then allowed myself to be drawn into a feathery embrace. The were-albatross smelled of fresh air and salt water, and I swallowed against a stab of sorrow. We'd spent longer on the ship than I'd ever expected, but on the whole the journey had been good for me. I'd been able to come off alcohol and to begin my reconnection with God.

'When you're back in Lloegyr,' I said, 'send us a rat. It'd be good to come and see you.'

Raven held out a foreleg, and I climbed up to my usual perch. The sacks holding my belongings bumped against my legs. I winced as I saw that the leather sides were rubbing against the dragon's sore spots. And he hadn't made a single complaint.

The two gryphons leapt over to take perches on my shoulders. For the last time, Raven filled his gas chamber and lifted us from the ship. The crew called out final farewells as we flew away, several were-puffins darting around us in an aerial send off. Raven turned his head towards the island, and soon *The Morning Star* was far behind us.

At a grassy area out of sight of ship and village, Raven landed. I reached down and pulled Clyde out of his case. 'You really are paranoid,' Morey commented as Raven took us upwards again. 'Do you still think anyone will trace a thin place over this island back to Clyde?'

'It's not paranoia if they're really out to get you,' I retorted. 'Better to be safe than sorry.'

'Any other clichés you want to throw in there, Black?'

'A mother will do anything for her child?'

Morey snorted but said nothing more.

In a valley between two hills, Raven pulled up into a hover. 'Time for Clyde to take us to Lloegyr.'

'Near to Saint Raphael's,' I told Clyde. 'But not too close.'

The snail hummed an affirmative. I held him out, and Raven lowered us down slowly as Clyde's sharp teeth carved out a thin place. Once it was large enough to accommodate a dragon, I pulled the snail back and tucked him into my coat. I was sweating under my layers of shirt, sweater, and jacket, and almost couldn't wait to be back in wintry Lloegyr.

Raven backed off and up, gaining height. Then he aimed his muzzle at the crossing. One moment, we were in afternoon sunshine under blue skies. The next, we were flying in twilight. Grey clouds added to the gloom. The sweat on my face cooled, and I shivered at the chill.

We had emerged over the woods near the main building. Lights shone through the windows of the house. Raven took us over the trees and landed on the gravel area by the front door. Morey flew off, closely followed by Jago. I clutched Clyde as I slid to the ground. Although it pained me to do so, I placed him on the stones so my hands were free to open Cornelius' case so he could fly free. My fingers started to numb from the cold, but I still managed to undo the buckles of Raven's harness. The straps and my bags fell from his sides.

'I'm going to visit the search dragon settlement,' Raven said, touching my shoulder with his nose. 'Do you want me back in the morning, or would you rather speak to Llewelyn on your own?'

The gold bracelet on his foreleg glimmered in the light spilling across the path. My own band was hidden under several layers of clothing. 'I'll speak to him on my own. That seems kinder, somehow.'

Raven dipped his head in a nod. 'Call for me when you're ready.'

I picked up Clyde as the dragon launched himself away. Spending my first night in Lloegyr away from my husband wasn't ideal, but he was too large to enter the house. And the middle of winter wasn't the time to suggest that we bed down in the woods or in a barn.

Morey rapped on a window with his beak. A moment later, the door creaked open to reveal Miriam's large figure. 'Morey, Jago, Penny, Clyde! Wondrous to see you.'

Cornelius was standing next to the gryphons. 'Perhaps we didn't meet when I was last at this establishment. I am Cornelius Eleanor Winchester von Gockelspruch the Third.'

'And a magnificent name it is,' the were-bear replied. 'Come in, all of you. I shall call for Llewelyn.'

'Very kind of you,' Morey said as we entered the warm house. 'Give the chaplain my regards, but I shall head up to see my wife.'

'Me too,' Jago said. 'I've missed Mam.'

The two gryphons flew up the stairs. I managed to put a smile on my face as Llewelyn hurried down the hallway. 'Penny. It's good to see you back. And you look so well.'

I managed to avoid a hug by stepping back to shake his hand instead. 'We've been enjoying winter sun. It's taken a little while, but we finally found an air thin place.'

'The benefits of having a search dragon as a friend,' Llewelyn said cheerfully. I managed to keep smiling, although the gold band around my left wrist pricked at my skin and my conscience. 'You're in time for dinner. Or have you eaten?'

'Just had lunch,' I replied. 'But I'd better eat on Lloegyr time. It's the only way to get past jet lag. I mean, the best way to adjust to a new time zone is to eat and go to bed at the new time.'

'And my manners have escaped me.' Llewelyn bent his head to the mantis. 'Greetings to you as well, Cornelius. It will be too cold for you to sleep outside. We can find lodging for you here, if you require it.'

'Seeing as I don't have a pot to piss in or a window to throw it out of,' Cornelius said, 'I would appreciate that very much.'

'And Clyde?' Llewelyn asked. 'Where would you like to reside?'

Clyde opened his mouth in a sharp-toothed grin. 'With Penny.'

'Cornelius, please come with me,' Llewelyn said. 'Penny, do you have any belongings which need taking up to your room?'

Miriam took Clyde from my arms. 'I'll put Clyde inside the house, and then I'll collect Penny's things.'

'My, my, my,' Cornelius commented as he followed the chaplain down the hall. 'What a friendly place we have here. I'm grinning like a possum eating a sweet tater.'

'Saint Raphael's welcomes everyone,' Llewelyn said in response. 'This is a place of sanctuary and healing.'

Miriam returned a moment later, a sack over each of her broad shoulders. I followed the were-bear up the stairs, looking forward to the evening. A hot bath, fresh clothes, and a dinner which was certainly not going to feature fish. Despite the challenges ahead of me, I was suddenly very glad to be back to what was the closest I had to a home.

I stopped in the doorway to the dining room, surprised to find five people already sitting at the table. Llewelyn rose from his chair. 'Father Penny, these are the kind clerics who have come to assist us with our work. They have heard much about you, so perhaps each of them can introduce themselves.'

A red-haired woman gave me a nod. 'Angharad.' A were-fox, I decided.

'Rhodri,' said the short man next to her. Not only his height but his thick hands marked him out as a dwarf.

The next woman along sprang to her feet. 'Sorcha Grey.' Her smile exposed the sharp teeth of a vampire.

'I know a Grey,' I said warmly. 'She is--was--might still be my curate. It's complicated.'

'Greys usually are,' said the were-badger on Sorcha's left. 'I should know, I'm her husband, Glynn.'

The sight of another mixed-species marriage was reassuring. 'It's good to meet all of you. My Associate, Morey, is upstairs with his wife and son. I'm certain you'll be able to meet them in the morning.'

'And the snail shark?' Sorcha asked eagerly. 'I've heard so much about Clyde.'

'We've been told,' Rhodri added as a were-badger carried food into the room, 'that his singing is a wonder to hear. I do hope, once he's ordained, that he sings the liturgy.'

I glanced at Llewelyn as I took a seat. 'Are they all this well informed?'

'We wanted to know, you see,' Angharad said. Her pronounced Welsh lilt made me suspect that English was her second language. 'We've heard so much about all of you.'

Beef casserole was ladled onto plates. Boiled potatoes and mixed vegetables were brought in a moment later. I took a deep breath of the thick scents, and decided that I didn't want to see a single piece of fish for at least three months.

After dinner, whilst we were relaxing over a heavenly cup of coffee, Llewelyn said apologetically, 'We have already met together for Evening Prayer, before dinner as is the practice at Saint Raphael's. I would like to suggest that we go to the chapel again and offer prayers of thanksgiving for the safe return of Penny and her companions.'

'That would be nice,' I agreed, although my cheeks had warmed. Llewelyn's kind attention was making me dread more and more the moment I told him that I was now married to Raven. But I had determined to tell him before the day was over. I couldn't face him resuming his attempts to court me.

We piled into the simple chapel. Candles flickered against the bare walls and the wooden pews. Llewelyn handed out the service books for Compline. I relaxed as we said the ancient office together. When I'd left Saint Raphael's, I could barely tolerate attending worship. Now I felt God's presence hovering in the scented air and vibrating through the voices of my colleagues.

When we'd finished, we sat together for a minute in silence. As people prepared to leave, I asked Llewelyn, 'Could you stay behind for a moment?

There's something I need to tell you.'

The others filed out, placing their orders of service back into the book rack. Llewelyn moved to a pew just in front of mine, and turned so he could look back at me. 'Yes?'

I found it hard to meet his eyes. The were-wolf had only ever shown me kindness. Perhaps, under different circumstances, we might have dated each other, maybe even developed a relationship which led to marriage. 'You made me an offer, many months ago. I need to tell you that I'm declining it. I won't be marrying you.'

Llewelyn accepted the news with a grave nod. 'Have you and Raven come to an understanding?'

'We have.' I cleared my throat. 'We held our wedding on the ship.'

The were-wolf gave me a bittersweet smile. 'My congratulations. I had wondered whether that would happen during the course of your voyage.'

'He and I have been through so much together.'

Llewelyn held up a hand. 'Penny, there is no need to justify yourself. You have made your decision, and as your friend and colleague, it is my place to be pleased for you. I know you well enough to realise that you did not make it lightly.'

'"Not by any to be enterprised, nor taken in hand, unadvisedly, lightly, or wantonly,"' I said, quoting from the Book of Common Prayer's service for Holy Matrimony. 'Bishop Aeron won't be happy, though.'

'No, she will not.' Llewelyn shrugged. 'We already have several mixed-species marriages here, including that between Sorcha and Glynn. The Church will simply have to accept yours as well.'

'But your funding from the diocese--'

'Ended some months ago,' Llewelyn said. 'The Guild of Saint Raphael's is not beholden to the Diocese of Llanbedr, or its bishop, either for our ministry or for our funding.'

I paused a moment to make sure I could make my tone casual. 'So where is our funding coming from?'

'A very generous benefactor.' The chaplain grinned. 'I shall give you the full tour tomorrow. Our work has expanded dramatically.'

I couldn't think of how to probe more closely without causing suspicion, so I said instead, 'I suppose I'd still better go tell Bishop Aeron.'

'Yes, you must do that.' Llewelyn ran a hand through his dark hair. 'My suggestion is that you meet her on your own, rather than have Raven accompany you. Dragons have a tendency to spark off each other.'

I nodded. 'I've seen that for myself. Raven, by the way, wants to be confirmed. I'm not certain what Bishop Aeron will say to that.'

'We shall prepare him alongside the other candidates, and present him at the due time,' Llewelyn said. 'The Bishop would not deny him that sacrament. This I know for certain.'

'Good.'

He touched my shoulder with gentle fingertips. 'As disappointed as I am not to be one to partner you in marriage, I have seen that Raven is dedicated to you and to what you regard as important. God has brought you together, no matter what a bishop might say.'

'Thank you.' I quickly wiped a tear from my eye. 'Anyway, her chaplain once told me that Bishop Aeron doesn't incinerate anyone. She wouldn't risk setting her books on fire.'

Llewelyn laughed. 'Yes, I can well imagine Aldred saying such a thing, but that's to be expected from a Bishop's Chaplain. Remember this. Entering a mixed-species marriage does not remove the grace of ordination. You are still a priest. The Bishop cannot take that away from you.'

Chapter Seven

'And so,' I finished, keeping my gaze on the red dragon in front of me, 'we had our wedding ceremony on *The Morning Star*. It was the modern Church service. Captain Johno officiated.' I'd thought it best not to mention Morey's involvement.

Bishop Aeron's horns and ears were drawn back to lie almost flat against her head. Small wisps of smoke rose from her nostrils, filling the room with the acrid scent of angry dragon. 'You and Hrafn Eydisson have married. That was not what I'd hoped to hear, when I agreed to this very early and very quickly arranged meeting.'

'Yes, we're married.' I wished that her office boasted the luxury of a chair. On the other hand, perhaps it was best that I stayed on my feet. Despite Llewelyn's assurances, the Bishop might think losing a few books was a small price to pay in order to rid herself of a troublesome priest.

'Which I had specifically warned you not to do.'

'You did.'

'You put me in a very difficult position, Father Penny.'

'Not really,' I pointed out. 'I've returned to my role at the Guild of Saint Raphael's. Raven and I aren't front and centre in a church. You can pretty much ignore us.'

Lips drew back from her long teeth. 'I have no desire to ignore any of the priests in my diocese. Whatever choices you make, I am your Father-in-God, even if currently a very disappointed one.'

The thickening atmosphere in the room was threatening to make me sneeze. 'I'm not the first clergyperson to enter into a mixed-species marriage in the Diocese of Llanbedr.' Then I decided to throw all caution to the wind. Or at least into a dragon's smoke. 'And there may be many more. Bishop Aeron, if there's to be any sort of future for the Church, and for your country, the different races will have to learn to live together.'

The Bishop narrowed her eyes. 'They already do.'

'They might mingle during the day, in the cities,' I said, 'but look what happens at night. Most of them go back to their single-species enclaves. They might go to church together, or work together in offices or factories, but they don't associate with each other outside of that. They aren't reaching out to make friends with each other.'

'The humans who live in Llanbedr,' Bishop Aeron pointed out, 'have also decided to live separately. Their other representative to the Llanbedr City Council, Fred Wiseman, only attended one meeting.'

'Which is why those who do reach out to other races, who even marry outside their own species, should be encouraged,' I said quickly. 'We need to be breaking down barriers rather than building them up. I've seen this in action, on an island we recently visited. People *can* live side by side in harmony.'

A flash of purple-grey past the window told me that Morey had chanced a quick fly past to see if I were still alive. My Associate had insisted on coming to Llanbedr with me. Although he had kept his beak shut on the flight over, I could sense that the meeting he'd had with Bishop Aeron, after his first marriage to a were-fox, was still a painful memory.

'You are, of course, unable to be objective in this regard.'

'And so what?' I glared at her. 'Is a discussion somehow better if it's detached from emotion, or from personal experience? Doesn't this "objectivity" come from being in a privileged position? You're a bishop, a dragon, someone who isn't affected by the prejudice which I face. Your privilege gives you emotional distance, but not expertise.'

If Morey were in the room, no doubt he'd be hiding his head under a wing. I straightened as the Bishop raised her head. 'You are a most interesting person, Father Penny. Did you usually speak to Bishop Nigel in this manner?'

'I aim for respect,' I admitted. 'Deference isn't always my strong point.'

'So I've noticed.' Her ears and horns lifted. 'I cannot give you another parish position. But you are correct, you can continue in your ministry at Saint Raphael's. And I know that you are not the only priest there in a mixed-species marriage.'

I nodded. 'By the way, Raven wants to be confirmed.'

'I'm very pleased to hear that, and I shall be even more pleased to confirm him.' The Bishop sighed, her breath blowing stray strands of hair from my face. 'Go, Father Penny, before Trahaearneifion crashes through my window. His wingtip brushed the glass on his last flight past.'

'Thank you, Bishop Aeron.' I turned on my heel, opened the door, and somehow managed to keep to a steady pace as I left the room. But it was only when I was in the entrance hall that I felt able to breathe freely again.

The winter cold hit me once I was back outside. I quickly buttoned up my new jacket, a homecoming gift from Llewelyn. The blue outer layer was waterproofed, and covered a thick fur lining. Although I had mixed feelings about wearing the skin of a dead animal, there was a lack of alternatives in Lloegyr. And the coat certainly kept me warm.

Morey landed heavily on my shoulder. 'Well, you're alive.'

'She wasn't best pleased.' I started to walk to the cathedral, my boots crunching on ice-crisped gravel. The sun was just rising, casting a weak light over a frosty morning. 'But she's not going to pull me out of Saint Raphael's.'

'What would she do with you if she did?' Morey asked. 'She won't put you into a parish, will she?'

'She could have just dismissed me from ministry altogether.'

'Although I've had my own issues with the Bishop,' Morey said slowly, 'I don't think she would've done that. She does care about her clergy.'

The thick wooden doors at the west entrance to Llanbedr Cathedral were shut, no doubt an attempt to keep out the chill. I wrestled briefly with the metal handle, and pulled the right hand one just far enough to be able to slip inside.

The high ceilings and muted lighting inside the large building eased some of the tension from my shoulders. A hint of incense hung in the air. Despite the early hour, several choristers were practicing their solos. The bright young voices rose and fell, echoing against the stone pillars.

Raven sat in one of the side chapels. As I drew near, I realised that he was talking to a dwarf wearing a clerical collar. The priest turned his head and I suddenly recognised him. 'Father Andras. I haven't seen you since my licensing to Saint George's.'

Andras gave me a grave nod. His beard was longer and greyer than I remembered, and slid across his black shirt as he glanced back at Raven. 'And to answer your question, yes, Clyde would be very welcome.'

'The Dean and I have had a very interesting conversation,' Raven told me. 'He's brought in many changes.'

'I was installed as cathedral dean in early December,' Andras said. 'Your husband has been telling me that we might gain a very good tenor to our choir, when the next lot of ordinands begin their studies in the autumn. Many come here on Sundays to worship, you see, those which can fly or ride dragons.'

I wished Raven had chosen a side chapel which possessed pews. Shock had weakened my knees. I couldn't say which had surprised me more, the Dean's easy acceptance of my marriage to Raven, or his willingness to allow Clyde to join the choir. 'He's a snail shark, you know. Ordinand Clyde.' The dwarf laughed. 'All of the Diocese of Llanbedr, perhaps even all of the Church of Lloegyr, knows that Clyde is a snail shark. Others might hold on to their old prejudices. As for me, I believe that Jesus meant it when he said that we should love everyone.'

I smiled. Andras obviously had a very different attitude than the previous dean. 'I'll let Clyde know. He's sung in the choir at Saint Raphael's, and I'm certain he'll be thrilled to sing here. If the other members will accept him.'

'The cathedral community knows that their new dean will not accept any form of prejudice,' Andras said firmly. 'Several mixed-species couples have started to worship with us, as well as vampires from the colony which you helped to settle in Llanbedr. While I'm dean here, this cathedral will welcome all.'

Somehow I managed not to rush over and give him a hug. Holding my arms firmly behind my back, I said, 'I'm very pleased to hear it.'

'This cathedral,' Morey added, 'now has the opportunity to become a place where diversity is accepted.'

'Not only accepted, Father Trahaearneifion,' the Dean replied. 'We rejoice in diversity. It is all of God. As I have learnt from Father Penny.'

'Me?' My voice came out as a squeak.

'In your advocacy of snail sharks, refugee vampires, and not-weres,' Andras said. 'Ironic, perhaps, that it took someone from another world to make us look more closely at our own.'

'I've had good friends along the way,' I mumbled, staring down at my boots. 'I'll have to come to a Sunday service when I'm not on the rota at Saint Raphael's.'

Andras nodded. 'Please do. I'd love to have you preach at the main Eucharist.'

Morey lifted his wings. 'How much longer will you stay in the cathedral, Raven, Penny? I have a meeting in a few minutes with Bishop Aeron. I could fly back to Saint Raphael's myself, if you want to go.'

I nearly asked him what the meeting was about, but managed to bite back my words. If Morey had wanted me to know, he would have told me. 'Raven, if you don't mind, I'd like to see how Fred Wiseman and the rest of my fellow humans are getting on. I don't know how long we'd be.'

Raven chuckled. 'Sorry, Trahaearneifion, but the desires of a wife outweigh those of a friend.'

'Of course they do,' Morey agreed. 'I'm married myself. I'll see you back at the Guild. Taryn would probably say that the exercise will do me good.'

I winced at that. Months on a ship had done little for my own physical fitness, even if the rather basic diet had kept the weight off my hips. Maybe I should ask Raven to take me to someplace warm where I could do some walking or, better yet, swim.

'Send a rat when you can come and preach,' Andras said, reaching up to grip my arm.

I watched him stride away. A bat fluttered down and changed into biped shape to walk alongside him. 'He's very different to his predecessor.'

'Thank goodness,' Morey grumbled. 'I'd better be off. Tell me later on whether Fred Wiseman still fails to live up to his name.'

The gryphon flew out of the chapel. Raven and I followed more slowly. 'What did the Bishop say?' my husband asked as we headed outside.

'She's not happy. But I can still live and work at Saint Raphael's. And I told her that you want to be confirmed.'

'What was her response?'

'She looks forward to confirming you.'

Raven waited until we were a dozen paces away from the cathedral entrance before he stopped to allow me to climb up his neck. 'My mother has heard of our marriage, and has sent her congratulations.'

I settled into my place and tightened my coat around my chest. 'That's very kind of her.'

'She adds that, should you ever tire of me, she will hunt me down on your behalf. But she will allow you to feast on my heart or my eyes, whichever you prefer.'

'And that's very generous of her.'

'It is,' Raven agreed, spreading out his wings. 'Those are the choicest parts of a dragon.' A moment later we were in the air and heading away from the cathedral.

The cold wind whipped through my hair. 'You know where we're going?'

'I've been there before,' he reminded me. 'That mansion near the river.'

The city was quiet beneath us. The frost had obviously discouraged denizens from lingering outside. Smoke rose from the chimneys of the brick buildings, filling the air with the thick scent of burning coal. I found myself missing the activity of warmer months, when merchants erected stalls to hawk their wares and people strolled through the parks.

Raven tipped a wing and took us away from the river. Grand mansions set behind carefully tended gardens lined either side of the cobbled street. The tall trees lining the avenue were bare, but the ground was free of even the smallest leaf.

We landed in front of an imposing building of grey stone and marble. The height, at five storeys, was greater than any of the other dwellings nearby. I slid down to the paved path.

'Not built for dragons,' Raven commented. The floors were designed for nothing taller than a were-bear.

'Perfectly adequate for humans, though.' I patted his leg. 'Do you want to take off or will you wait?'

Raven lifted his head and sniffed. 'There are no air thin places near here. I'll wait.'

'You won't get too cold?'

'I managed to survive in the Arctic,' he reminded me. 'Go. Speak to your own kind.'

The path contained spots of ice where puddles had frozen overnight. I wandered over to the grass to avoid the slippery sections. The worn ground revealed that many others had done so before me.

The steps up to the wide portico were dry. I climbed them with more confidence than I felt. It'd been many months since the humans stranded in Llanbedr had been re-located to this mansion. The Consortium had arranged everything. Had the rat king made any moves to call in the debt?

The door opened as I reached the top of the steps. The not-were standing just inside looked familiar. 'Father Penelope White,' he said, face shifting between human and bear. 'Whom have you come to see?'

'Fred Wiseman, if he's in.'

'Mr Wiseman has his office in this building.' The were-bear moved aside so I could enter. 'Wait here, and I'll see if he's free.'

The warmth of the house was very welcome. I unfastened my jacket and blew my nose. The small entrance hall always reminded me of a student residence. A set of stairs led to the next floor, and corridors led off left and right. All of the flats, I recalled, had been built with outward facing windows, so there was very little natural light in this public area.

The not-were padded back a few minutes later. 'Mr Wiseman would be happy to see you. May I bring you a coffee, or some tea?'

'Coffee, please.' I'd been without my favourite non-alcoholic beverage for long stretches of time. I had a lot of catching up to do.

I was led to a room just a dozen paces away from the entrance. The not-were knocked on the door, opened it, and stepped back. I peered inside.

'Penny.' Fred was sitting behind a large desk, papers covering the dark surface. 'Come on in.'

He made no move to rise as I entered the room. I sat down in the chair facing him. Through the window behind him, I could see Raven studying the nearby trees. 'This looks comfortable.'

'It's archaic.' Fred waved a hand over his work. 'It seems some computer systems were brought over from our world, but they ground to a halt when the crossing places were closed off. They were relying on batteries, of all things. You would've thought someone might have installed solar panels.'

'You seem to be coping, though.'

The light from nearby oil lamps cast a yellow gleam over Fred's grey hair as he nodded. 'I started in business back in the days of shorthand, typewriters, and Rolodex files. I prefer a laptop, but needs must. What can I do for you, Reverend?'

The were-bear chose that moment to appear with my coffee. I was able to gain some thinking time as he placed the mug on the desk and checked that Fred didn't need anything. As the door shut behind the not-were, I picked up the cup and wrapped my hands around its warmth. 'Oh, I just wanted to see how everyone's getting on.'

'Anyone willing to work has a job.' Fred grimaced. 'Some people thought what they were being offered was beneath them. We give them the basics, lodging and food, but nothing extra unless they're bringing money into the Firm.'

'The Firm?'

'That's what people have decided to call this place,' Fred said. 'Not what I would have chosen, but I'm not going to fight over it. The Consortium found people jobs in their factories, some as workers, others as managers. A percentage of everyone's salary pays for the upkeep of this place, as well as our food and people like cleaning staff and cooks. It's not luxury, but no one's homeless or starving.'

The coffee had been whitened with milk. I allowed myself a few seconds to enjoy the warm roast. 'And you?'

'I run the place, of course.'

'Of course,' I said brightly. 'You're used to being in charge.'

'Precisely.' Fred pushed a map towards me. 'Everyone knows that I'm doing my best to get us out of here. We're not really happy living in this city. The Consortium's got some towns which might suit us better. We're hoping to move in the spring.'

'And what would you do there?'

'Set up our own businesses. That's what we want to do.' Fred tapped the crude drawing. Hills, a river, streets, and clusters of houses had been inked across the paper. 'Of course, we'd all rather go home. But I've said to everyone, we can't sit around waiting for a crossing to stay open.'

As I had expected, the bottom of the mug held coffee grounds. Someone needed to invent cafetieres. 'So still no thin places leading through to Great Britain?'

'New ones form all the time,' Fred said. 'The big ones, those seem to disappear quickly again. The small ones hang around. So we use those to send rats through.'

'To do what?'

Fred stared at me. 'To send messages to those we've left behind, of course.'

'But most people on Earth can't see anyone from Lloegyr. They need to have the Sight.' I had a sudden thought. 'What about all of you? Are you making sure you touch someone from Lloegyr regularly, so you can keep the Sight?'

'No need, not anymore,' Fred said. 'Some vampires brought over that strange winged unicorn, what's her name, Epona? Told us once we saw her, we'd keep the Sight forever. Seems to be working.'

'She seems to have that effect on humans, yes. But most people in Britain haven't seen her. So how can they hear the rats recite their poetry?'

'We've convinced the rats to fly through with written messages. The first message tells the recipient to respond in the same way, with a letter no longer than a single rolled up piece of paper. The rat swings by a few days later and retrieves the message. And so the correspondence begins. Not as quick as emails, or the Royal Mail, but it means we can communicate between our two worlds again.'

Inwardly I was making many mental notes. Outwardly I grinned and said, 'I'm really pleased to hear that. Maybe I could use a rat to send my brother a message?'

Fred studied me for a moment. 'I think we could arrange that.'

'I do wonder, however,' I continued, 'how people are coping with these messages just appearing in their houses.'

'Fairies? Aliens? God?' Fred shrugged. 'Some of our people tried to tell them the truth, but they found their families just didn't believe a word of it. My PA, of course, knows about Lloegyr, so no problems writing to her. But trying to run a multinational company through flying rat messengers does have its challenges.'

'I can imagine,' I said, although to be truthful I really couldn't.

Fred rapped the desk with his fingers, and seemed to come to a decision. 'Look, Reverend, you and I have had our differences. But a lot of the people here, well, either they're religious or they have their problems, sometimes both. We could probably use a vicar at whatever town we fetch up, if you think you'd be interested.'

'There might already be a church there.'

'Not the town we have in mind.'

'And I'm married to a dragon,' I said, watching him closely.

'I don't care what you're married to,' Fred replied. 'That's your private life.'

'That's commendable ,' I said. 'But Bishop Aeron won't grant me a license to serve in a parish church.'

'So we'll take you on.' Fred waved my concerns away. 'We'd find the money to pay you. You're human, so you're one of us, Reverend. I'll send you a rat when we're ready to make our move.'

'Thank you,' I said, and even managed to sound sincere. 'Are people usually around in the evening or weekends? I'll try to drop in.'

'Come and eat with us,' Fred said. 'We dish up dinner around seven o'clock on weekdays, six on weekends. We even have a decent Sunday roast, if you can get here by one o'clock.'

'I'll bear that in mind.' I rose from my chair, and this time he rose too. We shook, my hand nearly as warm as his. 'I'm glad to see that you've decided to try to make a go of it here.'

'Only until we can find a way to return home,' Fred said grimly. 'In the meantime, we'll do what we need to survive.'

The were-bear saw me out. I tightened my coat as I walked back down the steps and across the lawn to Raven. The dragon swung his head to me as I drew near. 'How is Fred Wiseman?'

'Trying to make a good life for the humans stuck here,' I said. 'I guess we have to admire him for that.'

'If we must.'

'There's something he told me, though, which bothers me.' I leaned in close to Raven, drawing warmth from his body. 'He says that the large crossings to Great Britain still disappear, but the small ones are remaining open.'

Raven snorted. 'I'll visit the search dragon settlement and ask why that's the case. I wouldn't be surprised, though, to find out it's deliberate.'

'Really?' I asked. 'I thought they were supposed to close up any thin places which form, no matter how small.'

'My gold is gone,' Raven said matter-of-factly. 'Whatever they do now is simply to protect themselves. They know that your country might try to use the large ones for dangerous purposes, but perhaps they feel the small ones aren't worth shedding blood over.'

'Maybe they're not,' I admitted. 'I guess it could be tiring, trying to sort out every thin place which forms. I have most of the gold the merpeople gave me. We could use some of it to pay for the small ones to be shut off, but…'

'But?'

I sighed. 'The humans here are able to use them to send messages by rat to their families in England. I'd hate to cut that off for them. And, really, what harm can it do?'

'I shall make that visit to the settlement,' Raven said, 'but suggest that only the large crossings are closed. Are you willing to part with some of your gold? That would give extra incentive to continue.'

'Of course,' I said, although part of me was already regretting my offer. It had suddenly occurred to me that a small nest egg might have come in handy, should I need to leave Saint Raphael's for any reason. 'Once we're back at the Guild, I'll fetch some down for you.'

'Time we were heading back.' Raven lowered his head to my chest. 'I can hear your stomach complaining.'

'Breakfast feels like a long time ago.' I climbed up to my usual seat. 'I'll grab a snack when we're back. Llewelyn wants to give me a tour of the new developments.'

Raven glanced back at me. 'Make sure he shows you the rodents.'

'I beg your pardon?'

'Rodents.' The dragon lifted his head and made a dramatic sniff. 'There are at least twenty rodents living in one of the barns. Rats or mice, I can't quite tell. But I'd like to know why. They're definitely not were-rodents.'

'Rodents,' I said slowly. 'Flying ones? That's not what the Guild was set up for. You're right, we need to know why Saint Raphael's taken them in. Maybe I'll find out later today when Llewelyn shows me around.' Then I took a deep breath and braced myself for the cold flight ahead of us.

Chapter Eight

Although I'd had glimpses of the expansion at Saint Raphael's from the air, to be shown around on foot brought home exactly how much work had been undertaken during my absence. Llewelyn was almost bouncing with excitement as he showed me the new barns and outbuildings. The sun had warmed the ground during the morning and now, early afternoon, my boots were darkening from the water clinging to the long grass.

'We have been able to provide housing for many more not-weres,' the chaplain said as he waved at the nearest barn. 'A pack of were-foxes came out of the hills a few weeks ago, all of them outcasts from the packs of their birth. That building is our new medical facility. We can now afford to employ two unicorn healers. They live at the rear of the premises. I know they're a bit busy today with some new arrivals, but we will introduce you to them very soon.'

'That's another new one,' I said, pointing at a smaller barn nestling between the hospital and the barn which, I assumed, still held the were-rabbits. 'Who's in there?'

Some of the spring left Llewelyn's stride. He paused and ran a hand through his dark hair. The thick eyebrows drew together. 'They are a special case.'

'A special case of not-weres?' I felt my stomach jolt. 'I've not taken letherum for ages, but if they're really that bad, maybe I should have a tablet first?'

'No, they're not not-weres.' The chaplain straightened. 'But you do need to know about them.'

With quick, determined steps, Llewelyn led me to the small door. To my surprise, a lock glinted in a metal latch. The were-wolf pulled out a key. I tried to ask a question, but he shook his head. 'I'll explain later.'

When he pulled the door open, warm air rushed out, along with the harsh scent of urine and faeces. I nearly gagged, and quickly dug out a cloth handkerchief from a trouser pocket. Holding it over my nose and mouth helped as I followed Llewelyn inside.

The interior was dimly lit. As Llewelyn shut the door behind us, I stood still and waited for my eyes to adjust. The lanterns which hung from the walls glowed with the bright yellow light of *creigiau tywynnog,* a type of rock which was activated either by fire or dragon flame. A few high windows allowed in cold air and a limited amount of natural light.

Long platforms ran down both sides of the barn. Plastic washing-up bowls rested on the wide shelves. Llewelyn gave me a nod, and I followed him to the nearest bowl on the left. Bits of straw had escaped the bright blue enclosure and straggled across the platform.

A head rose from the matted bed. Whiskers twitched in my direction. Black wings shuddered against the rat's thin sides as she tried to stand.

'No, no, stay down,' Llewelyn said softly. 'I've brought Father Penny to see you all. She's known many a rat in her time.'

The rat curled back into herself. The eyes were sealed shut, grime forming a crust across the dark lids. Her voice was very weak, and I had to lean close to hear her. 'Father Penny. We've met. I represented the Zygaton Network. I danced for you.'

I searched my memory. 'That's right. A group of you gave presentations to help me decide which rat king to consult over a missing submarine.' I looked over at Llewelyn. 'I had to choose between eighteen different performances. All of the losing rats were terribly upset that I hadn't chosen them.'

'The Zygaton Network was very displeased with me,' the rat said sadly.

'What happened?' I nearly reached out a hand to touch her sparse fur, but the stench made me decide otherwise. 'Did he do this to you?'

'No, no, no!' The rat shook with the force of her response. 'My rat king has always been good to me. I'm just old.'

'There is a cost to interacting telepathically with a rat king,' Llewelyn explained, keeping his voice low. 'The mind begins to crumble under the effort. There are also many flights, sometimes into dangerous situations, for a messenger. So the body is also prematurely weakened. Celyn is just one of many. The Guild has taken in nineteen others just like her.'

'Celyn,' I asked softly, 'how old are you?'

'I am not Celyn,' the rat snapped, sudden strength in her voice. 'I have no rat king, so I have no name.'

'She's seven years old,' Llewelyn said. 'And, separated from her rat king, she won't live to be eight.'

I slipped my handkerchief back into my pocket and placed several fingertips on the rat's bald head. 'Celyn, you were loved by God before the world began. You still have a place. You still have a name. No rat king can take that away from you.'

But Celyn had retreated back into herself. I stepped back and looked down the length of the barn. Twenty washing up bowls were staggered along the shelves. The building could easily hold many more. 'As much as I believe in giving help to anyone who needs it,' I told Llewelyn, 'I thought Saint Raphael's was established to help not-weres.'

'We couldn't leave the rats to suffer.' The were-wolf sighed. 'We do our best to keep them comfortable.'

'The bedding needs to be changed more often.'

'It's changed every few hours. Their physical state means that food simply passes straight through them.'

'The chaplain is right.' Bastien had landed on the platform to our left. 'Even if you changed the straw every hour, it wouldn't make much of a difference. The slow, drawn-out death of a rat is very messy. Especially the deaths of those whose minds have been devastated by a rat king.'

I glanced back at Celyn. 'Devastated from regular contact with a rat king?'

Bastien lifted his black wings. 'No, not by regular contact. Come with me.'

As the rat flew further into the barn, Llewelyn placed a warning hand on my shoulder. 'Prepare yourself, Penny.'

I gave him a nod before following Bastien. The rat stood near a green bowl. Inside was a white rat, his eyes closed and his breathing irregular. Dried blood crusted around his ears and snout. His legs were twitching, and his tail curled and uncurled.

'If a rat particularly displeases his rat king,' Bastien explained, 'the rat king strikes the rat's mind with a powerful telepathic pulse.'

'Their mind is burnt out?' I asked.

'Not immediately,' Llewelyn said. 'It is more like a sickness implanted into the brain. The rat is disabled, but usually able to fly away. Within hours, the damage has spread, and the rat loses all ability to communicate. Within a day, the unlucky ones become as you see here, unable to move.'

Bastien blew a soft breath across the rat's sparse fur. 'The lucky ones die a few hours after the telepathic blast.'

'We can do little more than keep this one comfortable.' Llewelyn leaned in closer. 'The jaws are locked shut. He can't even take in liquid, never mind food.'

'Would it be kinder,' I asked quietly, 'if you didn't let him starve to death? Or is euthanasia not allowed in Lloegyr?'

'Not in Saint Raphael's,' Llewelyn said firmly. 'I would like to give them letherum, to ease their suffering, but we have so many other demands on our supplies. We simply don't have enough to treat the not-weres and to also ease the rats' pain.'

I glared at Bastien. 'Are you proud of the Consortium now?'

'He is my rat king,' Bastien replied calmly, as if that explained everything.

The barn was quiet once we stopped speaking. I swallowed against the

—

bitterness forming in my throat. The lack of noise from the suffering rats somehow made the situation seem all the worse. Llewelyn gave me a nod, and we walked back outside.

'So part of the Guild has become a hospice,' I said. 'Don't get me wrong, I think it's good that the rats are being taken care of. But that wasn't Saint Raphael's original brief.'

'We seek to bring healing,' Llewelyn replied. 'Even if that healing is only the final one of death.'

Bastien landed on my shoulder. 'Penny, may I speak with you?'

'I'll wait for you at the next barn,' Llewelyn said. His long strides quickly carried him away.

'What do you want?' I asked Bastien, my voice sharp in my own ears. 'Sorry, let me try again. What can I do for you?'

'I need to have a difficult conversation with Jago.' Bastien's dark eyes glittered, and I wondered if I saw tears. Could rats cry? 'Would you be willing to be there? I think it would make it easier for him.'

'Have you spoken to Jago since our return?'

'I've been avoiding him,' Bastien said. 'Before we resume our relationship, there's something he must know.'

'Are you willing to let me know what it is, just so I'm prepared?'

'Certainly,' Bastien said. 'I'll be dead within the next year.'

The strength left my legs. I looked in vain for a bench, and had to resort to leaning against the rough wall of the barn. 'What's happened?'

'Service to my rat king, that's what's happened.' Bastien spoke matter-of-factly. 'I'm seven years old. I've seen what lies ahead of me before I reach eight.'

I hesitated as I searched for the right words. 'So you're not ill right now, not at this exact moment?'

'At this exact moment, I feel well and healthy.' He pointed his snout at the building. 'But twelve months ago, those rats would have said the same.'

'"One day I'll stand by your grave and weep,"' I murmured. 'Raven will outlive me.'

'But you'll have at least several decades together. We won't even have a year.'

'Understood.' I took a deep breath and pushed myself away from the barn wall. 'When do you want to do this?'

'This evening. After you've had dinner. We'll meet in the chapel.'

'Jago doesn't always come to dinner.'

'Then you'll just have to tell him,' Bastien said with a growl. 'I'll join you both there.'

I kept my own voice calm. 'Are you sure you want to do this in the chapel?'

Bastien's whiskers twitched. 'Why not? A chapel is surely just the place to contemplate love, life, and death.'

'After dinner, then.'

The rat took off as I hurried after Llewelyn, my heart already aching for Jago.

The growth in number of ministers was still a bit disconcerting. After lunch, as we enjoyed a hot drink, I studied my fellow priests over my mug of coffee. They were all friendly and obviously committed to Saint Raphael's, but part of me missed the days when it had just been Llewelyn, Morey, and me. Or perhaps I was just recovering from many months on a ship where I had come to know everyone.

A wind had started up during our meal, and I was glad of my warm coat when Llewelyn took me outside to continue our tour. My steps quickened as we headed to the were-rabbits' barn. 'It's been ages since I've seen them,' I said to the chaplain. 'How've they been getting on?'

Llewelyn halted and turned to face me. 'Penny, I am very sorry not have to told you before this, but the were-rabbits are no longer with us.'

My sudden chill had little to do with the air temperature. 'What happened?'

'Oh, the very best outcome happened,' Llewelyn hurried to reassure me. 'They blended their warrens, healed physically and emotionally, and left us to form a new life further south. Theirs is a success story for Saint Raphael's, and your art therapy played a large part in their recovery.'

'I suppose I should be happy for them,' I said glumly, 'but I wish I could have been here to say goodbye.'

'Surely your husband can find the warren? A search dragon can find anything.'

'Their abilities aren't always as great as their reputation,' I admitted. 'Raven might be able to, if he's formed a close enough connection with one of them.'

Several were-hedgehogs lived in the barn. Spines bristled from their human faces, and their bodies shimmered between animal and human. I took deep breaths, using the pleasant smell of clean hay to help calm my stomach. After we'd spent a little time talking to the not-weres, Llewelyn led me back outside.

'I might need some letherum tablets,' I said apologetically. 'I really didn't feel well in there.' Llewelyn hesitated, and I felt my face warm. 'Look, I know I abused my use of them when I was fighting hangovers, but I haven't touched alcohol for months and I'm not planning to take up drinking again. It's only so I can do my work with the most affected not-weres.'

'I do trust your use of letherum,' the chaplain reassured me. 'My concern is that we have very little left in stock. The plant from which letherum is distilled is not common, and there has been such a heavy demand on our supplies. Sorcha is well-trained in relaxation techniques. Perhaps she can help you learn to control your reaction to not-weres?'

'I'll give it a go,' I agreed, hoping Llewelyn was right and the vampire could help me. 'I'd prefer not to need a drug.'

We finished our tour at the corrals which held the were-horses. Maxence, whom I'd first met when he was travelling with Elthan's vampire colony, galloped in full horse shape inside the enclosure. When he pulled up in front of me, he changed into biped form. I clapped my hands. 'You can finally choose to be fully one or the other,' I said happily. 'How do you feel?'

'Whole,' Maxence replied, dropping back into horse form. He brought his grey head near my own, and I rubbed the soft muzzle. 'I'm staying on, though. I'd like to help others become whole as well. Dr Wyn is going to run training sessions for people like me.'

'It'd be good to have laity working alongside the clergy,' Llewelyn explained. 'Particularly those who themselves have been through the experience of being healed.'

'I can walk alongside them,' Maxence agreed, 'until they are ready to gallop on their own.'

I grinned at them both. 'That's fantastic. Where I come from, we call it "the wounded healer." Someone who's been through tough times themselves can offer help to others facing similar problems.'

'That's me,' Maxence said. And with a happy snort, he dashed away to once again run around the corral.

Tour finally complete, I went to my room to sort through my belongings. The Guild had continued to pay me during my absence, so I had the funds for much needed new clothes. I also wanted to make a trip to the warehouse which sold human toiletries. My toothbrush was in dire need of replacement.

All of the priests and several of the laity reported to the chapel for Evening Prayer. Afterwards, the other ministers chatted quite happily over dinner. I spoke when necessary, but my mind was on the upcoming meeting in the chapel. Most of my colleagues seemed not to notice, but I did catch Morey studying me. He knew me better than the others, of course, and I wondered if I'd have to face some awkward questions.

As I rose from the dinner table, Morey flew over to land on my shoulder. 'You can't come with me,' I said as I left the room.

'I know.' His voice was low. 'Jago told me that he's meeting with you and Bastien. The lad's very nervous about telling Bastien about Dancer. Has Bastien guessed?'

I paused in the hallway. 'I can't tell you that. Bastien's taken me into his confidence.'

'Of course.' Morey cleared his throat. 'Taryn's going to be back early tonight. Bring Jago to our flat if it all goes terribly wrong.'

'Will do.' I waited until the gryphon had returned to the dining room before continuing my journey to the chapel.

Jago was already waiting inside. His short fox tail thumped against his pew, the blue and turquoise feathers which trailed past the furry tip sweeping across the dark wood. His crest flopped against his grey neck. 'Auntie Penny, do you think Basty will be very angry with me?'

'I don't know,' I said. 'But you're doing the right thing in talking to him. Do you still want to be with him?'

'Yes. More than anything.'

'Then that's what you tell him.' I looked around the room, and found a chair to place in front of the pew. Then I took a seat next to Jago.

Bastien flew in a few minutes later. At my nod, he settled on the chair so that he and Jago faced each other. 'Hello,' he said quietly. 'I'm glad you returned safely from the voyage. I missed you.'

'I wanted to come talk to you,' Jago said in a rush. 'But things happened out there, and I didn't know how to talk to you. Auntie Penny knows all about it.' He pressed against my right leg and looked up at me.

'Auntie Penny,' I told him, 'is here to help. But you two need to do the talking. Right, Bastien?'

The rat drew himself up to his full height. 'Jago, I need to tell you--'

'I didn't mean to do anything wrong,' Jago interrupted. 'It's just, I haven't met many gryphons my size. It's so hard being really small, sometimes, even smaller than gryphons like Mam and Tad. I know that it's supposed to be wonderful to be a *griffwn glas*, the most beautiful of all gryphons, but I'm always having to fly harder just to keep up with anyone else, and I'm always worried that a full-sized gryphon like my great-grandmam might accidentally step on me. Dancer was my size, you see, and also she was…'

'Very pretty,' Bastien supplied. 'I saw how you looked at her when you first met.'

'She's pretty, and smart, and brave,' Jago said. Then his tone lowered into misery. 'But she wasn't who I thought she was. She led the other hummingbird-gryphons to fight and kill honey bees. She wanted me to fight alongside her! But I don't hunt, I don't kill. I thought she knew that. I thought we had the same values. And that's what matters in a relationship. Having the same values.'

Bastien sighed. 'Thank you for being truthful with me. Now I need to tell you--'

'Please don't,' Jago begged. 'I know you wanted us to get married before I left, and that's what I want some day. But a gryphon doesn't reach maturity until he's thirty-five--'

'Thirty-five,' Bastien breathed, his voice low in amazement.

'So there's no hurry, we have lots of years yet.' Jago stretched out his neck, bringing his beak inches from Bastien's nose. 'But I want to spend those years with you. Only you. Dancer and I spent time together, we bathed together, we preened each other, and I know I shouldn't have done any of that. Please forgive me. I love you, and we've been apart too long already. I want to be with you.'

The rat's whiskers twitched, and a tear rolled from each eye. 'And I love you, Jago. Whatever time I have to live, I want to spend it with you.'

The gryphon's crest rose high over his head. 'Oh, Basty, I'm so glad! Let's go for a flight. I haven't flown at night for ages.'

'I'll join you in a moment,' Bastien said. 'I need to talk to Penny first.' Jago hesitated, his gaze alternating between the two of us. Bastien hopped over to the pew and gave him an affectionate nudge. 'Don't worry, I won't be long.'

Jago stretched out his blue-feathered wings and flew from the chapel. I looked down at the rat. 'Bastien--'

'I have less than a year to live,' he growled. 'Why should I care if he's preened someone else?'

'You didn't tell him.'

'How can I?' Fresh tears glittered in his dark eyes. 'Not now, not after everything he said. He's chosen to be with me because he loves me. I don't want him to be with me because he feels sorry for me.'

I sighed. 'Raven once told me, "One day I'll stand by your grave and weep, but why should I sacrifice present happiness to future grief?"'

'Exactly.' Bastien shook out his black bat wings. 'And you're not to tell him. Understand? No one's to tell him.'

'Bastien--'

He bared sharp white teeth in my direction. 'I expect you to honour my decision.'

'I won't tell him,' I said heavily.

The rat leapt into the air and flew from the room. After he'd gone, I pulled a handkerchief from my pocket to dry my own eyes.

Chapter Nine

After that final exchange with Bastien, I wanted nothing more than to summon Raven and take shelter under his wing. But I forced myself to climb the stairs to the top floor. Morey and Taryn would be wondering whether they were needed to console a heart-broken son. It wasn't right to leave them fretting.

I hesitated outside the door to their room. Someone was speaking inside, and although I couldn't catch the words, the voice was unfamiliar. I knocked and called out, 'It's Penny. May I come in?'

'Yes, come in,' Morey replied.

The gryphon's flat was very similar to my own. Morey and Taryn sat on the double bed, feet nearly hidden under the furs which covered the mattress. A squirrel was stretched out on the settee, her red fur contrasting with the blue cover. Clyde rested on the desk.

'Jago and Bastien have gone off for a night flight together,' I said as I closed the door behind me.

Pinks and greens swirled through Clyde's body. 'Good.'

'I told you Bastien would forgive him,' Taryn said to her husband. 'I have mixed feelings about that rat, but this speaks well of him.'

'Hmph,' Morey said, sounding unconvinced. 'Well, they have plenty of time to become reacquainted.'

I turned away, using the excuse of retrieving a chair to hide my face until I had myself back under control. As I took a seat, I asked, 'I take it we've been sent a message?'

The squirrel rose to her feet and took a bow. 'Sioned, from Saint Canna's Seminary. I have brought a message from the Warden for you and Ordinand Clyde.'

'We were going to send for you,' Morey explained. 'She'd only just finished telling us when you knocked on our door.'

'Seminary,' Clyde said happily. 'Visit.'

Sioned's gave the snail an indulgent look, her whiskers twitching as she smiled. 'Warden Liliwen invites you both to visit Saint Canna in two Wednesdays' time. She likes to meet ordinands and their sponsors before the ordinands begin their training. You'll be shown around the college and Ordinand Clyde can meet with some of his fellow students. If you're both free to stay overnight, you'll be able to join the community for worship and dinner. Rooms are available for you.'

'I visited before I started my training,' Morey said. 'It was very useful.'

'Of course we'll go,' I told Clyde, forcing back my worries as to whether the other students would accept a snail shark. 'What time should we arrive, Sioned?'

'Ten in the morning would do nicely,' the squirrel replied. 'Go to the main house and speak to the porter. The Warden will be waiting for you.'

Clyde was waving his tentacles in great excitement. 'Seminary!'

'Does the Warden know that a translator will be living with Clyde?' I asked. 'That's Jago. He's a small gryphon.'

'No doubt Warden Liliwen does know,' Sioned said. 'Would Jago be able to visit with you?'

'That should be possible,' Morey replied. 'I'll talk to him when he's back from his flight.'

Sioned nodded. 'I'll advise the Warden. May I stay in the house tonight? It's cold outside and I don't know where to find a warm roost in your woods.'

I moved to the door. 'You can join Clyde in my room. He's inside for the winter as well.'

'When you have escorted them to your flat,' Taryn said, 'please return to ours.'

'Of course.' Somehow I managed to keep my tone positive, although I wondered if I were in for another tongue-lashing from the falcon-cheetah gyphon. I knew from bitter experience that her temper could be as sharp as her beak.

Clyde led the way to my lodgings. 'Do you need anything?' I asked Sioned as she and the snail made themselves comfortable on the settee. 'Food, water?'

'Strong tea and burnt toast at breakfast,' the squirrel replied. 'Nothing until then, but thank you for asking.'

Good thing I hadn't assumed she'd want acorns. I closed the door and took a deep breath as I prepared to return to the gryphons. For the first time in weeks, I longed for a shot of whisky. Just as well that there was none available.

The two gryphons broke off a conversation as I entered their room. Our long sea voyage had made me forget that Taryn was larger than her husband, but I believed it wasn't size alone which made her the dominant one in their partnership.

'Summoned, I come,' I said with forced cheerfulness as I resumed my seat.

Taryn snorted. 'You needn't look so worried. I haven't summoned you to an execution. I wanted to thank you for bringing Jago safely home.'

'I was with him as well,' Morey protested.

His wife didn't even flick an ear in his direction. 'My son can be rather impulsive, which no doubt comes from his father's side of the family.'

Morey muttered, 'That's the pot calling the kettle black.'

'He's a good lad,' I said. 'Well, both of them are. I'm sorry if I seem cautious. I'm just remembering how angry you were about my decision to close off all the thin places between here and Britain.'

'On balance, it was the right decision,' Taryn replied. 'What I objected to was that you made this decision without reference to anyone other than the search dragons. You have the tendency to act unilaterally, Penny, when there's no need for you to do so. During your time in Lloegyr, you've built up a community of friends and confidants. I do wish you'd deign to consult us from time to time.'

'Noted,' I said sheepishly. 'I am sorry that you'll be losing Jago again, when he goes off to the seminary with Clyde.'

Taryn lifted her wings in a shrug. 'He'll only be an hour's flight away, closer than our other eyasses.'

'And how are your other children? Doing well?'

'All well. Eiddwen resumed her training once I'd recovered from my injuries and could return to duty. Rothgen and Annest are proving to be great hunters. Gwilym's poetry has moved even Matriarch Ercwiff to tears.' Taryn sighed. 'For some reason, I seem to worry about Jago more than the rest of my children combined. The other *griffoniaid glas* in our family line were blessed with beauty and intelligence, and cursed in matters of the heart.'

I rubbed my face and let out a yawn, hoping that between the two I hadn't given anything away. 'Bastien seems to have forgiven Jago, so that's good. Anyway, I'd better go. I obviously need my rest.'

Squirrel and snail were both curled up in sleep when I carefully tiptoed into my room. I brushed my teeth in the bathroom, and tried to change as quietly as possible before slipping into bed. As I fell asleep, I wondered when I'd ever be able to share a room with my husband instead of friends and visitors.

The barn gave some protection from the cold wind, but I still pressed against Raven's warm side. 'I don't know what I'm meant to do here,' I said. The were-horses were grazing in their nearby corral, so I kept my voice low. 'The were-rabbits are gone, so Llewelyn's been very good about giving me time to think over which group I should work with next. I know he'd like me to help him with the worst-off not-weres, but I can't face them for long without feeling sick in my stomach.'

'Not without taking letherum,' Raven commented. 'Has Llewelyn offered you any?'

'I asked. He said it's rare, and he doesn't have that much in stock.' Raven's silence pulled at me. 'You still think there's something dodgy going on?'

'Letherum is valuable. Saint Raphael's has come into money. Are the two linked?'

'I don't know. I hope not.' I slipped the glove off my right hand to give his neck a rub. 'I'm sorry I haven't flown off with you to bed down somewhere warm at night. Llewelyn prefers me to be at Saint Raphael's in case there's an emergency.'

'Another month and I'll be back in the woods,' Raven said calmly. 'I don't expect you to join me there either.'

I took a step back to look him in the eyes. 'You don't want us to sleep together? I know there's no indoor space suitable here--'

'Nothing with indoor plumbing.'

'Or warm enough. I've managed to scrounge a hot water bottle for tonight. My room was very cold last evening.' I shivered at the memory. 'But I thought we'd eventually work something out.'

Raven chuckled. 'We had very few nights together on the ship.'

'I saw that as temporary.'

'Why?' He cocked his head. 'Dragons rarely sleep alongside their mates.'

'When matriarchs have the tendency to eat their drakes, I'm not surprised.' I sighed. 'It's a human custom, at least in my culture, that a husband and wife share the same bed. So, for me, it feels wrong that we're apart.'

'If it's important to you, then we'll find a way.' He gave me a gentle nudge with his snout. 'I'm more concerned that you're finding it difficult to fit in here.'

'I guess it'll just take a little time,' I said. 'Things have changed so much whilst we were gone.'

'Do you miss being a parish priest? Maybe Bishop Aeron would find you a church to look after.'

'Not while I'm married to you.' I gave him a grin. 'And you are non-negotiable.'

Raven arched his neck. 'Of course I am.'

Morey flew past, arrowing down to the corral. Mariam strode over to speak to him. A were-wolf trotted across the fields, and I could hear Sorcha's voice in the distance. 'There was a time,' I said slowly, 'when I would have given anything to live in a country filled with beings such as dragons and unicorns. My life in Beckeridge seemed so dull and boring. I can hardly believe it myself, but I'm missing that village, that church, those parishioners. I'm even missing Holly, although she could make my life hell.'

'Clyde could cut us a crossing back to your world,' Raven offered, 'and we could both settle there.'

I moved my cold fingers to touch the soft skin around his nostrils. 'I know what it's like to be separated from your own country. I don't want to inflict that on you. Oh, how I wish we could open lots of thin places between here and England so we could go back to travelling between the two. Drat that Minister without Portfolio and her dreams of a new British Empire.'

'We could live in the search dragon settlement,' Raven offered. 'I've started carving obsidian again. We could buy a tent and you could start a church there.'

I was tempted for all of ten seconds. 'I don't feel God is calling me to evangelise search dragons. Thanks for the offer, though. I'll just keep plugging on here. Maybe something will turn up, like the were-rabbits did. I am glad to hear you're carving again.'

'I'm enjoying it.' Raven sighed warm air across my face. 'I only wish you were happy as well.'

'I'm not desperately unhappy either,' I reassured him. 'Just feeling, well, a bit lost.'

'I could fly us somewhere warm and relaxing.'

'Could you hold that offer until my day off?' I gave his snout a final pat. 'Morey keeps looking over at us. I think he wants a word.'

'You could speak to Llewelyn,' Raven said as I reluctantly pushed myself away. 'He might be able to advise you.'

'I still feel a bit awkward seeing him on his own. He asked me to marry him, and I came back the wife of someone else.'

Raven chuckled. 'I wouldn't worry about that. He and Mariam have started hunting together. There might be another wedding at Saint Raphael's by the summer.'

'Llewelyn and Mariam,' I mused with a smile. 'Yes, they could be very good for each other. You're right, I'll talk to Llewelyn.'

My Associate was perched on a wooden post near Maxence. The were-horse's head hung close to the gryphon. Muscles bunched under Maxence's neck and shoulders, and he pawed the ground with a hoof. Their conversation halted as I approached, and I wondered for a moment if they'd been talking about me.

'Maxence is worried about Llewelyn,' Morey said, his casual tone sounding slightly forced. 'I've been trying to set his mind at ease. Why don't you tell Penny what's bothering you?'

The were-horse huffed and sighed several times before speaking. 'Most of the herd sleep inside the barn this time of year, see. But I like being outside. And my winter coat is a bit thicker than theirs.' He turned his head and nibbled at the shaggy hair growing along his back.

'Very useful, I'm sure,' I agreed.

'I usually stay in the corral, because it gives extra protection if something nasty was to come out of the woods.' The wide-eyed glance Maxence threw at the trees reminded me that were-horses were prey animals. 'But the other night, I went for a walk around. I stopped, though, when I realised that Dr Wyn was by the barn that houses the really poorly not-weres.'

'You knew it was him?' I asked. 'It wasn't too dark to be sure?'

The horse flared his nostrils. 'I know his scent. And there was a full moon.'

'You didn't greet him?'

'Well, he was talking to someone. A bear not-were. I didn't recognise her.' Maxence snorted. 'I couldn't hear what they were saying, but Dr Wyn sounded very unhappy. The bear seemed to be bothering him.'

The were-horse shifted his weight from foot to foot. My right hand was still gloveless, and I lifted it to give his head a comforting scratch. 'It was just as well you were there to keep an eye on things.'

'I would've helped Dr Wyn, if he needed it,' Maxence agreed, although there was a tremble in his voice. 'But he gave the bear a small sack, and she went away. Dr Wyn still wasn't happy, though. His sweat was very sour.'

'Maybe the not-were is refusing help,' I suggested, 'and Dr Wyn is worried for her?'

Morey caught my eyes and gave a quick shake of his head. 'Tell Penny what you said about the sack.'

'When the bear took it, she tipped it a bit, and whatever was inside made a noise. A sort of rattling sound, like when hail hits a barn roof.'

'Thank you for telling us about this,' I said soothingly, giving him one last scratch before I slid my cold hand into a coat pocket. 'We care about Dr Wyn very much, just like you do. We'll do our best to help him.'

'I knew you would. I knew I could talk to you.' Maxence flicked his tail. 'Thank you.'

As he charged off, releasing his tension in a gallop, I looked down at Morey. 'Letherum is stored in wooden boxes.'

'And pills rattle,' Morey agreed.

I glanced at the barn, but there was no sign of the dragon. 'Raven was just reminding me of his theory that letherum is paying for all the improvements here.'

'Or Llewelyn could simply be helping out a not-were who won't approach the Guild openly,' Morey said. 'That could be the simple explanation.'

'I need to know more about letherum. Who's the best person to talk to?'

'Taryn.' Morey leapt up to my shoulder. 'She put in a day's leave to visit her clan this morning. Why don't we go up to the flat? She should be back by now.'

'Does visiting family put her in a bad mood?' I asked as I started walking towards the house.

'Not since her father died, a couple of years ago.' Morey added quickly, 'Best not to say anything about that.'

'Noted.'

As it was still several hours before our evening meal, we went to the kitchen to make a pot of tea and collect several biscuits. I carefully carried the tray up the stairs, sweating in my warm coat as I fought not to spill any liquid or lose a mug. But the happy prick in Taryn's ears as I handed her a cup of tea made the journey worthwhile.

'It's a bribe,' I warned the peregrine-cheetah gryphon as she tucked into a ginger biscuit. 'Morey says you can tell me all about letherum.'

'I was put onto light duties after my tangle with the rats,' Taryn said. 'I undertook administrative duties for the police medics in Llanbedr. What do you want to know?'

'Everything. Where does it come from, how is it refined, who can get hold of it, and anything else I don't know to ask.'

Taryn took a long sip of tea before speaking. 'Letherum is a blend of several plants which only grow on Ennor, an island off Kernow. Harvesting is limited to a few weeks in June, and the mixture of flowers and leaves are dried out in barns over the course of the summer. The exact blend is a fiercely kept secret by the *Tylwyth Teg*.'

'Who are they?'

Morey cocked his head. 'The Fair Folk.'

I nearly spilled my tea. 'You mean fairies? Cute little people who live in the woods and have gossamer wings?'

'Black, I'm shocked,' Morey said sternly. 'You're not usually one for racial stereotypes.'

'They're around the height of an elf,' Taryn continued calmly. 'Very thin, and their skin is a deep green. Not all of them have wings. No males or females.'

'They have just one gender?' I asked.

Taryn shook her head. 'The *Tylwyth Teg* are without gender, neither male nor female. For the last two centuries, they have only lived on Ennor.'

'Why?'

My question hung in the air. Morey turned his head away, his flattened ears telling me that the question made him uncomfortable. Taryn took a bite of her biscuit. Only when she had picked up the crumbs from the bed did she answer. 'It was the only place the Church could not reach when the priests were trying to exterminate them.'

'That's the rumour,' Morey protested. 'The Church's own records say that the Fair Folk agreed to put themselves into exile.'

'All institutions try to put the best possible interpretation on their actions,' Taryn said. 'I've seen this in my own profession.'

'Is letherum in short supply in police stations?' I asked, cutting off Morey's continued attempts to defend the Church.

'I'm not certain.' Taryn pointed her beak at the tea pot, and I refilled her mug. 'I monitored delivery of the Llanbedr supplies in November. Each station received the amount they'd requested, which admittedly isn't that much. We only use it on criminal vampires or weres. I do know that some species can use it for pain relief.'

'Peter gave me my first tablet,' I recalled. 'He said it was "over the counter", but of course it isn't.'

'Our station's medic probably didn't see any harm in giving tablets to a human for future use.' Taryn narrowed her eyes. 'Is letherum in short supply elsewhere?'

Morey's ears had finally returned to a relaxed angle. 'Llewelyn's said it's in short supply here.'

'Saint Raphael's has greater need of letherum than the police,' Taryn said. 'And the Guild has expanded operations. Penny, perhaps you should take a request to the Fair Folk asking for another shipment.'

'*Me?*'

'The Fair Folk bear no grudge against humans, although it's unfortunate that you are a priest.' Taryn glanced at her husband. 'I suggest you remain here.'

'They won't know I'm a clergyman,' Morey protested.

'They will, and would you be able to keep your beak shut if they complain about the Church?'

'Even now?' I asked. 'I mean, you said everything happened over two hundred years ago.'

'The *Tylwyth Teg* are long lived, and their grievances last even longer.' Taryn's head bobbed in a brisk nod. 'You go, Penny, with Raven. The Fair Folk have an affinity with dragons.'

'I'll go on Friday,' I said slowly. 'That's my day off. Do I need to somehow let them know I'm coming?'

'They'll know you are coming. They are very far-sighted.' Taryn hesitated, then added, 'Take iron with you, and your own food and water. Do not eat or drink anything you might be offered. And above all, do not ride with them, no matter how beautiful the horse they show you.'

'Sounds similiar to warnings in Earth legends,' I said. 'What would happen if I did any of that?'

'You and I have had our differences,' Taryn replied. 'But I would not want to see you trapped on their island forever.'

My throat was suddenly dry. I took a quick sip of cold tea. 'Right. Noted.'

Chapter Ten

Tentacles traced a thin line of slime across my right cheek, waking me from my sleep. Even with my eyes closed, the lack of natural light in my room told me it was still early. 'Clyde,' I groaned, 'the sun hasn't even come up yet.'

'Seminary day!' he announced cheerfully, my pillow jerking under his happy bounce.

'We're not due there until after breakfast.' I deliberately rolled onto my left side. 'Just because you can't sleep doesn't mean I have to get up before dawn.'

'Prayer. Chapel.'

'After breakfast.'

'Important,' he insisted. 'Prayer.'

'Remember what it says in the Psalms,' I said. '"Even upon my bed my heart instructs me."'

'"At *night*",' Clyde corrected me.

'Great,' I muttered into my blankets. 'It was bad enough just having Morey correcting my Bible quotes. Having two of you around is going to make my life impossible.'

'Study more?'

'Maybe I should go to seminary with you.'

'Chapel?' Now the entire bed jolted as Clyde bounced.

I had a sudden flashback to the broken sleep I'd endured the first few months after my parents had died. James had suffered nightmares and bedwetting. At least Clyde only left slime behind. 'All right, all right. I'll get up. But don't expect too much from me until I've had some coffee.'

The flickering flame of a single candle gave just enough light for me to change into day clothes. I used the bannister to steady my steps as I went down the stairs. The larger windows on the ground floor added light to that of my candle, and I was able to find my way to the kitchen and pour myself a mug of coffee. A flask was always left out overnight for anyone who had to make an emergency pastoral call. I decided going with an excited snail shark to the chapel came under that category.

My steps slowed as we approached the small room at the end of the corridor. Light stretched down the stone floor from the half open door. Clyde hung back as I stepped into the doorway and looked inside.

Llewelyn was knelt in prayer in front of the altar. A large fur coat rested on the step beside him, and I wondered whether he'd come in from an early morning visit to a not-were. I tried to back away, but the sole of my shoe squeaked against the floor.

The chaplain looked up, blinking as he focussed on my face. 'Penny. Please, do come in.'

I crept inside, Clyde close behind. As Llewelyn closed his eyes and bent his head, I found a seat several pews back. Clyde clambered up next to me.

The smell of my coffee slowly added a warm note to the slightly acrid scent of candlewax and the smokey traces of incense. I sipped as quietly as I could, and expressed extreme gratitude to God that Lloegyr offered such a necessity. Giving up alcohol had been hard enough. To have given up coffee as well would have been unbearable.

The room brightened as the sun rose. I studied the stained glass window of Saint Raphael, the healer, glowing in its place behind the altar. The angel's white wings were spread open over a huddled group of not-weres. Clyde might be excited about our visit to the seminary, but even the coffee couldn't warm the chill I felt in my stomach. How would the other ordinands react to the snail shark?

Voices echoing down the corridor announced the arrival of kitchen staff. Clyde slid from the pew and left the chapel. I hoped he'd go outside to hunt. He probably wouldn't have time to catch any birds during our visit, and I had no idea what the seminary might offer a snail shark to eat. I started to rise from my pew.

'Penny.' Llewelyn's quiet voice made me sit down again. The were-wolf's head was still bent. 'Do you think that some sins are unforgiveable?'

'Of course not,' I said. 'God forgives anyone who repents.'

'I have been pondering what Christ said. "Whoever blasphemes against the Holy Spirit never has forgiveness, but is guilty of an eternal sin."'

'I've never understood that passage,' I admitted. 'What does it mean to "blaspheme against the Holy Spirit"?'

'Perhaps one does so if he continues to commit an act which he knows to be sinful. What is the point of repentence if he knows he will sin yet again?'

'Sometimes it's hard not to do something over and over again,' I said slowly. 'I mean, we all have faults, things we end up repeating, even though we try very hard not to. Look at how much I used to drink, for example.'

'Yes. We become trapped by our earlier actions into sustaining them.'

'Llewelyn.' I waited, but he didn't look at me. 'Is there something you want to talk about?'

The door suddenly swung fully open, making me jump. Miriam stared at us, a white cloth clutched in her large hands. 'My apologies. I thought I'd do a bit of polishing whilst the clergy were having breakfast.'

'That's very good of you,' Llewelyn said, rising to his feet. 'Penny and I were just about to leave.'

'I haven't interrupted anything?'

'Nothing that can't wait,' I assured her, clamping down on my annoyance. Just one look at Llewelyn's face told me that the moment had passed. A studied calmness had smoothed his cheeks and evened out his eyebrows.

After breakfast and Morning Prayer, I collected my coat, slipped on my backpack, and scooped Clyde into my arms. Raven was waiting for us outside, his green-black hide gleaming in the early morning sunshine. I paused for a moment, drinking in the sight of my gorgeous husband.

Raven arched his neck and rustled his wings. 'Yes, I am the most handsome dragon in all of Lloegyr.'

I laughed as I strode over to his side. 'Well, I'm not going to argue with you.'

He glanced down at the snail shark in my arms. 'Shouldn't Clyde travel in his container?'

'No,' the snail said firmly. 'Dignity.'

Jago landed on my shoulder a second later. 'Uncle Clyde says that he doesn't want the other ordinands to see him arriving in a basket.'

Raven snorted. 'That's understandable. It's an hour's direct flight to Saint Canna's. I suggest Clyde rests deep inside Penny's coat. I feel a wind starting up.'

'Room for two?' Jago asked hopefully.

'There's enough give in my coat,' I said. 'Just don't wriggle.'

A passing were-bear took Clyde from me before I clambered up Raven's side. She passed the snail over, and I tucked him inside my coat before Jago dropped down on top.

Raven was right about the wind. The strength increased as we flew over a series of fields and forests, buffeting us from the left. I gave up trying to keep my hair in any sort of order, and as my ears froze I regretted my lack of woolly hat.

Saint Canna's Seminary was set in a valley surrounded by gently rolling hills. Four buildings made of stone, brick, and wood created a square, with a grassy quadrangle in the middle. A wide cobblestone path surrounded the buildings. To one side, bare trees huddled together, the regular planting making me wonder if it were an orchard. Fields stretched around two other sides. A barn and attached corral completed the scene, and several cows grazed inside the enclosure. Did the seminary strive to produce all its own food? And did students undertake manual labour alongside their studies?

Raven backwinged to land in the quadrangle. I remained on his back for a moment, glancing around the buildings now we were at ground level. The one made out of grey stone on my left, I decided, must be the chapel. It was the only one with stained-glass windows. To my right was probably the ordinands' accommodation, a three-storey building of red brick broken regularly by small windows. Behind me was a wooden structure, and I found it hard to identify its purpose. The fourth building, a mixture of dark timber and brown brick, struck me as most likely to be the administration and teaching block.

Jago crawled out of my coat and flew over to land on Raven's head. I lifted Clyde out and placed him behind a spine before lifting my right leg over the dragon's neck and sliding to the soft ground. Clyde carefully made his way down to my upstretched hands.

The large oak door of the brown building swung open. A unicorn stepped out. Her white coat was shaggy with winter growth, but she still looked elegant as her silver hooves rung out against the flagstones. She halted a few feet away, and bright blue eyes studied us each in turn. Then her spiral horn pointed at the snail shark in my arms. 'Ordinand Clyde. You are most welcome. I am Liliwen, the Warden of Saint Canna's. Perhaps you could introduce me to your companions?'

Now that we were here, a strain of yellow swirled through Clyde's body. 'Penny. Raven. Jago,' he said, pointing his tentacles at each of us in turn.

'Didn't you know our names already?' Jago asked from his high perch.

'I did know,' Liliwen agreed. 'Sometimes it's courteous to ask another to effect introductions.' Her tone was mild, but Jago's crest dipped at the rebuke. 'Please, follow me to my study. Let's have coffee and come to know each other better.'

'I'll stay outside,' Raven told her. 'I've only come as transport.'

'All of our rooms are built to accommodate dragons,' the unicorn said, 'but you can wait here, if you prefer. I'll send some coffee out to you.'

I placed Clyde on the ground. Jago flew down to ride on his shell. As they followed the Warden, I hung back to whisper to Raven. 'Do you think you can hang around until tomorrow, when we leave? Just in case anyone thinks of causing trouble for Clyde.'

The dragon sighed, his warm breath disturbing my wind-swept hair even further. 'Penny, I can't stay here for all of his three years in training. Clyde will have to find his own way with his fellow students.'

'I know, I know.' I watched the snail shark enter the building. 'I worry about him.'

'And you always will.' He lowered his snout to nudge my back. 'You'd better catch up with the others.'

I nodded and set off across the grass. My friends were in the entrance hall when I stepped through the door. Liliwen had halted to speak to a young-looking elf. As he hurried away, the unicorn pointed down the corridor on our right. 'This way.'

The sound of hooves striking tiles echoed off the high ceilings. I heard snatches of music, and a droning voice which sounded like a lecture. Liliwen took us into a wood-panelled room, with a large window that looked out onto the quadrangle. A couple of sofas and a set of mismatched chairs formed three sides of a square around a small table. A desk set into the opposite wall was covered with various papers and a pile of books.

'Please, make yourselves comfortable,' the Warden said. 'As you can see, the tea has already arrived.'

A coffee pot with a mug and three bowls rested on the low table. I busied myself with pouring out a portion for each person. Jago and Clyde placed themselves on the table by their bowls. A small stand rested beside one sofa, and I placed Liliwen's drink on the dark surface.

'Thank you for coming,' the Warden said after a quick slurp of tea. 'I think it helps a new student to settle in if he and his sponsor have visited before term starts.'

'It's very kind of you to invite us.' I nodded at Jago. 'I hope you already know that Clyde needs a translator? Jago will be coming with him.'

'That's okay, isn't it?' Jago asked hesitantly. 'I'm looking forward to learning all about the Bible and everything.'

'Arrangements are already in hand,' Liliwen assured him. 'I understand that you're a vegetarian? Our cooks are used to catering for wide variety of diets, so that won't be a problem.'

'Hunt?' Clyde asked hopefully.

'Only if you can do so off site,' the Warden said. 'We need to encourage wildlife in the area to keep down the pests in our fields and orchards.'

'He's eaten pre-caught meat before,' I told Liliwen. 'And I assume, when I come for a visit, Raven and I can take him away from here to hunt?'

'Certainly. We ask that the distance be at least ten miles.' She turned her gaze to the snail. 'So, Clyde, please tell me about yourself. How has God worked in your life to bring you here?'

Clyde's tentacles writhed and colours swirled through his body. Jago translated the snail's attempts to give a short autobiography. I sipped my coffee as Clyde started with the death of his mother, the Noble Leader, and how he came to live with me. Jago's voice trembled slightly as he delivered Clyde's matter-of-fact statement on how he had sacrificed his wings for the sake of peace. Clyde flushed pink as he spoke about his confirmation and receiving communion for the first time. Our trip to les Etats-Unis was summed up in a few sentences. 'And now I'm looking forward to learning more about my faith and preparing myself to serve God as a deacon and a priest.' Jago turned his head and whispered to Clyde, 'And one day a bishop!'

Liliwen's ears flicked, and I was certain she'd heard the gryphon's comment. 'I have heard many an ordinand's story, but yours is one of the more memorable ones. You are the first snail shark to train here, and we'll need to discuss how we can make your bedroom accessible. For tonight, I understand you're all willing to share? We've given you a room with three beds.'

'That'll be fine.' I lifted my backpack from the floor. 'Would you mind telling me what we'll be doing today? I'd rather leave this somewhere than carry it with me.'

'Our plan is for you to join today's schedule here at Saint Canna's,' the Warden said. 'One of our second year ordinands has been assigned to guide you around. Lachlan will take you to your room, and you have a few minutes before mid-day prayers at noon. Lunch is served afterwards, and we do ask students to attend all meals, even if they don't eat daily or hunt for themselves. We consider the coming together to be important for community life.'

'Fine,' Clyde agreed.

'After lunch, you'll go with Lachlan to a preaching workshop. Several ordinands will be delivering sermons in the chapel, and these will be assessed by the group.'

'I did that in my theological college,' I commented. 'It was a bit daunting, but we all learned a lot from it.'

'You'll then have some free time before Evening Prayer,' Liliwen continued. 'A number of the ordinands like to use the grass field to play a quick football match. You might like to join them. Normally the time after the evening meal is free, but tonight we have a guest speaker, and you're all welcome to attend.'

'What's the talk about?' Jago asked.

'The Archdeacon of Hammtun will be speaking to us about developing a welcoming and inclusive church.' The unicorn's voice softened. 'I should think you'll have some personal observations to make, Clyde.'

The snail's colours darkened to browns and greys. 'Yes.'

'Morning Prayer is at eight o'clock,' Liliwen said. 'Breakfast follows, then you will go with Lachlen and the other second years to a lecture on the New Testament. I believe it'll be about the Letter of James. After a coffee break, the next lecture will be on church history. Then mid-day prayers, lunch, and we four will meet up again to reflect on your visit. We'll discuss what particular adjustments Saint Canna needs to make to help you live and study here.'

I rose to my feet as she backed away from the table. Slinging my backpack over one shoulder, I followed her to the door. Jago flew to my left shoulder, and Clyde slid along at my side.

A touch of Liliwen's silver horn undid the door's catch and it swung inwards. A young man waiting outside immediately straightened. He was slightly taller than me, with dark red hair and a brave attempt at a moustache adding fuzz to his long face. I looked in vain for pointed elf ears or the shimmer of a were. 'You're human,' I blurted.

'Och, aye, that I am.' He held out a hand as thick as his Scottish accent. 'Lachlan MacLeod.'

'MacLeod? Like from *Highlander*?'

His grip was warm and firm, despite the confusion on his face. 'I know not what you mean.'

I could imagine the sarcastic comment Morey would have released at this point. 'Sorry, a TV series from awhile back. My name's Penny.'

'What is this "TV"?'

'Lachlan,' Liliwen explained, 'fell through a thin place when he was only nine years old. He was found half-starved on an island off Alba.'

'Discovered by a dragon,' Lachlan said. 'She brought me to the kirk and they gave me hearth and home.'

I frowned. 'Why didn't someone take you back to your home in Scotland?'

The man's face darkened. 'I didnae want to go back there.'

The tone was sadly very familiar. In my time as a priest, I'd heard stories of childhoods which had brought me to tears. 'So you were raised in Alba?'

'Aye, with brocks.'

'Were-badgers,' Liliwen translated for me. 'They're very proud of their son.'

I smiled down at Clyde. 'I'm very proud of my son as well.'

The snail flushed bright pink and muttered an embarrassed, *'Mam.'*

Lachlan crouched down to address the snail. 'My mither be the same. Best just to let it pass.'

'I'm Jago,' said the gryphon on my shoulder. 'I'll be coming to seminary too. I translate for Uncle Clyde.'

'You all be very welcome.' Lachlan threw out an arm to our right. 'This way to your room.'

Our accommodation reminded me of my cell at Saint Thomas's. Plain walls, three beds, rugs to cushion the stone floor, a small desk, and a shared toilet and washing facilities down the hall. Lachlan said he'd wait for us, and closed the door behind him as he returned to the corridor. I dumped my backpack, tried to tame my hair, and let myself out to visit the loo. Then we followed the young man to the chapel.

Mid-day Prayer was short and sweet. The reaction from some of the students and staff was the opposite. The scowls and mutters we encountered when entering the cold building made me want to pick up Clyde and head straight back to Saint Raphael's. But the snail shark ignored them and entered whole-heartedly into the service.

The chapel was large, with seating at the front and empty space at the back for the larger species. Dragons, unicorns, and full-sized gryphons peered over the heads of dwarves, elves, vampires, and various weres. During the hymn, I made a quick count. Over sixty people were present, though it wasn't obvious which were the students and which were staff.

The stained glass windows held images from Jesus' life and portrayed various Lloegyr saints. The one behind the altar showed a female vampire, which I assumed was the Saint Canna after whom the seminary had been named. She held a spear in her hands and a unicorn huddled behind her. I made a mental note to ask Morey to tell me more about the saint.

The refectory was similarly designed to accommodate species large and small. Unfortunately, this meant a forced separation similar to what I'd seen in the chapel. The larger species once again congregated together to one side, and the smaller staff and students sat at the tables.

Lunch was vegetable soup and thick bread. Clyde sipped politely at his, Jago consumed a portion with great delight, and I managed to spoon half of the tasty mixture down my throat despite the fact that the elf on Clyde's left was doing her best to ignore him. Fortunately, Lachlan, who sat between Jago and Clyde, happily talked to the snail about student life.

The preaching workshop was held in the chapel. The stone building was surprisingly warm. I winced in sympathy as the first ordinand, a dwarf, made the same mistake to which I'd once been prone, namely trying to deliver four different sermons in twelve minutes. The tutor, a unicorn who had not offered up his name, asked for responses from the other twenty students in the room.

When it was his turn to comment, Clyde prodded Jago, who looked half-asleep on the chair next to him. 'I'm interpreting for my Uncle Clyde,' the gryphon hurriedly informed the group. 'He says that the subject of the Temple of Jerusalem has filled volumes of books, so he thought Chesten did very well to bring so much into a short sermon. The most interesting angle was about Jesus' body being the new Temple. Clyde thinks, when she works on the sermon again, she should focus on that and leave the other ideas for another time.'

Chesten flushed slightly, and I warmed to the dwarf. The smile she directed at Clyde seemed genuine.

Three sermons later, Jago wasn't the only one struggling to stay awake. I did my best to remain charitable. My early sermons hadn't been very good either. Actually, if I'd had a busy week, sometimes a congregation still had to cope with whatever I managed to cobble together late on a Saturday night.

After ninety minutes, the tutor declared the session was over. As ordinands shuffled to the exit, Chesten made her way over to our pew. 'Some of us are going off for a quick game of footy,' she said. 'You coming?'

'Yes,' Clyde said firmly.

And so, with a gryphon on my shoulder and a snail at my heels, I followed the dwarf out of the seminary complex to the field outside.

The sun was shining and the air held a hint of warmth. Jago jumped temporarily to my head as I pulled on my coat, then dropped back down to dig his claws into the leather. The shaggy grass was solid underfoot, but I was certain that a bit of rain would soon turn the field into a soggy mess.

'We never saw any sports when we were in les Etats-Unis,' Jago commented as we joined the students who had ventured outside. 'Do you think they play football over there?'

'Perhaps, although they might play what we call "American football" rather than what Americans call "soccer".'

'What's American football like?'

'From what I've seen, it's like rugby, but with more padding. And cheerleaders. And takes forever because of all the commercial breaks.'

The football field had been marked off with ropes, and the goals were no more than webbing strung up between poles. The grey-white football looked worn, but it was fully inflated. A vampire held it in her hands as she talked to a gryphon and a unicorn.

The three of them finished their conversation, and the vampire raised her voice. 'All right, whoever wants to play, join us on the pitch. If you want to watch, stay outside the boundaries.'

Of the forty students, only nineteen stepped forward. The vampire spoke again. 'We need one more to make up two sides.'

Clyde sped forward. 'Me. Clyde.'

'Should he do that, Auntie Penny?' Jago whispered in my ear, echoing my own concerns. 'What if the ball hits his shell?'

'We have to let Clyde make his own decisions,' I said, although lunch was curdling inside my stomach.

A number of students were scowling or showing the equivalent with drawn back ears or whisking tails. But the vampire smiled at the snail. 'Good to have you with us, Clyde. Let's number off the players and give the captains a moment to assign positions.'

I was pleased that the umpire simply divided the group in two rather than allow the captains to pick their team mates. The horror of always being chosen last, throughout my time in school, still gave me the occasional nightmare.

My relief was only short-lived. Clyde had ended up with the unicorn as his captain, and it was obvious that she didn't quite know where to assign him. Finally, the position always suggested for the least well regarded player was shouted out. 'Goalie!' Somehow I managed to suppress a groan. I'd always ended up in goal as well.

The teams formed up behind their captains. The vampire pulled a whistle from her pocket and blew on it once. She released the ball and quickly backed away.

The match soon became rather messy and very enjoyable, which was often the way when the enthusiasm of the players was greater than their skill. For several minutes, most of the action happened in the middle of the pitch. Clyde waited in the goal area on my right, his tentacles at full stretch as his eyespots followed the ebb and flow of the game.

Some of the four-legged players were able to dribble the ball between fore and hind legs, making it more difficult for an opponent to kick it away. The smaller weres had a distinct advantage in this regard. One were-badger in particular changed several times into animal form to scoot underneath a large gryphon to steal the ball.

A throw-in from the far side brought the ball close to the gryphon captain. He used a mixture of head and beak to bring it to his feet, and then he charged towards Clyde's goal. His taloned forefeet kept the ball moving forwards, weaving past a were-squirrel and an elf. A dwarf defender ducked in and kicked the ball towards Clyde.

The snail rose high on his foot as the ball bounced in his direction. At the last moment, he threw his weight onto his head and slammed his foot against the ball. It arced through the air, landing only a yard away from the gryphon captain. He brought the football under control and passed it to a vampire team mate.

'Well done, Clyde!' I shouted out, clapping my hands together.

The action moved to the other side of the pitch. The other team's goalkeeper, a painfully thin elf, threw herself at the ball as a dwarf headed it towards the goal. Her hands closed briefly around the football. Then it slipped from her grasp and bounced into the net.

Cheers erupted around the field. The elf kicked the ball to the umpire, and she restarted play. The gryphon captain pounced on the ball and darted towards the right-hand goal. Clyde's body swirled with blues and purples as he watched the gryphon racing towards him a second time. His team's defenders tried but failed to halt the captain's progress.

The gryphon kicked the football. Clyde opened his jaws wide. I winced as the ball slammed into his teeth. The force knocked him backwards, and he ended up in the net. The make-shift goal collapsed around him, burying him in a tangle of brown webbing.

I looked to the umpire, wondering whether she would rule this as a 'save' or a 'goal'. But even as the vampire started to open her mouth, the gryphon charged. He galloped over to the floundering snail shark and used his forefeet to wrap the netting even tighter around Clyde's body. 'Let's lift him up' he told the players who surrounded him. 'Maybe it's time to make a snail fly!'

Chapter Eleven

The gryphon extended his wings and leapt upwards. Other flighted students quickly joined him, digging feet or teeth into the webbing. My heart skipped several beats as the still-struggling snail was hoisted from the ground, carried aloft by a mixture of gryphons, vampires in bat form, and several were-birds.

'We need to stop them!' Jago said to me, his own wings out. 'I can't do it on my own, I'm too small. Call for Raven!'

My hand had slipped into my pocket to fumble for my pocketknife. Clyde was only twenty feet from the ground, but still far enough for his shell to be damaged in a sudden drop. And what if the gang took him even higher? I could only hope that Raven wasn't far away.

The vampire umpire blew her whistle and waved her arms. 'Stop this at once! Do you hear me? Bring him back down immediately!' She changed into bat shape, her abandoned clothes falling to the ground as she flew up to the group. Despite the smaller form, her voice had lost none of its strength. 'This is not how we treat a fellow Christian, an ordinand at this college! You should all be ashamed of yourselves!'

'Yes, she is right,' the unicorn captain added, stomping her hooves. 'Bring the snail back down before someone is hurt!'

I forced myself to leave the knife unopened while Clyde was slowly lowered back to the field. The students grumbled as they detached themselves from the net. 'Was only a bit of fun.' *'Chafodd neb ei frifo.'* 'He's all right.'

The vampire returned to human form the moment she landed. Although she shivered, no doubt from being naked in the cold air, she hurried over to Clyde to extract him from the webbing. Once he was clear, she straightened to glare at the other students. 'What do you say, Clyde? Was it only a bit of fun?'

The snail spat the ball and several teeth out of his mouth. His body was a dark shade of red-brown. 'No. Bullies.'

The gryphon drew back. 'I'm sorry you can't take a joke.'

Jago flew over to land on Clyde's shell. 'Uncle Clyde says risking someone's life is not a joke, and it's not what he expects from a follower of Jesus. Uncle Clyde thinks that all Christians are called to act like Jesus would.'

Clyde reared up on his foot and opened his jaws. '"Forth in your name, O Lord, I go, my daily labour to pursue, you only, Lord, resolved to know in all I think or speak or do."'

A dwarf had brought the umpire's clothes over. The vampire paused in pulling up her trousers to smile at Clyde. 'What a wonderful singing voice you have.'

'Uncle Clyde can sing easier than he can talk,' Jago told her. 'That's why I translate for him.'

Fully dressed again, the vampire retrieved the deflated ball. 'Game over for today. I declare the match a tie. And all of you who hoisted Clyde into the air are banned for the next three games. For conduct unbecoming a Christian.'

Several of the students started to complain. A fierce look from the vampire silenced them. I quickly decided two things. One was that I never wanted to get on her bad side. The second is that she was bound to be at least an archdeacon one day, if not a bishop.

'My name's Carys Grey,' the vampire told Clyde. 'As a Grey, I know what it's like to be an outsider. This lot are mostly decent, but they're not perfect. I'm sorry, that should never have happened to you.'

'All sin,' Clyde replied solemnly.

Carys stared at the gang. 'Apologise to him.'

The gryphon snorted, his ears flicking. 'All right, all right, sorry about that, Clyde.'

'Forgiven,' the snail said.

'And you're a good goalie,' the unicorn captain added. 'I hope you're on my team at our next match.'

Clyde opened his jaws in a wide smile. The missing teeth made me wince, although I knew that it wouldn't take long for new ones to take their place. 'Forgiven.'

'We have some time left before Evening Prayer,' Carys told him. 'Would you like to go to the Common Room for a coffee?'

'A cup of tea would be great,' Jago said from his perch on the snail's shell.

'If you don't mind,' Carys told him, looking apologetic, 'I was hoping for just the two of us, Clyde and me.'

'Oh, okay, right.' Jago extended his wings and flapped back over to my shoulder. His beak lowered to my right ear. 'How's she going to understand him?'

Carys and Clyde were making their way to the buildings. The snail's body swirled with a combination of colours, pinks and golds and greens, which I had never seen before. 'I think they'll find a way.'

I was less certain what I was meant to do until Evening Prayer. Jago and I retired to my room. A flask of hot water rested on the desk, and I made us each a cup of tea. He helped himself to a biscuit and visibly cheered up again. 'I mean, it's good for Uncle Clyde to make friends. I'll make friends here, too. I need to talk to Warden Liliwen about having a room of my own, once Basty joins me here.'

Somehow I managed not to choke on my drink. After a careful swallow, I asked with equal caution, 'Bastien plans to live here?'

'Why not? They use rats to send messages just like other people. That could be Basty's job.' Jago made happy noises as he crunched his biscuit, seemingly unconcerned at the mess he was making on the desk. 'I know it'll be for three years, but I know he won't mind.'

'You sure he won't mind?' I asked cautiously, fighting back the voice screaming in my head that I had to tell Jago the truth about his boyfriend's health.

'It doesn't matter where he serves his rat king.' Jago cocked his head, causing his blue and purple crest to trail through the biscuit crumbs. 'Might as well be here. Do you think you could mention it to the Warden? She could put in a request to the Consortium.'

I shivered slightly at the rat king's name. 'After the way the Consortium treated you, I'm surprised you'd want to ask any favours of him.'

'Only because of Basty.' Jago shook himself. 'And remember he sold himself to the Consortium to keep me safe.'

'To keep you safe from *Cadw ar Wahân,*' I said. 'You know, I've never asked Bastien why his bondage would keep you safe. Has he told you?'

'No.' The gryphon's voice was low. 'I've not wanted to ask him. There's all sorts of stuff going on with the rat kings that I try not to think about.'

I tried to make my tone casual. 'Like what?'

'You know I can't tell you, Auntie Penny,' Jago said miserably. 'I swore on Basty's life that I wouldn't.'

'Sorry, that's right.' I looked up at the sound of a distant bell. 'I think it's time for Evening Prayer. Coming?'

Jago leapt up to my shoulder in response, and we left the room together.

Clyde sat next to Carys for Evening Prayer, and her soprano singing voice was nearly as pure as his tenor. To my surprise, we had a short sermon, delivered by the Warden. Her few words on Psalm 121, pointing out that we didn't look to the hills for our help but in God, made the ordinands nod studiously. I fought back a sudden urge to chuckle, remembering all too well how courteous I'd been as a student. Only later, out of earshot of the tutors, would we compare notes on what we'd really thought about a sermon.

Dinner was a lovely piece of fish for those who ate meat, and a mixture of beans and vegetables for those like Jago who didn't. I shared a glance with Clyde, certain he too felt he'd had his fill of fish during our voyages on *The Morning Star.* But we both ate our portions without grumbling.

It'd been some while since I'd seen Rhis Cadwalader, the Archdeacon of Hammtun. As I entered the chapel for his lecture, the vampire came over to greet me. 'Father Penny, good to see you here with Ordinand Clyde. And his friend and interpreter, Master Jago.'

'Hello,' I said guardedly, remembering all too well that the Archdeacon had argued against allowing Clyde to train for ordination.

Rhis wore a dark three-piece suit. Immaculately trimmed hair matched the grey of his eyes. Oil lamps spread across the stone walls glanced light off his glasses as he bowed to kiss the back of my hand. Then he crouched lower to address Clyde. 'I trust all has gone well during your visit?'

'Not really,' Jago replied. 'Some bullies had a go at him on the football field.'

'Jago,' Clyde growled. 'Quiet.'

The Archdeacon's dark eyebrows drew together. 'Do you wish to make a complaint, Ordinand Clyde?'

'No,' the snail said emphatically. 'Sorted.'

'Good.' Rhis nodded. 'Best that these things are settled peacefully. As I'm certain you can appreciate, not everyone in the Church is quite ready for a snail shark ordinand. Now, if you would please excuse me, I'd like to look over my notes one last time.'

As he walked back to the lectern, I rubbed the back of my hand against my trousers.

To my surprise, the Archdeacon's address was very good. He spoke about the various prejudices which had affected the Church in the past. 'Most obviously, the one against humans, understandable when our patron saint and martyr, the great dragon Saint George, was killed by a pagan human knight when Saint George refused to renounce the Christian faith. But we have had a human, in recent years, serve a parish church. Father Penny is here tonight, visiting us from her important work at Saint Raphael's.'

'And you're stuck there,' Jago muttered in my ear, 'because the Church doesn't like you being with Raven.'

Rhis moved on to the dates at which different races had been admitted to ordination. 'Vampires were only admitted a decade ago. A number of opponents argued that my kind would never be willing to settle for preserved blood or solid food, and our own parishioners might find themselves put under pressure to offer themselves for our sustenance. This was, of course, proven to be utterly untrue. And now, in this very seminary, you will have the first snail shark training for ordained ministry.'

After admitting that churches still had the tendency to reflect, in their membership, the communities in which they resided, the Archdeacon added that churches set in more mixed areas saw a greater diversity in the worshipping congregation. 'Father Penny served for several months in Caer-grawnt, in a mixed and fully integrated congregation. That's the challenge which many of you will face once you're ordained and serving in your parishes. How can we ensure that anyone who comes through our doors is made to feel fully welcome? This has implications wider than just the Body of Christ. As more and more people move out of their home enclaves and into our towns and cities, the different races are being challenged to live in peace and co-operation with each other. The Church is called to be a shining beacon which flourishes because of differences, not despite them. This will be a large part of your service to God in the Church, and in this we remember our Lord and Saviour, Jesus Christ, who reconciled all things to God on the Cross. Thank you.'

Staff and students expressed their appreciation by clapping hands or stomping feet against the stone floor. The Warden left her place at the back of the chapel and joined Rhis. 'Any questions for the Archdeacon?'

'I have one,' Jago said from my shoulder. 'If that's okay?'

Liliwen dipped her head in a nod. 'You'll be a member of our community when you and Ordinand Clyde join us in September. What would you like to ask of Archdeacon Rhis?'

'Actually, it's a question for you.' Although Jago sounded calm, I could feel the tension in his body. 'Do you agree with him that the Church should be happy with difference?'

'Of course. You need only look at the students and staff assembled here.'

'You must have rooms large enough for a dragon, because you have dragons as tutors and students,' Jago continued. 'So why didn't you offer Penny, and her husband Raven, one of those?'

'Quite simply,' the Warden replied calmly, 'I did not know that they are married, and they didn't ask.'

'And if they had asked?'

Confusion rippled through the room. Most of those present had no idea who Raven was. I wanted to reach up and clamp Jago's beak shut. Perhaps he was concerned about my marital sleeping arrangements, but I also suspected that he was thinking about the welcome he and Bastien might be given. I cleared my throat. 'Raven's my husband, a dragon, and we're used to sleeping apart.'

Mutters and whispers filled the chapel. Jago raised his voice to speak above them. 'So, if Auntie Penny and Uncle Raven had asked, would you have given them a room together?'

'The Church has come a long way,' Rhis responded before the unicorn could speak. 'But you must know, Master Jago, that we are still against mixed-species relationships. This is not the time or place for a fuller discussion, but I'd be very happy to sit down with you tomorrow morning to work through the scriptural references.'

He stepped back to glance at the Warden. Liliwen studied the Archdeacon for a moment. Then she said, firmly and clearly, 'Had I known that Father

Penny is married, I would certainly have found her and her husband a room large enough to accommodate both of them.'

A few gasps echoed against the stone walls. The Archdeacon's firm voice cut through the chatter. 'Warden, this would go against the Church's long-held position against such relationships.'

'Saint Canna's has long enjoyed the freedom to question scripture, tradition, experience, and reason,' Liliwen said calmly. 'Our ordinands are encouraged to challenge tradition when new understandings emerge from experience. Scripture and reason are not meant to battle one another. This seminary does not depend on Eglwys Lloegyr for funding nor approval. Our students must be able to engage in such study without threats hanging over them or our institution.'

Rhis glared at her. 'And if the Church decides not to ordain graduates from this seminary?'

'Llanbedr Diocese might decide not to ordain our students.' The unicorn remained calm, although some of her tutors were showing signs of alarm. 'Other dioceses would be very happy to take them instead. Threats do not become you, Archdeacon. I would hope you would be more concerned to stamp out prejudice. Only a few years ago, the first Grey who began her studies here had to face down several vampires from other blood groups. And this afternoon, an ordinand was bullied during a football game. Prejudice is like an infection. There can be no toleration of even the smallest example. Otherwise, like a disease, it spreads throughout the entire body and threatens all.'

'I like her,' Jago said into my ear. 'I'm really happy Uncle Clyde is going to be here.'

'We don't try to convince our students to accept mixed-species relationships,' an elf said quickly. 'Saint Canna's tolerates a wide range of theological stances.'

'Thank you, Misstral,' Liliwen said. 'Father Penny, would you like to change your room?'

My face was hot as I rose to my feet. 'That's very kind of you, Warden, but remember that my husband is a search dragon. He prefers to find a warm country in which to sleep during the Lloegyr winter.'

Chuckles and comments of 'Can you blame him?' broke the tension. Rhis moved to Liliwen's side and her ears twitched as he spoke to her. Then, after an exaggerated bow to his audience, the Archdeacon stalked out of the chapel.

I found myself yawning as students and tutors prepared to leave. Some formed groups, obviously intent on discussing the evening's events. Others headed for the door. I reached up a hand to tap Jago's beak. 'I'm off to my room. You coming, or did you want to stay here?'

'I thought I might talk to Uncle Clyde...' The gryphon's voice trailed off, and I followed his gaze. Carys and Clyde looked to be deep in conversation. 'Yes, I'll come with you. I don't think he needs me right now.'

'It's good that Clyde's making new friends.'

'Yes, it is,' Jago said, but his uncertain tone undermined his words.

Clyde came to the room shortly after I'd brushed my teeth, and all three of us had an early night.

Lachlen appeared after breakfast to escort us to the two scheduled lectures. After lunch, he took us to the Warden's office before wishing Clyde well.

I filled bowls and cups with tea before settling into my seat. Liliwen studied us each in turn. 'The incident during the football match should not have occurred. I understand that the other ordinands have sorted sanctions, and unless you wish otherwise, Clyde, I'll take no official action. But be assured, a repeat of such an action will bring harsher consequences.'

The snail wriggled his tentacles and various colours flashed through his body. Jago translated, 'It's been sorted out for now. Saint Canna's doesn't need to do anything more.'

Liliwen dipped her head in a nod. 'And I believe you've already made some friends in the course of your short visit?'

'Some,' Clyde said, his body pulsing pink and gold.

'Good.' The Warden took a sip of her drink. 'We need to discuss practicalities. I assume a ground floor room would be better for you. We'll speak to a carpenter about installing a door knob at your height. Are you planning to share your room with Jago?'

The gryphon hopped down to her desk. 'Actually, I was wondering about a room for me and Basty. He's my boyfriend.'

'This is a Christian establishment,' Liliwen said. 'Only married couples may share a room.'

'He's a flying rat,' I added quickly.

'I did not ask about his species. I'm only concerned about their marital status.'

'So, if we're married,' Jago asked slowly, 'it'd be okay for us to live together here?'

'We would make a room available, yes.'

'And I'm sure Basty would deliver messages for you,' Jago said. 'So it'll be good to have him here.'

The sound of a hoof scraping against floor screeched through the room. 'We prefer to use squirrels, but I'll keep that in mind. If we have sorted your requirements, Master Jago, I would like to now hear from Ordinand Clyde. Are there any other adjustments we need to make before his arrival?'

'I won't be able to open most of the doors in the seminary,' Jago translated for Clyde. 'Otherwise, I can't think of anything else at the moment.'

'There are a number of doors which I can't open without assistance,' Liliwen replied. 'We expect all staff and students to assist one another in this regard.'

'It must be a challenge,' I said. 'Your staff and students come with such a wide range of shapes and sizes.'

'And all have their place in the body of Christ.' The Warden fixed her gaze on me. 'When you next visit, a dragon-sized room will be ready for you and your husband.'

'Thank you,' I said politely, wondering whether Raven would want to trade a warm beach for a room in a seminary.

We exchanged a few more polite comments, and then I opened the door to let us out. After a quick trip to collect my backpack, the three of us headed outside to the quadrangle.

Raven was already waiting for us, his head lowered to talk to an elf. She made a comment to which the dragon responded with a chuckle. As I walked over, zipping up my coat against the evening chill, Raven looked over the elf's head to address me. 'Fraunchoun knows a good source of high-quality obsidian. She's agreed to take me there in the spring.'

I grinned. It was good to see Raven so excited. 'That's fantastic. I'll enjoy seeing your new carvings. Fraunchoun, could you lift Clyde up to me once I'm on Raven's neck?'

The elf obliged. I settled snail and gryphon inside my jacket, made sure my backpack was secure, and gave Raven a nod. We took off into the darkening sky.

Night had fallen by the time we landed at Saint Raphael's. A passing were-horse took Clyde from me and opened the door of the main building so the snail could go inside. Jago followed a moment later. I slid to the ground, and rested a moment against Raven's warm side. 'I think Clyde will be all right at Saint Canna's.'

'The other students accepted him?'

'There was a bit of trouble,' I admitted. 'I nearly called for you. But the students managed to sort it out themselves.'

Raven snorted. 'Good. As I've said, I can't be his protector. I have no desire to spend three years living in a seminary.'

'Nor do I.' I sighed. 'The Warden said that she'll take action if something like that happens again. But I'm hoping that Clyde will find his own way to deal with any prejudice.'

'By biting off the nearest appendage of the offender?'

I gave his shoulder a push. 'You know that's not how he handles things. Anyway, the Warden says that when we next visit, she'll arrange a room for us to share together.'

Raven brought his head closer to mine. Warm breath stirred the hair from my face as he asked, 'Is that why you're unsettled here? Because we can't share a room?'

'What makes you think I'm unsettled?'

'Benighted Penny, you may hide it from yourself, but you cannot hide it from me.'

I lowered my voice. 'It's not the same, not since we got back. Not with all the changes Llewelyn's brought in. And, I think, I actually miss being a parish priest. In England. I never thought I'd say this, but I miss my vicarage, and my church, and those people.'

'You long to return to your own country.'

My eyes were moist. I pulled out a handkerchief and blew my nose. 'But I can't. For all the reasons why I decided to stay on this side when you closed up the last air crossing.'

'Part of that longing,' Raven mused, 'might come from missing those you love. Didn't you say that the rats have been able to take messages through small thin places? Perhaps Bastien can help you contact your brother.'

'I've been thinking about using a rat. You're right, I'll ask him.' I shivered and moved away. 'I need to go inside and warm up.'

'Do so.' Raven stepped back and unfurled his wings. 'Penny, if you want to return to England, I will take you there.'

'No.' Of this I was certain. 'I'm not letting Sue Harkness get her hands on a search dragon.'

'She would have to catch me first.'

'She doesn't have to catch you,' I said bleakly. 'She only has to catch me.'

Light from the building's windows glittered across Raven's eyes as he turned his head. 'Yes. You are right. Until tomorrow, my beloved Penny.'

His words warmed me, and I bitterly regretted that we were separating once again. I waited until his wings had carried him out of my sight. Then I went in search of a late dinner.

Chapter Twelve

Friday, also known as my day off. But there was no chance of a lie in. Raven had agreed that we'd sneak down to Ennor and visit the Fair Folk. No one would ask any questions about me heading off with my husband on my rest day.

I joined the others for breakfast, but made my apologies and skipped Morning Prayer. A quick visit to the kitchen provided me with a packed lunch. I grabbed my jacket from the hooks near the door and headed outside into a sunny morning.

Raven stood on the gravel path, Bastien perched on his neck. I strode over. 'Hello, both of you. Lovely day.'

'I know what you want,' Bastien said. 'Raven told me. The Consortium controls a small thin place which leads through to Northampton. What message do you want me to deliver to your brother?'

I reached into a pocket and pulled out a folded piece of paper. 'I've written it down for you to carry through.'

'"Written it down"?' The rat's whiskers twitched with indignation. 'We deliver verbal messages.'

'Not to humans without the Sight,' I pointed out. 'And if James can see you, then feel free to add a poem. But please do give him the note.'

Before I could hand over the paper, Jago landed on my outstretched arm. 'Great news, Basty! I talked to the Warden at Saint Canna's, and she says we can live there together, once you've married me. I was thinking of maybe a wedding in June? It's a lot warmer then and so we can have it here, outside, just like Halwyn and Aldona. I was thinking of Clyde and James as my best men, if it's okay for me to have two, and you should think who you want for yours. You don't have to do something like ask your rat king first, do you?'

'No,' Bastien said slowly. 'I don't have to ask the Consortium. The rat king doesn't care what a rat does in his private life. Not so long as I obey him in everything else.'

My arm bounced with Jago's excitement. 'So, June, right? What do you think?'

'You pick the date.' As Bastien stretched out to take the note from my fingers, I noticed that some fur was missing around his neck. I opened my mouth, and he gave me a glare. A priest was required to keep confidences. I swallowed my words.

'Well,' Jago huffed after the rat had flown away, 'I thought he'd be a bit more excited about marrying me.'

'Maybe it took him by surprise,' I said. 'I mean, you turned him down when he'd asked you. Maybe he wasn't expecting you to bring it up again so soon.'

'I guess so.' Jago made his way up to my shoulder as I lowered my arm. 'You could be right, maybe it was a surprise to him. I'll do something more romantic when he gets back. I know I want us to spend the rest of our lives together, and that's years and years, so I'll make sure I get this right.'

I turned my head, worried about controlling the expression on my face. 'Don't worry about that. Bastien loves you. You don't need to prove anything to him.'

'We should start our journey,' Raven said. 'You'll want to make the most of your day off.'

Jago hopped over to the dragon. 'Where are you going? Can I come too?'

'Of course not,' Morey said firmly as he emerged from the house and landed on my shoulder. 'Married couples need time alone together. You can help me with the were-horses. I know the foals like to see you.'

'And I have something to tell you, Tad.' Jago's crest rose high above his head. 'Basty and I are going to get married.'

'Congratulations.' Morey's voice was steady, but his fur and feathers slicked at the news. 'We'll talk about this further tonight when your mother is home.'

'There's so much to plan,' Jago agreed happily. 'I've told Basty that June might be a good time.'

'As good a time as any other,' Morey muttered. 'Come along, son, time to do some work.' The gryphons flew off.

I clambered up to Raven's neck. 'How long will it take us to reach Ennor?'

'That depends,' Raven said. 'Do you want a quick trip, or a comfortable one?'

'Quick,' I replied pulling gloves from my coat pockets.

We ducked through a number of thin places in quick succession. I shivered over an ice field, roasted for ten minutes as we flew along a hot beach, and crouched down inside my jacket as rain poured down from a dark sky. When we finally emerged over cool but sunny coastline, all I wanted was a hot shower and a large mug of coffee.

Although I had been on holiday to Cornwall, the landscape below me was unfamiliar. Instead of fields and crumbling tin mines, I saw forests interspersed with moorland. The cliffs and the sea, however, were the same. I smiled at a happy memory of a young James building a sandcastle on a golden beach, and hoped that I would hear from him soon.

Raven stretched out his wings to catch at the wind. We wheeled away from the mainland and headed out to sea. My wet gloves chilled in the breeze, and I pulled them from my hands.

At first the island was nothing but a gleaming speck in the dark ocean, the yellow cliffs shining in the winter sun. As we drew nearer, a green and brown landscape was revealed, bushes alternating with fields. A dozen large stone houses, each surrounded by an elaborate garden, rested in the centre of the island.

'How do we ask permission to land?' I called out to Raven as he lowered us towards the settlement.

'Like this.' He pulled up into a hover, and bellowed, *'Gawn ni ganiatâd i lanio?'*

For a long moment, the only sound was the crashing of waves against the cliffs and Raven's wings beating in the air. Then the ground suddenly moved. Green detached from green, and figures emerged from the fields and bushes. Blue-green faces framed by long blonde hair looked up at us. The points of long ears twisted in our direction. Their eyes were silver-white, with small grey pupils. Robes of blue and green flowed around their thin bodies.

One separated from the others. I recalled what Taryn had said about the *Tylwyth Teg* being without gender as I gazed down at a broad face which struck me as neither male nor female. *'Pwy sy'n galw arnom?'* shouted up a deep voice. The Welsh was heavily accented, and it took me a moment to translate it. 'Who calls upon us?'

'Hrafn Eydisson, a elwir yn Raven. A Penny White.'

The gleaming eyes narrowed. *'Mae croeso i ddreigiau yma. Beth ydych chi'n ei gario?'*

'I'm pleased that dragons are welcome,' I replied in Welsh. 'I am human. May we both land?'

'I sniff something on the human,' was the response. 'Land and bring yourself closer.'

Hoping I'd interpreted correctly, I slid to the ground as soon as Raven's feet touched the soil. I forced myself to hold still as the *Tylwyth Teg* approached. Nostrils flared in the large nose as the green face was brought close to mine. 'Christos,' the *Tylwyth Teg* declared, and spat at my feet.

'I am a Christian priest,' I affirmed, doing my best to smile as I wrapped my tongue around the Welsh words. 'But I come from England, the sister country to Lloegyr on the world of Earth. My kind had nothing to do with your exile.'

'And she is my wife,' Raven added. 'I ask that you welcome both of us.'

'For the sake of the dragon, you may speak,' the *Tylwyth Teg* growled. 'Why have you come here?'

This was obviously going to be a meeting without coffee. Just as well, since Taryn had warned me against eating or drinking anything. 'I represent a Guild which is dedicated to the treatment of not-weres. You've been very kindly supplying us with letherum. Our supplies have run low. I've come to ask if we can arrange to buy some more.'

The thin mouth pulled down into a frown. 'We have nothing to offer you.'

I worked through the Welsh in my head. 'You have no more in stock, or you are unwilling to let us have any that you have?'

Another *Tylwyth Teg* spoke. 'We are unwilling to offer anything to a Christos.'

'I understand that the Church treated you badly in the past,' I said calmly. Another twenty *Tylwyth Teg* had come close, and I forced myself to stand still while several of them touched my arms and back with elongated fingers. 'But I'm asking you to help people who had nothing to do with that persecution.'

'The not-weres are suffering,' Raven added. 'The work Penny and the other Christos carry out is worth your support.'

'We are offering to pay for the letherum.' I pulled out my coin bag and opened it to show the gold glittering inside. Despite the payment I'd made to the search dragons, I still possessed half of what Abella had given me.

The first *Tylwyth Teg* let out a haughty sniff. 'We won't accept gold from your hands.'

If pleading didn't work, nor the offer of payment, what could I say which might change their minds? I tried to remember what else Taryn had told me. *Take iron. Don't eat or drink. Don't ride with them.* I raised my head. The island was small, and I'd seen all of it from Raven's back. 'I've heard your horses are beautiful. May I please see them before we leave?'

Eyes and hands dropped away. One *Tylwyth Teg*, half the size of the others, started to sob. 'Our last horse died years ago.'

'And you haven't bought any new ones?'

'It's a long way from the mainland from here,' Raven pointed out. 'And the settlement is high up from shore. I don't know how they brought the original herd, but I should think dragons would be needed if they wanted any more.'

The sudden silence was intense. More *Tylwyth Teg* emerged from the buildings, pale eyes wide, mouths half-open. 'We could bring you horses,' I said. 'If that's what you want instead of gold.'

An ancient looking *Tylwyth Teg* moved through the group. The one in front of me bowed aside, allowing the elder to come close. 'Walk with me,' the *Tylwyth Teg* commanded, and set off towards the nearest field.

I hurried to obey, happy to leave the crowd behind me. Raven matched my pace, his feet squelching as his weight drove each step deep into the soft soil. An earthy note rose to join the clean scents of salt and grass.

We halted at a row of bushes. The *Tylwyth Teg* ran a hand over the spiked leaves and pulled off several red berries. I was offered one, and I shook my head.

'Very wise.' The *Tylwyth Teg* ate them instead.

'We have given you our names,' I said politely. 'May I have the holding of yours?'

'They call me Unhynaf.'

Raven grunted. '"Oldest One."'

'That is what I am.' The Welsh was easy to follow, spoken with a soft sing-song lilt. 'I remember the driving out from our own lands. The Christos showed us no mercy.'

'I'm very sorry to hear that,' I said. 'There is still prejudice in Lloegyr, and in the Church, I'm sad to say. My own adopted son is a snail shark, and he's had to face hostility from the Church. But there's hope. He's been accepted for training to become a Christos.'

A smile eased the deep lines in the broad face. 'Our small ones would ride snail sharks in our processions. Should you ever return, bring your son with you.'

'If I can, I will.' I nodded at the bushes. 'These are part of the ingredients for letherum?'

'All that we grow here is.' Unhynaf pointed back at the gardens. 'Only there do we grow our own food. All else is for the healing herbs.'

I glanced around the flat landscape, noting how the small settlement was surrounded by fields and bushes. 'Letherum is worth the effort?'

'Yes. We are building up our stores of gold.' White teeth flashed in a grin. 'When we return to Lloegyr, we will be able to afford protection.'

'I don't know what Lloegyr was like, hundreds of years ago,' I said carefully. 'But I don't think you would need to worry about protecting yourselves. Many species now mix together, and it's mostly peaceful.'

'There are those who are working against that peace.'

'There's organisations such as *Cadw ar Wahân,'* I agreed. 'But, on the whole, like I said, it's peaceful.'

'There are those who are working against that peace,' Unhynaf insisted. 'We see them clearly. Letherum was meant for healing, but it has been used for destruction.'

'It was used to kill vampire children,' Raven agreed, his voice tight. 'I saw that for myself.'

'And against the resident akhluts when we were on Tarkik's ship,' I added. 'Letherum has been used against weres and vampires.'

'We sent sufficient letherum to the Guild of Saint Raphael for your needs.' Unhynaf removed a few more berries, bruising leaves along the way. A garlic scent filled the air, reminding me of the distinctive smell of gaseous letherum. 'You should be asking where that has gone.'

'We've wondered about that.' I gave Unhynaf my widest smile. 'I've been told that the *Tylwyth Teg* are very far-sighted. What have you seen?'

Unhynaf stilled. The bright eyes shut for a moment. When they opened again, the pupil had all but disappeared, leaving shiny silver orbs to stare into the distance. 'I have seen letherum resting in places full of soft voices planning violence. Wings rustle past, boxes are taken into teeth, and are gone. I know not where, only that it's a place beyond my sight. And my sight stretches across all of Lloegyr.'

'To another country?' Raven asked.

I took a deep breath against a sharp stab of fear. 'Or to another world?' Unhynaf looked at us again. 'Bring us horses. A fine breeding stallion and four young mares, from the Seraphixon bloodline. For now, I will send you back with two sacks of prepared letherum. Keep the herb under your personal protection.'

I nodded. 'Saint Raphael's has a locked cabinet.'

'That cabinet is no protection.' Unhynaf placed a hand on my chest. Although there were several layers of clothing between our skins, a chill still spread through my body. 'I am trusting you, Christos. This supply must not be used for harm.'

'I'll look after it personally,' I promised, although I wondered how I was going to explain that to Llewelyn. 'Thank you for trusting me.'

The hand fell away. 'You have a snail shark for a son and a dragon as a husband. For those reasons, you will be given the letherum.' Unhynaf's voice hardened. 'But when we return to the mainland, be warned, we will not allow the Church to exile us a second time.'

'Why were you exiled the first time?' Raven asked, voicing the question I had not dared to raise.

'For keeping to our own beliefs,' Unhynaf growled. 'The Church wanted us to bow the knee to their God. A much older spirit inhabits Lloegyr, and we would not break faith with her.'

'There were times, and there still are places on my own world, in which different faiths fight one another.' I placed my hand on Unhynaf's chest. The blue and green robe was smooth, like silk, and to my surprise was warm to the touch. 'I have always argued for tolerance, and I'd do so for the *Tylwyth Teg.*'

Unhynaf studied me for a long moment before moving away. 'The letherum is kept near my home. Follow me.'

We squelched back to the settlement and Unhynaf led us into a large narrow building. The smell of pressed garlic and vinegar told me, even before my eyes adjusted to the light, that I was in the presence of letherum. The dim light revealed what looked to be a processing line. Bundles of various dried herbs hung at one end of a long table. Pestles and mortars spread across the scarred wooden surface. A press at the far end was open, revealing small hollowed out sections used to create pills.

A breeze slid through the open door, lifting dust into the air. I sneezed. A few seconds later, the usual effects of letherum took over. I stood still as the sound of Raven's breaths became purple swirls, and the acrid scent of letherum filled my mouth with the taste of chocolate.

Unhynaf walked to a wooden trunk. The creak of the hinges sparkled orange and red in the air. Unhynaf lifted out two large leather sacks before closing the heavy lid. I could hear the pills rattling inside their containers.

'I'll need a rope or a harness to carry those,' Raven commented. 'We won't want to get the letherum wet, so I'll have to do more direct flying on the way back. Penny can't hold on to them for the time that'll take.'

'We have rope.' Unhynaf reached up to a shelf and pulled down a long coil of twisted leather.

My senses settled once we were back outside. Several other *Tylwyth Teg* helped to wrap the rope around Raven's neck and attach the sacks. I climbed up to my usual seat, and leaned down to double-check the knots. 'Thank you,' I said from my perch. 'Please give me a few weeks to sort out the horses, but they will come, I promise you.'

Raven kicked us away from the island. I waited until we were out of earshot to ask, 'Do you have any idea where we're supposed to find this Seraphixon bloodline? And how much five horses will cost in gold?'

'We'll find them,' the dragon reassured me. 'And how much can a horse cost?'

'Quite a bit,' I fretted. 'And I expect I'll have to pay for transport. You'll need help to carry them.'

'*We* will have to pay for transport,' Raven corrected me. 'And if your gold isn't sufficient, then I'll have to sell a few more carvings to make up the difference.'

I patted his warm hide. 'This is my problem.'

'I am your husband,' Raven replied. 'Your problems are my problems, and we solve them together.'

I blinked back tears. 'You're right. Together.'

The return flight took several hours. Raven landed a couple of times to give both of us a break. The few crossing places he used led to deserts, keeping our precious cargo safe and dry. The weather in Lloegyr also behaved, although it was always a shock returning to the cooler temperatures after a session above hot sands.

'What do you plan to tell Llewelyn?' Raven asked as we rested one last time. We were on the outskirts of a small town, and the thick scent of coal fires thickened the air.

'I'm going to say that I managed to find some supplies the police weren't using.' I stomped around the dragon, trying to bring some feeling back into my numb legs. 'I'll say that part of the agreement was that I monitor its use. So I'll keep the sacks in my room.'

'Do you have a lock on your door?'

I halted and stared up at him. 'Do you really think Llewelyn would break into my room to steal letherum?'

'I don't know. But I think you should take precautions.'

'Okay.' I rubbed my forehead. 'There isn't a lock at the moment. I guess I could ask for one because I'm storing letherum. The cabinet in the not-weres' barn has a lock, after all, so it's not like I'm implying anything.'

'One day,' Raven said, 'you might have to do more than imply. If Llewelyn is selling letherum...'

'I know.' I leaned against his side. 'But if that's how he's been funding the expansion of Saint Raphael's, it's only to help others. It's not like he's been using the money to pay for private jets or expensive holidays. Or whatever is the Lloegyr equivalent.'

'It's still wrong.'

'I know,' I said miserably. 'Especially if that's how letherum is getting into the hands of people who use it against vampire children and resident akhlut.'

'If I find out that the chaplain was responsible for the letherum which killed those children,' Raven growled, 'I will lift him to a great height and drop him.'

'No, you mustn't do that.' I reached up and laid my hands on either side of his head. 'Please. Llewelyn has done a lot of good.'

'I still see them.' His ears and horns sagged. 'When I sleep, I sometimes dream of children dropping past me. As hard as I try, I can't save them. I hear them screaming as they fall, and the crunch of their bones as they hit the ground. Then there's nothing but terrible silence.'

'You've said that knowing me has been bad for your skin,' I said sadly. 'I think it's also been bad for you in other ways.'

'I'm not the dragon I was from before I met you.' Raven chuckled, and my mood lifted. 'But I am happy with what I have become.'

I slid my arms along his neck to draw close to him in a hug. 'I liked the dragon you were before, and I love the dragon you are now.'

After a long moment, I released him and climbed back to my usual seat. Raven took us back into the air and aimed his head towards Saint Raphael's.

The sun was still bright and the air held a hint of warmth as we approached the main building of the Guild. Many of the not-weres were outside, making the most of this break in winter. As Raven took us down, I looked around for my companions. Clyde was seated on a fence post by the were-horses, Jago at his side. Morey emerged from the rats' barn, followed by Bastien. One of the new priests was inside the corral, but I could see no sign of Llewelyn.

Raven's claws crunched down into gravel. I dismounted, and pulled out my knife to cut through the leather straps holding the sacks in place. The contents were heavier than I'd expected, and I grunted as I lowered each one to my feet.

Morey landed on my shoulder. 'I take it your visit was successful?'

'It was,' I agreed. 'But now we need to find a stallion and four mares from the Seraphixon bloodline. Any idea how we go about that?'

'I know a horse breeder near Llanbedr,' Morey said. 'We could send her a rat and ask if she knows who breeds from that bloodline.'

Bastien swooped over my head to take up a perch on Raven. 'Welcome back from your day off, Penny. I delivered your message to James, and he gave me a note to bring to you in return.' The rat reached around to a piece of string wrapped around his body, and pulled out a folded piece of paper.

'What, no poetry?' I asked as Raven lowered his head to bring Bastien in reach.

'What's the point?' the rat asked grumpily. 'I don't know what you wrote to him, or what he's sent in response.'

'Really?' I held up the note. 'It's not sealed.'

Bastien's dark eyes glittered. 'Perhaps you'll read it out to us.'

I tucked the note into a trouser pocket. 'I haven't had any contact with my brother for six months. I'm reading this in private.'

'Fair enough,' Raven said. He touched my shoulder briefly with his nose. 'I'm off to warmer climes, Bastien.'

The rat shook out his wings and flew over to join Jago and Clyde. Raven took off a moment later, scattering gravel as he left the ground. I watched as he climbed into the sky and disappeared through a thin space.

'Why don't you go with him?' Morey asked. 'It's your day off. You wouldn't be expected to be on call tonight. You could stay overnight.'

'I tried that a couple of times. Once at the search dragon settlement, where they expected me to use the dragon midden when I needed the loo. The other time was on a beach, and the sand flies ate me alive.' I hoisted the sacks and headed to the building's entrance. 'Come on. It's time to find out what James has said.'

'I thought you said you wanted to read his note in private?'

'I didn't want Bastien to see me read it. I'm hoping James will tell us something important.'

'In a note which anyone could read?'

I stepped inside the house and Morey hovered while I removed my coat. 'I'm hoping James followed my lead. I don't think anyone will have worked out the real message.'

The gryphon returned to my shoulder as I climbed the stairs to my room. My arms were aching by the time I lowered the sacks onto my bed. I headed over to my desk, took a seat, and brought out James' note. A grin spread across my face as I read his response. 'He got it! Well done, James.'

'Got what?' Morey demanded, taking a seat at my right hand.

'Here's what I sent him.' I pulled out a copy of my message and read it out loud.

> '*Dear James,*
>
> '*I hope you're well. I miss you very much. It's like you were eight again and at camp, or when you were ten and visited our Uncle. You skipped out the door each time, without a single look back at me. Never mind Doctor Who, is there any new Sherlock to bump "The Empty Hearse" off your list of favourite TV episodes? Do you still fancy Amanda Abbington?*
>
> '*Sorry, now I've embarrassed you. Just pretend that this letter begins with the next paragraph.*
>
> '*Anyway, you're old enough not to be worried about me. After all these years I should be over worrying about you. Can't help you from Lloegyr, can I? I'm also rather busy with the human exiles. Although they have found homes and jobs, are humans going to be stuck in Lloegyr forever? It's safe in England, compared to here.*
>
> '*Sorry, I'll stop now. How are you? Please write back.*
>
> '*Penny.*'

Morey cocked his head. 'You haven't told him you're married to Raven.'

'That's something I'll only tell him face to face.' I studied the gryphon for a moment. 'You didn't get it?'

'Get what, other than the fact that you just can't resist mentioning TV programmes whenever possible?'

'Did you ever watch *Sherlock?*'

'No. And we're too far away for me to scan your DVDs.'

'In "The Empty Hearse", Amanda Abbington's character works out that a text is in a skip code. You're meant to just read certain words to find out the real message.'

'Eight and ten,' Morey said thoughtfully. He shifted slightly to read the note. 'So, if I go down to the third paragraph, and pick out words eight, ten, eight, ten, and eight again…'

'You have what I've really said to James.'

'"Worried over Lloegyr exiles are safe."' Morey thrust out his chest and the feathers around his neck and cheeks fluffed. 'Well done, Black. I'm impressed.'

'Oh, well, it worked,' I said awkwardly, although his admiration had made me blush. 'Here's my brother's reply.' I cleared my throat and read it out.

Hello Sis

We're all okay over here, and missing you, of course. By the way, I was ten when I went to camp, but I had my first sleepover when I was six.

'So how are things over there? I know that Lloegyr wasn't always easy, but the people were mostly good. After a while, I was really taken with them. It's hard being away from all that. And I think it's harder for Skylar. A vampire, she's used to hiding what she is but sometimes she wishes she could come out with it and very soon.

'But I guess that's enough of that. I'm glad we can send messages to each other.
James.'

'Words ten and six,' Morey said. 'What's James said?'

I took out a pencil and circled the skip words. '"Lloegyr people taken away Skylar hiding come soon."'

Morey cursed in Welsh and then in English. I fought back the temptation to follow his example. Once he'd finished, I pointed out, 'We heard from EBM, I mean Colin Shoemaker, that people from Lloegyr were being rounded up. I'm not really sure what I can do about it.'

'It could be that James wants you to bring Skylar back here, where she'd be safe.'

'You're quite right. I didn't think of that.' I straightened. 'I have a full roster of duties until Sunday afternoon. I can't go until then.'

'Which gives you time to send another message to James.' Morey pointed his beak at the clean sheets of paper on my desk. 'Let's work on it together. I've never written a skip code before.'

'And after we've done that,' I said, 'you can help me on how to explain to Llewelyn that I'm locking supplies of letherum in my room.'

Morey's ears sagged. 'I hate to think that we can't trust him.'

'So do I. But we have to be careful.' I put pen to paper as we began to craft our message.

Chapter Thirteen

'And so that's what I promised,' I said, forcing myself to keep my eyes on Llewelyn's face. 'It was the only way the *Tylwyth Teg* would let me take the letherum away.'

Despite the flames crackling in the fireplace, the chaplain's office still felt cold. A sadness tugged at the were-wolf's long face. 'Did they say why you are not to store it with the rest of our supplies?'

'They're worried about what else letherum's been used for,' I said apologetically. 'I've seen it for myself, when it's been turned against vampires and were-orcas. I tried to tell them that we only use letherum to help people here, but that wasn't enough for the *Tylwyth Teg.*'

'I see.'

'Because we only use it for people who are here, don't we?' I gave him a smile. 'Organisations which have legitmate need, like police stations, source their own supplies.'

'As you know, we've struggled to match supply to demand,' Llewelyn said. 'I'll have to put in a request for more in the spring. Our expanded operations mean we need more letherum.'

I so much wanted to believe him. My head was pounding with the urge to ask him outright whether he'd been giving away or even selling letherum. But that would only put him on the alert if he were guilty, and possibly jeopardise our relationship if he were innocent. And I needed a place to live and work in Lloegyr. 'Clyde's keeping watch in my room at the moment, but I guess we'd better put a lock on my door. For the same reasons you keep a lock on the supplies cabinet.'

'Understood.' And as he turned his head away, I wondered if he did indeed understand more than I'd intended.

'And in the meantime,' I said brightly, 'I've managed to send a message to my brother, and he replied. I'm glad the rats have found a way to go through to England.'

'Family is important,' Llewelyn agreed. 'I am glad to hear that you're in contact with your brother again. Did he congratulate you on your marriage to Raven?'

I coughed. 'Actually, I haven't told him yet. He'd only worry. *Cadw ar Wahân* and all that.'

'Mixed-species couples are safe here,' Llewelyn said firmly.

'You seem very certain. Why?'

The were-wolf rose from his seat. 'Nearly time for lunch. You're visiting the were-horses this afternoon?'

I also came to my feet. 'Yes. Several want to talk about baptism. I was thinking of putting together a baptism preparation course. Other not-weres might also be interested.'

'That would be good.' Llewelyn held the door open so I could go out ahead of him. I stalked down the hallway to the dining room, taking deep breaths as I fought to bring my frustration under control.

The other ministers filtered in, and we all helped ourselves to bread, meat, and cheese. Once we were all seated, Llewelyn held up a hand to still conversation. 'Penny has managed to source more letherum, a welcome boost to our dwindling supplies.'

Nods and murmurs of approval went around the table. 'Llewelyn and I've agreed that it'll be kept in my room,' I said. 'So you'll have to ask me for tablets. I don't know who needs what, but I'd like to start offering some of it to the rats we've taken on.'

'That's a good idea,' Rhodri said. 'It's my turn to tend to the rats. Could we take some letherum over after lunch?'

'Of course,' I told the dwarf.

'May I come too?' Morey asked from his seat on my right. 'I've been too busy to visit the rats, but I have some free time this afternoon.'

So, after a fortifying cup of tea, I went upstairs to fetch a container of letherum tablets from my room. 'Llewelyn's going to arrange a lock,' I promised Clyde as I rummaged in one of the sacks. 'I think Jago's going to take on guard duties later on?'

'Yes.' Clyde's colours were calm greens and blues. 'Soon.'

I pounded back down the stairs. Once I'd pulled on boots and coat, Morey hopped over to my shoulder. We followed Rhodri from the building and into the grey day outside.

'I should warn you,' I said to Morey as we approached the barn, 'that many of the rats are in very poor health. It's not a pretty sight. Or smell.'

'I'm a hunter,' Morey replied. 'I have a pretty strong stomach.' But his feathers slicked as I pulled my handkerchief from my pocket and held it over my mouth and nose.

Rhodri unlocked the door and opened it for us. I felt my eyes water as the acrid scent of urine rushed out. Morey gurgled, and he shoved his head into my hair.

The dwarf seemed to be unaffected by the stench. After closing the door behind us, he led the way to the closest rat on the left-hand platform. Celyn lay in her blue bowl, her breathing quick and shallow. Almost all of her fur was gone, and her ribs pushed through the thin skin.

'She mostly sleeps now,' Rhodri said, holding out his hand. I opened the box of letherum, and he removed a tablet. A mortar and pestle rested nearby, and the dwarf crushed up the pill before adding water to make a thin solution. With great and gentle care, he opened the rat's mouth and spooned the liquid inside. Celyn swallowed several times. Her breathing slowed, and her body uncurled from its tight shape.

'Wonderful.' Rhodri sighed. 'So good to see her without pain.'

'What's happened to her?' Morey asked, his voice low and tense. 'What's happened to all of them?'

'Service to their rat kings,' Rhodri said. 'It wears them down, both physically and mentally. Most messengers only live seven or eight years. May I have more tablets, Father Penny? I'd like to give each rat a dose. Well, those who can still swallow, at any rate.'

I trailed behind him, occasionally helping out by moving a rat into a better position or gently forcing a mouth open. The obvious difference the letherum made reassured me that I'd made the right decision in going to the *Tylwyth Teg*. Whatever the horses cost me, in terms of gold and gratitude to dragons, was worth it to see the rats finally gain some relief from their constant pain.

Finally we had treated all the rats we could. Rhodri and I thoroughly washed our hands with a strong-smelling soap before leaving the barn. The dwarf clicked the lock back into place, thanked me for my help, and strode off towards the next barn.

'Penny.' Morey's voice was a strangled whisper. 'Bastien has been losing fur. And there's been a smell around him which, well, I thought came from a change in diet. But those rats had the same odour.'

'Oh,' I said. 'Right.'

The gryphon moved down my arm to stare into my face. 'You know something.'

'I can't tell you. It's confidential.'

'This affects Jago. My son. What will he be taking on when he marries Bastien?'

'A rat,' I said miserably, 'who loves him very much.'

'But for how long? Okay, yes, I know, you can't tell me that.' Morey pondered for a moment. 'What's the average age of the rats in that barn?'

'Seven to eight years old.'

'And how old is Bastien?'

I took a deep breath. 'Promise me you won't fly off and do something foolish, like immediately say something to Jago.'

Morey growled. 'I'll handle this with my usual tact and diplomacy.'

'And that's what I'm worried about.'

'All right, all right,' he snapped, 'I'll take time to think everything over.'

'You'll talk to Taryn first,' I said firmly.

'I'll talk to Taryn first. How old is Bastien?'

My throat closed. I had to swallow hard before I could speak. 'He's seven years old.'

Morey swore, long and low. 'How dare he plan to marry my son? Jago doesn't know about this, does he?'

I picked my words carefully. 'As far as I'm aware, no. And it was Jago who pretty much told Bastien that they're going to get married. Morey, it's really up to Bastien to sort this out, don't you think?'

Morey's wings sagged. 'I've known heartbreak. I'd rather my son did not.'

'It's not something any parent can prevent.' I reached out to scratch the feathers around his head. 'You can always encourage Bastien to come clean with Jago.'

'He's already showing signs of going the same way as that lot.' Morey sighed. 'Jago's going to notice, sooner or later, that something's not right.'

'There is that.' I lowered my hand. 'In the meantime, we both have work to do. Again, promise me that you'll not do anything hasty.'

'I've promised.' Morey opened his wings. 'But I can't be held responsible for what Taryn does when she finds out.'

And he flew off before I could say anything more.

There was no eruption from Morey and Taryn's room that evening. Jago's mother, it appeared, agreed with me that Bastien should be the one who spoke to his fiancé. As I went about my duties, it was obvious that Morey was unhappy and distracted. I had only brief glimpses of Bastien, usually in Jago's presence, and so had no opportunity to speak to him.

I took the service in chapel on Sunday morning. My sermon was on the waiting and watching of Lent, waiting for Jesus to reveal himself at Easter. I carefully did not look at Morey as I spoke, just in case he might think I'd written my words for him alone.

After lunch I went to my room. I unlocked the door and, as was my practice, checked the letherum supplies. I'd been assured that I had the only key, but I had no way to verify that. So far, the number of boxes in each sack were what I expected. I'd spent several evenings putting candle wax seals on each container, and these were also still intact.

'Guard?' Clyde offered from his position on my bed.

'That's kind of you, but I'm not going to ask you to spend the next few months staying in my room.' I slipped my iPhone into trouser pocket. 'Besides, I need you to cut a way through to England today, remember? We're going to meet up with James. He sent a note through on Friday.'

'Jago?'

'I know he would love to see James again,' I agreed. 'But not this time. It's only you, me, and Raven.'

I scooped up the snail and headed downstairs. Other members of the Saint Raphael's team were still in the dining room, talking and laughing as they drank coffee. They were obviously at ease in each other's company, in a way which I didn't yet feel. I went to the door, pulled on my coat, and headed outside.

'Penny?' Raven asked, ears and horns twisting. 'You look unsettled again.'

'I'm all right.' There was no one else in sight, so I placed Clyde on Raven's head before climbing up to my seat. The snail made his way down the neck, and I took him into my arms. 'So, Clyde, a thin place over EBM's house. Then, Raven, you can fly us to James?'

'I can find him, certainly,' Raven agreed. 'But why not simply ask Clyde to carve a crossing directly to James?'

'Connection,' Clyde agreed.

'Because I don't want a thin place near James, just in case he's been followed. I don't want Harkness stumbling across it. Who knows what she'd do to keep it open.' I rubbed my face with my free hand. 'And we must make sure we close the new one up once we're back through again.'

'I will,' Raven said. And he launched us away from Saint Raphael's.

Once I was convinced we were away from any watching eyes, I held Clyde out so he could create a dragon-sized thin place. Raven backwinged, paused a moment to allow me to tuck Clyde into my coat, and took us through.

We exchanged a cold grey day for a slightly warmer one. Earls Barton was spread out below us. All Saints' Church rose proudly from its hill, as if protecting the mixture of old and new houses nestling between fields of green. Although we were several miles away from my house, I still felt as if I were home. I could nearly forgive the town its lack of the possessive apostrophe.

Raven swung his head from side to side. 'Found him. James is about ten miles west of here.'

We flew towards Northampton, the A4500 a dark ribbon of asphalt below us. The density of housing increased as we came into the airspace above the town. I recognised Weston Favell Shopping Centre, the dark-roofed building surrounded by smaller retail outlets and car parks. We passed over more housing areas before Abington Park came into view.

Raven landed on the eastern side of the park, near the larger lake. Ducks took fright, complaining loudly as they exited the water. I'd forgotten that birds could see people from Lloegyr, and I sent apologetic thoughts their way.

I placed Clyde on Raven's neck before sliding to the ground. The snail made his own way down, leaving a long trail of slime across Raven's green-black hide. The dragon grumbled as he nosed at the glistening mucus. I hid a smile.

A man standing on the path near the lake lifted his head to look at us. There were a few touches of grey in his brown hair, and a moustache straggled along his upper lip. But it was unmistakeably James.

I hurried along the wet grass and took a set of steps down to the lakeside. Without a word James opened his arms, and we pulled each other close into a long hug. My eyes prickled as I pressed my cheeks against his coat, and I took in a deep breath of his scent.

'You've changed aftershave,' I said shakily when we finally released each other. 'It's a bit more fruity.'

'Skylar bought it for me.' James rubbed his upper lip. 'A bit of a waste, now that I have less to shave.'

'The moustache suits you,' I lied shamelessly. 'I'm glad we managed to understand each other's messages.'

James lowered his voice. 'My mobile phone is off. Is yours?'

'Yes.' I stared at him. 'You think we could be tracked through them?'

'I'd rather be paranoid than sorry.' James glanced around. 'Come on, let's get under the trees.'

The small wood was already greening with signs of spring. 'I used to bring you to this park as a boy, remember?' I asked him. 'A groundskeeper tried to tell you that the Pogles lived here.'

James smiled. 'And I didn't have a clue what he was talking about. When was that programme on TV, the late 1960s?'

'But you were very polite and even thanked him.' We halted by one tall tree. 'How's Skylar?'

'Bishop Nigel's been great. Skylar's hidden away in a retreat house, somewhere in Cornwall, I think. I've asked him not to tell me where.' James cleared his throat and held up his left hand. 'I guess I need to tell you something.'

A gold band glinted on his ring finger. 'You're married!' I nearly hugged him again, then remembered that I needed to tell him my news. 'Well, I'm married, too. Raven and I did the deed a few months ago.'

James threw back his head and laughed. 'Why am I not surprised?'

'You don't mind?' I asked carefully. 'Me and a dragon?'

He shrugged. 'Look at me. I've married a vampire.' Then his mouth pulled into a frown. 'It's not good for Lloegyr people right now, Sis.'

'I've heard that they've been rounded up.'

'The vampire colony in Saint Wulfram's is gone,' James said. 'A group of soldiers fired some horrible smelling gas inside, and all the vampires stumbled out in human shape and were stuffed into vans.'

'You were there?'

'Skylar was. She was checking the graveyard when the soldiers came. They saw her dog collar, told her to keep out of the way, and stormed the church.'

'The gas was probably letherum,' I said. 'It wouldn't have affected Skylar because her solid food diet has already fixed her in human shape. The villagers must have wondered what was going on when a bunch of naked people were removed from the church.'

'The local news said they were victims of human trafficking, and were taken away for their own safety.' James shook his head. 'Skylar tried to interfere, but they just told her that it was none of her business. At least they didn't spot she was a vampire, too. I don't know what I would've done if she'd been carted off.'

'You would've contacted me,' I said firmly. 'And I would've promised Sue Harkness anything she wanted to make sure Skylar was safe.'

'That's what worries me.' James ran a hand through his already rumpled hair. 'How much am I being kept an eye on because I'm your brother? I check my car for tracking devices every time I set out, I took all sorts of random turns to come here today, but this is still a risk.'

I glanced back to where Raven and Clyde were waiting, but couldn't see them through the trees. 'Maybe you and Skylar should come back to Lloegyr with us?'

'I suggested that to her, while we were waiting with the Bishop for her to be smuggled away. But she reminded me that people also need to stay and fight. She's doing her best on a laptop with the tightest internet security I could find.' James looked down at his feet. 'I'm doing what I can, too. Have you heard of the "Friends of Aslan"?'

'Colin Shoemaker told me about it. Now that he has the Sight, he seems keen to help out.'

James winced. 'Almost too keen. His wife took some photos of Epona when the unicorn was in their back garden. When Colin told her about the "Friends of Aslan", she decided to post them in our Facebook group. It took me hours to track down and remove the photos from all the places they'd been shared. Seems even seeing an image of Epona gives people the Sight forever.'

I sighed. 'Good thing you jumped on that so quickly. So, what's your alias in the network?'

'I'm Susan,' James said. 'Skylar is Lucy, and you're Jewel.'

I had to think for a moment. 'The unicorn? That's a bit rich, knowing how I feel about unicorns.'

'And Sue Harkness is Jadis, in case you ever wander on to our website.'

'The White Witch. Very apt.' I slipped my cold hands into my trouser pockets. 'It's so frustrating, being in Lloegyr when all sorts is happening over here. Maybe I should stay.'

'Reverend, how good to find you here.' Only as the Minister without Portfolio emerged from the trees did I realise the mistake we'd made taking refuge in the woods. 'There's so much we need to talk about.'

Chapter Fourteen

'How did you find us?' James asked. 'Was it through my iPhone?'

'A dragon appeared in the sky over Earls Barton,' Sue said smugly, patting down her long black coat. 'I keep someone on watch in areas Penny is known to frequent.'

My stomach, which had already soured, did a flip-flop. I thought it highly unlikely that the Minister would have revealed such information unless she were planning to take me into custody. My fingers dug deeper into my trouser pocket to locate my penknife. Four casually dressed men had taken up places alongside Sue, and I didn't want to pull out a knife and alarm them into taking action. Could I open the blade inside the pocket without stabbing myself?

'Riley, please keep an eye on Penny,' Sue said in a pleasant tone. 'You never know what sort of creatures might come to her aid. That's why I arranged for your guns to be loaded with silver bullets.'

'Normal bullets work just as well.' And Peter stepped into the small clearing. 'Hello, Penny.'

For a moment I feared I might throw up. A few quick breaths helped the feeling to pass. 'Hello, Peter. Working with the Minister now, are you?'

'I'm a police officer,' he reminded me. 'I did my duty for Queen and country.'

I gazed sadly at the man I had almost married. He was as handsome as ever, a bit more grey around the temples and a bit more weight bulging against his belt, and I felt a tug at my heart. Seeing him standing beside Sue felt like a betrayal. 'Doesn't your duty include protecting the weak and helpless?'

'Weak and helpless *people*,' Sue snapped. 'Not creatures which prey on humans, like vampires and snail sharks. You can't trust anything that comes out of Llocgyr.'

'If you're here with anyone else,' Peter said, 'tell them to lay down their weapons and come in peacefully, like the wolves of winter.'

Somehow I managed to keep my face still, despite the warm hope which suddenly surged through my chest. Of course I recognised the *Doctor Who* quote, since it came from my favourite episode of all time, 'The Curse of Fenric.' Was Peter signalling to me that he was still on my side? 'Always winter,' I said, 'and never Christmas. This is some present you're giving me, Peter. I thought better of you than this.'

'I know who my friends are,' he replied with a shrug. 'I'd be lying if I didn't. But we need to return to the main event.'

Was he trying to make me think of 'lion' and 'mane'? Was he too a 'Friend of Aslan'? 'Yes, indeed,' I said, deciding to trust him. 'What do you want from me, Minister?'

'I have a lot of questions I'd like to have answered.' Sue looked around the grey woods. 'Why don't you come with us and we can talk somewhere a bit warmer and more private?'

Not for the first time, Sue reminded me of an old poem. *'Will you walk into my parlour?' said a spider to a fly.* I finally managed to open my penknife, the blade scratching against the thin lining of my trouser pocket. 'I'm quite happy out here, thank you. But if you want to send your soldiers off to fetch us some coffee, that would be great.'

Her fixed smile began to slip. 'I'd rather keep them here with me. Wherever you are, Penny, creatures from Lloegyr are rarely far behind.'

'Very true,' I said as tree branches began to shake on my right and Raven came into view. 'But the people of Lloegyr rarely attack unless they're provoked.'

'So it's best not to provoke me,' the dragon told her, stopping beside me. Clyde still clung to his neck. 'James I know, and Peter. Who are the others?'

'The woman in black is Sue Harkness,' I said, 'Minister without Portfolio in Her Majesty's government and in charge of matters relating to Lloegyr. The men are from the military. And, it seems, all of them can see you.'

From the startled looks on at least three of the soldiers' faces, they had not been expecting to encounter a dragon and a snail shark. The fourth was doing his best to hide a wide grin. I immediately warmed to him and, catching Peter's eye, jerked my chin in the man's direction. The soldier could be a potential ally. Peter gave me the briefest of nods.

'Of course they can,' Sue said. 'I make sure all of my people retain the Sight.'

'But not always yourself,' I noted. 'You can see Raven?'

'I can always see dragons,' she retorted bitterly. 'And what is this one doing?'

Raven had extended his neck, bringing his head within ten feet of Sue's. The soldiers straightened, hands hovering near their holstered pistols, as the dragon opened his nostrils and drew in a long breath. 'You seem familiar, somehow, although we've never met. The way you stand, your voice, your

THE HUMILITY OF HUMANS

smell... Who are you?'

I suddenly realised that I'd never thought to tell Raven that Audrey had produced a daughter. *Dear Lord,* I prayed, *help us to get out of this in one piece and I promise to tell Raven as soon as we're safely back in Lloegyr.* 'As I told you, Sue Harkness, Minister without Portfolio. She thinks I should go with her. I have other ideas.'

But Raven didn't appear to have heard a word I'd said. 'Do I know you?'

'I shouldn't think so,' Sue replied, her voice tight. 'I can't stand dragons.'

'Intriguing. There are many dragons I'd rather eat than meet again, but I don't hate my entire race. Why do you?'

'One of you dragons ruined my mother's life,' Sue said bitterly. 'That's all I heard about, for years and years. The dragon she rescued from a lake, how she raised him, how he brought her back to London, how she was sorry she'd let him go. My father and I, how could we compete with such memories?'

Raven pulled back his head and stared down at her. 'This dragon, did he have a name?'

'She said it was "Raven".'

Peter stiffened. James whistled, low and long. Clyde's body swirled orange and green. I placed a hand on Raven's leg. The dragon was the one to break the silence. 'You are Audrey's daughter.'

'Yes. How do you know my mother's name?' Sue glowered. 'Do you dragons tell stories and laugh about her?'

'Your dam was a courageous and resilient woman, who managed to survive on her own in a remote valley in Alba,' Raven said. 'But she could also be cruel and selfish. It seems we have both suffered at her hands. I have not given you the holding of my name. By birth I am Hrafn Eydisson. However, within hours of my birth, Audrey renamed me. I am Raven.'

'But that can't be,' Sue said unsteadily. 'That was over seventy years ago.'

'Dragons live far longer than humans, which will one day cause me great sorrow.'

Sue took a step back, leaving Peter and the soldiers closer to Raven. 'Men, I want that dragon incapacitated. Go for the legs or the wings, your choice.'

I immediately moved to place myself in front of Raven. James did the same, and my right arm brushed up against his left. His hand found mine, and gave it a comforting squeeze.

Three of the soldiers glanced at the fourth. Although their clothing carried no insignia, he was obviously their commanding officer. I was relieved to note that he'd been the one to grin when Raven had appeared. 'With all due respect, ma'am, the dragon hasn't shown any signs that he plans to attack us. On what grounds do you want him shot?'

'Revenge,' I told the officer. 'As you've already heard, she blames Raven for her mother's neglect.'

'We were both poorly treated by Audrey,' Raven said softly. 'Once I brought her to London, she discarded me like a beast who had done his duty. She broke my heart.'

'You deserved it.'

'No, I did not. And neither did you.'

'Ma'am,' the officer said to Sue, 'if you want me and my men to assist the Reverend to your car, we'll do so. But whatever your private feud is with this dragon, he's given us no reason to go on the offensive.'

I ducked back and quickly mounted Raven. James followed, climbing up with an ease which reminded me that he'd done a lot of horse-riding in New Zealand. As my brother settled into place behind me, I said, 'If Raven had decided to "go on the offensive", he could have flamed all of you before you could draw your guns. Just be grateful that he thinks before he attacks. Minister, I might have been happy to answer your questions if you hadn't sprung my former fiancé and the military on me. Send me a rat, and I might reply.'

The trees were too close together for Raven to take flight. My back crawled as he turned and went back the way he came. But no one made any threats as we retreated. I heard Peter say, 'I tried to tell you that this wasn't the way to deal with Penny. Why not send a rat with your questions, like she suggested? Add a bottle of single malt and I'm sure she'll respond.'

I grimaced at the last sentence. Then Raven kicked us away from the ground, his wings pounding as he took us up in a rapid ascent. Clyde slid down the dragon's neck, and I reached out to grab him. It was only James' firm grasp on my belt which stopped me from falling off myself.

Once we were several hundred feet above the park, Raven levelled off and I was able to catch my breath. 'I don't think you can go home now,' I said to James. 'Do you want to come to Lloegyr? Or should Raven find out where Skylar is hiding, and take you there?'

'I can find Skylar,' Raven confirmed. 'Our connection is strong enough.'

'I'd like to be with her, if we can make sure we're not followed,' James said. 'I'd like to see our daughter.'

'I know I've been away for a while,' I commented, 'but that seems rather quick.'

James laughed. 'I can't get Skylar pregnant. I mean, the plumbing is compatible, but the DNA isn't. We've adopted a four-year-old vampire, a Grey, whose parents died fighting capture. Not everyone from Lloegyr allowed themselves to be rounded up without a fight.'

'A daughter.' I smiled to myself, marvelling how much my brother had changed in the last couple of years. 'What's her name?'

'Dwysil.'

'Well, congratulations.'

'It's about a three-hour flight to Skylar if I fly straight,' Raven said. 'Unless Clyde can shorten the journey for us?'

'Connection,' the snail confirmed from his place in my lap.

'Let's go back through to Lloegyr,' I told Raven. 'We can sort out a crossing from there. Is that all right, James?'

'Whatever takes me to my wife and child is fine by me.'

Northampton was soon behind us. Raven alternated between gliding and flying as we followed the A4500 back towards Earls Barton. We wouldn't need the dragon for the next crossing, I reflected. No doubt Clyde would simply create a thin place leading directly to wherever Skylar lived, and James could step through. Did we have the time to let him have a short meeting with Jago? I knew how much the small gryphon missed his namesake.

A distant thrumming sound brought me out of my thoughts. 'What's that?' Raven asked, his horns and ears pointing at a long black object hovering in the sky.

'It's a helicopter,' I reassured him. 'I'm a bit surprised you've never seen one before. We use them for transporting people quickly. It's probably taking some rich person to an important meeting.'

'Actually, Sis,' James said, 'I think it's coming our way.'

'Then we'll just keep out of its flight path,' I replied. 'There's plenty of air space between us.'

'Really?' James pointed at the helicopter. 'I think it's coming for us.'

'We're not far from the crossing,' Raven said, abandoning his glide to pound his wings. 'We'll be there in a few minutes.'

The helicopter was still heading in our direction. The smooth black sides, bare of any markings, made me shift uneasily in my seat. I lowered Clyde into my coat.

Raven changed direction, taking us towards the town. The helicopter followed suit, tracking us from around a hundred feet away. Wind from the whirling rotor blades blew my hair around my face. I flinched as a voice blared through loudspeakers. 'Enemy combatant, land now!'

The dragon reared into a hover. 'I'm not your enemy! And I recommend you don't make me into one!'

'Land now!' the voice ordered. 'Or we will bring you down!'

'I can outfly your mechanical thing!' Raven scoffed. 'You leave, before I flame you out of the sky!'

A side door slid open, revealing several people crouching inside. A strap was stretched across the open space, and the nearest woman pulled out a large rifle to rest on the green material. She crouched and lowered her head to look through the mounted scope.

'Raven, dive!' I shouted.

The loud crack of gun fire ached across my ears. Raven bellowed. Red blood blossomed from the top joint of his left wing. His chest expanded under my legs. A moment later, he opened his jaws and spewed bright fire at his attacker.

The helicopter peeled away as the woman hurriedly shut the door. But Raven too was falling away, unable to maintain his hover with only one good wing. 'The thin place, the thin place!' I urged him, terrified at the prospect of the dragon being trapped in England. 'Take us through to Lloegyr!'

Raven's groan of pain made my heart skip several beats. I tightened my legs against his neck, willing strength into my husband. The dragon spread out his wings and aimed us towards Earls Barton. We rocked wildly from side to side as he fought to compensate for his injury. Blood was flowing freely from the large hole, and the top fifth of the wing was unusable.

'I'll have to dive sideways,' Raven warned us as we neared the house of Colin Shoemaker.

'Why?' James asked me.

'Because he's bleeding,' I said, too worried to do anything other than tell the truth. 'The blood of search dragons seals up thin places.'

Surely we were nearly at the crossing? I wiped tears from my eyes and looked for a shimmer in the air. Just as I spotted it, Raven turned and dropped towards the thin space. His right wing was first to go through, followed by his head and those of us riding on his neck.

The cleaner smells of Lloegyr wrapped around me. I glanced to my left, breath catching in my throat as I watched Raven pull his wing through. The tear in the sky was closing, reacting to the dragon's blood. The shimmer wrapped around the last bit of wing, and Raven bellowed as the clawed tip was left behind in England.

The ground rushed up towards us. Raven's body shuddered as he wrenched himself into a horizontal position. He extended both wings, and once again the uneven thrust made me cling to the spine in front of me as we jolted from side to side. But he had halted his fall, and Saint Raphael's was visible in the distance.

'Bring us down,' I urged Raven. 'Don't try to take us all the way there.'

The dragon stretched out his legs. The speed of his descent forced him into a jog as soon as he landed. By the time he was able to stop, my back ached and I wondered if I'd be ever be able to sit comfortably again. I passed Clyde to James, dismounted, then took the snail back again as my brother joined me. A moment later, Raven sank to the earth with a groan.

'Run to the main building,' I urged my brother. 'Tell them to send a unicorn immediately.'

James obeyed, his jacket flapping as he charged off towards Saint Raphael's. I hurried to kneel beside the bleeding wing, placing Clyde on the ground before dumping my coat over the wound in an attempt to staunch the flow.

'I'm not going to die,' Raven reassured me. 'I've had worse wounds.'

'I'm not worried about that,' I said as blood soaked through the fabric. 'Will you be able to fly again?'

'Of course I will.'

The sound of hooves thudding against the turf made me lift my head. The unicorn shone against the grey sky, and I could almost feel the power she drew from the ground beneath her silver hooves. Despite her quick gallop, her voice was steady as she pulled up next to me. 'Father Penny, please remove your clothing so that I may see the wound for myself.'

'He was shot,' I said, wondering how to explain guns to a person from Lloegyr. This country was still using blades and spears rather than firearms.

Her long beard trickled across my ear as she lowered her head to the dragon. 'I do not understand your words, but I can clearly see the damage. Please move to one side.'

I scrambled out of her way. The unicorn straightened. Her horn pointed upwards for a moment, drawing light from the hidden sun. Then she lowered the sharp tip to Raven's wing.

Clyde pressed up against my leg, and I rubbed his shell without taking my eyes off the unicorn. Blue fire twisted down the silver spiral and flowed from the tip, erupting like cold flame along the jagged edges of the wound. The skin puckered, then smoothed. New growth flowed across the hole, a lighter blue-green than the older hide.

Several sets of footsteps made me glance up. James had returned, along with Llewelyn. The were-wolf swept his eyes over the scene before addressing the unicorn. 'Revnassa, what can we do to help?'

'Straighten out the upper portion of the wing,' the unicorn replied. 'We want the muscle and bone to heal in the correct position.'

James and Llewelyn knelt beside the tip. Raven snarled as they carefully manipulated the wing, and I reached out to rub his shoulder. The healing flames spread to encompass the area between man and were-wolf. Cold blue light revealed the grimace in James' face, and the deep lines etched across Llewelyn's.

Revnassa lifted her horn and stepped back. 'The wound is sealed and the muscles and bone lie back in place. But the structure was much weakened, and blood has been lost. Raven must not attempt to fly for at least a fortnight, and must restrict himself to short flights at first until he has built up his strength.'

'But he will fly again?' I asked fearfully.

'There is no reason why he should not.'

Raven brought his head to mine. 'Good. A grounded dragon is not a real dragon.'

I placed my hands on either side of his jaws. 'I would have loved you just the same.' And I lowered my face to his soft nose, wetting the skin with my tears.

Chapter Fifteen

'Do you mind spending the night here?' I asked James as we walked beside Raven. The dragon had reluctantly agreed to take shelter in one of the barns. His injured wing was spread out across the backs of three were-horses as they supported his trip to the shelter.

'I've not seen Skylar or Dwysil for over a month. Another night isn't going to make much difference.' Even in the dimming light, I could see the suspicion on James' face. 'From the way you've been talking, you have a way to take me directly to her. Something to do with Clyde?'

'I'll tell you later,' I said, glancing at the horses.

We saw Raven into the barn. The weres inside gave him welcome, and those supporting his wing changed to biped shape to help him lower it carefully to the ground. 'I'll come back at bedtime,' I told him.

Raven snorted. 'You'll sleep much better in a bed. Come back in the morning.'

'I won't sleep at all, worrying about you,' I said firmly. 'I'll see you later tonight.'

'They weren't trying to kill him,' James said once we were back outside. 'I think the whole idea was just to bring him down.'

'Sue Harkness,' I muttered, biting back a curse. 'She's proved once and for all that she's no friend to me.'

'Or to Lloegyr.'

A small blur of blue and purple whizzed over my head. 'James, James, James!' Jago shouted as he landed on my brother's shoulder. 'It's really you!'

James laughed as the small gryphon rubbed feathers against chin. 'It's good to see you too. I bet you have lots of adventures to tell me about.'

'Oh, yes, we went to les Etats-Unis on a sailing ship, and we stopped on a lovely island, and there was a big battle against bees, and that was very sad, and--'

'And you can tell James all about it inside,' I said, urging them on. 'It's getting cold out here.'

I left them in the dining room and made a trip to the kitchen. The cook on duty nodded when I asked her to cook an extra portion for another human. A quick chat with the housekeeper gave me access to a spare room, and he agreed to make up the bed for my brother.

'And the wedding's going to be in the spring,' Jago was saying excitedly when I re-joined them. 'Do you think you can come? It'd be wonderful to have you there. I want you and Clyde to be my best men.'

'If I can come back safely, I will,' James promised, glancing at me. 'Right, Sis?'

I jerked my chin at the door. 'Morey usually heads to his flat to clean up before Evening Prayer. I'd like him to hear what's been happening in England.'

'I'll find Basty and tell him you're here,' Jago said eagerly. 'Maybe now he'll agree to fix a date for our wedding.'

'The rat's a bit shy, is he?' James asked as we headed up the stairs.

'It's a bit more complicated than that.' I led him to Morey's door and knocked. 'Hi, it's Penny, and I've brought a surprise!'

'A pleasant one, I hope?' Morey's voice answered. The door opened a moment later, and the gryphon backed up and flew to my shoulder. 'Oh, well, it's James.'

'Pleasant surprise?' my brother prompted with a grin.

'I'm sure it has been for Jago.' Morey fluttered over to the fur-covered bed. 'Come on in.'

I shut the door firmly behind us and took a seat next to Morey. James pulled over a chair. 'I hear Jago's getting married.'

'Seems everyone's piling into marriage,' I said lightly, pointing at the golden ring on my brother's left hand. 'We don't have that much time before Evening Prayer. James told me a little of what's been happening in England before Sue Harkness interrupted us.'

'Lloegyr people are being rounded up,' James said. 'I think I've located some of the places where they're being kept. It's mostly in large abandoned buildings, like old aircraft hangers. A few have managed to escape, usually smaller weres like squirrels and hedgehogs. From what they've said, although it's a bit crowded, everyone's being fed and the place is kept clean. But they're not allowed to go outside, and no one knows how long they're going to be forced to stay there.'

'Or why,' I added darkly. 'Morey, Raven flew James and me away from Harkness. But a helicopter came after us, and Raven was shot in his left wing. One of the Guild's unicorns has healed him--'

'But that's not the point.' The gryphon's back was arched and fur and feathers bristled. 'This just goes to prove that she has no concern for the welfare of Lloegyr citizens. We must try to rescue all those she's holding hostage. Could Clyde create some escape routes?'

'And how would Clyde do that?' James asked.

'Clyde can create air crossings,' I said quickly. 'But very few people know that. Please, you need to keep it to yourself. Can you imagine what someone like Sue Harkness would do if she knew?'

'Kidnap you to make Clyde do whatever she ordered him to do,' James answered. 'And maybe she thought she could use Raven as leverage against you, if she managed to capture him.'

I shook my head. 'That would never happen.'

'Really?' James asked. 'If someone had Skylar hostage, I'd do anything to protect her.'

'Where is Skylar now?' Morey asked.

'Safe. Somewhere.' James rubbed at his chin. 'I'll be joining her in hiding, now. But that's okay. My business collapsed after Lloegyr was sealed off. I've tried to set up some other fair-trade deals, based on Earth, but nothing's worked out so far. I've been living off the *wergild* Bodil gave me. So long as I can access a computer, I can still do my work for the "Friends of Aslan". And maybe I'll take on some IT consultancy.'

'That sounds really good,' I said encouragingly.

'About all the thin places closing up,' James continued. 'None of us could understand what'd happened.'

'It was with search dragon blood,' I admitted, unwilling to lie any further. 'Raven and I organised it.'

James looked away. 'I hope you had a really good reason to destroy my company and trap Lloegyr people in England.'

'Sue found out that search dragons can find air thin places,' I explained, forcing myself not to reach out to him. 'At first she was only talking about using them to transport goods. Then she realised the military uses. James, I couldn't let the British government use search dragons in that way.'

Morey had calmed down as we talked, and his voice was steady as he spoke to James. 'Although I take issue with the fact that Penny made this decision single-handedly, I believe that, in the circumstances, it had to be done. Penny neglects to mention that the Minister had also come to an agreement with the rat kings. British detention centres were to be emptied, and those held inside sent to work in factories here in Lloegyr. Slave labour, in effect.'

'You couldn't have allowed that.' James finally faced me again. 'But new crossings have opened up, haven't they? That's how the rats are taking messages between our worlds.'

'The search dragons seal up the large thin places,' I said. 'They've let the small ones stay open. After all, new land crossing places open up all the time, usually where something terrible has happened. Remember the one Sue took us to, in that cellar in London? She warned us that several people had been hanged as traitors there.'

James shuddered. 'It was horrible. It felt like the rope was around my own neck. And the terror of the men…' He gulped down air. 'Well, at any rate, we need to do something to help people from Lloegyr.'

'Those camps are bound to have guards and cameras,' I said. 'I don't know how we'd manage to get anyone out, especially if the guards are armed. They didn't hesitate to shoot at Raven.'

'I guess you're right,' James said. 'The weres who've managed to escape told us that the larger ones, like gryphons and unicorns, are locked away. As far as we're aware, any dragon in England is still free.'

'Teeth, claws, and flame make dragons rather formidable.' I rubbed my forehead. 'We saw Peter, by the way.'

'Working with Sue,' James added.

'I don't think he is,' I said. 'He dropped some hints. I think he's another "Friend of Aslan".'

Morey stood and stretched. 'The Peter I know is an honourable man and would never work against Lloegyr. I refuse to accept that he has changed. It's time for Evening Prayer. James, if you'd like to go to the dining room, the rest of us will join you after worship.'

'Actually, I'll go with you.' James smiled. 'Church reminds me of Skylar when I can't be with her.'

After dinner, five of us crowded into my room. Taryn and Morey pressed for details about Dwysil. Clyde said little but the calm blues and greens swirling through his body were occasionally lightened by slashes of happy pink. Jago pressed himself against James' ear and I feared that the gryphon would want to return to England with my brother.

'I have some good news for you, Penny,' Taryn said when James had finished catching everyone up with his news. 'I have tracked down several horse breeders who specialise in the Seraphixon bloodline. One has herds grazing near a longhouse, so her horses are comfortable in the presence of dragons. She's willing to provide you with a stallion and four mares for five ounces of gold.'

'They'll be comfortable until they're lifted into the air,' Morey noted glumly. 'With Raven out of action, we'll have to find some other way to hire dragons.'

'I'll talk to Raven about it,' I said as I wandered over to my desk. My bag of gold was inside a drawer. 'There must be some way to contact the other search dragons.'

'Thin place,' Clyde reminded me. 'Find.'

I nodded as I weighed the bag in my hand. How many ounces did I possess? 'That's right, we don't need a search dragon to find air crossing places. Even a tacsi dragon can do it, if Clyde's at the front to pick out the short cuts to Ennor.'

'I'll ask for the names of some trustworthy dragons, preferably search dragons,' Taryn said. She rose to her feet and stretched. 'Time to go, Trahaearneifion. James, I will have to leave for Llanbedr before dawn. I wish you and your family well.'

James flushed. 'Thanks.'

When the others had gone, I said to James, 'Maybe you three should come over to Lloegyr. What if Sue Harkness finds out where you're hiding?'

James shook his head. 'I'm the IT person in the "Friends of Aslan" network. I'm staying to fight for Skylar, and Dwysil, and everyone from Lloegyr.'

'Should I also be over there, I wonder?'

'No. You belong here.' James reached over to give my hand a squeeze. 'Find out who's been sending letherum over to England.'

'The rat kings, I shouldn't wonder,' I muttered. 'Sue climbed into bed with them over shipping immigrants to their factories.'

'And,' James said slowly, 'the rats might be delivering more than messages through those small thin places. Strikes me a rat could easily carry a gun, for example.'

I groaned. 'Bother. I'm not sure I can convince the search dragons to go back to sealing those up as well.'

'But what's the rat kings' game?' James asked. 'What would they gain from taking letherum to the British government? I mean, why does Harkness want it? Okay, yes, they've used it to capture people from Lloegyr. But why would they want more?'

'Who knows what scheme rat kings or politicians might come up with next?' My sigh turned into a yawn. 'I need some sleep. Before you go to your room, will you help me carry stuff to Raven's barn?'

James helped me to strip blankets and pillows from my bed. After collecting a lantern from the front door, he led the way to Raven's shelter. The dragon was asleep, and I tried to be as quiet as possible as I did my best to make a nearby stall comfortable. As I settled down on the thin layer of straw, still wearing my regular clothes in an attempt to keep warm, I resigned myself to a fitful night. But at least I'd be only a few feet away from Raven, close to hand should he need me.

To my surprise, I did manage to sleep. The smell of coffee pulled me out of my cocoon of blankets. Early morning light spilled through the half-open barn door, revealing the tall form of my brother. As I rose to my feet, dusting bits of straw from my trousers, James held out a steaming mug.

'How are you feeling?' I asked Raven, wrapping my cold fingers around the warm drink.

'The wing joint feels stiff, but I'm in no pain,' he assured me. 'And you?'

My back ached from a night spent on flagstones. 'I'm fine,' I lied, looking in vain for somewhere to sit. A glance at my wristwatch told me that I had an hour before breakfast. Perhaps I'd have time for a quick bath? 'I'll go over to the house, and I'll come back after Morning Prayer. Unless you need anything now?'

'Some water when you return,' Raven said. 'And if the weather is fine, perhaps the were-horses would help me outside.'

'I'm sure they will.' I took a few gulps of coffee, welcoming the warmth sliding down my throat. Thus fortified against the cold morning, I left the barn.

The sound of leathery wings pounding against air made me look up. A moment later, the downdraft whipped the hair from my face. The search dragon landed in front of me, her form a slightly thinner version of Raven's own. As the green-black head swung in my direction, I recognised the torc of translucent glass resting around her neck. 'Tyra,' I said resignedly. 'You could at least have waited until I'd finished my coffee.'

'Is it true?' she demanded, smoke puffing from her nostrils. 'Hrafn lost his wing from an attack on your world?'

I raised my free hand. 'No, no, he was injured, but he still has his wing and he'll be fine.'

'Tell me who did this to him,' Tyra growled, 'and I will eat the *tramgwyddwr* immediately.'

James gave me a nudge. 'That would solve a lot of problems.'

'And create many others,' I replied. 'Tyra, thank you for the offer, but that's not the answer. Did you want to see Raven?'

Tyra arched her neck. 'Yes. Remember, Father, I've known him longer than you have. He will always want to see me.'

I fought back the temptation to throw the rest of my coffee at her. After gulping down the lukewarm liquid, I placed the mug on the ground and rolled up the left sleeves of my coat and jumper. The gold bracelet gleamed even in the dull light. 'Raven and I are now husband and wife. We married several months ago.'

Tyra stared at me for a long moment, blue-green eyes wide and nostrils flaring. Then she lifted her head and laughed. The high-pitched sound was quickly joined by the worried whinnying of were-horses and a low growl from a were-bear. Tyra shook her head and, gasping for breath, said, 'So he's finally done it. Given himself over to a human.'

James placed his hands on his hips, reminding me for a moment of the Third Doctor. 'And I'm really pleased for them.'

Tyra snorted. 'And who is this?'

'My brother, James,' I said. 'You knocked him down when you kidnapped me at the Frost Fair.'

'And are you also now wed to a search dragon?'

'A vampire, actually.' James bent down to retrieve my mug. 'I'll see you back at the house, Sis.'

'This way,' I said to the still-chuckling dragon. 'He's in that barn.'

Both doors needed opening to allow Tyra inside. My back creaked as I pulled at one, then the other. 'Visitor for you!' I announced as I stood back.

Raven raised his head. 'Tyra. As you can see, I still possess two wings.'

'You heard me?'

'The whole community will have heard you.'

Tyra pointed her muzzle at the gold bracelet on Raven's left leg. 'Now I understand the meaning of that bauble you've taken to wearing.'

'It's a sign that I have plighted my troth to Penny.'

I rubbed my face, hiding my smile at Raven's archaic language. 'So, Tyra, as you can see, he's being well looked after.'

'Do you require anything?' Tyra asked Raven. 'I could bring you a fresh kill.'

Raven cocked his head. 'The were-bears have already offered to bring me regular meals. What we do need is help in recruiting ten dragons to provide transport. We are obligated to deliver five horses to an island called Ennor.'

Tyra narrowed her eyes. 'Who wants these horses?'

'The *Tylwyth Teg*. Penny has arranged a trade with them.'

'The *Tylwyth Teg* were willing to meet with an *offeiriad*?'

'Penny,' Raven declared proudly, 'is no ordinary *offeiriad*.'

'Obviously not.' Tyra studied me for a moment. 'What does Hrafn's matriarch think of your marriage?'

I cleared my throat. 'Actually, Eydis gave me permission to marry him.'

'Why would she do that?' Tyra dipped her head in a nod. 'To draw you to the attention of the *Cadw ar Wahân*. She has hopes that they will rid her of Hrafn.'

'Ten dragons, nine if you are willing provide transport,' Raven said. 'Will you assist us?'

'For enough gold, yes.'

I thought nervously of my rapidly diminishing store of gold and tried to keep my voice calm. 'Could you get a quote and come back to us?'

'Certainly.' Tyra raised her eyes to Raven. 'You keep your hide safe in the meantime.'

She stalked from the barn and I closed the doors behind us. Once Tyra was in the air, I hurried to the main building. No time for a bath now, but perhaps I could squeeze in a quick wash and a change of clothes before breakfast.

Chapter Sixteen

My duties meant that I wasn't able to take James back to England until late morning. When I was free, we met up in my room. As I picked up Clyde from my bed, my brother asked, 'We can go from here?'

'Clyde can carve a crossing between any two points,' I said. 'Well, within reason. He has to have a connection with the end point, either through having been there before or through someone he knows well.'

'Then could we go first to my flat? I'd like to collect some clothes and my laptop.'

I shook my head. 'Don't you think Sue and her lot will be keeping an eye out for you?'

'How will they know we're there?' James asked. 'We'll stay away from the windows.'

'And if they've put cameras up inside? They'll see us step through a thin place.'

James rubbed his chin. Several days away from a shaver had given him the outline of a beard. 'They won't have them in the bathroom, I should think. People are usually squeamish about that. And you don't have to cross over with me, do you? You stay over on this side, and I'll just take a few minutes. I'll be in and out before the British government can storm my flat.'

'Okay,' I said reluctantly. 'But do be quick. I don't have much of this.' I held up a small bottle, the red liquid already congealing inside. 'Raven lost plenty of blood yesterday, so I didn't dare draw off any more.'

'Is the connection strong enough?' James asked Clyde as I held up the snail. 'You've never been to my flat.'

'Enough,' Clyde confirmed. He opened his jaws, and his teeth sliced through reality as I lowered him towards the floor.

James gingerly poked a hand through the slight shimmer in the air. His fingers disappeared. 'Wow. Can all snail sharks do this?'

'Only lefties like Clyde, we think,' I said. 'Make sure you mark where the crossing is before you leave the bathroom. It's not always easy to spot one when you've taken your eyes off it.'

'Got it.' James climbed through the thin place.

I studied my wristwatch and tried to calm my nerves. James had always had a flexible arrangement with time, and 'a few minutes' could be anything up to an hour. Ten minutes ticked by, and I was about to go after him when his head appeared in my room. 'Whew, found it. Coming through.'

At least my brother knew how to pack light. All he brought with him was a backpack. Once he was back in Lloegyr, I unstopped the bottle and flung dragon blood at the crossing.

'Gone,' Clyde confirmed a moment later.

'Can you find Skylar?' I asked, placing the bottle on my desk.

'Of course.'

I lifted Clyde again. Once he had finished slicing the air, I stepped through with him in my arms.

We emerged into a small sitting room. A large window ahead of us looked out across fields and a small hill. A desk and chair was positioned to take advantage of the view. On my right was a blue settee, on which Skylar was sitting. She looked up as I stepped to one side. 'Penny--'

James nearly trod on my heels as he came through the crossing. Skylar rose from her seat, and the two moved into a tight embrace. I listened to the sound of a clock ticking and the baas of sheep as I placed Clyde on the floor.

Of course, Skylar was never silent for very long. She freed herself from James to address me. 'I'm so sorry, Penny, I knew I should have asked first, as you're the head of the household, but we didn't know how to find you and with everything that's been going on we wanted to set a date. And then we still couldn't find you and we needed to keep to our plans, you see Bishop Nigel had agreed to officiate, and his diary is pretty full, so we went ahead. I'm really sorry and I hope you can forgive me.'

I was well practiced at cutting through Skylar's verbiage. 'You mean, you should have asked my permission to marry James?'

The look of embarrassment on my brother's face was one I knew I'd long treasure. 'I kept trying to tell her it doesn't work that way in England.'

'Of course it works that way,' I said brusquely. 'Well, Skylar, let's talk about this. You mustn't let him get away with you doing all the housework. He's perfectly capable of cooking a meal, so make sure you take it in turn. Shiny gadgets turn his head, so for goodness' sake don't let him buy any technology magazines.'

'Sis,' James protested in a strangled voice.

I grinned. 'But he's grown up to be a loyal man, a good friend as well as a brother, and I couldn't be happier with his choice of wife. You have my backdated permission to marry him. Welcome to the family, sister-in-law.'

Skylar ignored my offered hand and drew me into a tight hug. I grunted as the air was squeezed from my lungs. 'Oh, Penny, that's just wonderful! I did wonder if you'd be happy with his choice, since I was your curate and everything, but as I'm not now, your curate I mean, I guess it's all okay. Although I did enjoy being your curate, of course.'

'Feeling's mutual,' I managed to gasp. 'You can let go now.'

'How long are you staying?' Skylar asked James as she obeyed.

'For as long as we have to stay in hiding.' James lowered his backpack to the ground. 'Harkness found me and Penny talking together. It's not safe for me to go home. I'm going to have to join you here.'

Another long hug between husband and wife. Clyde's tentacles traced a circle over his head, and I wondered if this were his equivalent of an eye roll. 'Will that be okay with whoever owns this place?' I asked.

'I'm sure it will,' Skylar said, her voice muffled against James' shoulder. 'I've been so worried, James. I'm so glad you've come here.'

A door next to the settee opened. A small girl toddled out, her pyjamas and short dark hair rumpled. She rubbed her eyes, then fixed them on James. 'Daddy?'

'Dwysil. Come here, Pumpkin.' James knelt down, and the girl rushed into his arms. 'Daddy's going to stay with you, now. And I've brought someone to meet you. This is my sister, your Auntie Penny.'

Dwysil pulled back just far enough to look up at me. Although she bore no physical resemblance to James, her mixed expression of welcome and confusion reminded me of him at the same age. I lowered myself to her height. 'I'm very pleased to meet you, Dwysil.'

The girl gave me a smile. 'Present?'

I laughed. 'Now I definitely know that James is your father. I'll bring something next time. Okay?'

'Okay.' Dwysil walked over to Skylar.

James unzipped his backpack and pulled out his Macbook. 'Before you go, I want to show you what we've been up to. Skylar, what's the wifi code for this place?'

The computer chimed into life. James placed the laptop on the desk and entered his password. 'Here's the website for the "Friends of Aslan." We all use fake names, of course. I'm going to activate yours, just in case you find yourself over here and need to contact us.'

'I know you've already given me "Jewel".' I peered over his shoulder. 'I would've preferred "Polly".'

'Who's that?'

'Polly Plummer. One of the two children who watched Aslan sing Narnia into existence.' I grinned. 'Looks like Digory's already been taken. Who is that?'

'Good question. I don't know the real name of everyone who's on the site.' James clicked through to a comments section. 'But he's written something since yesterday. "I'm more of a Peter than an Edmund." Wonder what that's all about.'

I took a deep breath. 'You don't think Digory could be our Peter? Edmund betrayed his brother and sisters to the White Witch. Maybe he's letting us know that he hasn't betrayed us to Sue Harkness?'

'I hope you're right.' James tapped at the keyboard. 'We have several thousand people signed up. Of course, not all of them are part of our network. Some of them think it's just a website with linked social media for Narnia fans. Well, that's done. Now let me show you something else.'

James entered a string of numbers and letters into the web browser. A page came up, white print on black background. I moved closer. 'Is that the royal seal?'

'I'm in a government website. It's supposed to be hack-proof.' James laughed. 'Bless them.'

'Won't they be able to spot you and trace you back here?'

'Don't worry, I've made sure they can't.'

I nodded, deciding to trust his IT skills. 'What are you looking for?'

'This.' A few more clicks brought up a list. 'Here are the places where people from Lloegyr are being held.'

Clyde charged across the floor. 'Free them!'

'There's no way we could get them all out before being captured ourselves,' I told him sadly. 'Is there anything there about the government's long-term strategy? I can't see Sue wanting to house and feed them forever.'

'Nothing's been published so far. But it may be too sensitive even for a secure site.' James closed the browser window and turned to face his wife and child. 'Penny's offered to take us all through to Lloegyr. I want to stay here and do what I can for the detainees. But you two could cross over.'

'No,' Skylar said firmly. 'I'm a "Friend of Aslan" too. I'm staying here until we've freed everyone trapped in those camps.'

I looked at them, my precious family, and wondered how safe they could be in England. 'Maybe we should leave the thin place open, just in case you need to get away?'

'No,' James said, shaking his head. 'What if Harkness and her goons trace us here and stumble across it? We can't take that risk.'

Clyde nudged at my foot. 'Wall. Hide.' He pointed his tentacles at the settee.

'Great idea,' I said. 'A crossing just at the wall, below the height of the settee. Clyde, can you make sure it leads to a wall in my room on the other side? I'd rather not fall through in the middle of the night when I'm searching for the loo.'

James and Skylar helped me to move the piece of furniture. Clyde cut carefully and precisely as I lifted him from floor to around three feet high. I poked my head through, found myself looking into my room, and smiled in satisfaction. We pushed the settee back into place.

'You could send Jago over once a day,' James suggested. 'He can take messages between us. Or you can just shout from behind the settee.'

'I'll use Jago. He'll be pleased. And it's more dignified than the alternative.' I bent down to pick up Clyde. 'We'd better go.'

'Present,' Dwysil reminded me from her father's arms.

'Present,' I promised solemnly before stepping back through the original crossing. Once back on my side, I closed it up with Raven's blood. With some effort, I placed my own settee across the remaining opening. Two pieces of furniture would also help to dull the noises from each other's flats.

'Job done,' I told Clyde. 'And I even have time to visit the were-sheep before lunch.'

Raven insisted that I spend the night in a comfortable bed, so I was in a much better mood the next morning when Tyra turned up after breakfast. 'I have found ten dragons willing to carry horses for gold,' she said, arching her neck proudly. 'Payment is half an ounce of gold per dragon, so five and half ounces due to us.'

'For ten dragons?'

'You'll need an eleventh one to carry you. Me.'

Tyra's flying had proven to be even more erratic than Raven's, but I could see that I had little choice. And, having taken the opportunity to weigh my gold last night, I knew that I had enough to cover both horses and transport. 'Okay, done. Could you go to the horse breeder? I'd rather not use rats. Let's try for Friday morning to take the horses to Ennor.'

With the help of Taryn's directions, the necessary messages were passed back and forth. And so, on a bright and crisp March morning, eleven search dragons landed outside the Guild's main building. Ten of them already wore harnesses. A dragon in the settlement had agreed to prepare mats to carry the horses, and these were currently rolled up and slung below half of the dragons' bellies.

I zipped up my coat, patting once again the pocket which held my gold coins. My other pocket held bread and cheese, plus a filled water bottle. Taryn had renewed her warnings that I must not eat or drink anything the *Tylwyth Teg* might offer me.

Raven emerged from his barn, his left wing raised awkwardly above his back. 'Carry her carefully,' he warned Tyra as I climbed up her neck.

'Of course I will,' the other dragon retorted. 'She's not paying us until the end of the trip, and I want my gold.'

Clyde sat in the doorway of the house, his body a dull grey. Although he had wanted to come with me, I needed to concentrate on clinging to Tyra and watching the horses. Morey was accompanying me instead, as another pair of eyes to monitor our precious cargo.

'Quick to the horse breeder's,' I told Tyra. 'But a comfortable route to Ennor when we have the horses.'

'We'll earn our gold,' she assured me. And then took off so abruptly that I had to grab a neck spine to keep my seat.

Morey landed on my shoulder just before Tyra led the way through a thin place. I coughed as we emerged in thick smog over a modern city somewhere on Earth. Our next crossing, over a serene forest, gave me time to clear my lungs just before we emerged into frigid night. Just when I thought I might lose my fingers to frostbite, we returned to Lloegyr.

A series of barns and corrals stretched out below us. Horses grazed on clumps of grass and pulled at mounds of hay. Although I knew little about horses, the elegant heads and strong bodies spoke of good breeding. Only a few bothered to look up as the dragons flew past.

A tall elf waved at us, pointing at a clear area of land near a small corral. Tyra took us down, landing a moment before the other dragons.

'Croeso i chi,' the elf said, her thin face serious as she studied us. 'Rydych wedi dod am y ceffylau?'

'We have come to buy the horses,' I agreed in Welsh. 'I have brought the gold.'

'A fyddant yn cael eu trin yn dda?'

I slid to the ground and walked up to her. 'I promise you, yes, they will be treated well.'

She nodded, then called out several names. Five elves emerged from a nearby barn, each carrying a rope. The mares, three brown and one nearly black, waited calmly as the leads were slipped through their halters. The grey stallion was less patient, tossing his head several times before he allowed the elf to attach the rope.

The dragons had paired off. More elves appeared, and helped me to remove the mats. We rigged them up between each dragon, forming slings to carry the horses. The grooms brought the stallion over first, carefully placing his hooves in the holes cut out of the thick material. The horse snorted a few times, but made no further protest. The mares followed.

'We need to buckle the slings around the horses,' Morey said from his place on my shoulder. He repeated his statement in Welsh, adding, 'Will that panic the horses?'

'Not after this,' the elf said. She pulled sugar cubes from her pocket, and offered one to each horse. A minute later, their heads sagged, and they looked half asleep. 'That will keep them quiet until you reach their new home.'

'I'm supposed to deliver horses in prime condition,' I said. 'Their new owners might not accept them looking like this. What have you done?'

The elf went into a long technical explanation. The Welsh was beyond me, and I only blinked as she handed me a small bottle and a grey cloth. Morey told me, 'It's all right, it's a tried and tested concoction she's used many times when horses need to be kept calm. You just smear liquid on their tongues at the other end and they'll be fine.'

'They'd better be,' I muttered, glancing at the horses now safely tied up in their slings. I removed my coin purse and slipped the antidote into my pocket. 'There. Five ounces of gold, as agreed.'

The coins glittered in her long fingers. 'As agreed.'

'What do people use horses for, anyway?' I asked Morey as I walked over to Tyra. 'Isn't it more convenient to use a *tacsi* dragon for getting around?'

'You have cars and planes, but you still have horses,' the gryphon pointed out. 'They're used for transport, ploughing, and some of the towns have racecourses. I also understand they're very tasty.'

I tapped his head. 'Just keep your beak off these ones.'

Tyra chuckled as I mounted. 'Horse does taste nice. But we also will keep our teeth clean.'

My back protested as she kicked us into the air. I glanced back at the other dragons, wondering how they were going to lift off with their burdens. Their sides expanded, harnesses stretching as they filled their gas chambers. A gentle push from the ground sent them after us. The slumbering horses rocked slightly between the dragon pairs.

'Careful with the crossings,' I reminded Tyra. 'Nothing too hot or too cold.'

'Understood!'

Of course, no dragon could predict the weather. So I gritted my teeth as rain soaked us over a set of dreary fields, and fretted when high winds jounced the horses and harnesses rubbed against scales and skin. A short blast of heat was welcome and didn't last long enough to cause me any worry for our cargo.

My watch and my bladder informed me that we'd been airborne for just over three hours when the dragons reached the Cornish coast line. The island was a welcome sight as it emerged from the ocean.

'Not very large, is it?' Morey commented as we drew near. 'How many *Tylwyth Teg* live here?'

'I'm not entirely certain.' I scanned the settlement. 'There, Tyra! Land us near that *Tylwyth Teg*!'

The broad face looking up at us remained expressionless as I gave a quick wave. Tyra backwinged into an elegant landing. The wind from her wings blew the long blonde hair away from Unhynaf's pointed ears. 'We could use some help bringing the horses down,' I said as I dismounted.

More *Tylwyth Teg* emerged as the dragons hovered. They reached up their thin arms as the horses were slowly lowered, the dragons releasing lighter-than-air gases in bouts of small flames. The horses, although still under the influence of whatever the elf had given them, were able to stand upright.

'What is wrong with them?' Unhynaf demanded in Welsh.

'Nothing,' I said with more confidence than I felt. 'Let's get them out of the slings, and I'll bring them back around.'

Eager hands dug at the buckles and straps. As the material fell away, sighs of wonder went up from the *Tylwyth Teg*. The dragons stepped back.

'Can you help me?' I asked Unhynaf as I pulled bottle and rag from my pocket. 'Hold open their mouths while I wipe their tongues with this.'

The *Tylwyth Teg* obeyed. As I poured liquid on the cloth and smeared it across each pink tongue, the horse slowly returned to full consciousness. When all five had been restored, I backed away and smiled at Unhynaf. 'All yours. You might want to grab on to their leads before they trot off.'

'No.' Unhynaf produced a knife. Four other *Tylwyth Teg* followed suit. They cut through the halters, leaving the horses bare-faced. 'Our horses live free. They will choose to be with us.'

One of the mares whickered. The stallion answered back. The *Tylwyth Teg* moved out of their way as the horses wandered off to a patch of thick grass. Tears glistened in many of the pale eyes and tracked down their blue-green faces.

I excused myself and made use of an outhouse. When I returned, more of the community had emerged to admire the horses and talk to the dragons. Unhynaf, Tyra, and Morey were discussing the stallion, although I feared their interest in his muscle tone stemmed from rather differing reasons.

'You bring us double joy,' Unhynaf told me. 'Horses and dragons.'

Tyra arched her neck. 'And even better than that. Search dragons. Superior to all others.'

'We are whole again.' Unhynaf turned to look at the horses. 'A Christos kept a promise.'

'Thank you for trusting me,' I said. 'The letherum has already been used to help others.'

'A Christos kept a promise.' The *Tylwyth Teg* spoke as if tasting something new on the tongue. 'I would like to also meet your son, the snail shark.'

'If you will permit me to visit again,' I said, 'I'll bring him. For this journey, I wanted to concentrate on the horses.'

Morey leapt down from Tyra's neck to my shoulder. 'I too am a Christos. I hope you welcome me as much as you do Penny.'

'He's my Associate,' I added. 'We work together.'

'Then you are welcome.' Unhynaf laid a hand on my arm and pulled me away from the dragons and other *Tylwyth Teg*. 'When you were last here, you asked a question which I didn't answer.'

'I seem to recall that I asked several questions which you didn't answer.'

'This is the one which you most need answering. Letherum has been taken out of this world.'

'I know it has,' I said. 'We know that it's been used against vampires in my own country. Can you tell us who has been taking it through?'

'I can taste that other world on fur.'

Morey's tail thumped against my back. 'Flying rats? Are the rat kings involved?'

'I see many bodies tied together by tails,' Unhynaf said slowly. 'Many voices, but just one mind. And just one intent.'

Dragons and other *Tylwyth Teg* seemed to be paying us no attention, but I lowered my voice anyway. 'Which is?'

White teeth were bared to the bright sun. 'When we return to Lloegyr, we will be able to afford protection.'

'The Church,' Morey said strongly, 'is not your enemy. Not any longer.'

'We have nothing to fear from the Church.'

'Then from whom?' I asked. Unhynaf simply stared at me. 'How many horses would it cost for an answer?'

'You speak of peace between the different species,' the *Tylwyth Teg* said. 'As I have said before, there are those who do not want peace. Ask yourselves, what do the rat kings value most?'

'Secrets?' I offered.

Morey shook his head. 'No. Above all, they value money.'

'But peace allows for a growing economy,' I protested. 'And surely that's how the rat kings can best become rich. Through all of their factories and messaging services.'

'I've not known anything but peace,' Morey said quietly. 'You tell me, Penny, who becomes rich through war?'

My knees suddenly felt weak. I stumbled over to a nearby boulder and sat down. 'People who sell weapons. Arms traders. Countries which build tanks and fighter planes. Dear Lord, save us.'

Chapter Seventeen

Morey walked down to my arm. 'You think that might be happening here?'

'Something one of the humans trapped in Llanbedr said to me.' I paused to dredge up the memory. 'Mark. He said he worked in "defence procurement". In other words, an arms dealer. And, now I remember, Fred once told me that the rat kings were particularly interested in him. I didn't think anything of it at the time. Morey, Lloegyr hasn't developed guns yet, has it?'

'No projectile weapons of any form,' the gryphon said glumly. 'Most of us use teeth and claws, or swords if those aren't strong enough. But what's the worst that could happen? Maybe rats would carry through pistols, or push rifles through a thin place. The openings are very small, aren't they? It's not like they could bring anything big through, like a tank or a fighter jet.'

'And there would have to be a demand for such arms,' I added. 'Like you said, things are peaceful between the different species. It'd take something to stir them up.'

Unhynaf's face became even more solemn. *'Cadw ar Wahân.'*

'They've killed people in mixed-species relationships,' I agreed, giving Morey's head a comforting scratch. 'But how would that set people against each other? It hasn't so far, and most still marry within their own kind.'

'Be aware, and take care,' Unhynaf said. 'One close to you knows more.'

Morey snorted. 'Bastien isn't about to betray his rat king.'

'Not only him.'

'And I ask again,' I retorted, 'how many horses would it cost me to get a straight answer out of you?'

The *Tylwyth Teg* looked away, and I immediately felt embarrassed by my outburst. 'You have brought us what was agreed, and we're grateful to once again live with horses. But you are still a Christos. I have given you all that I am willing to give.'

I pulled out my water bottle to wash down my frustration. 'Fair enough. Thank you once again for the letherum. Come on, Morey, time to head back.'

Paying the search dragons reduced my wealth down to three gold coins. I deposited their wages into a bag strapped to one dragon's harness, then stood back as they flew away. Tyra hesitated for a moment, her horns and ears twisting. 'Take care, Father Penny. Watch out for *Cadw ar Wahân.*'

'I thought you'd be glad if something happened to me,' I said, keeping my tone light. 'It'd free Raven, wouldn't it?'

'Hrafn will only ever look to humans for his mate. After you die, he will find another human woman.' And she took off before I could think of a suitable reply.

'Poor loser,' Morey commented. 'Raven did right not choosing her.'

I straightened. 'She sorted out our transport, though. And I think she does really care what happens to Raven. Just not so much for what might happen to me.'

Morey chuckled. 'Surely the feeling's mutual?'

I laughed. 'Okay, yes, it is. How very unchristian of me. I'll confess and repent of it later.'

'Do so at Evening Prayer.' Morey glanced up at the darkening sky. 'Which must be nearly upon us.'

I glanced at my watch. 'About thirty minutes to go. I'll give Raven a quick visit, then come over.'

My husband turned his head as I opened the barn door. Lanterns cast yellow light across the interior, and revealed Miriam sitting on a nearby bench. 'Just taking his meal order,' the were-bear said cheerfully. 'He wants to have a living deer brought to the barn, but I've talked him out of it.'

'Seems the were-sheep wouldn't approve,' Raven grumbled, his ears and horns twisting. 'They don't like to hear the sounds of slaughter.'

'You'll be hunting again soon enough,' I said soothingly.

Miriam rose to her feet. 'We'll bring over a fresh doe carcass tomorrow. See you at Evening Prayer, Father Penny.' She left the barn.

I walked over to the bench. 'This is new. I approve.'

'I've had a lot of visitors. They decided it was more comfortable to have a seat available.' Raven brought his head to mine. 'The horses were delivered safely?'

'Well and sound,' I confirmed. 'The *Tylwyth Teg* seemed very happy with them. But not happy enough to stop being cryptic and give straight answers to straight questions.'

'What did you ask of them?'

My hands had bunched into fists. I forced my fingers to relax, and laid them on Raven's warm muzzle. 'Unhynaf confirmed that letherum's been taken to England by flying rats, and also warned me the rat kings don't want peace between the species in Lloegyr.'

'What would they want instead?'

'I'm worried that they might prefer conflict, maybe even war,' I said slowly. 'One of the humans trapped in Llanbedr, Mark, he worked in the arms trade, the sale of weapons, back in England. I'm wondering if he's been speaking to the Consortium.'

'What type of weapons do you mean?'

'Not swords or spears.' I rubbed my forehead. 'Guns, like what was fired at your wing. Or larger. We humans have invented large weapons like missiles and bombs, which can kill lots of people at once.'

'Why would you even *want* to kill many people at once?'

'All sorts of reasons, sadly.' I shook my head. 'Humans fight each other because of religious differences, for land, or for resources like food and water. Sometimes conflicts go a long way back in history, and bringing peace can be almost impossible.'

His snort was warm on my face. 'You're the same species. You'd think you could get along with each other.'

'You'd think,' I agreed. 'So far, Lloegyr's remained mostly peaceful, even if the different races have a tendency to segregate themselves. I said as much to Unhynaf. And he warned me about *Cadw ar Wahân.*'

Raven pulled his head away. His eyes were more green than blue in the lantern light. 'Perhaps you need to speak to this Mark you've mentioned.'

'With care,' I said. 'I don't think, "Hey, are you planning to introduce mass warfare into Lloegyr?" would be the best approach.'

Raven chuckled. 'Possibly not.'

'But I do have an open invitation to join the Firm for Sunday lunch,' I mused. 'Oh, that's what the human community in Llanbedr call themselves. Fred Wiseman said I should come around sometime. Why don't I take him up on the invitation?'

'And hope that Mark will be there?'

'If he's not, then we'll just have to try something else.' I grimaced. 'Sorry, Raven, but I guess I'll have to use a *tacsi* dragon.'

'Only until I'm healed,' Raven said grandly. 'Until then, you'll have to cope with inferior transport.'

'No one flies quite like you,' I agreed, resisting the urge to rub my back. 'It's nearly time for Evening Prayer. Is there anything you want me to bring over after dinner?'

'Just yourself.' Raven touched my forehead with his snout. 'But you are to sleep in your bed again. It'll be cold tonight.'

'I can't bring myself to argue with you.' I patted his muzzle one more time before leaving.

'Are you sure that's a good idea?' Morey asked. He was sitting next to

Taryn on the bed in their flat. Both had bowls of tea near their feet. Clyde rested on the desk, sipping at a drink of his own. 'How are you going to approach Mark? Ask him outright if he's arranging for weapons to be brought to Lloegyr?'

'Of course not,' I said, my chair creaking as I leaned forward. 'Give me a little more credit than that. I plan to go to lunch, ask people how they're getting on, what sort of work they've been doing, whether they've been able to send messages home.'

'What is the normal size for these guns you mention?' Taryn asked. 'Can they be brought through the small thin spaces which the rats use?'

'Possibly,' I said. 'But I should think it'd be a slow process.'

'And there would have to be a market for them,' Morey added. 'How are things in Llanbedr, Taryn?'

'There is always some friction between the different communities,' she answered. 'Occasionally we have to intervene in a fight between individuals. But there haven't been any major incidences between species.'

'Maybe I'm fretting over nothing.' I took a swallow of tea. 'Maybe there isn't a market for human weapons here in Lloegyr.'

'Go,' Clyde said. 'Ask.'

'You'll feel better if you've done some poking around,' Morey agreed. 'Just be tactful.'

'Says the gryphon,' Taryn commented sharply, 'who is renowned for his tact and diplomacy.'

Morey nodded. 'Exactly.'

Clyde chuckled. I moved my chair closer to the desk so I could give his shell a rub. 'I'll ask Bastien to take a message to Fred Wiseman about me joining them for Sunday lunch. I'd like to arrive in good time, so I'm thinking I'd better skip the Eucharist. Could we do a swap, Morey? You preach in the morning, and I'll take Evensong?'

'Certainly,' Morey said. 'But are you sure you want to use Bastien? Why not send a squirrel? You have enough time.'

I shook my head. 'Remember that the Consortium has been very generous to the humans in Llanbedr. I don't want Fred to wonder why I haven't used a rat messenger.'

'And if we have exhausted this topic,' Taryn said, 'I'd like to discuss the impossibility of Jago marrying Bastien unless he knows the truth about the rat's condition.'

'We don't think Bastien has told Jago yet?' I asked. The two gryphons were silent. I turned to the snail shark. 'Clyde, has Jago said anything to you about Bastien?'

Hues of orange and yellow were sliding through Clyde's body. 'Bastien?'

Morey sighed. 'He doesn't know. Clyde, rats only live to around eight years old. Bastien's seven, and he's starting to show signs of age.'

'That information is confidential,' I said quickly. 'Bastien told me, but Morey worked it out for himself.'

'Jago knows?' Clyde asked.

'Bastien needs to tell him,' I said. 'But we don't think he has. I can't imagine Jago wouldn't have come to one of us if he had.'

Morey growled. 'Maybe we need to force the issue.'

'Penny could talk to Bastien when she asks him to send the message to Wiseman,' Taryn said. 'Bastien chose her as his confidant. Perhaps he will listen to her advice as regards Jago.'

'And Jago might still decide to marry Bastien,' I pointed out. 'Raven decided to marry me, although the lifespan of a human is far shorter than that of a dragon.'

'But you should still have decades together,' Morey said. 'My son might only have months with Bastien. He needs to know the truth about his fiancé.'

I drank down the last of my tea and rose to my feet. 'I'll talk to Bastien. If he agrees to talk to Jago--'

'When,' Taryn insisted.

'--we might want him to tell us when that's going to happen, so we can be around to support Jago.' I collected the empty tea bowls and stacked them on a tray. 'Ready, Clyde?' And the snail and I left the gryphons to grumble to one another.

As I stepped out of the main building the next morning, I saw Bastien sunning himself on one of the nearby rocks. For a moment I hovered near the door, hoping for some sudden emergency which would pull me away from speaking to the rat. But when no one hurried up to me, I forced myself to walk over to the boulders.

'Good morning, Father Penny,' Bastien said, opening his eyes as I stopped beside him. We were nearly the same height. 'You have a message to impart to me?'

I glared at him. 'I do hope you're not reading my mind.'

'There's no need. I can't remember the last time I've seen you stand so stiffly.' He yawned, revealing yellowed teeth. 'Go on, what do you need to tell me?'

'I'd like you to carry a message to Fred Wiseman, please. Some time ago, he said I'd be welcome to join the Firm for Sunday lunch. I'd like to know if this Sunday would be okay, and what time I should come.'

'You'll also need a *tacsi* dragon,' Bastien said. 'I can sort that out for you.'

'Thank you.' I shifted weight from foot to foot. 'And, also, I need to talk to you about Jago.'

The rat narrowed his eyes and thrust his nose towards my face. 'What have you told Morey?'

'Nothing,' I insisted. 'He went into the barn with the other rats, asked me how old they were, and how old you are. I didn't break my promise, I kept what you told me confidential. But other people might start to work it out as well, maybe even Jago himself. You're looking a bit, shall we say, ragged?'

'Thank you,' Bastien said sarcastically.

I sighed. 'You're losing fur, your teeth don't look great, and I think the skin on your wings is flaking.'

Bastien folded his wings tight against his body. 'I'm dying. I would have hoped a priest might care about that, rather than just on how this will affect her friend.'

I wanted to protest that I also considered Bastien to be a friend, but I couldn't force the lie out of my throat. 'I do care about that. All of us are here for you.'

'But you're primarily concerned for Jago.'

Guilt always left a bitter taste in my mouth. 'I know you're young, but he's even younger. Gryphons aren't considered mature until they're over thirty-five.'

'I'll tell him, but in my own time,' Bastien said. 'Tell Morey and Taryn that I expect them to honour my wishes and not to tell Jago themselves.'

'All right.' I lifted a hand, but the rat backed out of reach. 'Is there anything we can do for you? Maybe one of the unicorns should see to you?'

'Even a unicorn can't heal old age.'

'I'm sorry, Bastien.' And I meant it. 'No one's suggesting that Jago shouldn't marry you, if that's what you two want. We want you both to be happy.'

'And how would knowing that I'm dying increase Jago's happiness?' Bastien asked. 'What if I decide it's better that he not know, so we can simply enjoy whatever time I have left?'

'Is that fair to Jago?'

'This is my life.' Bastien bared his teeth. 'And my death.'

'But don't you think--'

Bastien rose onto his hind legs. 'Enough for now. Jago is flying towards us.'

A moment later the small gyphon landed next to the rat. 'Morning, Auntie Penny! And it's a really nice one, don't you think? Spring is coming. Months and months of warmer weather to look forward to.'

'That'll be good,' Bastien said, his voice strained.

'What're you doing this morning?' Jago asked him. 'I thought we could fly over to the meadow. I bet the flowers are starting to come out now.'

'I have a message to take to Llanbedr, but I'll be back by the afternoon. We can have a look then.' Bastien gave Jago an affectionate poke, then extended his wings and flew away.

'I'm sure you'll have a good time,' I told Jago, doing my best to keep frustration out of my voice. 'I'd better go and check in on Raven.'

The main building's door opened and shut, and a moment later Morey thumped onto my shoulder. He dipped his head in greeting to his son before asking, 'Was that Bastien I saw leaving?'

'He has work to do,' Jago said. 'But we're going to have the afternoon together.'

'Really?' Morey tilted his head to look at me. 'Are you two planning to do anything in particular?'

'Look at flowers and discuss wedding plans,' Jago said happily. 'Isn't it wonderful that everything's starting to bloom again? And, look, what a pretty bird.'

A white bird floated down towards us. Her body was plump, like a dove's, but a crest rose from her elegant head and the feathers of her long tail ended in elaborate curls. She swooped in low, singing a tune which made my heart lift and my eyes tear at the same time. Jago danced happily as she circled over him, her song rising and falling with her wing beats.

A shift on my shoulder made me glance at Morey. Never had I seen him so shocked. His feathers and fur were pulled so close to his body that he seemed only half his normal size. My back shuddered under his trembling.

'That was lovely,' Jago sighed as the bird flew away. 'Have you ever seen one like that before, Tad?'

'Never.' Morey sounded strangled. 'Penny, shall we go see Raven?'

Taking the hint, I walked away from the still-entranced Jago. Only when I thought we were well out of earshot did I hiss, 'What's the matter?'

'Into the barn,' Morey said. 'We'll talk in there.'

The dragon raised his head as I let us in. 'Morning already?'

'Morning and a nice one,' I said quickly. 'Right now, Morey needs to tell me why his claws are destroying my coat.'

'A white *llatai*,' Morey told Raven, 'has just circled my son three times.'

Raven drew his head back, nostrils flaring. 'Was she singing?'

'The entire time.'

'And for the mere mortals amongst us,' I said, irritated, 'can you explain what a *llatai* is and why both of you are so alarmed by it?'

Morey leapt from my shoulder to land by the dragon's feet. 'A white *llatai* only appears to lovers, and always in warning to the one who will soon lose the one he loves.'

'How did Jago react?' Raven asked.

'He thought the *llatai* was beautiful.' Morey snorted. 'He's spent too much time in England. There's so much about Lloegyr that he doesn't know.'

'Maybe that's a blessing,' I said.

'It would have forced the issue,' Morey grumbled. 'He would have probably gone to Bastien to demand the truth from him.'

Raven glanced between me and the gryphon. 'And what truth is that?'

'Bastien's dying,' Morey said before I could stop him. 'He probably has less than a year to live, and yet he's still talking about marrying my son.'

'I can understand that,' Raven said quietly. 'I know that I will most likely outlive Penny. But I won't let my future grief affect my current happiness. Perhaps Bastien thinks as I do.'

Morey shook his head. 'Penny married you knowing all that. It's not right that Bastien doesn't tell Jago.'

'Really?' Raven asked. 'Perhaps it's best Jago doesn't know. Let him have his time of happiness with the one he loves.'

'Bastien was saying pretty much the same thing,' I told Morey. 'I don't think he wants to tell Jago.'

Morey growled. 'I do hope I won't be forced to.'

'I must spend more time with Bastien,' Raven said thoughtfully. 'He will need the support of his friends.'

'Of course he will,' Morey said quickly. 'It's good that you'll be there for him.'

Raven narrowed his eyes. 'What about you? Or Penny?' Our awkward silence gave him the answer. 'Jago isn't the only one we should consider. Has no one thought to offer comfort to Bastien?'

'I've been more worried about my son,' Morey admitted gruffly.

I found it hard to meet Raven's gaze. 'Me too.'

'Ask the were-horses to help me outside when they've finished their morning graze,' Raven said. 'If you see Bastien before I do, ask him to come and see me.'

'Will do,' I said awkwardly. 'I'll go talk to the were-horses now. Anything else I can do for you?'

'Yes.' His ears and horns were drawn back, showing how annoyed he was. 'Both of you can start acting like Christians and be as concerned for Bastien as you are for Jago.'

I stiffened my back to walk out of the barn, although I felt like slinking. Morey came to my shoulder as I was shutting the door. 'I feel quite ashamed of myself,' he admitted into my hair.

'As do I.' I started walking towards the were-horses' corral. 'So, we repent, we ask for forgiveness, and we decide to do better with Bastien from now on. That's how we start acting like Christians.'

'I will arrange to meet with Bastien,' Morey said. 'Give him time to talk about his future and my son.'

'And not try to talk him into telling Jago the truth?'

'I will restrain myself. With great difficulty.' Morey sighed. 'Goodness knows what Taryn will say. I do hope she doesn't decide to shred my other ear.'

Chapter Eighteen

The weather turned colder on Saturday night. I had some warning on Sunday morning when I emerged from my bed into my chill room. Despite fastening up my coat and pulling on a hat and gloves, I still shivered in the icy wind as I stood outside the main house. The *tacsi* dragon was late.

By the time the dragon emerged from the early mist, I was tempted to call off my trip to Llanbedr and go back into the house for another cup of coffee. As the yellow dragon settled on the ground in front of me, I tried not to grouse. 'Morning. Are you the *tacsi* taking me to Llanbedr?'

'One passenger from St Raphael's to the human colony in Llanbedr,' the dragon confirmed. She lowered her belly to the frosty grass. 'Ready for boarding.'

I climbed up the metal rungs which led to the saddle. After all these months of riding search dragons, it felt odd to have leather between me and a dragon's hide. 'I'm ready.'

'One to the Firm,' the dragon announced. 'One hour flight time due to weather conditions. Payment already arranged. Please hold on to the grab handles and, in the unlikely event of nausea, do not vomit upwind.'

She went for a running take-off, her feet slapping at the hard ground. I tried to drop my chin down into my jacket, chilled even further. It was too late to go back into the house for a scarf. I resigned myself to a freezing flight.

Fog hindered our journey from time to time, the dragon slowing her wing beats as she navigated through. Clearer sections revealed mostly empty grasslands. I looked down at the still frozen grass and didn't blame anyone for taking shelter under trees or rocks.

It was very different as we approached the city. The sudden cold snap this close to spring hadn't stopped merchants from setting up their stands near the river. The water was running deep and clear, and merpeople offered fish for sale from the banks. Smoke puffed into the air from nearby houses. I brightened as I realised that our destination was coming into view. Even if the welcome turned out not to be warm, at least the building would be.

The *tacsi* dragon landed in front of the five-storey mansion. I slapped life into my stiff legs before dismounting. Once on the path, I turned to the dragon. 'Thank you for a very smooth flight.'

She dipped her head in a brief nod. I stepped back as she crouched and leapt upwards.

I straightened and headed up to the house. The door opened before I even reached the steps. Fred Wiseman smiled, looking warm and comfortable in his shirt sleeves and trousers. 'Reverend. I'm so pleased you've taken up my invitation. Come on inside.'

The glory of central heating enfolded me as I joined him in the entrance hall. The were-bear I'd met on my previous visit hurried over to take my coat. I stuffed my gloves and hat into the pockets before allowing him to hang it up. A cup of coffee was pressed into my hand, and I took several grateful gulps.

'Leave some room for sherry,' Fred chuckled, an outthrown arm indicating that I should go down the left-hand corridor.

The sound of many human voices led me to a large room facing the front garden. Tables had been pushed together to make one long dining area. I decided that there must be around sixty people gathered by the windows, drinking amber liquid from small glasses as they chatted to one another. Not-weres bustled from the nearby kitchen, placing cutlery and plates on the white tablecloths.

'Dry or sweet?' Fred asked, escorting me to a nearby table laid out with bottles and goblets.

'Orange juice, please,' I responded, although not without a momentary pang of regret.

'How very healthy of you.' Fred poured me a drink and indicated the room. 'We try to come together every Sunday.'

'But this isn't everyone, is it?' I asked. 'I thought a lot more humans lived here.'

'Some people prefer to eat on their own, or they have Sunday jobs which keep them away.' Fred shrugged. 'And those who refuse to contribute to the community pot are only offered bread and cheese on Sundays.'

'Even if they're sick?'

'Oh, we take that sort of thing into account,' Fred said grandly. 'I'm talking about shirkers. Everyone who's fit, well, and able should pull their own weight.'

'Penny!' Gwen hurried over, sherry sloshing in her glass. 'Glad you could join us!'

The elderly woman's effusive welcome took me by surprise. 'Good to see you too,' I said as she gave me a half-embrace. A hint of perfume hovered around her immaculate grey hair and elegant blue cardigan.

The high-toned ringing of a small bell stilled conversation. 'Ladies and gentlemen, please take your seats,' a were-bear intoned. 'The first course is ready to be served.'

'With me,' Gwen insisted, placing her free hand on my arm.

There appeared to be no assigned seating. People simply settled themselves on the wooden chairs. I glanced around, and was pleased to find Mark. He was at the far end of the long table, so I would have to try to catch him after lunch.

Soup was brought out, filing the room with the smell of tomatoes. I was about to tuck in when Fred rose from his seat. 'Before we start, and since the Reverend has kindly joined us today, perhaps she would like to say Grace?'

Most of my fellow diners put down their utensils and closed their eyes with a grimace of resignation.

'Loving God,' I prayed, 'thank you for all of your good gifts to us. Bless this food to our use, and us to your service. Amen.'

A few 'Amen's rose in response. Then the clatter of spoons into bowls and new discussions filled the room. A were-wolf walked along the tables, offering either white or red wine. I opted for another orange juice.

'What have you been up to?' Gwen asked me. 'We've not seen you for some time.'

'I made a trip to Daear's equivalent of the USA,' I told her. 'I've been away on a ship for months.'

'And do I hear that you've married a dragon?'

I pulled back shirt sleeve and sweater to reveal the golden bracelet on my left wrist. 'Yes, I have. His name is Raven.'

'You're not worried about *Cadw ar Wahân?*'

'What have you heard about them?'

'An organisation which is against mixed-species relationships.' Gwen patted my hand. 'Not that we've had any trouble here, even though some of our members have started courting Lloegyr people. Fred thinks this is "going native", but it's none of his business so we just ignore him.'

I studied her carefully. *'We?'*

Her giggle was of a woman half her age. 'I've met quite a nice vampire. We've had a few lovely evenings out. Never expected to find romance at my time of life.'

'Good for you,' I said warmly. 'My brother has married a vampire. They've adopted a young girl.'

'If only we had more of these sorts of interactions between Lloegyr and Britain,' Gwen commented. 'I'm beginning to wonder why we've all felt we had to keep everything so secret.'

I lowered my voice. 'To keep Lloegyr safe, I've always thought. Fred was interested in taking over land for agriculture, for example. I'm worried that humans would end up exploiting this world.'

'The British don't have a good record when it comes to colonisation,' Gwen mused. 'But surely that's from a different era? I should hope that most of us wouldn't allow Lloegyr to be exploited. Not with today's concerns about the environment and the rights of indigenous people.'

We drifted into other topics as the main course, beef with rather flaccid Yorkshire puddings, was served. The gravy was a bit salty, but the roast potatoes were perfect. I enjoyed the contrast between crispy outside and the fluffy interior.

'And so it's not a bad life,' Gwen concluded after detailing her responsibilities as Fred's personal assistant. 'Goodness knows it's much less stressful than my job at Waters, Clueit, and Stephens. But I do miss my home in Norwich and my cats. My daughter's taken them in and she says they're fine, but she does ask questions I can't answer.'

'You've been communicating by rat?'

'Yes, for some time now. But we're careful what we say. Some people told their families the truth, and the government made life difficult when a few actually believed them and started asking questions.' Her mouth quirked. 'My daughter's convinced I'm running some sort of undercover operation for my old company, although she has a hard time working out how my letters to her just appear, and hers to me just disappear. She doesn't have the Sight.'

The delicious smell of chocolate made me lift my head. The dinner plates had been removed, and now the not-weres carried bowls of steaming desserts into the room. I sighed with appreciation as I dug my fork into the dark pudding.

'Sundays are rather special here,' Gwen said. 'We don't eat like this the rest of the week. It's more like cafeteria food Monday to Saturday. But I'm not complaining. It's wonderful not having to cook for myself. You can ask for seconds, you know.'

'I'd better not.' I patted my stomach. 'I can feel the calories starting to settle as it is.'

'That is the problem,' Gwen agreed. The were-wolf walked past, and she held up her glass for a refill of red wine. 'It's better now that spring's coming. I try to take a walk every day.'

I had kept an eye on Mark. Much to my delight, he regularly arranged for his wine to be topped up. I could only hope that this would make him more ready to talk after lunch. 'Exercise is important.'

People began to shove chairs back and place napkins beside their bowls. I rose to my feet and wandered over to the drinks table to pour myself some water. Much to my relief, no one seemed to be making quick dashes for the exits. Better yet, Mark himself was wandering over, his eyes fixed on the half-empty bottle of wine resting near the sherry.

'Hello, Penny,' he said as he helped himself to a drink. 'How are things?'

'Fine, all good with me. And with you?'

'Can't complain.' He wasn't slurring his words, but there were signs that he was rather merry. 'God business still working out for you?'

'Still plenty of opportunities for "God business" here in Lloegyr,' I agreed, keeping my tone light. 'What about your line of business? What was it again?'

'Defence procurement.' Mark took a swig of wine.

'Not much call for that in Lloegyr, I should think.'

'Oh, you'd be surprised.' He gave me a wink. 'Not everyone has great teeth and sharp claws. But that's what defence procurement is all about. Just levelling up the playing field so everyone can feel safe. Makes the world a more peaceful place.'

Somehow I managed not to splutter water all over him. Instead, I ended up coughing as liquid went down the wrong way. Mark kindly held my glass whilst I pulled out a handkerchief. 'Sorry,' I gasped.

'It happens,' he said. 'Can I get you anything else? Maybe something stronger?'

Whisky would be wonderful for my throat, but not for my sobriety. I fought back the all-too-familiar thrill of desire. 'I'll be okay.'

'It's not been too bad, spending time here,' Mark continued. 'I've learned a lot from working with Mr Wiseman. He's a great negotiator. You should see him go head to head with the Consortium. Me, I think I'd clam up around a rat king. But Mr Wiseman just takes them in his stride.'

'Rat kings can be a bit unsettling,' I managed to say.

'But great businessmen. Businesspeople? Businessrats?' Mark shrugged. 'Mr Wiseman says they're easier to work with than your average politician, at any rate. The Consortium's been pretty generous, I have to say that about him.'

I took back my water and managed a few slurps. 'To you?'

'Oh, it's been worth my while.' Mark grinned. 'The Consortium has been very appreciative of my advice. And my contacts in England.'

My ongoing voice difficulties kept me from demanding, *'And are you arranging for weapons to come to Lloegyr from England?'* Which was probably just as well. The Lord definitely worked in mysterious ways. 'Good.'

'Yes, all good.' Mark downed the rest of his wine. 'And it'll be even better when we can go back home. My boss has already promised me a promotion.'

Why did I think that rats would only be used for personal messages? Of course Mark would be in contact with his employers. I nodded enthusiastically. 'Congratulations.'

'Thanks,' Mark said happily. 'Well, it's been great seeing you again, Penny. Don't be a stranger.' And he wandered off.

There was still some wine left in the nearby bottle. I tore myself away from its siren call. Of course, I had no proof, no outright statement from

Mark that he was bringing weapons to Lloegyr. But there was enough in what he'd said that left me pretty certain that he was involved in plans to do so.

Coffee and tea was brought into the room. I claimed a cup of the latter, added milk, and walked over to Fred. He was talking to a young woman, and I hung back until they'd finished. 'Thanks for lunch,' I said. 'It's good to see how you are all doing. I'd better get back. Can someone send for a *tacsi* dragon?'

Fred raised a hand, and one of the not-weres drifted over. 'Not a problem. Where's your usual dragon?'

'Raven's temporarily unavailable,' I said. 'I have some coins with me.'

The man shook his head. 'You won't need those. We have an account with a local firm. Let's make sure you get home safely. You're the only reverend we have. We don't want to lose you.'

'That's very kind of you.' I hesitated, then added awkwardly, 'Particularly if you still want me to head up a church in your new town.'

'If we still need that new town.'

I softened my tone with a smile. 'Your plans have changed? Llanbedr isn't that bad after all?'

Fred tapped the side of his nose, and turned away to speak to someone else. I realised that I'd been dismissed. So I finished my tea, collected my coat, and went outside to await the arrival of the *tacsi* dragon. Although it was still cold outside, I'd suddenly had enough of being with the Firm.

I spent the rest of Sunday with Raven. By afternoon, sunshine had warmed the air enough that it was comfortable to sit outside. Revnassa came over to check his wing and general health, cheering Raven up by telling him that he should be able to fly 'slowly, cautiously' within another week. 'Don't strain the skin,' the unicorn warned him. 'If it splits, you'll be back to barn rest.'

'I hate being earth-bound,' Raven grumbled.

'Dragons are not known for their patience,' Revnassa commented. 'I suggest you do your best to cultivate some.'

'You'll be back in the air soon enough,' I said as the medic trotted away. 'Let's not push it.'

Raven rustled his wings. 'I don't like you using *tacsi* dragons.'

'It won't be for much longer,' I reminded him. 'And it's not like any of them can match you.'

'Certainly not.' Raven brought his head closer to mine. 'Bastien came to my barn this morning.'

I lowered my voice. 'You were able to have a chat?'

'Of course. We've been friends for some time.' Raven sighed. 'He feels age creeping into his bones. Flight is becoming painful for him. He thinks he will not see another winter.'

'And Jago?'

'He wants to enjoy his time with Jago, rather than plunge him into worry before it's necessary.'

I shook my head. 'I don't think that's fair to Jago.'

'I can understand Bastien's point of view,' Raven said. 'Perhaps because it is so close to mine.'

'So you think we should let Bastien decide when to tell Jago.'

'I do indeed.'

'That might not go down well with Taryn and Morey,' I pointed out.

'Who has the greater right in these circumstances?' Raven asked. 'The parents, or the fiancé?'

'Good question.' I glanced at my wristwatch. 'I'm on duty for Evensong, so I'd better go. Do you need some help getting back into the barn?'

Raven arched his neck. 'Not at all.' Slowly, with great care, he half-folded his injured wing along his back. I smiled as he walked himself back to his accommodation. It was good to see that he was indeed healing. I could only hope he'd be patient and not push himself too far when he once again could take to the air.

I went to the house and divested myself of coat and shoes at the front door. My clerical robes were hung up in my flat, so I headed up the creaking stairs. When I unlocked the door and pushed it open, I was taken aback to see Cornelius standing next to Clyde on the settee.

'How did you get in?' I demanded.

'Clyde opened the door for me,' the mantis replied calmly. 'And good afternoon to you, too.'

I glanced down at the clever contraption the locksmith had put into place to enable the snail to open the door from the inside. 'And to what do we owe the pleasure of your company?'

'I thought it was about time I caught up with Clyde.'

The snail's colours swirled blue and pink. 'Friend.'

'I'm glad you two had a chance to spend time together.' I forced myself to smile. 'Could I ask you to wrap it up? I need to change for Evensong.'

'Don't mind me,' Cornelius said grandly. 'I'll turn around.'

'Actually, I do mind,' I replied. 'I'd rather dress in private.'

Cornelius flexed his forelegs. 'That's certainly a lady's prerogative. It was good for me to spend time with a friend.'

I felt a pang of guilt. 'I'm going to go brush my teeth. You can have a few more minutes yet. I'll leave the door open so you can see yourself out.'

'I was just fixin' to go,' Cornelius said. Then he cocked his head. 'By the way, is this place here haunted? I've heard some voices coming, well, I'd say through the wall.'

Despite regular reminders, my brother and his family still seemed to forget that we only had a couple of pieces of furniture to deaden noises from each other's flat. 'Morey and Taryn are next door,' I said quickly. 'And, like all married couples, sometimes they have rows.'

I grabbed my toiletries bag and headed off to the bathroom. After a bit of a clean up, I felt better and ready to face Evensong. I rinsed the sink and headed back into the hallway.

Clyde was waiting for me outside the room. 'Cornelius. Friend.'

The door was nearly shut, and I quickly pulled it open. I'd left my key on the desk. 'Really?' I glanced into the flat, but the mantis was nowhere to be seen. He must have left the room with the snail shark. I followed Clyde inside and closed the door. 'He didn't show any loyalty to you when you were in charge of the Nation.'

'Stopped Nation.'

'He went to the Community for his own selfish reasons.' I pulled on my black cassock and concentrated on doing up the buttons. The surplice went over the top, and I smoothed down the thin white fabric. I draped the black stole over my arm. The scarf was just a bit long, and I didn't want to risk tripping over it as I went back down the stairs. 'Come on. Time for Evensong.'

Chapter Nineteen

Leaning back in my chair, I sipped at my coffee and smiled at my fellow ministers. Breakfast was becoming my favourite meal. Llewelyn had somehow managed to staff St Raphael's with morning people, and they all sparkled as toast and bacon was brought in. I had finally memorised all of their names, and even most of their biographies. Although it had taken a while, I was starting to feel comfortable around them.

We went together to the chapel for Morning Prayer. Llewelyn led the service, and I felt the calming words of Psalm 121 wash over me. 'The Lord is your keeper; the Lord is your shade at your right hand. The sun shall not strike you by day, nor the moon by night. The Lord will keep you from all evil; he will keep your life. The Lord will keep your going out and your coming in from this time on and forevermore.'

Morey led the intercessions. In the midst of naming those who particularly needed our prayers, Miriam burst into the room. 'Dr Wyn, Fathers, everyone, I'm sorry, but you need to come outside now.'

The were was shifting between human and bear in her distress, the size difference threatening to tear apart her shirt and trousers. I rose from my seat and hurried down the corridor, Morey landing on my shoulder as I reached the door. Llewelyn had been quicker, and he was already pulling it open. Shoving my feet into boots and grabbing my coat, I followed him outside, the rest of our group close behind me.

Miriam rushed past us and led the way around the building. Once the barns came into view, I stopped so suddenly that one of my fellow ministers bumped into me. My attention was fixed on the red letter painted on each of the barns' wooden sides. Stylised 'W's bristled in the morning light.

'Cadw ar Wahân,' Morey said grimly. 'There's a mark I'd hoped to never see again.'

'But not here,' Llewelyn was muttering. 'It was never supposed to come here.'

Fear tightened my chest. I'd not fastened up my boots, and they threatened to trip me up as I raced over to Raven's barn. 'Raven? Raven? Are you all right?' I yanked the door open.

The dragon raised his head from his forelegs, blinking in the light. 'Why wouldn't I be?'

Morey flew over to land by his claws. '*Cadw ar Wahân* visited St Raphael's during the night. They've left their symbol on all of the barns.'

Raven snorted. 'I'm more than a match for *Cadw ar Wahân*.'

'I'd rather not have to test that,' I said worriedly. 'Remember that they've used poison in the past.'

The dragon lifted his injured wing. 'We could leave here, once I'm healed. *Cadw ar Wahân* won't be able to touch us at the search dragons' settlement.'

'Let's not do anything hasty,' Morey said. 'This is exactly the sort of reaction a terrorist would want people to have. We need to keep calm and think through how to best protect people here at Saint Raphael's.'

'I'd be happy to take all those who feel unsafe somewhere else to live,' Raven said. 'All they need to do is ask.'

I shook my head. 'That's very kind of you, but I'm not certain that's the answer. People have lives here, ones they might not want to give up. I know they're your type of dragon, Raven, and you have a place there, but I'm not certain whether I'd want to live in the search dragon settlement.'

'It'd be useful to know,' Morey continued, 'whether Saint Raphael's has been singled out, or if *Cadw ar Wahân* have spread their particular type of cheer further afield. Taryn should be able to tell us when she returns from Llanbedr this evening.'

My loose boots were beginning to bother me. I bent down to lace them up. 'In the meantime, I guess we'd best carry on with our usual duties.'

'Yes,' Morey agreed. 'Otherwise the terrorists win.'

I walked to Raven and buried my face in his neck. He smelled of fresh grass and woodsmoke, and the familiar scent steadied my heart. 'Nothing will happen to either of us,' he rumbled. 'I won't let it.'

'I know you won't,' I said with more confidence than I felt. I forced myself to let him go. 'I'll come back later.'

Morey returned to my shoulder as I headed outside. Llewelyn was standing nearby, his gaze fixed on the nearest 'W'. People were already at work, standing on ladders as they scrubbed rags against the paint.

'We need to make sure everyone stays calm,' Morey told the were-wolf. 'It might be a good idea to call a general meeting, maybe later on this morning? Just to reassure everyone that there's no need for panic.'

'There is no need for panic,' Llewelyn agreed. He rested balled hands on his hips. 'I suggest we all attend to our morning duties. We'll have that meeting just before lunch. Perhaps by then I will have managed to think of what to say.'

As he strode away, I muttered to Morey, 'He seems thrown by this.'

'Didn't we all think mixed-species couples would be safe here?'

'I never did.' I shivered, and Morey's claws dug deep into my coat. '*Cadw ar Wahân* managed to kill Odlia, even though she was far away in the Arctic with her husband. Whoever *Cadw ar Wahân* are, I'm not certain anyone's safe from them.'

All those who wished to hear Llewelyn's address were invited to come to the area outside the main building at 11.30am. A bell was rung five minutes beforehand for the many who didn't wear watches.

The not-weres who left barns, fields, and corrals to make their way over to the already gathered ministry team looked calm enough. A few flicking ears and extended nostrils spoke of fear, but those were in the minority. *Most of them aren't in mixed-species relationships,* I reminded myself. *They don't have any personal reason to be concerned.* For a moment I wished that Raven had come as well, although he had explained to me that it would have been too painful for his wing to walk that far.

Llewelyn waited until the last of the stragglers had made it to the meeting. Because I was standing only a few feet away, I could hear him saying the psalm from Morning Prayer under his breath. Then, as all faces turned towards him, he raised his voice. '"The Lord will keep you from all evil; he will keep your life. The Lord will keep your going out and your coming in from this time on and forevermore." My friends, we have seen evil in our midst today. An evil which denies that diversity should be celebrated, that difference is to be enjoyed rather than feared. This group, which calls themselves *Cadw ar Wahân,* came like cowards in the night to place their contemptible mark on the buildings of our community.'

'Who is this *Cadw ar Wahân?*' a were-sheep asked.

'An organization which is against people of different species coming to love one another, and who decide to celebrate that love by the sacrament of marriage.' Llewelyn nodded at a couple who stood nearby. 'For example, in our own community we have Aldona and Halwyn, whose wedding was held here only last year. Father Penny and Raven have also entered holy matrimony. *Cadw ar Wahân* condemns these relationships.'

'Their marriages have nothing to do with *Cadw ar Wahân,*' a were-bear growled. 'Let them come here in daylight, and give me a reason to test my teeth and claws.'

'They are cowards who prefer to cause fear rather than face anyone openly,' Llewelyn said. 'How do we fight them? Not with teeth and claws. No, we fight them by remaining true to our calling as Christians. We extend the love of Christ to everyone, regardless of their species or whom they choose to wed.'

'But they won't hurt people who keep to their own kind?' a were-wolf asked.

'They never have, but that's not the point,' Morey snapped. 'We can't let them set us against each other. That's how they'll win.'

'I'll support whatever you decide, Dr Wyn,' a were-sheep said. 'If you want the couples to stay, then just say so.'

'Of course they are to stay,' the chaplain said. 'They are part of our community.'

'But if they might bring danger to us--'

'They are the ones in danger,' Miriam retorted, standing tall and grim at Llewelyn's side. 'And we will shelter them here, even as Saint Raphael's has always offered welcome to anyone who seeks our help.'

Some of the not-weres looked unconvinced. I was trying to decide whether I should try to add something when a were-horse lifted her head. 'Dragon incoming.'

The yellow dragon bore the saddle of a *tacsi*, but seemed to be without a passenger. As he drew near, however, I saw that a red squirrel clung to the seat. The flat ears and drawn in tail led me to suspect that she wasn't used to flying.

The dragon circled once, head sweeping from side to side. He tipped a wing, and came down to the left of the gathering. As soon as he touched the ground, the squirrel called out. 'Father Penny! Father Penny! Could you please come to the Bishop's Palace as soon as possible? Bishop Aeron needs to see you.'

Morey's claws dug into my shoulder as he called out, 'Does she want both of us, or only Penny?'

The squirrel rose to her hind legs. 'She only asked for Father Penny.'

I nodded over at Jago and Bastien, who were huddled together on the nearby rocks. 'You stay and talk to those two. I'll go see what the Bishop wants.' I raised my voice to address the squirrel. 'Give me a moment to grab a few things, and I'll be with you.'

Ten minutes later, I mounted the *tacsi* dragon. The squirrel placed herself behind me, riding on the saddle's cantle. I glanced at the broken clouds above, noted the lack of wind, and hoped that the calm conditions would follow us to Llanbedr.

The fields, forests, and signs of habitation as we approached the city were familiar landmarks which I used to count off the time. As we flew along the river, I knew that something was amiss. The market stalls were out, people walked the streets, but at a much-reduced level of noise. The traders sounded almost apologetic as they mentioned their wares. Those striding past seemed to be avoiding each other's eyes. I shifted uneasily in my seat.

The cathedral came into view. As the dragon took us down to land by the

Bishop's Palace, I noted the lack of visitors on the cathedral green. A hush seemed to hover over the city, and I found myself suppressing a shudder.

The *tacsi* dragon was smaller than Raven, and I took a moment to judge the distance to the ground before I dismounted. A lifetime of being polite to bus drivers made me turn my head to say, 'Thank you.' Then I lifted up my arms, offering the squirrel a lift down.

The large door to the Palace opened as I followed the squirrel across the cobblestones. Aldred stood inside. Although he was the same yellow as the *tacsi* dragon, he was nearly a third larger. The twist in his ears and horns made me straighten and slow my strides. The body language of the Bishop's chaplain told me that he was very worried about something.

'Father Penny, many thanks for abandoning your duties to come to the Palace,' he said as I stepped inside. 'The Bishop is waiting for you in her office. I'll send in a pot of coffee.'

'I'll take care of that,' the squirrel squeaked, hurrying off across the tiled floor.

I made my way down the hallway. The door to the Bishop's office was ajar, and the scent of smoke trickled through the air. I wasn't surprised, as I knocked on the heavy wood and entered, that Bishop Aeron looked as concerned as her chaplain. Even her red-orange hide seemed to have paled.

'Father Penny, I am grateful for your quick response,' the dragon said. 'Is everything well at Saint Raphael's?'

'The usual things going on, dealing with not-weres…' I trailed off as an elf brought in a chair and indicated that I was to use it. 'Okay. No, it's not. *Cadw ar Wahân* left their mark on our barns last night.'

'It wasn't only Saint Raphael's which they targeted,' Bishop Aeron growled. 'Their symbol was painted on buildings across the city. Communities known to have mixed-species couples were singled out. The cathedral and all of our churches were left untouched.'

I managed to bite back the first three comments which came to mind. 'Congratulations.'

'I read nothing good into our escape. The Church does not agree with the persecution of those who marry outside of their own kind.'

'But you don't allow those marriages either,' I pointed out. 'No wonder *Cadw ar Wahân* doesn't see the Church as a threat. In fact, they might even see you as allies.'

'"You"?' The Bishop lowered her head to mine. 'Not "we"?'

'In this issue,' I said firmly, rising from the chair, 'I'm not in accord with the Church, so I am not one of you.'

Bishop Aeron studied me. The elf returned with a small table and then a tray. The smell of freshly brewed coffee eased through the smoky scent of annoyed dragon. I waited until I'd poured myself a mug before sitting again.

'We have our theological differences,' the Bishop acknowledged. 'But that does not mean that I support the stance of *Cadw ar Wahân*. The Church does not accept prejudice.'

'But you won't let me serve as a parish priest,' I said. 'Not now that I'm married to a dragon.'

'A higher standard is expected of clergy.'

'I've never understood that argument.' I took a sip of coffee, forcing myself to swallow yet more words. 'What's been the reaction in Llanbedr? It did seem a bit quiet as I flew in.'

'I fear for this city,' Bishop Aeron said quietly. 'I fear for this country. *Cadw ar Wahân* left their mark across Lloegyr. My fellow bishops report of panics in some communities, the arming of others. Here in Llanbedr, the council will be meeting at three this afternoon to discuss the situation. Are you still one of the human representatives?'

'I think so,' I replied. 'I know I've been out of the country for a while, but no one's told me that I'm not.'

'No doubt the council is arranging for rats to be sent,' the Bishop continued. 'I wanted to meet with you beforehand to discuss how you can best represent the Church's stance.'

I bought some time by drinking from my mug. 'I don't represent the Church.'

'Not officially, perhaps. But the council knows that you're a priest. You are in a position to speak on our behalf.'

'To say what?'

'That the Church does not condone any acts against those in mixed-species relationships.'

'Oh, yes, I'm sure that'll help,' I retorted. 'The average person will clearly understand that the Church isn't prejudiced, even though it won't ordain anyone in a mixed-species marriage. Is this your version of "Hate the sin, love the sinner?" Because, from where I'm sitting, it doesn't much feel like love.'

A small curl of smoke rose from her nostrils. 'We obviously continue to disagree on this matter. I've studied the theological issues in great depth. Have you?'

I placed the empty mug on the table and stared into her large eyes. 'If I had, I'm certain it would have given me great comfort when my life and those of people I love are in danger.'

A long silence. I was determined that Bishop Aeron would have to be the one to break it. She finally spoke. 'Please make it clear that the Church condemns any hostility shown to mixed-species couples.'

I nodded. 'I will do. Anything else, my Lord Bishop?'

The dragon growled. 'I have already accepted quite a bit of disrespect from you today, Father Penny. Don't push me too far. You may doubt this, but we are on the same side.'

She was right. I rubbed my aching forehead. 'Sorry. To you, all this might

THE HUMILITY OF HUMANS

be academic--'

'Whilst you and those close to you are at risk,' Bishop Aeron said sympathetically. 'As I've said, we are on the same side. Please do what you can to impress upon the council that vulnerable people must be protected. Tell them that the Church will work alongside anyone with that goal in mind.'

'I will.' I took a deep breath. 'We're on the same side.'

'Precisely.' Her ears and horns straightened. 'We must do what we can to prevent panic and to provide reassurance. My chaplain is preparing a message which all clergy are to deliver this coming Sunday. Whereas we do not approve of mixed-species relationships, we are firmly against any abuse of couples in such relationships.'

'When I visited Durham Cathedral, a few years ago,' I said slowly, 'I was shown their sanctuary knocker. Centuries ago, anyone who was on the run could rap the knocker, and the cathedral would let them in so they had protection from the mob chasing them. It gave time for heads to cool and for them to establish their innocence.'

'Taken from Numbers 35, no doubt. God instructed Moses to designate asylum-cities.'

For a moment she reminded me of Morey. 'I was just wondering whether our churches could be known as places of sanctuary. Anyone feeling in danger from *Cadw ar Wahân* could come to their nearest church for shelter.'

The Bishop cocked her head. 'You're asking our members to put themselves at risk?'

'Sometimes words aren't enough,' I said. 'Sometimes we need to take action as well.'

'I can understand your concern, in your own personal circumstances.'

'There's a saying where I come from. The difference between being involved and being committed is like bacon and eggs. The chicken is involved. The pig is committed.' I sighed. 'Raven and I are the pigs.'

Bishop Aeron snorted. 'I shouldn't say that to his snout.'

'I have no intention of doing so,' I said dryly. 'I value my marriage.'

'Good to hear.' The Bishop raised her head. 'I should like to hear the outcome from the council meeting, if you are able to return to the Palace afterwards. If not, please give your report to a squirrel.'

'Not rat?'

'I've decided not to expose Church business to the rat kings.' The curl in her horns warned me against asking any questions. Her tone softened. 'I know that this is a frightening time for anyone who feels targeted by *Cadw ar Wahân*. I am your bishop, Penny, and therefore your Father-in-God. You only need ask, and we will find a place of safety for you and Raven.'

Some of the tension eased from my shoulders and I rose from my chair. 'Thank you. I'll do my best at the council.'

It was good to leave the Palace for the fresh air outside. The *tacsi* dragon was curled up on the grass, snoring softly. I glanced at my wristwatch. One o'clock. No point trying to go back to Saint Raphael's. I might as well stay in Llanbedr and return after the council meeting. But how to let the *tacsi* dragon know?

I returned to the now-closed door to the Palace. At my knock, a squirrel leapt up to the small window set into the thick wood. 'If the *tacsi* dragon asks where I am,' I said, projecting my voice, 'tell him that I'm attending a council meeting at 3pm. He doesn't have to wait for me, I'll arrange for another to take me back to Saint Raphael's.'

'His name is Huw,' the squirrel replied equally loudly, pointing at the sleeping dragon. 'He works for the Bishop. Come back here after the meeting, and he'll take you home.'

'Home.' And where exactly was my home now? 'Thank you. I'll come back here.'

As I walked over to the green grass which fronted the Cathedral, I had a moment's panic as I wondered if I could find the way to the Guildhall in which the council met. Perhaps I should return and awaken the *tacsi* dragon to give me a lift. But even as I pondered my options, a black rat swooped through the air to land at my feet.

'A message for Father Penny White,' the rat announced. She rose up to her hind legs, dark wings sweeping out behind her. 'Father Penny White, vicar of the Church Divine, you are summoned to a council meeting, and three o'clock is the time.'

I sighed. 'Do you think that maybe, one day, I'll be deemed worthy to receive a limerick? Or at least a haiku?'

The rat sniffed. 'No. Never.'

Well, that told me. 'Can you at least give me directions to the Guildhall from here?'

Her dark eyes glittered as she cocked her head. 'I will return to be your guide. Don't worry, there's no place you can hide.'

Then she was gone. My stomach growled, and I headed away from the Cathedral in search of some lunch. I'd not taken the time to pack anything before leaving Saint Raphael's, but I did have a few coins in a coat pocket.

I made my way down to the river. Various buildings had been marked with the 'W' of *Cadw ar Wahân*. Those who were scrubbing at the paint did so with grim determination. Passersby altered their steps to give a wide berth to any business which had been singled out. I bit back my anger, reminding myself that a lot of that came from fear.

The smell of roasting meat drew me towards the food booths set up on the pathways near the riverbanks. A number of vendors shouted out their wares, all of which were, of course, 'the best in Llanbedr.' Sausages sizzled on grills, steam rose from freshly baked bread, and the carcass of a large animal was cooking over a massive spit.

One stall was, in contrast, quiet and uncrowded. As I drew near, I saw the *Cadw ar Wahân* mark painted on the dark wooden sides. The proprietor stood behind a counter loaded with pies. Although he looked human, his hair and side-burns were the striped black and white of a badger's head.

'Hello,' I said, wandering closer. 'What fillings do you offer?'

'Eel, snail, or cockles.'

None of the options sounded appealing, but I was not going to walk away. I decided to go for the least worst option. 'Cockles, please.'

The were-badger bundled a pie into a paper bag. I placed a copper coin into his wide, hairy palm. 'Cockles harvested fresh this morning,' he said gruffly as he gave me my change.

A movement at the back caught my eye. An elf was working at the stove, stirring ingredients in a large pot. 'Is that your husband?'

'Yes.' The were-badger glared at me. 'What of it?'

I pulled back my left sleeve to show him my wedding bracelet. 'I'm married to a dragon.'

The elf abandoned his cooking and hurried to join the were-badger. 'Don't speak so loudly,' he hissed. 'It's not safe for people like us right now.'

'And it should be,' I said boldly. 'I'm going to the council meeting this afternoon. Officially I'm there to represent humans, but I'll also speak up on behalf of us who are in mixed-species relationships. We deserve to live without fear or harassment.'

'How long have you lived in Lloegyr?' the elf asked. 'How many years?'

'Not years,' I admitted. 'Months, here and there.'

'Then you don't know,' the were-badger said. 'The prejudice runs deep.'

'But things can change,' I persisted. 'And if we don't try, if we just give up, then we'll never see change.'

The elf gave me a quick smile. 'Your hope is to be admired. We wish you well.'

I nodded and wandered off with my pie. The crust was pleasantly crunchy, and the cockles were mixed in with pieces of potato and chunks of carrot. It made for a warming meal as I watched merpeople splashing in the river.

Some while later, whilst I was looking at a fabric stall, the rat swooped down to land on my shoulder. 'Time to show you where to go.'

'If I brushed up on my Shakespeare,' I asked, 'would I at least be worthy of a sonnet?'

The rat studied me for a moment, then chuckled. '"When to the sessions of sweet silent thought, I summon up remembrance of things past, I sigh the lack of many a thing I sought, And with old woes new wail my dear time's waste."'

'Oh, very cheering,' I grumped. 'Which way to the Guildhall?'

The rat directed me away from the river. I began to recognise some of the buildings as we drew near to our destination. The impressive meeting house for the city council hulked at the end of the street. The lead-paned windows, set in brown stone, gleamed in the afternoon sun. The height of the three storeys were tall enough to allow dragons inside.

The square in front of the Guildhall was sparsely occupied, with only a few Llanbedr citizens waiting to enter through the large front door. The rat took off as I joined the other councillors, not even giving me a chance to thank her. As we started to file inside, I removed my coat, grimacing at the blood stains which darkened the leather. Pity I hadn't dressed in something smarter than my grey sweater.

My shoes squeaked on the bright stones of the entrance hall. The white hides of the unicorns gleamed against the dark wood of the walls. I took a deep breath of the mixed scents of smoke, wax, and fur. The temperature inside was about the same as outdoors, and my hands began to chill. I decided that warmth was more important than image, and I pulled my coat back on.

I walked past the blue dragons which guarded at the end of the lobby. The council chamber extended the full width of the Guildhall, offering plenty of room for the gathered representatives. Through the clear glass windows I could see spring flowers in regimented beds, interspersed between bushes cropped into the shapes of vases and cubes.

The room filled. Each species was represented by two of their members, except for those such as merpeople who couldn't easily leave their watery environment. About thirty people spread across the tiled floor, smaller citizens taking advantage of the raised platforms set against the wooden walls.

Conversation ceased as an elf rapped the floor with his staff. 'I declare this special meeting of the Llanbedr City Council open,' he said in Welsh. 'Any members new to our gathering?'

'Sorry, everyone, I was held up by other business.' Fred Wiseman breezed in, looking immaculate in a dark business suit. 'May I ask that the session be held in English? I've been learning Welsh, but it really is a bugger of a language, isn't it?'

I quickly rubbed my face to hide a wince. As Fred came to my side, I whispered to him, 'I thought you'd decided council meetings were a waste of time?'

'I still can't stand this lot,' Fred replied. 'But I realised I'd rather be inside the tent than outside, if you catch my drift.'

'English it will be,' the elf said crisply, over a smattering of protests. 'Otherwise, as we well remember, the human representative will insist on translation, and none of us wish a long meeting. Do we?'

The murmurs died away. I felt my face warm as people glared at us both. This was not starting well. I could only hope that being the same species as Fred didn't sour our fellow councillors against me.

'This extraordinary meeting is called,' the elf continued, 'to discuss the overnight actions of the organisation which names itself *Cadw ar Wahân.*'

'Is that why we're here?' one of the dragons grumbled. 'I thought it was for something important.'

'It is important,' a were-sheep said indignantly, her long white hair floating around her slumped shoulders. 'Their horrible sign was painted on our houses.'

The dragon lifted his purple head and snorted. 'You have mixed-species marriages in your community? You should have known better.'

'Many of us have members who've married out,' a vampire said, lips curling away from his sharp teeth. 'My own daughter has. And her house was marked with their odious sign.'

'Then expel them,' the dragon retorted. 'Problem over.'

'I'm not about to expel my own daughter!'

'It's fine for you,' the were-sheep told the dragon. 'You have teeth and claws and flame. You can defend yourselves.'

The dragon's tail slapped the floor. 'Maybe you should learn how to use a sword.'

'I have something better than that.' The were-sheep reached into her coat pocket and pulled out a handgun. Light glinted along the metal barrel. 'I have this.'

Chapter Twenty

Fred and I were the only two in the chamber to freeze in place. The other councillors merely stared at the weapon. 'And what's that?' a dwarf asked. 'A short club?'

'Much more than that,' the were-sheep retorted, waving the gun around. 'With this, we won't have to be afraid of anyone ever again.'

'Please put that down,' I said, fighting to keep my voice calm. Was there any way to tell if a pistol were cocked and loaded?

The were-sheep turned towards me. A short curse slipped from Fred's lips, and he backed away. 'See,' she commented, 'the humans know what this is, and what it can do.'

I stood my ground, although every instinct screamed for me to drop to the floor. All sorts of images from movies and TV programmes swirled in my head. 'A gun can maim and it can kill, even by accident. Please, put it down.'

'We're tired of being seen as weak and defenceless,' the were-sheep continued. 'Never again.'

'With that thing?' a were-fox scoffed. 'That's too small to hurt anyone.'

'We'll only use them if we have to.' The were-sheep was still motioning with the pistol, and my stomach clenched as the barrel swept past me. 'So this is your warning, if any of you are thinking of coming after our flocks. We are armed. We are prepared.'

Her hand closed on the trigger. I felt more than saw Fred drop to the floor. The gun fired, the retort echoing through the chamber. The were-fox grunted as a hole opened in his chest and blood sprayed through the air. A moment later he was sprawled across the ground, his long howl of pain breaking the shocked silence.

'Quick!' I shouted at the two unicorns. 'He needs healing!'

They charged over, then hesitated. 'We've been too long in the city,' one said, tossing his head. 'Without connection to the land, we lose our powers.'

The staff-carrying elf exited the room, calling out, 'Medic! We need the medic!'

All the other counsellors stood still, even the were-sheep looking shocked as she looked down at the injured were-fox. I forced life into my legs and stumbled forward, tugging my coat from my shoulders. Warm blood soaked into my trousers as I knelt on the floor and pressed my jacket against the were-fox's side, trying to stanch the flow from the ragged wound.

The clatter of hooves against stone and tile made me look up. The unicorn charged into the room, counsellors darting out of her way. I scrambled backwards, clearing the area for her to work. She flicked my coat to one side, took a deep breath, and lowered her gleaming horn to the were-fox.

I collected my bloody jacket and rose to my feet. The were-sheep stared at me, pistol hanging limply from her fingers. Too angry to be afraid, I strode to her side and snatched the weapon from her hand. 'This,' I declared, 'is how even a small gun can bring down a were, vampire, elf, or dwarf. And there are larger weapons as well, called rifles, which can kill gryphons or dragons.'

'You seem to know a lot about these guns,' a vampire said. 'Do they come from your world?'

'This one certainly did.' I placed it carefully on the floor, uncertain how it was meant to be disarmed. Pity Peter wasn't here to take the gun into safekeeping. He would have known what to do with it. As I straightened, I had the strong desire to wash the metallic feel from my blood-caked hands.

'How many of you here present carry one of these devices?' the elf demanded, holding up his staff. 'Declare it now.'

Gryphons, unicorns, and dragons, who wore no clothing, merely looked at him. Others shook their heads. 'We prefer daggers and short swords,' a dwarf said. 'Fighting hand to hand, that's our way.'

'No weapons are allowed into council meetings,' the elf stated. 'That has always been a council rule, and the rule must be maintained.'

'Not fair to people like us,' the were-sheep complained. 'We have no way to defend ourselves.'

'Why would you need to defend yourself here?' a vampire asked. 'I've been a councillor for ten years now. This body has always discussed matters in a civilized fashion. Until today, no blood has ever been shed in this chamber.'

All voices stilled as the medic shuddered and backed away. The were-fox whimpered as he slowly and carefully sat up. 'I have managed to repair the damage,' the unicorn said, weaving on her hooves. 'But there was great blood loss.'

'And there was a great cost to yourself,' said one of the other unicorns. 'Please accept our thanks, and go take some rest.'

The medic stumbled away. A gryphon went over to the were-fox and held out her foreleg. The were-fox grabbed the yellow talons and pulled himself to his feet. 'That attack,' he hissed at the were-sheep, 'was unprovoked and will not go unavenged.'

I stepped forward. 'It was an accident. That bullet could have hit any of us.'

A unicorn snorted agreement. 'As far as I'm aware, there's no enmity between the were-sheep and the were-foxes. I agree with the human representative. This was an unfortunate incident, surely no malice intended. May we return to the business for which we were summoned?'

The elf rapped his staff on the floor. 'I call for a return to our proceedings. We are here to discuss the overnight actions of the organisation which names itself *Cadw ar Wahân.*'

'They're a threat to us,' the were-sheep said. 'A number of flock members have married out.'

'How is this council business?' the purple dragon demanded. 'These threats from *Cadw ar Wahân* only affect some communities, and then only a few in those communities. The answer is clear.'

'Which is?' I asked.

The dragon snorted. 'Expel those who have "married out". Then *Cadw ar Wahân* will have no reason to threaten the rest.'

The were-sheep marched up to the dragon. 'I'm not surprised to hear you say that. After all, you're a species which eats your own children. We value everyone in our flock. That's why we will defend them.'

'If that's your decision,' a were-badger said, 'you'll just have to live with the consequences.'

'Precisely.' Fred nodded at the badger and the dragon. 'Each race has to fend for themselves. You all made that perfectly clear to us humans. This isn't any different.'

I stepped away from my fellow representative. 'There's always been tension between the different species, which is understandable. Each of your communities have their own culture and customs. But I believe that we all have certain values in common, values which have enabled all of us to live together in this city of Llanbedr. I had thought that one of those values was respect for common decency, which is why dragons don't prey on weres, and vampires feed on animal blood or solid food. Shouldn't that common decency, the impulse to make sure everyone feels safe in this city, extend to anyone who feels threatened by *Cadw ar Wahân?*'

'You would say that,' a dwarf muttered. 'You're married to a dragon, aren't you?'

Fred glanced at me. 'I've wondered how that works.'

'I've long supported mixed-species relationships,' I continued, although I felt my face warm. 'And this council should, too. Aren't we here to serve all of the communities in Llanbedr, not just the ones which we represent?'

The dragon growled. 'We have our own people to think about.'

'Of course you do,' Fred said smoothly. 'At times like these, when you're under threat, that's the best thing to do. I'm very grateful that the Reverend doesn't live here in Llanbedr. I'm certain she and her husband feel much safer outside the city.'

'It's not like we chose to live outside of Llanbedr,' I said. 'I've been ministering at Saint Raphael's for longer than I've been married to Raven. And being outside the city didn't stop *Cadw ar Wahân* from painting their symbol on the buildings at Saint Raphael's. We're no safer there than here.'

'They can go back to their mountains and forests and fields,' the dragon growled. 'Send all those couples back to their original lands. Let *Cadw ar Wahân* pursue them, or leave them to live in peace. But that removes any reason for them to interfere with lives here in Llanbedr.'

'We do not eject people from our flock,' the were-sheep retorted.

The rapping of wood on tile brought our attention back to the elf. 'Many of our communities were targeted by *Cadw ar Wahân*. What should be our response? That is the reason for this meeting today.'

'Send them away,' the dragon said. 'Rid ourselves of the problem.'

'Defend them,' the were-sheep declared. 'It doesn't matter who they love, these people are still members of our families, and part of our flocks.'

'That's a noble thought, "defend them",' Fred said. 'But what if graffiti is only the beginning?'

A vampire nodded. 'This could be just an early warning. Who knows what *Cadw ar Wahân* might do next?'

'That's why we all need to come together,' I insisted. 'If all of our communities present a united front, if we all say that prejudice won't be tolerated, *Cadw ar Wahân* will realise that they can't intimidate us into sacrificing people.'

'Not all of us have to worry about *Cadw ar Wahân*,' a were-hedgehog said. 'Let the species with people who've married out worry about them. Some of our communities have enough problems as it is, without trying to take on those of others.'

'Precisely,' Fred agreed. 'Why should dragons care what happens to sheep? Or hedgehogs about gryphons? You all have your own people to think about.'

'Which is why,' the were-sheep said, pointing at the gun gleaming on the white tiles, 'we need those.'

'Surely the purpose of this chamber,' I asked desperately, 'is to help all of Llanbedr's citizens to work together?'

'We coordinate when policies which affect all have to be decided,' the elf said. 'But that is all.'

'Seems to me,' a vampire said, 'that we've come to a conclusion. If you're worried about members of your colony, then it's up to your people to decide whether you defend them or exile them. Whatever *Cadw ar Wahân* decides to do, it's not council business.'

I tried to think of something I could say, a way to change their minds. But even as I opened my mouth, the elf struck his staff against the floor. 'This emergency session is concluded. Rats will be sent should we need to meet again. Let us sing our usual song to our city, in your preferred language.'

The sound of voices, in a mixture of English and Welsh, filled the chamber in response. The unicorn nearest me sang out the English version.

> '"Llanbedr, Llanbedr our city so fair
> Fairest city in the world!
> We give you our lives and our work
> All the best of our hopes and dreams.
> Let us never be found wanting
> But always to strive unceasing
> To live side by side in harmony.
> Llanbedr, Llanbedr, the city we love
> Let us be the people you deserve."'

As the last notes died away, Fred retrieved the gun. His hands moved quickly and confidently over the weapon, and a moment later the unused bullets fell into his palm. He handed the gun to the were-sheep, but slid the bullets into his pocket, although he bent his head close to the sheep and whispered something into her ear. I gritted my teeth, too far away to hear what he was saying.

The blood on my trousers and jacket was drying and stiffening the fabric. As we shuffled out of the chamber, I forced myself to put on the coat. The temperature outside had fallen during proceedings, and a chill wind blew along the street.

I grabbed at Fred's arm as he tried to walk past me. 'What was all that about?' I asked him. 'Do you really want to see people in Llanbedr fighting each other?'

He smiled. 'Think about it, Reverend. If there's less of them, there's more for us. That's what I tell people.'

The response made me gape at him in disbelief. 'Really?'

'Let them tear each other apart,' he said dismissively. 'I'm only interested in the humans here.'

'*Cadw ar Wahân* will come after humans,' I snapped. 'I'm married to a dragon, remember?'

'The Firm has nothing to fear from *Cadw ar Wahân.*' Fred shook off my hand. 'Now, excuse me while I return to more important work.'

I watched him stride away. My rat guide dropped down to my shoulder, although her whiskers twitched at the state of my clothes. I sighed. 'Could you direct me to the Bishop's Palace?'

My feet ached by the time we rounded the Cathedral and took the path to the Palace. Hard cobblestones and solid boots were not a good combination. The sight of the *tacsi* dragon cheered me. Very soon, I would be heading back to Saint Raphael's. Never before had I been so eager to leave the city behind.

The rat gave me a quick nod and flew off.

'Thank you for waiting, Huw,' I said. 'Let me go and check whether Bishop Aeron's free for my report.'

'The Bishop left about thirty minutes ago. You could give a message to the entry squirrel.' He bent his head and sniffed at my trousers. 'Have you killed a were-fox?'

'No. I was trying to save his life after he was shot with a gun.'

'Is that a type of sword?

'It's a weapon, but nothing like a sword.'

I went up to the Palace door, quickly summarised the meeting to the squirrel, and then clambered up Huw's neck. As he sent us into the air, I tightened the jacket around my middle and settled into the saddle for the ride. I felt the tension lift from my shoulders as the buildings of Llanbedr disappeared behind us.

The miles passed below us. I smiled as the buildings of Saint Raphael's came into view. The *tacsi* dragon started his descent, obviously planning to land by the main building. But I saw Raven lift his head, ears and horns straightening at the state of my trousers and coat. 'Land by the search dragon, please,' I told Huw, worried that my husband might injure his wing in an attempt to join me.

The *tacsi* dragon slightly misjudged the ground, and hopped as his fore claws tangled in the long grass. I waited a moment for my spine to recover before I slid from his neck. 'The blood isn't mine,' I reassured Raven before turning to thank Huw. The *tacsi* dragon nodded and then took off again.

Raven stretched out his neck and took a deep sniff. 'Were-fox. What happened?'

'Can it wait until everyone's here?' I asked. 'I think the ministry staff should hear what happened.'

My back gave another twinge as Morey thumped onto my shoulder. 'You look like you've been in a battle, Black.'

'Were-fox,' Raven told him.

'I can smell that for myself.'

'Morey,' I said, 'I'd like to speak to all of the leadership team. Not just the clergy. Could you find Llewelyn and the others and bring them here?'

'Certainly.' His tail brushed past my ear as he launched himself away.

'What happened to the were-fox?' Raven asked.

'Shot with a small gun.'

The dragon growled. 'I don't like guns.'

I shook my head. 'Neither do I.'

Llewelyn was the first to arrive. 'Not my own blood,' I quickly reassured him, as I said several more times as others joined us. Morey returned to my right shoulder. Jago placed himself on the other side, and Bastien found a perch on the nearby open barn door.

'Where's Clyde?' I asked Jago. 'He usually finds his way to a gathering like this.'

'Oh, he went off to Saint Canna's this morning,' the gryphon answered.

'There's another ordinands' day going on?'

Bastien chuckled. 'A *tacsi* dragon took him to see Carys.'

My frown deepened. 'Carys? I know they're friends, but why has he gone to see her?'

Now it was Jago's turn to laugh. 'Why do you think?'

Morey peered around my chin. 'Who's Carys?'

'A vampire ordinand at the seminary,' I said. 'Jago, are you telling me that Clyde's dating her?'

'Yes,' Jago said. 'Ever since our first visit there.'

'How does she know what he's saying?' Raven asked.

'They asked me to come as well, a few times,' Jago explained. 'But Carys has picked up on his sign language really quickly. And it's better that I'm not around, after all.'

I was torn between being pleased for Clyde and worry that yet another person I loved could be in danger from *Cadw ar Wahân*. 'Llewelyn, anyone we should wait for?'

The chaplain looked around. 'Arne is visiting a unicorn herd, and Wyn is busy with a not-were. I will speak to them later.'

'Okay.' I cleared my throat. 'I've just come back from a special meeting of Llanbedr City Council. *Cadw ar Wahân* left their mark across the city, singling out communities which have members in mixed-species relationships.'

'What action did the council agree to take?' Llewelyn asked.

I shook my head. 'There won't be any coordinated response. Each community will have to look after themselves. One councillor suggested mixed-species couples should simply be exiled.'

'But that's terrible,' Jago protested. 'It's bad enough that *Cadw ar Wahân* goes after people just because they've fallen in love with someone. But not to offer them protection, well, that just means they're agreeing with *Cadw ar Wahân,* that some people don't deserve protecting.'

Raven met my eyes. 'If danger comes, we will face it side by side. You with your sword, me with my teeth and fire and claws.'

'The Guild of Saint Raphael's accepts anyone who comes here,' Llewelyn said firmly. 'And we will not allow *Cadw ar Wahân* to harm those who live in our community.'

'Even so,' Morey said into my ear, 'I think you should start carrying your sword. Just in case.'

One of the unicorns snorted. 'My fear is that people might turn against each other. There has always been tension in Llanbedr, I remember it well from when I lived there. This could spill over into violence between the different communities.'

A movement of green and brown by his hooves drew my attention. Cornelius had joined our gathering. Well, if the mantis wanted to listen in, I saw no reason to stop him. I turned my attention back to Raven. 'If fights do break out, and if there are significant numbers of deaths, that might open up new thin places.'

Morey took a quick intake of breath, and I suddenly remembered that not everyone listening in knew that search dragons could seal up crossings. Fortunately, Raven was more circumspect. 'Noted,' he said, waggling his ears. My message had been received and understood.

Llewelyn sighed, the lines deepening on his long face. 'We can only make plans for Saint Raphael's. I will ask some of the larger not-weres to patrol our grounds, taking it in turns throughout the night. Everyone must be ready in case of increased efforts by *Cadw ar Wahân*. Those who have weapons should carry those with them at all times. Were-wolves and were-bears should sharpen their claws and ensure their teeth are in good condition.'

'What if mixed-species couples come here?' I asked. 'Will we take them in?'

'Of course.' Llewelyn's glare defied anyone to disagree with him. 'Saint Raphael's has always been a place of sanctuary, and it will remain so.'

I shivered. Never had I expected the chaplain to issue a call to arms. The group broke apart, and I headed to my room to change clothes and collect my sword.

Chapter Twenty-One

A rasp against my bedroom door informed me that Clyde had returned. I let him in, then called out, 'Jago, are you at home? Could you come over, please?'

'Of course, Auntie Penny,' came a muffled voice from Morey and Taryn's flat. I waited as the door opened, and Jago flew out to land on my shoulder.

'I need to talk to Clyde,' I explained as I returned to my room. 'He needs to know what's been happening.'

The snail had crawled onto my bed, and his body swirled orange and green as I brought a chair over. Jago jumped down to sit beside Clyde.

'You know about the marks *Cadw ar Wahân* left on our buildings last night?' I asked.

'Yes,' Clyde answered. Jago added, on his behalf, 'Uncle Clyde says he saw them before the *tacsi* dragon took him to Saint Canna's.'

I narrowed my eyes. 'And just how are you paying for trips to the seminary?'

Jago translated, 'The Warden heard what happened at the football match, so she's arranged for me to visit several times a month. That way, the other ordinands will know me better before I start in September.'

'And it also gives you a chance to spend time with one ordinand in particular?'

Swirls of pink lightened the snail's tentacles. 'Yes.'

'*Cadw ar Wahân* didn't only leave their mark here,' I continued. 'Any community with mixed-species relationships in Llanbedr was also targeted. I attended the city's council meeting, but they decided that it's up to each community to look after themselves. Here at Saint Raphael's, Llewelyn has set up a rota to patrol our grounds at night, and those of us who don't fight with teeth or claws are to carry weapons with us.'

Clyde's body changed to a mixture of browns and yellows. Jago paused a moment before asking, 'But *Cadw ar Wahân* has never attacked anyone, have they?'

'They've mostly focused on intimidation,' I agreed. 'But they have poisoned people, and they killed Auiak's wife. We know so little about them that it's best to be prepared for the worst.'

'Prepared,' Clyde said, and opened his belly to show off his jagged teeth.

I rubbed his shell. 'I know you can defend yourself. Now that you're dating a vampire, you and she could be targeted by *Cadw ar Wahân*. Is Carys still on a blood diet?'

'Yes.'

'So she can change into bat shape if necessary.' I sighed. 'And, Clyde, I hate to remind you what the Church thinks of mixed-species relationships. If you two remain together, Bishop Aeron might not ordain either of you.'

'Early days,' Clyde said, but the yellow pulsing through his body belied his words.

'And you and Bastien need to take care, too,' I told Jago.

'Mam and Tad made that very clear,' the gryphon said glumly. 'They're really worried about me. I told them we'd be all right, they don't need to worry about us.'

Oh, for the confidence of youth, I thought. 'Just be careful, all right?'

'Yes, Auntie Penny.'

And Clyde wagged his tentacles in agreement.

The next week finally gave me a chance to do some real work at Saint Raphael's. I visited the rat barn, took letherum to the not-weres who needed the medication, and assisted Clyde in setting up singing therapy for a flock of were-starlings which had recently joined the community. Other than the sword pulling at my belt, I could almost forget that *Cadw ar Wahân* had visited us.

I was checking the hooves of a were-horse when I heard Miriam's voice call out. 'Dragon incoming!'

'So what?' I muttered as I frowned at the mixture of stones and mud which had dried inside the hoof. '*Tacsi* dragons aren't anything new.'

'It's not a *tacsi* dragon,' the horse told me. 'She's large, and dark blue, and she's not wearing a saddle. I think there's some grey along her muzzle.'

The were-horse grunted as I released his foot. Shading my eyes with my hand, I scanned the sky. The massive dragon dropping down towards Saint Raphael's was instantly recognisable, and I felt my heart pound. Raven's matriarch had decided to pay a visit. Alarm gave strength to my legs as I set off in a sprint towards my husband.

Raven was sunning himself outside his barn. The tilt of his head showed that he had spotted his mother, and the low angle of his horns and ears told me how little he welcomed her. I reached his side and tried to catch my breath.

Eydis landed fifty feet away. I'd forgotten exactly how tall she was. Her head could easily touch the top of the barn. The ground shook slightly as she strode towards us. 'Hrafn,' she hissed. 'You are injured. Why are you still alive?'

'So much,' I gasped, 'for motherly concern.'

'An injured dragon is a dead dragon,' Raven said. 'Such is the rule in the longhouses.'

The matriarch bared her teeth. 'A dragon who can't protect himself doesn't deserve to live.'

Raven reared back, wings spreading as he shifted his weight to his hindquarters. 'Try me, then.'

'If you want him, you'll need to take both of us,' I said grimly as I drew my sword. 'Search dragon and knifebearer.'

'Why should you fight for this one?' Eydis demanded.

I removed one hand from the sword hilt to pull up my left sleeve. The gold bracelet glittered against my pale skin. 'Because he's my husband.'

The matriarch's eyes shifted to the golden bracelet on Raven's leg. Then she broke into loud laughter. I allowed myself to relax slightly as she sat down. 'So. The *offeiriad* caught her dragon at last.'

'Or I caught her,' Raven said gruffly.

My arms were beginning to ache from the weight of my sword. As Raven dropped his battle-ready position, I decided it was safe enough to lower the blade tip-first to the ground. 'We caught each other. It was a joint catching. What can we do for you, Matriarch? Or did you only come here hoping to eat your son?'

Eydis turned her attention to Raven. 'You have brought trouble to our longhouse, Hrafn.'

He snorted. 'Again?'

'Two of your clutch-mates have been killed,' Eydis growled. 'And the mark of *Cadw ar Wahân* was carved into their carcasses.'

I found myself leaning heavily on my sword. 'Killed? How?'

'Large holes in their chests and wings,' she said. 'As if something had dug in deep, like a powerful spear.'

'A rifle?' I wondered aloud. Had more guns crossed over from my world?

'Why should you care?' Raven challenged. 'I'm certain they made good eating.'

'They were drakas, not drakes,' Eydis said. 'Drakes I have in ample supply. Sylvi and Gunhild were two of my possible successors. This is a severe loss to my house.'

A stab of pain went through my chest. I'd met Sylvi several times. 'My sorrow for your sorrow.'

'As well you should sorrow.' Eydis glared at me. 'It's your fault that they were killed.'

I straightened. 'You gave me permission to marry Raven.'

'I didn't realise it would bring death to my longhouse,' Eydis said. 'So.

This relationship must end immediately. The dragon way would be for Father Penny to hunt down and eat Hrafn, but as she is not a dragon, I will accept human practice. What is the human custom?'

'Long drawn-out arguments, terrible silences, and lawyers,' I replied dryly. 'Forget it. I have no intention of divorcing Raven.'

'And I,' Raven snarled, 'will not part from Penny.'

'Sorry am I to hear this.' Eydis rose to her feet. 'I will not allow your relationship to threaten my House any further. But there's no need for both of you to die. Which of you would like to volunteer?'

Raven opened his jaws, and I raised my sword. Then Llewelyn's voice cut through the tense atmosphere. 'Matriarch, I apologise that it has taken me so long to notice your arrival. All of us welcome you to Saint Raphael's.'

I glanced to my left. The chaplain's face was calm but resolute. Morey stood tall on one shoulder, and Jago on the other. Behind him were positioned a dozen of the strongest members of the community. I noted were-bears and were-wolves, a couple of full-sized gryphons, and the unicorns. Clyde slid into place at Llewelyn's feet, his body pulsing with reds and browns and his jaws wide open.

Llewelyn bared his own teeth. 'It is good of you to show an interest in your daughter-in-law's work. Would you like a tour of our facilities, Matriarch?'

The dragon's tail slapped the ground behind her. 'I have no interest in what you do here.'

'Then, if you have finished speaking to your son, there seems little reason for you to remain any longer.' Llewelyn turned his head to Raven. 'I am assuming that your discussions have come to a natural end?'

'The discussions have,' Raven said. 'We were about to discover whether another type of ending would follow.'

'Anyone who comes to Saint Raphael's,' Llewelyn declared, 'is guaranteed safety within our boundaries.'

'He's a dragon,' Eydis said crossly. 'Why do you care what happens to him, or to a *skrælingi?*'

'They are part of us,' one of the unicorns replied. 'And we are part of them. To harm them harms us, and we will not let harm come to us.'

The matriarch's eyes narrowed as yet more of the community joined us. 'How many of you are ready to take down a draka, I wonder?'

I looked up at the matriarch. 'We're all ready. I guess the question is, "Do you feel lucky, punk?"'

Eydis growled, low and long, and I tightened my grip on the sword. But she snapped her jaws shut and shifted her weight to her hindquarters. Grass and soil fell from her claws as she sprang into the air. Her tail swiped over Raven's head, and he had to duck to avoid being slapped with the flat end.

'Go aloft,' Llewelyn told the two full-sized gryphons. 'Make certain she leaves our domain.'

'And look out for a search dragon,' Raven added. 'She must have used an air crossing, and a search dragon had to find it for her. Warn that dragon that if he ever brings my matriarch here again, I will personally flame his hide!'

I sheathed my sword. My legs suddenly felt weak, and I stumbled over to my husband to lean against his foreleg.

Morey flew to my shoulder. 'I didn't think Clint Eastwood was your style. Couldn't you think of a good *Doctor Who* quote?'

'No, only one from *Babylon Five*,' I admitted. 'But somehow "Get the hell out of my galaxy" didn't feel right. Raven, you're certain she used an air thin place?'

'Yes. Saint Raphael's is too far from her longhouse for her to have flown straight.' Raven turned his head to look at me. 'I don't want to see her here again.'

'Neither do I.' I turned my attention to Llewelyn and his gathered troops. 'Thank you, everyone, for turning out to defend us.'

'We stand together,' a were-bear growled. 'We are a united community.'

The group began to disperse. I motioned the chaplain to come closer. 'This community stands together,' I said quietly. 'But how many others will defend their mixed-species couples?'

'Not if they hear that *Cadw ar Wahân* has managed to kill two dragons,' Llewelyn agreed. 'That would put fear into even the largest predator.'

Morey cocked his head. 'Perhaps we can hope that the news won't spread to Llanbedr?'

'It'll get out.' I rubbed my aching forehead. 'Bad news always travels fast.'

'Then we need to stop it,' Jago said. 'Tell people they have to protect each other, just like we did with Raven's matriarch.'

I sighed. 'If only it were that easy.'

'It should be,' Jago insisted, his crest rising past Llewelyn's ear. 'People are people. It shouldn't matter who they fall in love with. And other people shouldn't let it matter.'

My headache was deepening. 'What will the fallout be in Llanbedr? Do we think that communities will now exile anyone who has married out?'

'Worse than that.' Bastien swooped down to land on Raven's neck. '*Cadw ar Wahân* will target both communities of mixed-species marriages. If one community refuses to exile the couple, the attacks will continue, even on the community which has not given them shelter.'

I shuddered. 'But that could lead to species attacking each other.'

Bastien directed his gaze at Jago. 'You know. You saw into the Consortium's mind when he threatened to keep you captive. Tell them.'

'But I can't,' Jago reminded him. 'I swore on your life to keep the Consortium's secrets, remember? He'll kill you if I tell.'

Bastien, with great gentleness, said, 'Jago, I am dying anyway.'

Everyone froze. I struggled to breathe. The small gryphon drew back. 'What do mean? You can't be dying. You're still eating, and flying, and, well, you can't be dying!'

'I am in my seventh year,' Bastien continued. 'Few rats reach an eighth. Haven't you noticed? I'm shedding fur. My wings are thinning. My heart skips beats. Go into the barn which houses other flying rats. You'll see what's going to happen to me over the next few months.'

Jago looked around wildly. 'Is this true? Is Bastien right?'

'I've lied about many things,' the rat said quietly, 'and to many people. But I won't lie to you, Jago. I'm telling you the truth. So you might as well let everyone know what the Consortium is planning.'

I ached to take the gryphon into my hands and offer him some comfort. Jago looked very small, and very frightened, as he offered, 'It's more like impressions than images, although there were some of those too. It's not like I wanted to see, it's more like I couldn't look away. I didn't mean to know what the rat king is doing.'

He fell silent. Raven shifted restlessly, and I could feel my own anxiety nibbling away at my patience. I finally asked, 'Is it something to do with *Cadw ar Wahân?* Is the Consortium somehow mixed up with them?'

Bastien's laugh was low and harsh. 'More than that. Haven't you worked it out yet? The Consortium *is Cadw ar Wahân.'*

The last of my strength left my legs, and I found myself sagging against Raven. Jago had thrown his wings forward to cover his head, as if he were trying to shield himself from an unwelcome truth. Clyde went white, and Morey's claws dug deep into my shoulder.

'So,' Llewelyn said, 'the rat king is behind all this intimidation? Bastien? Jago?'

'You might as well tell them everything,' Bastien said to Jago. 'We have both betrayed my rat king, and my life is already forfeit.'

'All right.' Jago's voice was muffled behind feathers. 'It's not like the Consortium has always run *Cadw ar Wahân*. The rat king took it over a few years ago, killing off anyone there who wouldn't do what the Consortium told them to do. The Consortium's been happy to let *Cadw ar Wahân* tick over, occasionally doing some graffiti or killing someone, just to keep people aware of them. But when I was with him, the rat king was starting to plan something much bigger.'

'Killing dragons?' Raven asked.

'Not that specifically.' Jago flipped his wings to his back. 'I know they--he--was thinking what would make people sit up and take notice. I guess dragons being killed was what he decided on. Another option was full-sized gryphons.'

Morey growled. 'If the lives of your own clan were in danger, I would have expected you to tell us.'

'I couldn't,' Jago reminded him. 'I swore on Basty's life.'

'But why?' I asked. 'Why all this?'

'Because they want the different species to end up fighting each other,' Jago said miserably. 'That's their plan.'

'And if the Consortium can supply weapons,' I added, 'that could be quite lucrative for them. Is that how the were-sheep got a gun, I wonder?'

'Guns are only the beginning,' Bastien warned. 'My rat king wants to sell the large weapons which your world produces.'

'Well, that's not going to be easy for him,' I said. 'If he wants tanks and missiles, he's going to need much bigger thin places.'

Raven snorted. 'Which he must know would disappear soon after opening, as all the previous ones have.'

'And we still don't know how that happens,' I said, perhaps too quickly. 'So the Consortium is stuck with guns for the time being.'

Jago glanced at Bastien. The rat gave him a nod. 'Basty and I both know that he's working with the humans.'

'I thought as much.' I willed energy back into my legs and straightened. 'Fred Wiseman, and an arms dealer called Mark.'

Raven turned his gaze to the rat. 'How long before your rat king knows you've told us his plans?'

'I'm too far away for the Consortium to reach me here,' Bastien replied.

'How long,' Raven asked, 'are you able to remain out of contact?'

I sighed. 'Exactly. Once the Consortium finds out you've talked to us, who knows what he'll do.'

Raven's ears drew back. 'And what will happen to Bastien?'

My face warmed. 'That too. Bastien?'

'I usually fly into range every few days,' the rat said quietly. 'Last time was yesterday. So I can stay here two days, maybe three. But then I need to be in contact with my rat king.'

'You can't go,' Jago protested. 'You've got to stay here. Where you'll be safe.'

'I can't stay.' Bastien turned his head away. 'I have no choice. Two days, maybe three, then I'll have to go back.'

'But you can just do a quick fly-by,' Jago begged. 'You don't have to get into intensive contact.'

'I could, and that would be enough,' Bastien acknowledged. 'But if I let our minds touch more deeply, I'll be able to find out more of what the Consortium's planning. I'm dying anyway. Let me at least do something useful with the life I have left.'

My throat closed. I glanced around my friends, and saw that they too were struggling to work out what to say.

Jago unfolded his wings. 'Come on, Basty.'

Gryphon and rat flew away. I watched them disappear, my gaze blurring with tears.

Chapter Twenty-Two

Later that evening, a scrabble of claws against my door drew my attention away from my book. I glanced at my watch as I rose to my feet, wondering who might be wanting me at this late hour.

Jago stood outside, crest lying limp along his neck. 'Auntie Penny, I--' His voice broke off into a sob, and he leapt to my chest. I cradled him with one hand and shut the door with the other.

I sat down on the bed. Clyde, resting at the foot, emerged from his shell as Jago's soft crying filled the room. The snail waved his tentacles. 'Basty?'

My response was a quick nod. 'Jago, where's Bastien now?'

'He's staying with Raven.' The gryphon looked up at me. 'I asked and asked him to go somewhere, anywhere, where he could be safe from the Consortium. But he told me it doesn't work like that. A rat needs regular contact with his rat king. That's why he couldn't come to les Etats-Unis with us. And why he can't stay away from the Consortium.'

Clyde slid across the bed and onto my knee. Orange and green chased through his body as he reached up to touch Jago.

'When does he plan to go?' I asked.

'Three days from now,' Jago said miserably. 'That's as long as he can hold out.' A tremor went through his body, and then his crest rose. 'So that's why we want to get married. Could you do that for us tomorrow?'

Clyde flushed bright pink. My own emotions were more mixed. 'What did your parents say?'

'I haven't told them yet. They'll say I'm too young, I know that, but if Basty's going to--if I'm going to lose him, I want him to be my husband first. So, can you do the wedding tomorrow, in the chapel here? Please?'

I took a deep breath, preparing myself to find a way to let the gryphon down gently. But Clyde flashed his teeth at me, then told Jago, 'Yes.'

'Tomorrow,' I agreed. 'Anyway, it's rather late. Do you want to go join

Bastien?'

Jago yawned. 'Okay. We can talk about the ceremony in the morning. We just want something really simple, just Mam and Tad and our closest friends there. Right?'

'Got it.' I opened the door, and waited until he'd flown down the stairs before going to Morey and Taryn's flat. I didn't want Jago to hear the arguments his decision was bound to start.

Afternoon sun slanted through the chapel's clear windows. A table had been placed at the front, and the two grooms sat side by side on the dark wood. I stood between them and the altar, sweating slightly in my white cassock alb. Clyde was in the front pew as Jago's best man. Raven stood outside, his head filling a window. Although he was Bastien's best man, he was too large to enter the chapel. Morey and Taryn took up another pew, their slick feathers and fur a sign of their unease. But they had finished their shouting last night, and had agreed to be at the wedding. As much as James had wanted to attend, he had reluctantly agreed that his presence would raise too many questions.

Llewelyn came to the doorway to the chapel and gave me a nod. He took up a position just outside, Miriam to his right. Although we didn't expect anyone to rush inside to protest, the chaplain didn't want to take any chances.

Despite his oft-professed disdain for the Christian religion, Bastien had agreed to be married in a standard *Eglwys Loegyr* ceremony. The service book I held in my left hand had the service in Welsh on the left, and English on the right. As Jago understood very little of Lloegyr's native language, we'd agreed to use English only.

I began to read out the words, familiar to me after officiating at many a wedding, albeit never one quite like this. "'Marriage is a gift of God through which a couple may grow together in the knowledge, love, and service of God. It is given that, united with one another in heart, mind, and in body, they may increase in love and trust.'" I stumbled slightly over the next sentence. "'God joins two people together in life-long union as the foundation of family life in which each member of the family, in good times and bad, may find strength, companionship, and comfort, and grow to maturity in love.'"

I finished the introduction, then looked up at the small congregation. "'If you are aware of any reason why these persons may not lawfully marry, you must declare it now.'"

A slight growl emerged from Morey's throat, and Taryn's ears flicked. But no one spoke up.

After a short prayer, I read out the Bible passage which Jago had chosen. 'The Song of Solomon 8: 6-7.

"Set me as a seal upon your heart,
as a seal upon your arm;
for love is strong as death,
passion fierce as the grave.
Its flashes are flashes of fire,
a raging flame.
Many waters cannot quench love,
neither can floods drown it.
If one offered for love
all the wealth of one's house,
it would be utterly scorned.'"

I had fully intended to deliver a short sermon. But the phrases 'love is as strong as death' and 'passion fierce as the grave' left me struggling for words. So I took a deep breath and moved on to the declarations and vows. "'Bastien, will you take Jago to be your husband? Will you love him, comfort him, honour and care for him, and, forsaking all others, be faithful to him as long as you both shall live?'"

'I will,' Bastien said.

The same questions were asked of Jago, whose confident 'I will' resounded through the chapel.

I cast my eyes over the others present. "'Will you, the families and friends of Bastien and Jago, support and uphold them in their marriage now and in the years to come?'"

'We will,' they all responded.

Jago and Bastien turned to face each other, first Bastien, and then Jago repeating the vows after me. "'I, Bastien, take you, Jago, to be my husband, to have and to hold from this day forward; for better, for worse, for richer, for poorer, in sickness and in health, to love and to cherish, as long as we both shall live, according to the will and purpose of God. In the presence of God I make this vow.'"

The couple had decided not to exchange any sort of physical token of their marriage, so I moved on to the proclamation. "'In the presence of God, and before this congregation, Bastien and Jago have given their consent and made their marriage vows to one another. I proclaim that they are therefore husbands to one another. Those whom God has joined together let no one put asunder.'"

As I glanced down at the service book, Morey extended his wings and flew over to my shoulder. He raised a forefoot and traced a cross in the air. "'God the Father, God the Son, God the Holy Spirit, bless, preserve and keep you; the Lord mercifully look upon you with his favour; and so fill you with all spiritual blessings and grace, that you may so live together in this life, that in the world to come you may have life everlasting. Amen.'"

'Amen,' all those present echoed.

Morey returned to his wife's side. I placed the newly-weds on my shoulders, and Llewelyn and Miriam stood to one side to allow me to exit the chapel. I heard the rumble of voices as I walked to the building's entrance. As I opened the door, the members of the community gathered outside broke into cheers and the stomping of hooves and feet.

Jago ducked around the back of my neck to say something to Bastien. A moment later, they flew off, looping once around the crowd before disappearing into the nearby woods.

'Lovely service,' Miriam said behind me. 'You do weddings very well.'

'Thank you.' I turned to look at her, and noted that she was holding hands with Llewelyn. 'Always happy to help a couple tie the knot.'

I wandered back inside and went to my room to change out of my robes. As I reached out to the dark sweater lying across the settee, a piece of paper fluttered away from one sleeve. It landed face up, with just one word written on the white surface. *James.*

My brother must have pushed it through the crossing between our two worlds. I pulled the couch away from the wall and reached out a hand. Nothing but air met my fingers, so I knelt down and gingerly put my head through.

Dwysil, sitting on a rug where their settee had been, looked up at me with a solemn expression. 'Mummy and Daddy want to see you, Auntie Penny.'

My heart warmed at the title she had given me. But I had something important to confess first. 'I wasn't planning to visit today, so I don't have a present for you.'

The girl studied me for a moment before giving me a small nod. 'Okay. Mummy, Daddy, Auntie Penny is here!'

'Coming!' responded James from behind a closed door. A moment later, he hurried into the room, hands patting at dishevelled hair. 'Sorry, Sis, I was having a nap. Stayed up late last night. How did the wedding go?'

'Very well,' I said. 'Any particular reason for the all-nighter?'

Skylar emerged from the kitchen. 'I've put some coffee on, Penny. I think you might be here for a while, James has a lot to tell you, and I think we have some biscuits in. Do you have just milk or do you want some sugar too?'

'Just milk,' I said, dropping down on to the settee.

James retrieved his laptop from the desk before joining me. 'I've been monitoring communications from the Minister without Portfolio. It took me a while, but I've managed to hack a couple of their Whatsapp accounts. We have a "Friend of Aslan" at one of the detention centres, and he's smuggled tracers to some of the Lloegyr people held there. There's been movement between the centres.'

'The government seems to be organising people by species,' Skylar said as she carried a tray into the room. The smell of fresh coffee tickled my nostrils. 'The vampires and weres have been placed in four centres. Unicorns, gryphons, dwarves, and elves are in the other three. The merpeople are still in a pool facility which the military took over early on.'

'We don't know why they've been moved around,' James continued, the computer keyboard clicking under his fingers. 'It could be it's easier to put together people who are on similar diets?'

'Unicorns and gryphons don't eat the same things.' Skylar handed me a dark brown mug. 'And with weres, it all depends what type of were they are. There's a big difference between a were-wolf and a were-rabbit.'

James sipped from his coffee. 'There's a rumour going around that gryphons have had their wings clipped.'

'I hope their beaks claimed a strip of flesh for each feather,' Skylar muttered darkly. 'Or better yet, an eye or two.'

My hands were shaking. I placed my drink on the floor. 'You can't blame the guards for carrying out a government order.'

'Yes I can.' Skylar glared at me. 'I thought this world decided years ago that "Just obeying orders" wasn't a good enough excuse for an atrocity?'

'The coaches and trucks which moved people around are still parked up nearby,' James said. 'All with dark windows so no one can see what's inside.'

'So the British public doesn't develop the Sight.' I stared longingly at my coffee, but I was still trembling. 'Don't know why the government worries about that. The Sight wears off for most people after a week or so. Very few have it permanently.'

'Bishop Nigel does,' Skylar reminded me.

'And people who saw that winged unicorn.' James turned the computer towards me. The website for 'Friends of Aslan' was spread across the screen. 'Just as well no one's ever done a video of her. Here's the message left by Digory. "This weather is so nice, Jadis will go out in her summer carriage." That means Harkness has left her office in London. Always a bad sign.'

'A message from Digory,' I mused. 'If Digory is Peter, maybe it shows that he's still in her entourage.'

'I've been trying to track her phone,' James said, 'but so far no joy. Her personal security is tighter than the government's. Whenever she leaves London, something happens. Last time, people were swapped between detention centres. We're wondering what she's up to now.'

'I'm wondering if she uses her phone for important messages.' Skylar took a seat on the floor beside her daughter. 'She could be using rats instead.'

I had been about to retrieve my coffee, but now my hands were unsteady again. 'Do you think she could be working with the rat kings?'

'I wouldn't put it past her,' James growled.

'I've been told that rats have been taking letherum to England,' I said slowly. 'We know it's been used to help round up vampires. Perhaps the rat kings are the suppliers.'

'Or at least one of them is,' James agreed. 'The Consortium.' His fingers flew across the keyboard, and a new image came up on the screen. 'These are the coaches.'

I leaned forward for a closer look. 'And trucks parked up behind. I guess those are for unicorns and gryphons. If they've finished transferring everyone, why is the transport still there?'

'We think there are plans to move people somewhere else.' James rubbed his chin. 'We haven't been able to find out what, where, or why.'

'Any "Friend" close enough to the Minister to find out?' I asked.

'Peter, if he is Digory, seems to be the closest we have,' James said. 'But we don't think he's in the inner circle.'

'Maybe they think he's still close to you,' Skylar noted. 'I mean, you two separated and you both have someone else now, but he did spend enough time with you for the Minister to think he might not be as "Britain First" as she is.'

'Peter lived in Lloegyr for a while, long before I met him.' I finally dared to retrieve my drink. 'And he's a moral man. He'd want to keep Lloegyr safe for his own reasons, not just because he knew me.'

'I'm not happy about this.' James tapped the photo on the screen. 'Can you check your side of the crossing several times a day? I'd like to be able to get hold of you if I find anything out. Or if they start moving people again.'

'I'll check my settee regularly,' I promised, and gulped down the last of my coffee. 'And I'd better make sure I find a present to bring next time, right, Dwysil?'

In response, the girl stood up and held out her arms. I picked her up for a hug, and was surprised to find my eyes prickling with tears. 'She's very trusting,' I said to my brother. 'You two are doing a good job.'

'We're doing our best,' Skylar said.

'You were both orphans yourselves,' I continued. 'I guess that gives you some insight into what Dwysil needs.'

'I had Cynwrig and Eres,' Skylar reminded me. 'They raised me as if I'd always been theirs.'

'And I had you,' James added. 'I only hope I can do as good a job as you did.'

'You will,' I said quietly. 'You saved Jago, and you'll do right by this little girl, too.'

James smiled, then his expression sobered. 'And how is Jago? If he needs someone after, well, you know, Bastien goes to the Consortium, I'm here for him.'

'I'll let him know.' I put Dwysil down and headed back through the thin place. Despite the sunny evening outside my window, I found myself shivering.

Chapter Twenty-Three

Duty in the barn which held the flying rats was such a challenging task that the ministry team had agreed to a rota system. The mixture of despair and faeces left an odour which even a long bath couldn't quite eradicate. Two days after Jago and Bastien's wedding, I was taking the morning shift at the barn, changing straw where I could, providing food and water to those able to take it, and administrating letherum as best I could.

A sudden weight on my shoulder made me jump. I turned my head, and Bastien met my gaze. 'I thought you'd be with Jago.'

The rat looked away. 'He won't follow me in here. It's the only place where I can leave him behind.'

I washed my hands in a nearby bucket of soapy water. 'I suppose he wants to spend as much time as possible with you.'

'He wants to go with me to the Consortium,' Bastien said. 'And he can't. Not if he's going to outlive me.'

I found myself looking down the row of rats, and, to my horror, picking out where we could place Bastien. 'How much longer can you hold out?'

'I can't.' The rat was trembling. 'Being away from your rat king, it's like an ache that grows and grows. Do you understand?'

'I think so. It sounds like how I used to feel when I needed a drink.'

'It's a craving,' Bastien agreed. 'You can no longer think of anything else, except the need to feel your rat king in your mind again. I was free for a short while, when the Enforcer rewarded me with my freedom.'

'But then you signed up with the Consortium to keep Jago safe,' I said softly. 'Since the rat king is *Cadw ar Wahân,* you knew he wouldn't target you or Jago.'

'Precisely. And so long as Jago stays away from the Consortium, he will be safe.'

'But you won't be.'

'I know what will happen to me.' Bastien nodded at the rats curled up nearby. 'And still I must go. I need your help, Penny.'

I took a deep breath through my mouth. 'What do you need?'

'For you to distract Jago so I can fly away without him seeing me.'

'I can do that,' I said, amazed that my voice was steady. 'I take it he's outside now?'

'At the front of the barn.'

I nodded. 'There's a gap near the floor at the rear. You should be able to squeeze through.'

The rat lifted his wings and flew from my shoulder. Light streamed through the hole between plank and ground. Bastien landed beside it, and for a moment his small body was outlined with brightness. Not knowing how else to mark his courage, I straightened and moved my right hand in a blessing. He went through the gap and was gone.

I pushed past the heaviness in my arms and chest and continued to minister to the rats. One of our patients had died in the night, and I cleaned out her bedding, wondering whether Bastien would be taking her place. Or would he even be able to come back to us? I wiped my eyes on a sleeve.

These thoughts were still swirling through my mind when I finally left the barn. Jago, sitting on a fence nearby, lifted his head when he saw me. I shook my head. As I had hoped, he decided this meant that Bastien was still inside, and he settled back down to wait. I told myself fiercely that I hadn't really lied to Jago, but I hurried away before my face could betray me.

A hot bath and a thorough scrubbing still left my hair tinged with the sharp scent of rat urine. As I pulled on my clothes, I comforted myself with the thought that it'd be a week before I was once again on duty in the rat barn. I put my smelly clothes into a wash bag and left them on the landing outside my room. One of the benefits of living at Saint Raphael's was having someone else to do my laundry.

I was readjusting the hang of my sword when heavy footsteps pounded up the stairway. 'Bishop Aeron and her chaplain are here,' Miriam announced before bending down to scoop up the wash bag. 'Wyn is talking to them, but they want to see you as well.'

The door to the other flat opened. Morey flew over to my shoulder. 'Both of them? Here?' he commented as I hurried downstairs. 'Must be something major.'

'That's what I'm worried about,' I replied. 'By the way, Bastien went off to the Consortium an hour ago.'

'Oh.' Morey's claws dug deep into my shoulder. 'And Jago?'

'Bastien managed to fly off without Jago realising.'

The two dragons stood near the main building. I thrust my feet into my boots, smoothed down my wet hair, and stepped outside.

Llewelyn gave me a tight smile as I came to his side. 'Bishop Aeron has come with news.'

'There were attacks on mixed-species couples last night,' the Bishop told me, lowering her orange-red head near to mine. 'News has spread that two dragons from Hrafn's longhouse have been killed. Panic is building and the situation is becoming dangerous. So I'm advising all church members who have married outside their own community to leave Llanbedr. They must find places where they can be safe. Aldred will fly you wherever you and Raven decide to go. Can your husband make his own way?'

'He's been making a few short flights,' I said, trying to force back my alarm. 'You think we won't be safe here?'

'You've already had a visit from *Cadw ar Wahân,*' Aldred pointed out. His yellow hide glowed in the sunlight. 'Is there anyone else who needs to be evacuated?'

'Why are you sending people away?' Jago demanded, landing on my free shoulder. 'Shouldn't you be trying to keep them safe instead?'

'My son,' Morey told the Bishop, 'has married Bastien.'

'And I think we have the right to live wherever we like without worrying about *Cadw ar Wahân,*' Jago said. 'Why isn't anyone standing up for us? Do you really think this is the right thing to do, just send us away, like we're the problem? *Cadw ar Wahân* is the problem. Why isn't the Church taking a stand?'

'The Church,' Bishop Aeron said, 'does not support mixed-species marriages, although we do not condone violence against anyone.'

'But that's part of the problem!' Jago's crest rose high, tickling past my ear. 'Why do you think *Cadw ar Wahân* can get away with what they do? Because no one speaks out against them! If anyone dies, you're going to be as much to blame as *Cadw ar Wahân.*'

Bishop Aeron directed her gaze at Morey. 'Your son has quite a temper.'

'Only because he's right,' Morey retorted. 'The Church says we follow a God of love, but then refuses to protect someone because of whom they love.'

'Exactly,' Raven boomed from fifty feet away. 'I sometimes wonder about this God to which I was so forcibly introduced. Doesn't your own Holy Book say we're supposed to love one another?'

Morey nodded. '"By this everyone will know that you are my disciples, if you have love for one another."'

Raven walked over to join us, his left wing folded awkwardly along his back. 'I have often wondered--' His head snapped up, eyes narrowing as he looked into the distance. I followed his line of sight, but could see nothing.

'Rats,' Aldred declared. 'A group of them, hurrying this way.'

'Jago,' Morey said calmly, 'would you mind flying to the ground?'

The smaller gryphon's ears twisted in confusion, but he did as his father had asked, landing on the grass near Bishop Aeron.

'Bishop,' Morey added in the same tone, 'would you mind imprisoning my son in your claws?'

The dragon acted without hesitation, shifting her weight to her hindquarters even as her forefeet whipped forwards. Jago squawked as her talons closed around him. Bishop Aeron sat back, raising her captive into the air. 'Done. May I ask why?'

'Because I can see seven rats.' Morey extended his wings. 'Six are chasing the seventh, and the one in front is Bastien.'

Grass and earth flew around us as Raven flung himself upwards, Morey following only a few wing strokes behind. 'Basty!' Jago called out, throwing himself against the dark claws which held him secure. 'I'm here, Bastien!'

Now I could make out the rat and those chasing him. Bastien's flight was erratic, his body rising with several quick wing beats, then falling as he faltered. The rats snapping at his tail showed no such difficulties. Their teeth gleamed as they closed in on their prey.

Raven roared a warning, and flung out a foreleg. Morey swooped past him, his own teeth bared as he snarled at the rats. Bastien folded his wings and fell into Raven's upturned foot. The dragon dropped down, landing heavily, still holding up the rat.

Morey tore into Bastien's pursuers, claws ripping across wings and flesh. The rats scattered. As Morey flew after one, Raven sent a quick blast of flame at two others. With a mixture of squeaks and snarls, the rats turned and headed back the way they'd come.

Raven hopped back to us, Bastien gasping in the dragon's forefoot. My breath caught in my throat as I saw his state. Very little fur was left on his body, just a few dark tufts on grey skin. His eyes were enlarged, as if something were pushing against them from deep within his skull. Blood trickled from a series of bite marks along his legs and tail. One ear was shredded, and the other was missing altogether.

'Penny,' the rat wheezed. 'Need to talk to Penny.'

I forced my numb legs to take me to Raven's side. 'I'm here, Bastien.'

'I saw it,' the rat croaked. 'Just before the Consortium turned on me. Thin places. They need large crossings. And your government is going to provide them.'

'How?' came Clyde's voice. I glanced down, and found him standing near my boots, a panting Morey at his side.

'Lots of deaths at once.' The rat's voice was beginning to fade. 'Lloegyr people.'

'The detention centres?' I asked. 'They're going to use the people in the detention centres?'

'Yes.' A white film was spreading across Bastien's eyes, and his hind legs began to jerk. 'The Minister. She's arranging. Letherum to control vampires and weres. Military to follow behind. Will protect crossings from closure.'

'Basty,' Jago begged from his cage. 'You can stop now. Where's a unicorn? He needs help!'

'Nothing can help this,' Bastien croaked. 'Mind blast.' With great difficulty, he managed to pull his legs under his body and rose to his feet. 'Please. Take me away from here. Away from Jago.'

Bishop Aeron asked gently, 'Wouldn't you rather have your husband at your side?'

'No,' I answered, suddenly understanding. 'If Jago's close to someone, he can feel what they're feeling. If he's close to Bastien now--'

'Take me away!' Bastien screamed. 'Don't let him feel me die!'

Raven leapt from the ground. I ducked as one wing came down near my head. The dragon headed straight up, Bastien held securely in his foot.

'Basty!' Jago screamed. 'Basty! Basty! Come back! Basty!'

High above us, Raven halted, his wings beating heavily as he hovered. The injured wing seemed to be holding firm. His head was lowered close to the rat, and I found myself quietly praying the Nunc dimittis. '"Lord, now lettest thou thy servant depart in peace, according to thy word. For mine eyes have seen thy salvation; which thou hast prepared before the face of all people. To be a light to lighten the Gentiles and to be the glory of thy people Israel."'

Raven raised his snout to the sky and roared a burst of flame. Extending his wings, he started a slow spiral down to us. I glanced at Jago. He was slumped down in the Bishop's foot, his eyes closed.

'I had no idea,' Llewelyn said miserably, 'that letherum would be used in this way.'

'You.' My fists clenched as I turned to him. 'You've been selling letherum to the Consortium, haven't you?'

'It was so we could expand our work here,' he pleaded. 'There were so many in need, and we had not enough space for all of them. And the Consortium said that we would be protected from *Cadw ar Wahân.*'

Raven landed and lowered Bastien's body to the ground. Bishop Aeron opened her foot, and Jago flapped down to the rat. The gryphon spread his wings over Bastien and began to sob. 'Oh, Basty, why? Why? You should've just checked in with the Consortium and ducked away again. You didn't have to pull all that stuff from his head!'

Bishop Aeron said quietly, 'He did it because he loved you.'

'No,' I retorted. 'Bastien did it because, by loving Jago, he learned to love all of us. He wanted to help us.'

'"No one has greater love than this,"' Morey added, '"than to lay down one's life for one's friends."' He flew to his son's side, and spread his own wings over Jago and Bastien.

'I never thought,' the Bishop said, 'that I would see a rat sacrifice himself for others.' She turned her head to Aldred. 'Summon the city council to meet me in the Cathedral. Send squirrels, not rats, and tell them to come when the bells are tolled in an hour's time.'

Her chaplain set off in a run, lifting into the air several strides later.

'I would ask that you come with me, Father Penny,' Bishop Aeron added. 'You should be at my side when I address your fellow councillors. I shall fly you to Llanbedr myself.'

'I can carry Penny,' Raven said.

I walked over to place a hand on his warm side. 'You've already used your wing quite a bit today. Please, don't overdo it. I'll go with the Bishop.'

'I'll keep Father Penny safe,' the Bishop said.

Raven snorted. 'Penny can look after herself. She knows how to handle her sword.'

There were times when I wished Raven didn't show such confidence in me. I glanced down at Morey. He shook his head. 'My son needs me here.'

Bishop Aeron lowered herself to the ground, and I winced as I noted the short gaps between her neck spines. This was going to be an uncomfortable trip.

Once I'd climbed up and slotted myself into the tight space, the Bishop rose to her feet and spoke to Llewelyn. 'I haven't forgotten your confession. Once this immediate crisis is over, expect a formal Visitation to Saint Raphael's.'

'And my resignation,' Morey said grimly. 'I cannot bring myself to work for a drug dealer.'

Llewelyn looked up at me. 'And you, Penny?'

As disappointed as I was in him, I couldn't quite bring myself to hurt the were-wolf any further. 'One thing at a time. I'll talk to you later.'

The Bishop set off at what she might have considered a gentle trot, but which bounced tender parts of my anatomy against her hard spines. I was relieved when we were finally in the air, and rearranged myself as best as I could. Never again would I complain about Raven's suitability as a mount.

Steady wingbeats carried us quickly to Llanbedr. We flew in low over the Cathedral, a number of councillors looking up to wave or bow their heads to the Bishop. The deep sound of the bells echoed against the nearby buildings. I gripped the thin spine in front of me as the dragon tilted her body, backwinging to land us on the green.

I slipped to the ground, and stepped away from Bishop Aeron's side. A squirrel dashed from the Cathedral, her long red tail lashing as she plunged to a halt by the dragon's feet. 'We've managed to find all of the councillors,' she wheezed. 'Most have agreed to come.'

'Most?' the Bishop rumbled. 'Not all?'

The squirrel glanced at me. 'The male human councillor refused.'

'That's okay,' I said. 'I'm the other representative for the humans in the city.'

Bishop Aeron shook her head. 'In this matter, I need you to be my priest, not a councillor. The humans will simply have to be unrepresented.'

'But--'

'Do I need to say the words "canonical obedience", Father Penny?'

I swallowed back my words. 'No, Bishop Aeron.'

We traded warm spring day for the cooler atmosphere inside the ancient building. A faint smell of incense hung in the air. I glanced at the side chapel set aside for personal prayer. The reality of Bastien's death was breaking through the initial numbness, and I longed for a few minutes alone to light a candle and shed a few tears. But I followed close behind my Bishop as she marched through the Cathedral, councillors quickly moving out of her way.

The thick walls cut out most of the noise from the bells. As the dragon turned, her tail sliding across the stone floor, the voices of the assembled crowd stilled. I moved to her side.

The elf who officiated at council meetings stepped forward, his fingers wrapped tightly around his staff. 'Bishop Aeron, the city council is only summoned to the Cathedral at the gravest of times. Why have you called us all here?'

'Father Penny,' the Bishop asked me, 'are the majority of the councillors present?'

I made a quick count. 'Most, yes. The merpeople are never represented, nor the rat kings.'

'Then we can begin.' Bishop Aeron inclined her head at the elf. 'Cledwyn, would you like to signal a start to this meeting?'

The elf faced the gathering. The sound of wood against stone rang out as he rapped the staff against the floor. 'I declare this special meeting of the Llanbedr City Council open.'

'Thank you, Cledwyn, councillors, for coming at my request,' the Bishop said. 'Each of you lives in close contact with your own species, in our unified yet divided city. Perhaps those who were affected by the latest actions of *Cadw ar Wahân* would like to address this gathering?'

There was a shuffle of feet and a few coughs. Then a were-sheep spoke up. 'Several of us were set upon last night, by ruffians disguised behind hoods and cloaks. Annabelle and her vampire husband were both injured, she very badly. Their house was set on fire.'

'We are aware of this attack,' a vampire said. 'Eurion's parents live in our community, and their house also had firebrands thrown through the windows.'

A were-wolf stepped forward with a growl. 'We saw off several attackers last night. Our pack leader nearly captured one, but she had to release her grip when a sword nearly sliced off her ear.'

'And us, and us, and us too,' a were-hedgehog squeaked, jumping up and down. 'We had someone come after us too.'

'We were brought warning by the police,' a unicorn said. 'We set up a guard, and no doubt our horns and hooves warned off any attempt on our lives.'

'Was any community unaffected?' Bishop Aeron asked.

'We weren't,' a dragon answered. He glanced over at me. 'But that may not remain the case.'

'Very few communities have not seen intermarriage,' Cledwyn commented, leaning on his staff. 'At our last council meeting, we could not reach agreement on whether such couples should be protected.'

The Bishop growled. 'They should indeed be protected. All of them are children of God.'

'Not that the Church has set a good example,' the dragon councillor stated. 'You don't allow your own clergy to marry out.'

'The Church does not condone violence against innocents,' Bishop Aeron declared. 'And those who have entered into holy matrimony, whatever the species, are not guilty of a crime. Therefore, I tell you, the Church stands ready to defend such couples. All churches in this diocese are hereby declared to be places of sanctuary. Any person threatened by *Cadw ar Wahân* who enters a church will be defended against any attacker.'

'By whom?' a were-sheep asked.

'By the Church, any clergy or laity who are able to offer teeth or claws or blades.' The Bishop bared her sharp teeth. 'I may be a bishop, but I am also a dragon. And a dragon always protects her own.'

Although I knew that Raven's matriarch happily ate both suitors and hatchlings, I decided this was a moment to keep my mouth shut.

'Well said, Bishop.' The unicorn archdeacon made her way through the Cathedral to our side. 'We do not seek this fight, but we will not allow the innocent to suffer. I stand ready to defend anyone who seeks sanctuary in this Cathedral, the mother church of our diocese.'

'Agreed.' The other archdeacon, Rhis Cadwalader, joined us. 'There are times when we are called to be the church militant.'

'And how do you feel about this?' the dragon councillor challenged me. 'Weren't you exiled to outside the city?'

'As someone in a mixed-species relationship,' I said slowly, 'I've found it difficult to serve in a Church which didn't recognise the committed love my husband and I have for each other. But the Church has acted before to save innocents, as when a vampire colony tried to seek refuge in Llanbedr. We all serve God, who is bigger and greater than our disagreements. And in this, the Bishop and her senior staff have shown that, in the name of God, the Church will continue to protect those who come to us.'

'We will call upon the police to work with the Church,' Bishop Aeron said. 'Those who have dared to act against the peace of our city will be caught and held to account.'

Cledwyn swept a gaze around the group. 'I support the Church's stance, and I will recommend that the elves in Llanbedr do as well. Our community will protect elves, their partners, and their families from any who would do them harm for their love choices. Who will join me?'

'We will!' the were-sheep stated.

The unicorns struck silver hooves against the floor. 'As will we.'

'And us,' a dragon said. 'I will encourage our brothers and sisters to aid in the defence of anyone in danger.'

'I'll need to speak first to our colonies,' one of the vampires stated. 'I can't pledge anything at the moment.'

'We can't either,' said a were-hedgehog. 'We need to speak to our nests.'

'Those of you who can pledge support,' Cledwyn said, 'send a message to the Bishop.'

'By squirrel, not rat,' Bishop Aeron added.

Cledwyn turned to face the dragon. 'Have you any more to add, or shall we draw this meeting to a close?'

'Nothing more for now.'

The elf struck the floor with his staff. 'I declare this meeting over. Keep yourselves and your communities safe.'

Aldred made his way over to me as the cathedral began to empty. 'Bishop, shall I fly Penny back to Saint Raphael's?'

'Yes, please do so.' She sighed. 'This unrest has not taken place in Llanbedr alone. I shall be speaking to my fellow bishops about setting up sanctuaries in their own cities. And thank you for your assistance, Father Penny.'

I shook my head. 'I don't think I did very much.'

'You are a living example of what we have decided to protect,' the Bishop said. She turned her head to Cledwyn, who obviously wanted to speak further with her. I followed Aldred out of the building.

Would today mark the beginning of a greater tolerance for mixed-species relationships? I could only hope and pray that it might.

Chapter Twenty-Four

Bastien's funeral was held in the woods near Saint Raphael's. Jago had decided that the agnostic rat would not have wanted the service to take place in the chapel, so a graveside memorial was arranged. In accordance with Jago's wishes, most of the community stayed away, with only the gryphon's closest friends and family present. Jago had rather pointedly excluded Llewelyn.

Raven dug out a small hole the evening before. The weather decided to be kind to us, and early morning sunshine filtered through the trees as we gathered around the grave.

Despite my severe misgivings, Jago had asked James to cross over. My brother carried the linen-wrapped body from the morgue to the place Jago had chosen as Bastien's final resting place. Even the bird song seemed hushed as James gently lowered the rat into the hollow, Jago swaying on my brother's shoulder.

Morey, with Taryn at his side, stood at the head of the grave. 'Bastien was not a Christian,' he said, 'and I won't dishonour him by pretending that he was. Nor can I say that I showed him much welcome when he and my son decided to marry. But in his final days, Bastien proved that he was a better person than many who call themselves Christian.'

'We wish that our son could have had years of happiness with his husband,' Taryn added. 'We have come to be proud that Bastien was our son-in-law. He was as brave as any member of our clans.'

Raven lowered his head to touch the white fabric that covered the rat. 'Bastien was a true friend to me.'

Clyde lifted his head and began to sing. We joined in after the first line.

> '"The day you gave us, Lord, is ended,
> the darkness falls at your behest;
> to you our morning hymns ascended,
> your praise shall hallow now our rest."'

Our voices fell away. I bent down to the mound of soil piled up next to the grave. The earth was moist, and slightly sticky, but I was still able to cast some onto the body. 'We commend Bastien to the mercy of God, and to the land of his birth. Earth to earth, ashes to ashes, dust to dust, committing his soul to the love from which he came and to which he has now returned.'

James followed my example. Taryn and Morey each ripped a feather from their chests and placed those in the grave. Clyde disappeared for a moment, and returned to add several flowers. Raven glanced at each of us in turn, then used a forefoot to shovel soil over Bastien's body.

Jago hopped down, his claws sinking into the grave. James and I walked away, followed by Raven. Taryn, Morey, and Clyde remained, pressing against the young gryphon to offer what comfort they could.

Once we were clear of the woods, James stopped me. 'I know, this is bad timing, but we need to talk about this before I head back. Like I said last night, we haven't seen any movement yet from the detention centres. If the government *is* planning to use Lloegyr people to create thin places, they must still be in the planning stage.'

Raven came to my side. 'You doubt what Bastien told us?'

'I don't know.' James ran a hand through his hair. 'It's just--look, I know Sue Harkness isn't on our Christmas card list, but would she really decide to kill a whole bunch of people?'

'She doesn't see them as people,' I pointed out. 'She's always referred to them as "creatures".'

'You have her mobile number, don't you?' James asked. 'How about you cross over with me and give her a call? Try to talk her out of this, if it's what she's really planning?'

I stared at him. 'Since when are you a fan?'

'I'm not.' James shook his head. 'But I just can't believe that anyone would do something like this. This is the British government we're talking about. Would they really arrange a mass murder? I mean, I thought we were the good guys.'

'The British government set up concentration camps in South Africa during the Boer War,' I pointed out, 'and killed innocent demonstrators in Amritsar, India. And that's just two things off the top of my head. Governments can justify doing terrible things, both to themselves and the general public.'

'This Sue Harkness sent a helicopter after us,' Raven growled. 'I would not be surprised at anything she might do.'

'Just try,' James said to me. 'We know for certain, now, that we have some people on the inside. They're ready to go into action if we need them to. But I don't want to put them at risk if we're not certain.'

I sighed. 'What do you want me to do? "Hi, Sue, it's Penny. Are you planning to murder people from Lloegyr?" Do you think she'd tell me the truth?'

James shrugged. 'Why not? She might think that there's nothing you could do about it anyway. Tell her you're married to Raven. You know she carries a grudge against him. Maybe that'll rattle her into talking.'

'Okay,' I said reluctantly. 'I'll come across and phone her. But won't she able to trace that to your place?'

'Nope,' he said with a grin. 'I've got the right kit now.'

Raven nudged my shoulder. 'Take your sword with you.'

I decided not to argue with him. So, once James and I were in my room, I slid the weapon onto my belt before we pulled the settee away from the wall. James shouted across to the other side. Once Skylar confirmed that the way was clear, we went through the thin place.

James opened a drawer and pulled out a small plastic device. 'Put this into the power slot on your iPhone. That'll keep Sue's people from tracing the signal back here.'

'Okay.' I turned the phone on, inserted the cube, and then pressed the number I had stored for the Minister without Portfolio.

The phone rang only twice before Sue answered. 'Penny. I do wonder how you manage to travel so easily to England. There must be a thin place you're using. Care to share its location with me?'

'Not after you shot at my husband,' I replied.

There was a moment's silence. 'Husband?' Some strange noises came down the line. 'Let me put you on speaker phone. I don't think I heard you correctly.'

'You did,' I said. 'The green-black dragon your helicopter tried to bring down, the dragon your mother named Raven, is my husband. But that shouldn't surprise you. His first love was a human woman, after all.'

'That damned dragon,' Sue hissed. 'I heard enough about him when she was still alive.'

'He makes a great husband,' I continued. 'Very thoughtful. Never mansplains or expects me to be the little woman at home. Pity your mother never really appreciated him.'

'Be very careful, Reverend,' Sue snapped. 'I wouldn't trust that dragon, or any dragon, for that matter.'

'Or anyone from Lloegyr?' I asked. 'You don't like any of them, do you?'

'Not a single one,' she said. 'We're wasting good taxpayers' money feeding the ones stranded over here. Good money which could be going to improve schools or ease the poverty of real people.'

'Pity you can't find any thin places,' I commented. 'Then you could send them back. End of problem.'

'The end of the problem is very near,' Sue said. 'They won't be a drain on our economy for much longer. Let's see what your precious dragon does about that.'

'I wish the Minister wouldn't fret about Raven,' came a familiar drawl. 'If his brains were dynamite, he couldn't blow his nose.'

My hand closed tight around my phone. 'Cornelius? Is that you?'

'Haven't missed me, have you? Course not. Bet you didn't even notice I'd gone.'

'What're you doing over there?'

'Making sure I'm on the winning side.' I heard the rasp of his forelegs opening and closing. 'I gave the Minister the solution to her little problem about crossings. What'd you say the other day? Lots of people dying at once creates thin places. Funny how she needed to be reminded of that.'

'Who are you talking to?' Sue asked. 'Penny? Are you still there? I hear a strange buzzing. Hold on, I'll be right back.' I heard the sound of heels against wood, and her voice came from a distance. 'Stanley? There's a problem with the phone line.'

'I have to pass everything through her bodyguard, that were-bear,' Cornelius continued. 'She has this blockage about seeing or hearing me. A bit tiring going around my ass to reach my elbow. But Pierre has been very good about helping me out. And he'll make sure that I'm as full as a tick when all this is over. Him and the Consortium both.'

Sue's voice was even harder to make out, and I wondered if she'd actually stepped outside the room. 'Stanley, please come to my office.'

I lowered my voice. '*You*, Cornelius? You're the one who gave her this idea of murdering everyone in the detention centres? But these are people from Daear, your own kind!'

'They are not my own kind,' the mantis retorted. 'And for every one who's ever given me the time of day, another six have treated me like gum on a boot heel. Once Lloegyr's run by this Minister, I'll be sitting pretty, and y'all will be lower than a snake's belly in a wagon rut. She's got plans, this Harkness woman. Just you wait and see.'

'But why now? There used to be lots of thin places. Why does she want them again now?'

Cornelius chuckled. 'Your country needs new opportunities, don't y'all? Wiseman Agricultural told her all about empty land ready for farming, minerals and forests lying around for the taking. And then there's those talks with the Consortium. It's going to keep everyone as busy as a one-legged cat in a sandbox.'

'I'm here again, Penny,' Sue said, sounding like her usual confident self. 'Was there any purpose to this call?'

'Yes, there was,' I replied quickly. 'Just to warn you to leave me and my husband alone. Next time, he won't hesitate to flame a helicopter if it's attacking him.'

My hand was trembling as I ended the call and lowered the phone. Three sets of eyes met mine. At some point during the conversation, Skylar and Dwysil had entered the room. My brother was seated on the couch, computer on his lap.

'So, do we now know for certain?' James asked. 'What did Harkness say?'

'Enough. Cornelius was in her office, and confirmed what she's planning. Kill off everyone from Lloegyr, open thin places, exploit the land and the people.' I handed him the device from my iPhone. 'How did that insect ever get loose in England?'

Skylar frowned. 'Remind me who Cornelius is.'

'A large praying mantis,' I replied. 'He comes from les Etats-Unis.'

'Is he a big bug who talks funny?' Dwysil asked. 'He was here. I opened the window for him 'cause he wanted to fly out. Was that wrong, Tad?'

'He must have crossed over from your place,' James said to me, then turned his head to smile at his daughter. 'You didn't do anything wrong, Pumpkin. Don't worry about it.'

'No point any of us worrying about it,' I agreed, although I was now regretting every word I'd ever spoken in front of the praying mantis. Later I'd try to work out how he managed to find his way to London. Did he receive help from flying rats? 'Sounds like Fred Wiseman and the rat kings are in on this as well.'

'All rat kings?' James asked.

'At least the one.' I sighed. 'The Consortium, the Firm, and the British government. What an unholy trinity.'

'Probably just as complicated as the holy one,' Skylar commented. 'And nowhere near as loving.'

I managed a small smile. 'James, those coaches and trucks, are they still outside the detention centre?'

My brother nodded. 'Last I looked, which was this morning before I crossed over.'

'Which probably means,' Skylar said, 'that your government is going to move them somewhere else first.'

'Somewhere out in the open, I should think.' James drummed his fingers on the laptop. 'If they want to send troops or tanks through, they'd want a large crossing, not something in a building. I think it's time. I need to ask our people to check all this out, even if it means they might get caught.'

I sat down on the settee. 'Please don't put anyone in danger.'

'They're willing to put themselves in danger,' Skylar said, 'in order to save the lives of others. As we all are.'

Dwysil raised her head. 'Me too.'

I gave her a smile. 'Your Mam and Tad will keep you safe.'

'My first Mam and Tad didn't,' the child reminded me. 'I hope my new Mam and Tad can.'

Skylar drew Dwysil into a hug. 'We'll do our best, but we've always said we won't make any promises we can't keep.'

Fear stabbed through my chest as I looked at my precious family. I wanted to urge them to hide, to keep away from any danger, but how could I ask them to do something I wasn't willing to do myself? James nearly dropped his laptop as I reached over to embrace him. I said into his shoulder, 'I'll send Jago over so he can pass on any news.'

Skylar frowned. 'You think he'll be up to that?'

'He'll want to be useful,' James said as I released him. 'And he'll want to help stop anyone else from being killed.'

'My sorrow for his sorrow,' Skylar told me. 'Please pass that on to Jago.'

'I will.' I was in desperate need of a cup of tea, but James had returned to his computer and Skylar was still holding their daughter. 'The next question is, if Harkness really does plan to murder people in order to create thin places, what can we actually do to stop her?'

The keyboard clicked under my brother's fingers. 'There's no point appealing to her better nature, she obviously isn't going to change her mind about Lloegyr people. We need to find some way of getting the British public on our side.'

'Trust the British public?' I remarked. 'That worked so well with Brexit, didn't it?'

'There was a time when I didn't think much of humans,' Skylar said slowly. 'But then I came to live in England, and I met people like Bishop Nigel and Rosie and you and James. I think that a lot of humans wouldn't just stand by if they knew that unicorns and gryphons and were-people and so on were going to be killed by their own government.'

James nodded. 'Harkness isn't going to swallow her pride and admit that humans aren't the most important beings in either world. But look at all the people who've signed up as "Friends of Aslan". We know that a lot of people know about Lloegyr and want to protect it. We just need many more of them.'

'Do we really want more people to know about Lloegyr?' I asked. 'You know how hard I've worked to keep Lloegyr secret.'

'You've worked very hard to keep Lloegyr *safe*,' James said gently. 'And I know how much that's cost you. But maybe keeping Lloegyr secret won't do that anymore.'

Skylar's smile softened the words she directed at me. 'Penny, you're not called to be the saviour of either world. God calls people into communities to work together, he always has, just look at the Israelites in the Old Testament or the disciples and Early Church in the New. That's what we need to do now. Pull people together into a community of action.'

I could see that they had a point. 'Okay, but how do we convince people that Lloegyr exists? Most of the general public don't have the Sight. Why should they believe in the existence of something they've never seen?'

'Sounds like the main reason why most people don't believe in God,' James commented. 'The good old, "Show me a miracle, and I'll believe." Where are we going to find a miracle?'

I found myself smiling at a favourite scene from *Buffy the Vampire Slayer*. 'Giles once said that he thought Buffy *was* a miracle.'

James straightened. 'That's it! We have to *Buffy* this!'

'I beg your pardon?' I asked.

Skylar laughed. 'I love how both of you say that.'

'Our mother's influence,' James said. 'Sis, remember how the TV series ended? All the potential Slayers were turned into Slayers for real. We need to bring the Sight to lots of people, and we know who can do that.'

'Epona.' I suppressed a shiver as I thought of the winged unicorn. 'Do you still have the photos which Colin's wife took of her?'

'I do, but we need something more than that,' James pointed out. 'Just giving people the Sight isn't going to be enough, not if we're going to have to talk them into doing something against the government. Give me time to hear back from our moles in the Minister's office, and think over what we could do.'

'I could visit Epona and take some video?' I suggested.

'I think we'll need something more dramatic than that,' Skylar said. 'Or people might just think it's something like those webisodes from your blog, you know, nothing more than some clever computer graphics.'

'We'll come up with something.' James stopped typing on his laptop and leaned back against the settee. 'Okay, that's it, I've told everyone "Christmas is here". That's like going on "Red Alert". It means anyone on the inside is to do whatever it takes to find out what's going on and to let me know.'

'Whatever the risk,' Skylar added grimly. 'What's the expression I've heard? The blow-up option?'

'The nuclear option.' I rubbed my face. 'Okay. I'll cross back over and ask Jago to come to you. And I'll go and find Epona. It might be worth having her at Saint Raphael's in case we need her at short notice.'

Dwysil pulled free from Skylar and walked over. 'Don't worry, Auntie Penny. It'll all be okay. You'll see.'

Warmth filled my body. I pulled her into a tight hug. In that moment, I knew I was willing to lay down my life for this child. 'Thank you.'

By the time I returned to my flat, lunch was over. I visited the kitchen to make up a cheese sandwich, which I consumed alongside a large mug of tea. Too unsettled to immediately return to my duties, I walked down the length of the building to enter the chapel.

Llewelyn was kneeling in front of the altar, head bowed. I quickly tried to retrace my steps, but his eyes opened and he looked up at me. 'Penny. There's no need for you to go.'

'I thought you might want to be on your own,' I said awkwardly. 'Well, you and God.'

'I find that God is saying very little to me right now.' The were-wolf rose to his feet and took a seat on a nearby pew. 'Unless he were planning to do so through you.'

'Not as far as I know.'

He crooked a smile. 'Then perhaps you could at least act as my conscience. Tell me, Father Penny, should I resign as Lead Chaplain at Saint Raphael's?'

I stifled a sigh and joined him on the wooden bench. 'Because you sold letherum to the Consortium?'

'Precisely. What did Morey call me? "A drug dealer"?' Llewelyn looked away. 'I thought I was acting in the best interests of Saint Raphael's and those whom we seek to serve. But to realise that my actions could lead to the deaths of dozens, if not hundreds of others... I cannot see how I can carry on.'

'I think you need to decide this for yourself,' I said, unwilling to add more misery to the obviously suffering were-wolf. 'Or maybe talk it over with your spiritual director?'

'Then answer me this, Father Penny.' Now the hazel eyes bored into mine. 'Are you willing to continue at Saint Raphael's if I remain here as Lead Chaplain?'

'I can't,' I told him. 'Not after Morey's made it clear that he won't. We're partners. We'd have to look for a new position together.'

'There is another option.' The words came slowly, painfully. 'Upon my resignation, I would recommend that you two were appointed joint Lead Chaplains. I know that the work we do here would continue to be successful under your leadership.'

I paused for a moment, acknowledging the great compliment he was paying to me and my Associate. 'If it comes to that, I'm certain Morey and I would give it a lot of thought.'

'Good,' Llewelyn said. 'I will return to prayer. Thank you for your assurances.'

As he returned to his position by the altar, I tiptoed out of the chapel.

Raven was sunning himself by the main building. I paused in the doorway to tighten my boots before joining him outside. 'I need to find Epona and ask her to come back here. Can we summon a search dragon?'

The dragon rose to his feet. 'I'll take you to her.'

'Really?' I looked up at his left wing. 'I'm assuming she's somewhere in Llanbedr. The vampire colony has moved on from the Bishop's back garden, but I'm not certain where.'

'I can manage Llanbedr and back again.' Raven flexed the wing. 'It'll simply take me a bit longer, if you demand that I take extra care. The unicorn medic has said that I will be at full strength soon.'

I weighed this up, adding in time it might take to find another search dragon. 'Okay. And I do want you to take it easy.'

'Noted.'

Glancing at the clouds gathering overhead, I retrieved my coat before climbing up his neck. After the uncomfortable flight on the Bishop, it was a relief to once again be seated between Raven's neck spines.

We set off at a gallop and gradually rose into the sky. I settled back and took pleasure at once again flying with my husband. Occasional glances at his left wing reassured me that the injured section seemed to be holding up well. If Raven were experiencing any discomfort, he was keeping quiet about it.

Llanbedr came into view. Raven swung to our left, skirting around the edge of the city's outskirts. We'd left the clouds behind, and I unfastened my coat as the sun provided some welcome warmth.

We followed the curve of the river. A collection of tents and small cottages appeared, arranged across close-cut grassland. I smiled as I recognised the gold and purple tent set in the centre of the cluster.

Elthan emerged as Raven circled the area. The dragon brought us down in a clear area between two buildings. The ground was soft, and my boots sank as I dismounted. I led the way to the colony's magister.

'Father Penny, Raven,' the vampire said, coming forward to grasp my arms in greeting. 'Be always glad to see you both.'

'And you as well,' I said. His grey hair was short and tidy, and his easy smile filled me with hope. 'This is your new home?'

'Aye, it be. Bishop Aeron did find us this land.' He released me to sweep a hand at our surroundings. 'Building goes slow, but steady. And what be the news of you and Raven?'

The dragon chuckled. 'We're married now.'

'At the last. She did take you on a merry chase.'

'But the catch was worth it,' Raven said.

'Once you've finished talking about me,' I commented, 'perhaps I could mention why we've come here? Magister, I need to speak to Epona. She still lives with you, I assume?'

Elthan sighed. 'Course she be here. She be welcome with us. Not many places else.'

I followed the line of his sight. A tent stood slightly back from the rest, the grass surrounding the woollen sides crisped to a dark brown. 'Keep well away,' I reminded Raven as we followed the magister over to the dwelling. 'You don't want her to touch you and take away your ability to fly.'

'Certainly not,' he agreed, dropping back.

The tent flap moved and Epona emerged. Her size reminded me of how long I'd been away from Lloegyr. She was no longer a small filly, but well on her way to full-sized mare. Her skin had darkened to full black, which made the red, green, and orange patterns striping her neck and swirling down her body almost glow in the sunlight. The horn had lengthened and the twists carried the same three colours. Her mane was still short-cropped, rising bright green from her curved neck.

'Epona,' I said, keeping my own distance. The one time I'd touched her, I'd been given glimpses of the future. 'How are you?'

The black-feathered wings rustled against her back. 'The colony have taken good care of me. I'm at home here.'

'I'm pleased to hear that.' I took a deep breath. 'I might need your help, if you're willing.'

The unicorn studied me. 'Depends on whom I'm helping.'

'When the crossings were shut between our two worlds,' I said, picking my words carefully, 'a number of people from Lloegyr were trapped in my home country, England. Their lives are in danger. The only way to save them is to give the Sight to the humans of my country.'

'I have little reason to love anyone from Lloegyr,' Epona said. 'Only the vampires have shown me any compassion.'

'And Father Penny,' Elthan said gently. 'Her friends be also good to you.'

'Yes, true.' Her green tail slapped against her hindquarters. 'What do you think, Elthan?'

'I be thinking that, whatever the Father asks of you, you be best to give.' He laid a hand on her side. 'She would not ask lightly.'

'I'm not certain what it might be, yet,' I added. 'But I'd be grateful if you could come back to Saint Raphael's with us. So you're nearby in case we have to act quickly.'

Silence. I forced myself to be patient, to wait, to pray that Epona would put aside her justifiable grievances and be willing to help protect her fellow citizens. I could hear the nearby laughter of children, and the distant gurgle of the river. A bird burst into song, notes rising and falling.

'Because it's you who's doing the asking,' Epona said finally, 'I will assist. But only for that reason.'

I nodded. 'Is there anything you'd like us to carry for you?'

'The colony has built a manger for my food, as I cannot graze.'

'We can offer you something similar at Saint Raphael's,' I assured her. 'And we can erect a tent.'

'She could share my barn,' Raven said. 'It's large enough for two.'

Just when I hoped that warmer weather might mean I could finally spend nights with my husband. I swallowed as I accepted the sacrifice. 'Anything else?'

'I have nothing else.' Epona turned her head to Elthan. 'I need only your blessing, Magister.'

The vampire traced a circle on her forehead. 'Clean running to your hooves, swift flight to your wings, and may earth and sky bring you safely back to this place, which be home to you and those who love you.'

I took my place on Raven's neck. As he prepared to take us into the air, I glanced down at the withered flowers near Epona's hooves. What exactly was I bringing to Saint Raphael's?

Chapter Twenty-Five

Raven kept his speed down during the return flight. Epona soon became bored by the pace. Within twenty minutes, she began to perform aerial acrobatics. I watched, my heart pounding, as she made loops in the sky and intricate curved patterns. 'You're quite the flier!' I shouted over to her at one point.

The unicorn dipped her wings to come closer. 'I like flying. I can't harm anything when I'm in the air.'

'So long as you don't come too close to them,' I said, nervous at her proximity to Raven.

'I can't harm anything while I'm in the air,' she repeated. 'I have to be connected to the ground to affect someone.'

'Glad to hear it,' Raven commented as one of her wings brushed past his. 'A sudden plunge to the ground would do neither Penny nor me much good.'

We reached Saint Raphael's without incident. Raven landed on the grass. After a moment's hovering, Epona settled down on the gravel. The weeds poking through the stones began to crisp.

Llewelyn finished a conversation with the were-horses and strode over to greet her. 'Welcome to Saint Raphael's. I am Llewelyn, currently Lead Chaplain here. May I have the holding of your name?'

'I have been given the name of Epona,' the unicorn replied. 'I suggest you keep your distance. Should you touch me, you would be stuck in your current shape for several months.'

The were-wolf smiled. 'You have been granted a special gift.'

'"Gift",' Epona echoed bitterly. 'Is it not a curse?'

'It would be a blessing to many of those who come here.' Llewelyn pointed at the nearest corral. 'Not-weres often struggle to maintain one shape. To be temporarily fixed in just one or the other, without the need for letherum, would be a gift indeed.'

I stared at him. 'Why haven't I ever thought of that before? Epona, you could be so useful here. I know you feel at home with the vampire colony, but maybe you'd be willing to visit from time to time to help us?'

The unicorn stared at us. 'I could be a blessing?'

'If you can indeed fix a were into one shape, yes,' Llewelyn said. 'May we ask you to visit some not-weres this afternoon? I would like to see if you can assist with some of our more difficult cases.'

'Yes.' Epona arched her neck. 'I would like to try.'

'She is going to stay in my barn,' Raven told the chaplain. 'And she'll need a feed trough and others to bring her grass and water.'

'All that can be arranged.' Llewelyn pointed at the corrals. 'Shall I give you an introduction to our work here?'

Once the two were out of earshot, I said to Raven, 'Just be careful around her.'

He chuckled. 'I will be, don't worry.'

I spent the next week fulfilling my duties, although sometimes it was hard to focus on the task at hand. The warmer weather meant I could leave my room's window open, so Jago could easily fly outside to find me. But I still went to the flat several times a day to check if he were waiting for me. Somehow I managed to resist the temptation to shout through the crossing to ask for any updates.

Several not-weres consented to being touched with Epona's horn. They rejoiced at being fixed in one shape, and the unicorn seemed overwhelmed at their gratitude. Offerings of flowers and apples were brought regularly to her feed trough in addition to fresh grasses.

At the end of the week, the Guild's trustees called a meeting to discuss Llewelyn's future. Raven and Epona made their barn available, as it was one of the few indoor spaces large enough to accommodate Bishop Aeron. Morey sat on my shoulder as we waited outside, as requested, whilst Llewelyn was questioned about his letherum dealings.

'Can you make anything out?' I asked after thirty minutes.

'Black,' Morey replied disapprovingly, 'would you expect me to eavesdrop on an important meeting like this?'

I turned my head to meet his eyes. 'Yes.'

He puffed out his cheek feathers. 'I've only picked up a few words. They must be at the far end of the barn.'

'My feet are starting to ache.' I sighed. 'I should have brought a chair.'

'No need,' Morey said, straightening. 'I think we're about to be called in.'

A moment later, the large door swung open. One of the trustees, a were-badger, blinked up at us. 'Fathers Penny and Morey, please join us.'

I entered the barn. Bishop and trustees were lined up on the left, Llewelyn facing them on the right. I stopped several feet away, not certain which side I was meant to join.

'We have discussed the situation at length,' a unicorn said, her skin gleaming even in the dull light. 'Father Llewelyn has expressed his sorrow at his actions. Although we accept that he sold the letherum not for any personal gain, it cannot be denied that what he supplied has been used to harm others.'

'In my capacity as Bishop Visitor to the Guild of Saint Raphael's,' Bishop Aeron added, 'I have advised the trustees that, in my view, Father Llewelyn can no longer continue as Lead Chaplain.'

The unicorn gave her a nod. 'The trustees are grateful for the Bishop Visitor's guidance, although the final decision rests with the trustees.'

Llewelyn glanced at me. 'I have already tendered my resignation.'

'His ability to offer wise leadership is in doubt,' the were-badger said. 'But not his undoubted talents as a healer. So we have decided that, although we accept his resignation from his role as Lead Chaplain, Saint Raphael's is still in need of his other skills.'

'So, Father Penny,' Bishop Aeron rumbled, a note of amusement in her voice, 'the trustees have decided that Father Llewelyn could continue to serve on the ministry team, so long as others are appointed Lead Chaplains in his stead.'

'Fathers Morey and Penny,' the unicorn continued, 'we invite you to become joint Lead Chaplains of Saint Raphael's.'

I had mentioned Llewelyn's idea to Morey, so I already knew his answer. 'We're both honoured by your offer. Before we accept, we'd have to discuss this with our spouses.'

'Understood,' the unicorn said. 'It would also be your decision as to whether you would accept Father Llewelyn as a member of the ministry team.'

'The Christian faith is based on forgiveness,' Morey said solemnly. 'Llewelyn has repented of his actions. Should I become a Lead Chaplain here, I would be pleased to continue to work with him.'

I nodded. 'I agree with Morey.'

'The community here needs to know that we have secured their future leadership,' Bishop Aeron said. 'Could you kindly make your decision by the end of the week?'

'We will,' Morey assured her.

I kept my mouth shut until we were back outside. 'Is this what you'd want, Morey? Or Taryn? Isn't she tired of commuting to Llanbedr every day?'

'The exercise is good for her.' Morey chuckled. 'I could use a bit more myself. No, we're quite happy here. But we're in our home country, in our own world. What about you? Wouldn't you want to return to England as soon as that's feasible?'

'With a dragon for a husband?' I smiled at the thought. 'It's taken some time, but maybe I'm starting to feel at home here. My main complaint is there's no place for Raven and me to live together. The barn might be all right in the summer months, but I'd want central heating in the winter. And plumbing.'

'Then demand that the Guild build an appropriate place for you both,' Morey said. 'That does mean you should consider serving for at least a couple of years in return for their investment.'

'On the other hand, I do miss England,' I admitted. 'Not that I can go there yet. I'll talk it over with Raven and see what he thinks.'

'As I will with Taryn.' Morey stiffened. 'A rat is coming.'

The white rat, grey wings spread wide as she glided towards us, was approaching from the direction of Llanbedr. I walked over to the nearest corral, giving her a place to land. She backwinged and dropped down onto a post.

'Who is your rat king?' I demanded.

'I serve the Consortium,' she replied with a sniff. 'A message for you, from Wiseman bold and true. Upon the end of the race, there will be for you a special place. Nearly over is the wait, so prepare for a new state. Remember where your loyalties lie, for whom you will live or die.'

'State of being?' Morey asked. 'Or state as in nation?'

The rat chuckled. 'Clever question. Which do you think?' She turned her gaze to me. 'Do you want to send a response to Fred Wiseman?'

'Tell him,' I said stiffly, 'that I do know where my loyalties lie.'

She dipped her head. With a quick flash of wings, she was aloft again and flying back towards the city.

I groaned. 'Why couldn't it be a straightforward message? "Dear Penny, we have planned some chaos and mayhem next Monday." Why does it have to be so cryptic?'

'It's clever to be cryptic,' Morey commented. 'Enough to tell you to be prepared, if you're on his side, but not enough for you to do anything to stop him, if you're not. At any rate, I think we can assume that Wiseman and company are about to make a move of their own. And it probably isn't too great a leap to also assume that it's linked to what your government is planning.'

'Don't call them "my government",' I said, walking us towards the main building. 'At the moment, they are definitely not representing me. And to think I voted for that party in the last General Election. First time ever, and I can tell you, it's the last time as well.'

'Glad to hear it.' Morey fluffed his cheek feathers. 'I'll speak to Taryn tonight. You'll have a chat with Raven?'

'Yes. Bishop Aeron was right. People here need to know what's going to happen next.'

'In some ways, Llewelyn hasn't acted very differently than the British government,' Morey said. 'Both he and Harkness believe that the ends justify the means. We have said we'll forgive the chaplain. Will we be so willing with the Minister?'

'I don't think she'll see anything wrong with what she does,' I pointed out. 'And repentance is part of the process.'

The door to the house opened, and the smell of roasting meat drifted out. My stomach growled in response. Time for Evening Prayer and then dinner. I took us inside.

The conversation with Raven took more time than I'd expected, and so it was very late when I finally went to my flat. My inability to come to a decision about the trustees' offer kept me awake for even longer. Raven was of the opinion that he could happily live anywhere in Lloegyr, now that he could fly again. It was easy enough for him to visit the search dragon settlement, using air crossings, wherever I worked. So the choice was entirely mine to make.

It seemed like I'd only just managed to fall asleep when a bounce on my arm pulled me out of a dream about rampaging were-hedgehogs. 'Auntie Penny, Auntie Penny,' Jago whispered insistently. 'You need to cross to the other side right now.'

'In the middle of the night?' I groaned, fumbling for the bedside candle. 'Tell James I'll be over in a minute. I'm not turning up in my pyjamas.'

The spluttering light was of little help as I searched for my spare boots. I didn't want to attempt the stairs in the dark to retrieve my usual pair from the front door. When I was finally dressed, I pulled the settee away from the wall and followed Jago through.

The bright lights of electric lamps made my eyes ache. I paused for a moment to allow my pupils to adjust. James was seated on the sofa, hunched over his laptop. Skylar came into the room and handed me a mug of coffee. I saw no sign of Dwysil and assumed that she was in bed.

'I've heard from Digory and the Badgers,' James said, sipping from his own mug. 'They started moving people from the detention centres around midnight.'

A deep gulp of coffee did little to ease the sudden chill in my stomach. 'Any idea where they've been taken?'

'Areas out in the countryside, but with good vehicular access. Digory's given me the GPS coordinates.' James frowned at his computer screen. 'He's also sent me a few photos.'

I took a seat next to my brother and looked at the pictures. Some were clearer than others, but I could see that high chain-link fences had been erected in fields. 'Basically those are large cages, aren't they? Shove the people in and lock the gate. They won't be able to get out, not even those with wings.'

'Not if they've been given letherum,' Skylar agreed. 'Mr Beaver sent a message that all of the vampires had been forced to swallow letherum tablets. They also gave tablets to any were-birds. Gryphons have had their wings clipped.'

Jago said something low and rude. I glared at the young gryphon. 'I agree with the sentiment, but I'm glad Dwysil isn't in the room.'

'Sorry, Auntie Penny,' Jago said, although his tone lacked any apologetic note.

'And there are reports of troop movements.' James brought up new images. 'Soldiers. Tanks.'

Skylar looked grim. 'Is this an invasion?'

'I think they'd arrange more firepower if they were planning to invade,' James said. 'More likely, they just want to make sure the thin places stay open while they plan their next move. They know that something keeps closing them off, even if they might not know that it's search dragons.'

'At any rate, the time to act is now.' I forced myself to stop chewing on my thumbnail. 'Any ideas?'

'We need to get Epona over to England, and make sure people see her.' James nodded at a nearby table. Three small black cubes rested on the wooden top. 'As many people as possible. Have her fly over London, and you on Raven alongside her. You'll wear a camera and capture the whole thing. I'll livestream the videos over social media, and try to get it to go viral.'

I frowned. 'So lots of people develop the Sight. But how does that help us stop Harkness from murdering detainees?'

'I'm going to include the co-ordinates of the cages,' James said, 'and tell everyone to get in a car or on a bike and get over there. I'll make it sound like the most exciting media event of the century, something no one wants to miss out on. If lots of people crowd there, all with their own smart phones filming away, the government's plans will be exposed. Harkness won't dare to carry it out.'

'From what I've seen,' Skylar continued, 'humans are fascinated by unicorns, dragons, and vampires. My hope and prayer is that you will all rise up to protect us.'

'That's what we're aiming for,' James said. 'Very helpful that Harkness decided to do this on a Saturday. I'd better get you rigged up with the camera, Sis.'

'And then I'd better hurry back,' I pointed out. 'We'll want more than just camera people flying alongside Epona. She'll need protecting.'

James paled. 'I never thought of that. You expect Harkness to send, what, fighter jets after you?'

'Helicopters, at least,' I said. 'Like last time. I'll take those extra cameras and put them on other people. Just in case something happens to me.'

Skylar nodded. 'I'll be one of them.'

'No, you won't,' I told her. 'Dwysil's already lost one mother. I'm certain I'll find volunteers at Saint Raphael's.'

James put down the laptop and rose from the settee. 'I'll show you how to rig it up on you, and you can do the same for the others.'

The harness was snug on my chest, and the camera rested in a small compartment at the front. My brother showed me how to train the lens to remain focused on a pre-determined subject. 'So if Raven has to duck and dive,' I commented, 'the camera will automatically do its best to track Epona.'

James grinned. 'Yes. And that's why my credit card is groaning. Top kit doesn't come cheap. But it's worth every penny.'

'Ha ha ha.' I picked up the remaining harnesses and cameras, and found another object underneath. 'And what's this?'

'Two-way radio.' James clipped it on the harness, and gave me an ear piece. 'It'll work here in England, and that way we can communicate with each other.'

'Even in the air?'

'No probs,' James said. 'You might have to shout so I can hear you. Just pretend I'm sixteen and I've raided the whisky cabinet again.'

'That'll do it,' I agreed. 'I'd better go.'

'Yes, I guess so.' James threw his arms around me in a tight hug. 'You keep safe out there, okay?'

'Don't worry, Raven won't let anything happened to me.' But I drew in a deep breath of his smell, a mixture of sweat and mint shampoo. Despite my brave words, I knew full well that Sue Harkness would not hesitate to shoot me down. Would this be the last time I ever saw my brother? It was with extreme reluctance that I left his embrace and walked back through the crossing.

Chapter Twenty-Six

Miriam, Llewelyn, and Sorcha stood beside me, all of us staring anxiously at the sky as we waited near Raven's barn. Miriam and Sorcha had been kitted out with the cameras, and we'd calibrated all three devices to follow Epona. To her credit, the winged unicorn had readily agreed to assist us, despite the dangers. 'For the sake of those who have given me shelter,' she said, 'I will forgive those who have rejected me.'

While it was still dark, Raven and I had taken Clyde aloft so the snail could cut a crossing through to London. Then Raven had left for the search dragon settlement, and I'd gulped down a quick breakfast and another cup of coffee. Now, two hours later, I realised that I could have taken my time. I pulled out an apple and bit into the wrinkled skin. The sharp taste filled my mouth.

'There he is!' Jago shouted from his perch on my shoulder.

The distinctive shape of my husband came into view. I strained my eyes to look past him. To my great relief, a half dozen search dragons followed close behind, including Tyra. Raven backwinged to land in front of me. The other dragons found room between the main building and the woods.

'We are ready to fly,' Raven announced. 'And we're ready to fight and die.'

'More of the fighting, though,' Tyra commented, 'and less of the dying.'

I looked past Raven at the other dragons. 'Have you been told what helicopters are? And what people in them might do to you?'

'I've explained all of that,' Raven said. 'That's why it's taken so long for us to return.'

I took a deep breath. 'Because of the danger?'

Tyra chuckled. 'Because so many wished to help. We are only the first group.'

The air groaned with the weight of dragons. At least twenty were hurrying towards Saint Raphael's, heads high, steam trailing from their nostrils. I straightened, hope warming my chest. And I tried to remember what the correct term was for a group of dragons.

The volunteers settled where they could. Weres rushed out of barns and other buildings, voices raised high in amazement. 'We'd better go,' I said to Raven. 'Never mind Sue's plans, we need to let this place calm down again.'

'Agreed.' He lowered himself, allowing an easy mount. Miriam climbed up to Tyra's neck and Sorcha chose another dragon nearby.

'I'm to fly in the middle,' Epona told the dragons. 'Make sure your riders have a clear view of me.'

'The rest of you,' Raven said loudly, 'are to protect us from all comers. If you see one of the human flying vehicles, flame it immediately.'

I bit my tongue, although my heart sank at the thought of lives which might be lost. But we couldn't take the risk of allowing any helicopter, or plane, to come too close. No doubt Sue and her people would quickly work out Epona's importance, and she would be their target.

Morey landed on my shoulder and nudged Jago with his beak. 'Go and join Clyde, now.'

The argument between father and son had raged earlier in the morning, until Jago finally agreed to stay behind. His ruffled feathers still showed his annoyance as he flew down to join the snail. I glanced at Clyde, who flashed encouraging colours of blue and green.

The dragons extended their wings, sunlight catching green and black along the folds. I was suddenly reminded of sails and ships. Never mind what the official group noun was for dragons. I decided that Raven and I were leading a flotilla. A flotilla of search dragons.

The assemblage leaned back on their hindlegs. Raven roared and kicked us upwards. The other dragons followed, Taryn dropping onto Miriam's shoulder as we headed away from Saint Raphael's.

Epona galloped across the now empty green, flinging out her wings to lift herself into the air. As she settled into place behind Raven, I checked the ear piece which James had given me. It felt snug, and I could only hope that the loop wouldn't become dislodged should my husband have to do any quick manoeuvres.

'Going through to London,' Raven called out. 'Be prepared.'

I flicked the camera on as we went through the air crossing. Clyde would have chosen a place which had a strong connection to Raven, so I was intrigued to see Buckingham Palace emerge beneath us. The Royal Standard fluttered in the breeze, revealing that Her Majesty was in residence. I wished we could drop in and let her know what her government was planning. Surely the Queen of Great Britain and Northern Ireland would not approve of any attack on her sister realm?

Telling myself to focus on reality, not fantasy, I held on as Raven dropped us back to fly on Epona's left. Tyra was on the unicorn's right. The dragon carrying Sorcha flew behind. All three cameras appeared to be tracking their target.

'I've got her, Sis,' James' voice came into my ear. 'Going out on Facebook now, copied across to Twitter, Instagram, and YouTube. The "Friends of Aslan" are going to share it everywhere. We're also contacting news stations and websites to let them know that they should keep an eye on social media, hashtag "flyingunicorn".'

'Do we know what's happening to the detainees?' I shouted at the small black receiver on my chest.

The pause made my breath catch in my throat. After a moment, James answered, 'Digory isn't communicating, so we think he's been rumbled. The Beavers say that the last of the Lloegyr people are in the pens. Oh, guess what, I'm getting some footage of the detainees. I think one of our people has managed to send a drone into the air. No, drones! There's a stream coming in from a second location. This is even better. People will definitely want to come when they see Lloegyr people in the pens.'

'It looks like nothing's happening yet,' came Jago's voice. I found myself smiling, pleased that the gryphon crossed over to help my brother. 'I'll keep watch on Skylar's laptop, James.'

'Good idea,' James said. 'Let me know if anything starts up. Pen, can you fly past Parliament? Epona with Big Ben in the background would be really great imagery. I can add all sorts of hashtags.'

'Houses of Parliament!' I told Raven. 'Epona, follow us there!'

Raven tipped his wing and turned left. The unicorn and other dragons followed. The Thames sparkled below us as we traced the river to the seat of the British government. Epona flew lower, allowing pedestrians on Westminster Bridge to see her. I saw jaws dropping open and smartphones aiming at us as our flotilla soared over human heads and past Elizabeth Tower. Big Ben tolled as Epona rounded the stone structure, we three camera-bearers hanging back to obtain the best images.

'That's great,' James told me. 'Twitter is going mad. "Flyingunicorn" is trending, along with "londondragons". Good work! Now have Epona fly past the London Eye.'

I shouted out his instructions. The unicorn obeyed, crossing over the Thames to the slow turning wheel. People in the observation capsules waved and pointed at us, cameras and phones raised. 'We should be carrying a banner with the hashtags,' I told James. 'Pity we didn't think of that. Lots of people are taking photos.'

'Don't worry,' he told me, 'it's already going viral. One of the London news stations has picked up the story.'

I raised my head at the sound of rotary blades chopping at the air. 'Don't attack!' I commanded as the blue and white helicopter drew near. 'It's here to film Epona! They're not a danger to us!'

A large camera on the chopper's nose swivelled in our direction. I gave a wave, before pointing at the unicorn. My fear was that the news crew might find dragons more interesting than Epona, yet it was she that we needed people to see. 'It's from the BBC!' I told James. 'Can you contact them with the locations of the detainees?'

'I'll try,' he said. 'They might not want to add it to the news report, but I'll do my best.'

I tensed at the sound of much larger blades chopping the air, raising a hand to shield my eyes from the sun. Morey was quicker than me. 'Military!' he shouted at the flotilla.

'We've got company,' I told James. 'Five helicopters.'

'Stick close to the Eye,' James instructed. 'They won't dare open fire on you there.'

A dozen dragons peeled off, heading towards the helicopters. Their chests expanded and they rose to face the dark green threat. Smoke trickled from their nostrils. The remainder of the flotilla drew in closer to us, their bodies a fleshy wall of protection around Epona and her camera crew. Morey climbed down from my shoulder to my chest.

Doors opened in the sides of the helicopters. Sunlight glinted off the dark rifle barrels. The sound of rapid gunfire made people below us shriek and flee into nearby buildings. The news helicopter turned and the camera was aimed at the dragons.

Several dragons roared as bullets tore through wings and bodies. They fell away, red blood streaming from their wounds. The uninjured dragons opened their jaws and blasted flame at the helicopters. The personnel behind the rifles screamed as fire tore across their bodies. The smell of charred flesh wafted across my nose and my stomach lurched.

One dragon crashed into the river. Another fell onto Westminster Bridge, her lashing tail knocking onlookers from their feet. A third came within a few feet of hitting the London Eye, somehow managing to pull away even though one of his wings was in tatters.

The damaged helicopters drew back. Two rose above us, doors firmly shut. 'Careful, Sis,' James said in my ear. 'I think they're sending for reinforcements. Can you get out of there? I have enough footage now.'

'Oh, no, it's Peter!' Jago's words made me start. 'James, do you see, there he is! He's in the pen!'

'I see Peter,' James confirmed. 'He doesn't look handcuffed or anything.'

'I bet he put himself in there,' I said, furious. 'He probably thought that that might stop Sue from carrying out her plans.'

Morey growled, 'He should have known better.'

'And it looks like Harkness is picking up the pace,' James added grimly. 'Soldiers are rushing out with guns and--what's that? Oh, that's just fantastic. Looks like they're planning to spray something inside the pens. Mr Beaver has just texted me. Petrol. They're going to spray petrol inside and then set the whole lot of them on fire.'

'What else is happening?' I demanded. 'Have any civilians showed up yet?'

'There's some movement, yes.' There was a pause, which only took seconds but felt like hours. 'Okay, I'm changing the message. I'm now telling people what's really happening, that their own government is planning to kill refugees and that we need lots of people to turn up to stop them.'

'We need more than humans,' I said. 'We need to have dragons there. Raven, can you locate Peter?'

'Of course,' the dragon rumbled. 'But he's at least an hour's flight from London, even at our top speed. The only air crossing is the one which we used to get here.'

'James, we can't stop them,' I said in despair. 'Not without air crossings. What're we going to do?'

'Head back to Buckingham Palace, for now,' James suggested. 'And keep low. Harkness might send some more airpower after you, but I bet they won't dare to attack you with the Queen there.'

'I could settle on the building,' Raven offered.

'I'm not certain the Palace was built to cope with the weight of a dragon,' I said. 'But if worse comes to worse, I suppose we could land in the gardens.' Would that be a treasonous offence? I could only hope not. I was in enough trouble with the government without upsetting my sovereign as well.

Raven shouted the new instructions across to Epona and the remaining dragons. We turned and headed back the way we'd come, keeping low to discourage any further military interference. The BBC helicopter continued to follow us, but at a greater distance than before. No doubt the dragons' attack had left the pilot rather nervous about coming too close.

'Any updates?' I asked James as Raven swerved around an office block.

'Looks like the petrol's being prepared,' my brother replied. 'Civilians are turning up, which is pulling soldiers away from the pens to do crowd control. But I don't think it's going to be enough. I'm sending the drone footage across all platforms.'

'It's too late,' I told Morey. 'What can we do now?'

The gryphon met my eyes. 'Pray. Like you've never prayed before.'

Dear God, I responded, *if you were ever going to send me a miracle, now would be pretty good time.*

The air shimmered on our left. A moment later, a search dragon emerged, Llewelyn seated on her neck. Clyde was clasped in the were-wolf's arms and Jago gripped his shoulder. The dragon dropped down as Clyde carved out another crossing. 'Follow us!' Llewelyn shouted.

'You go!' Tyra told Raven. 'Epona and I will land in that big garden!'

As Raven turned to follow Llewelyn's lead, I told James, 'I'm about to follow Clyde and Llewelyn out of here. And Tyra's going to drop down to Buckingham Palace.'

'I don't think it's a hanging offence,' James assured me. 'Where are the rest of you going?'

'I haven't a clue.' And then we went through the crossing.

The parks around the Palace were replaced with the view of a long field. Below us, their voices raised in desperate pleas for help, were a hundred Lloegyr citizens. Several clung to the rungs of the fence, hands bleeding from the sharp sides as they tried to climb their way out. Nozzles linked to large metal cylinders were aimed at the enclosure, and the chemical smell of petrol filled the air.

One of the search dragons tried to drop down to the enclosure. Rifle fire met her attempt, and she veered away. 'No flames!' I shouted at the flotilla. 'Not with all that petrol!'

'Pen, you won't believe this,' James said breathlessly. 'Epona landed in the private bit of the Palace gardens. And the Queen herself has come outside!'

'Her security people are allowing that?' I asked, searching for Peter in the crowd as Raven flew past. 'With a dragon there?'

'Why would she have bodyguards following her around when she's at home? Miriam's dismounted and her camera's still trained on Epona. And, oh wow, the Queen's gone up to talk to Epona and Tyra! Taryn's just landed on Her Majesty's shoulder. Talk about great footage! New hashtags coming up. "UnicornQueen" and "DragonQueen". I'll switch over to you in a moment. Aim your camera at the pen.'

'Doing it now.' I looked up as Llewelyn's mount flew off. A moment later, Clyde had cut another thin place, and they were gone.

'My wife,' Morey commented. 'Meeting Her Majesty Queen Elizabeth the Second. I trust they're telling the Queen what Sue Harkness is doing.'

'There aren't enough humans here,' I told James as the soldiers raised their guns and people stepped back. 'I think they're going to do this anyway.'

The air beneath us shivered as a new crossing appeared. A moment later, were-horses galloped through, followed closely behind by several unicorns. Members of the Saint Raphael's community had arrived.

'Blimey!' James said. 'Her Majesty's pulled out her phone and she's calling the Prime Minister. She's asking him what Harkness has been up to and if her government is really planning to torch innocent people.'

The soldiers stared at the sight of Lloegyr citizens outside the cage. Several civilians rushed at them, grabbing at the rifles. Shots flew into the air, and Raven quickly twisted to one side. More humans surged past and joined the snorting equines.

'Did you see that?' I asked James.

'Yes, I did. See, told you the great British public wouldn't let us down.'

The soldiers standing by the petrol cylinders had removed their hands from the nozzle controls. They made no move to draw their guns as the mixed crowd headed to the pen.

'Clyde's been busy,' James' voice broke through the shouts below me. 'I'm getting footage from drones above the second site. Bishop Aeron has appeared, along with some other dragons and a gryphon. They're having to avoid rifle fire--oh, Aeron's grabbed a man from the ground. That's stopped the others from shooting.'

'And the third site?'

'Not so good. I don't think there's a thin place yet, so no one from Lloegyr's got through.'

'Maybe Clyde doesn't have a connection to anyone held there,' I fretted. 'How far is it from the other locations?'

'It's about five miles west of you. Send some people over! I've looked at Google maps. They only need to follow the road, it pretty much leads straight there.'

Morey crawled back up to my shoulder. 'I'll tell Sorcha and her dragon. They can take a group to that site.' And he flew off.

'Dragons are going,' I told James. 'And maybe the Prime Minister will put a stop to all this.' A sound from the pen made me look down. 'They've managed to get the lock off. And there's Peter!'

I sighed in relief. Peter stood at the pen's opening, calmly controlling the people leaving the cage to stop any sudden rush. As they streamed out, more humans ran across the field, waving arms and aiming phones. One woman threw her arms around a unicorn. An elderly man stopped to chide a soldier, then turned to smile at a gryphon.

'I see Sue Harkness,' Raven growled. The Minister was striding away, her phone pressed against her ear. 'Gunnhild, capture that human!'

As the search dragon swooped after Harkness, I said to Raven, 'I'd have thought you'd want to go after her yourself.'

'Not a good idea. I might lose what's left of my temper and eat her.'

I smiled. 'That's good of you.'

'I was only thinking of my stomach. No doubt she'd cause me severe indigestion.'

Gunnhild dropped down and swiped her tail at the Minister, knocking the woman from her feet. At the dragon's roared command, a were-bear ran over. She removed her belt and used it to bind Sue's arms together.

Raven lowered us into a rough landing. A sigh escaped his throat as he folded his wings, and I patted his neck in sympathy. He had been flying for quite a long time. 'Just need a bit of rest,' he told me gruffly as I slid to the ground. 'And a fresh deer.'

'We've done it, Sis,' James said. 'The dragons arrived at the third site. All pens have been opened. A couple of soldiers were bitten, and I'm afraid a few people were shot. But unicorns are helping out, and I don't think anyone's died. Oh, and have a look at BBC One!'

I pulled out my iPhone and launched the BBC iPlayer app. And there, on my screen, was the Queen. She stood outside Buckingham Palace, Epona at her side, as a reporter repeated, 'So there's this entire parallel world alongside our own, and we're only just now hearing about it?'

'There is,' the Queen declared. 'We are entranced by these visitors from our sister country, and no doubt the entire nation will join us in welcoming them to our shores. We look forward to our government developing peaceful relations with Lloegyr.'

'Brilliant stuff,' James commented. 'Okay, you can turn your camera off. I'll keep the drone footage a bit longer but I think the Queen has cracked it.'

I forced myself to put the iPhone away. No doubt all the highlights from today would be pasted across social media and news channels and I could watch later. For now, I took in the sight of multiple species mingling in peace. One woman was speaking shyly to a unicorn, her eyes tearing as he gave her permission to touch his gleaming hide. A gryphon, his extended wings showing clearly where the feathers had been clipped, was being comforted by a vampire.

'What will happen to her?' Raven asked, pointing with his snout at Sue Harkness. The were-bear rested a large hand on the Minister's shoulder, and Gunnhild stood nearby.

'I'd like to see her thrown in jail,' I replied bitterly. 'But no doubt she'll just be moved to another department.'

'I don't think so,' Jago said as he landed on my shoulder. Llewelyn's dragon was landing nearby, Clyde still clutched in the were-wolf's arms. 'My mam told the Queen all about her plans. And the Queen's in charge, isn't she? She can have the Minister thrown into the castle dungeons, can't she?'

I gave his head a scratch. 'Remind me sometime to explain how a constitutional monarchy works. The Queen does have a direct line to the Prime Minister, though.'

Raven chuckled. 'Gunnhild might be happy for a quick snack.'

'There will be no snacking on humans,' I said firmly. 'No matter how tempting the idea. I firmly draw that line.'

'Penny!' Peter's familiar voice made me smile. He hurried over, making his way past a several dwarves. 'You'll have to fill me in some time on how all this came together.'

'But you played your part, didn't you?' I asked. 'As a "Friend of Aslan"? Are you Digory?'

'That's me.' He ran a hand through his greying hair. 'Penny, I'm sorry, but there's something I need to tell you. You see, well, Jenny and I have been seeing each other and, well, you see, she's pregnant.'

'Congratulations,' I said, and meant it. 'You'll make a great father.'

'Thank you.' Peter took a deep breath. 'We need Clyde to make some crossings so we can send people back to Lloegyr. Maybe Raven can spread his wings and hide Clyde from the crowd.'

'And then throw blood at the crossings afterwards,' the dragon commented glumly.

'Why can't we leave them open?' Jago asked. 'I mean, your country knows about us, now. Can't people just come and go between the two?'

Raven lowered his head to mine. 'That would free you to decide in which world to live, perspicacious Penny. I would easily be able to transverse between England and Lloegyr.'

I leaned against his side, suddenly giddy with the choices opening up in front of me. Becoming joint Lead Chaplain at Saint Raphael's still appealed. On the other hand, if Raven could travel between our worlds, I could look at returning to a parish in England.

'Both countries would have to decide how to treat the access points,' Peter mused. 'Whether as borders with crossing checks, or just leave it fully open. And I suppose, over time, we'd need to think about matters like dual citizenship.'

'And we'd want to change things in government,' Jago said. 'We'd want our own people in Parliament.'

'The chamber would have to be enlarged to hold dragons,' I noted. 'Or full-sized gryphons.'

Morey thumped onto my free shoulder. 'Well, at any rate, there's no way to keep Lloegyr secret anymore.'

Raven twisted his neck to look at me. 'How do you feel about that, valiant Penny?'

I smiled at the swirl of bodies surrounding us. People from England and from Lloegyr hugging, laughing, crying. Even the soldiers, their weapons now in a pile and guarded by several dragons, looked pleased. A weight lifted from my shoulders, and I threw my head back in a laugh. 'Free! I feel free!'

I hope you've enjoyed Penny's adventures!

Will you please take a moment to leave me a review at Amazon?

Thank you.

Chrys Cymri

About the Author

Priest by day, writer at odd times of the day and night, I live with a small green parrot because the upkeep for a dragon is beyond my current budget. Plus I'm responsible for making good any flame damage to church property. I love 'Doctor Who', landscape photography, single malt whisky, and my job, in no particular order. When I'm not busy with ministry work, I like to go on far flung adventures to places like Peru, New Zealand, and North Korea.

Discover other titles by Chrys Cymri

The Temptation of Dragons (Penny White # 1)
The Cult of Unicorns (Penny White # 2)
The Vengeance of Snails (Penny White # 4)
The Vexation of Vampires (Penny White # 5)
The Nest of Nessies (Penny White # 6)
The Weariness of Were-Wolves (Penny White # 7)
The Business of Bees (Penny White £ 8)
Dragons Can Only Rust
Dragon Reforged
The Dragon Throne
The Unicorn Throne
The Judas Disciple
The Monster Under the Bed

Connect with Me:

Facebook: **https://www.facebook.com/chryscymri?fref=ts**
My website: http://www.chryscymri.com
Goodreads:
https://www.goodreads.com/author/show/1076161.Chrys_Cymri

Printed in Great Britain
by Amazon

59053421R00139